Praise for Patricia Davids and her novels

"[A] wonderful tale…"
—*RT Book Reviews* on *An Amish Christmas*

"Davids' deep understanding of Amish culture is evident in the compassionate characters and beautiful descriptions."
—*RT Book Reviews* on *A Home for Hannah*

"Davids' latest beautifully portrays the Amish belief that everything happens for a reason, which helps one focus on the most important things in life."
—*RT Book Reviews* on *The Christmas Quilt*

Praise for Anna Schmidt and her novels

"A sweet story…"
—*RT Book Reviews* on *Family Blessings*

"Schmidt knows what readers expect…and delivers on all levels."
—*RT Book Reviews* on *Gift from the Sea*

"[A] poignant story…"
—*RT Book Reviews* on *Second Chance Proposal*

After thirty-five years as a nurse, **Patricia Davids** hung up her stethoscope to become a full-time writer. She enjoys spending her free time visiting her grandchildren, doing some long-overdue yard work and traveling to research her story locations. She resides in Wichita, Kansas. Pat always enjoys hearing from her readers. You can visit her online at patriciadavids.com.

Anna Schmidt is an award-winning author of more than twenty-five works of historical and contemporary fiction. She is a three-time finalist for the coveted RITA® Award from Romance Writers of America, as well as a four-time finalist for an RT Reviewers' Choice Award. Critics have called Anna "a natural writer, spinning tales reminiscent of old favorites like *Miracle on 34th Street*." One reviewer raved, "I love Anna Schmidt's style of writing!"

PATRICIA DAVIDS

An Amish Christmas

&

ANNA SCHMIDT

Family Blessings

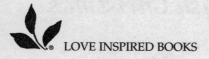

LOVE INSPIRED BOOKS

ISBN-13: 978-0-373-83895-0

An Amish Christmas and Family Blessings

Copyright © 2016 by Harlequin Books S.A.

The publisher acknowledges the copyright holders of the individual works as follows:

An Amish Christmas
Copyright © 2010 by Patricia MacDonald

Family Blessings
Copyright © 2011 by Jo Horne Schmidt

Recycling programs for this product may not exist in your area.

CONTENTS

AN AMISH CHRISTMAS 7
Patricia Davids

FAMILY BLESSINGS 227
Anna Schmidt

AN AMISH CHRISTMAS

Patricia Davids

This book is dedicated to women and men
everywhere who seek to mend fences
and to right wrongs within their families.

"Blessed are the peacemakers:
for they shall be called the children of God."
—*Matthew* 5:9

If thou, Lord, shouldest mark iniquities, O Lord,
who shall stand?
But there is forgiveness with thee,
that thou mayest be feared.
I wait for the Lord, my soul doth wait,
and in His word do I hope.
—*Psalms* 130:3–5

Chapter One

❧

"Our school program will be so much fun. We're going to do a play and sing songs. I have a poem to recite all by myself. I can't wait for Christmas." Eight-year-old Anna Imhoff leaned out the side of their Amish buggy to let the breeze twirl a ribbon she held in her hand.

Karen Imhoff listened to her little sister's excited prattle with only half an ear. Christmas was still eight weeks away. There were more pressing problems on Karen's plate, like buying shoes for three growing children, her father's mounting medical bills and finding a job until he was fully recovered.

Anna sat back and grabbed Karen's sleeve. "Look, there's a dead man."

Before Karen could respond to Anna's startling comment, the horse pulling the buggy shied violently, then bolted. Caught off guard, Karen was thrown back against the leather seat as the mare lunged forward. Anna screamed at the top of her lungs. Her brothers in the backseat began yelling. The horse plunged ahead even faster.

Regaining her balance, Karen grasped the loose reins.

She braced her feet against the floorboards and pulled back hard. "Whoa, Molly, whoa!"

Molly paid no heed. The buggy bounced and swayed violently as the mare charged down the farm lane. Mud thrown up by her hooves splattered Karen's dress and face. Gritty dirt mixed with the acid tang of fear in her mouth.

Anna, still screaming, threw her arms around Karen's waist, further hampering her efforts to gain control. The horse had to be stopped before they reached the highway at the end of the lane or upended in the ditch.

Muscles burning, Karen fought Molly's headlong plunge. A quarter of a mile flew past before Molly gave in. The horse slowed and came to a stop a few feet shy of the highway just as a red pickup zipped past. The brown mare tossed her head once more but didn't seem inclined to run again. Karen sent up a heartfelt prayer of thanks for their deliverance then took stock of her passengers.

Anna, with her face buried in the fabric of her sister's dress, maintained her tight grip. "I don't like to go fast. Don't do that again."

Karen comforted her with a quick hug and loosened the child's arms. "I won't. I promise."

Turning to check on her brothers, Karen asked, "Jacob? Noah? Are you all right?"

Fourteen-year-old Jacob retrieved his broad-brimmed black hat from the floor, dusted it off and jammed it on his thick, wheat-colored hair. "I'm fine. I didn't know Molly could move like that."

Ten-year-old Noah sat slumped down beside his brother. He held his hat onto his head in a tight grip with both hands. The folded brim made it look like a bonnet over his red curls. He said, "That was *not* fun."

"I thought it was," Jacob countered. "What spooked her?"

"I'm not sure." Karen's erratic heartbeat gradually slowed to a normal pace.

Brushing at the mud on her dress, Anna said, "Maybe Molly was scared of the dead man."

"What dead man?" Noah leaned forward eagerly.

"The one back there." Anna pointed behind them. They all twisted around to look. Karen saw only an empty lane.

Jacob scowled at his little sister. "I don't see anything. You're making that up."

"I am not. You believe me, don't you, Karen?"

Hugging the tearful child, Karen wasn't sure what to believe. Anna had been the only survivor of the buggy and automobile crash that had killed their mother, two sisters and their oldest brother four years earlier. The child worried constantly about death taking another member of her family.

Karen looked into Anna's eyes. "I'm sure you saw something. A plastic bag or a bundle of rags perhaps."

Jacob, impatient as ever, said, "There's nothing back there. Let's go. I don't want to be late for school."

"We can't leave him there," Anna insisted, her lower lip quivering ominously.

Noah started to climb out. "I don't mind being late. I'll go look."

Forestalling him, Karen said, "No. We'll all go back."

Anna could easily become hysterical and then they would get nowhere. It was better to show the child that she had been mistaken. After that, Karen could drop the children at their one-room schoolhouse and hurry to her interview at Bishop Zook's home. It wouldn't do to be late for such an important meeting.

When the wedding banns had been announced for the current schoolteacher, Karen knew it meant a new teacher would have to be hired. With money tight in the Imhoff household the job would be perfect for Karen and bring in much-needed funds.

The church-district elders were speaking to teaching applicants this morning. She had to be there. But first she needed to convince Anna they didn't have a dead man on their lane.

Turning the horse around, Karen sent her walking back the way they had come. As they neared the start of their reckless run Molly balked, throwing up her head and snorting.

Not wishing to have a repeat of the mad dash, Karen said, "Jacob, take the lines."

He scrambled over the seat back to sit beside her. After handing him the driving reins Karen stepped down from the buggy. Her sturdy black shoes sank into the ground still soft from last night's rain.

The morning sun, barely over the horizon, had started to burn away the fog lingering in the low-lying farm fields. Where the sunlight touched the high wooded hillsides it turned the autumn foliage to burnished gold and scarlet flame. A breeze tugged at the ribbons of Karen's *kapp* and brought with it the smell of damp grasses and fallen leaves.

Walking briskly back toward their farmhouse, she scanned the shallow ditch beside the road without seeing anything unusual. Turning around in the road, she looked at the children and raised her arms. "I don't see anything."

"Farther back," Anna yelled.

Dropping her hands, Karen shook her head, but started walking. Anna had been leaning out her side of the carriage. She would have had a good view of the ditch. Karen had been paying attention to the problems facing her family and not to the road. A mistake she would not make again.

A few yards farther along the lane she caught a glimpse of something white in the weeds. At first she thought she'd been right and it was a bundle of cloth or a stray plastic bag caught in the brush. Then the breeze brought her a new smell—the sickly metallic odor of blood. A low moan made her jump like a startled rabbit.

Taking a few hesitant steps closer, she saw a man sprawled on his back, his body almost completely hidden in the grass and wild sumac. His face looked deathly pale beneath close-cropped black hair. Blood had oozed from an ugly gash on the side of his head.

In an instant, Karen was transported back to that terrible day when she had stood beside the remains of the smashed buggy where her mother and sisters lay dead and her brother lay dying.

She squeezed her eyes shut. Pressing her hands to her face, she whispered, "Not again, Lord, do not ask this of me."

"Did you find something?" Noah yelled.

Jerked back to the present, Karen shouted, "Stay there!"

She approached the downed man with caution. He was an *Englischer* by the look of his clothes. The muddy white shirt he wore stretched tightly across his chest and broad shoulders while his worn jeans hugged a lean waist and muscular thighs. Oddly, both his shoes were missing.

He moaned, and she moved to kneel at his side. "Sir? Sir, can you hear me?"

"It *is* a dead man!" Noah stood on the roadway looking down with wide eyes.

She scowled at her brother. "He is not dead. I told you to wait in the buggy."

"Are you sure he isn't dead?" The boy's voice brimmed with excitement.

Laying a hand on the man's cheek, Karen became alarmed by how cold his skin was. He might not be dead, but he wasn't far from it. "Run to the phone shack and call for help. Do you know how to do that?"

Noah nodded. "*Ja,* I dial 9-1-1."

"*Goot.* Hurry."

She watched her brother climb over the fence and head across the muddy field of corn stubble. Their Amish church forbade telephones in the homes of the members, but did allow a community telephone. It was located at a midway point between their home and two neighboring Amish farms.

Jacob brought the buggy up. When Molly drew alongside the ditch, she snorted and sidled away. Apparently, she didn't care for the smell of blood. That must have been what frightened her in the first place. Jacob held her in check.

Karen looked up at him, "Go get Papa."

"We can't leave you," Anna protested.

Jacob drew himself up bravely. "I should stay."

Shaking her head, Karen said, "I'll be fine. Just go. And bring some quilts. This poor man is freezing."

Jacob slapped the reins sharply and sent Molly racing

up the lane toward the farmhouse. Settling herself beside the injured man, Karen took one of his hands and began to rub it between her own. How had he come to be here?

He groaned and moved restlessly. She squeezed his hand. "You will be okay, sir. My family has gone to get help."

He responded by turning his face toward her. His eyes fluttered open. They were as gray as rain clouds. Encouraged, Karen continued talking to him and rubbing his hand. "My name is Karen Imhoff and this is our farm. Can you tell me who you are?"

He mumbled something. Leaning forward, she positioned her ear near his mouth. His faint, shaky whisper sounded like, "Cold."

She quickly unbuttoned her coat. Pulling it off, she tucked it around him. Raising his shoulders slightly, she scooted beneath him so his head rested on her lap and not the chilly ground. It wouldn't help much. His clothes were wet from the rain as was the cold ground he was lying on. Using the corner of her apron, she folded it into a pad and pressed it against the wound on his head.

He moaned again, opened his eyes and focused on her face. "Help me."

His voice was barely audible but the words he whispered were the same words, the last words, her brother Seth had uttered. She cupped the *Englischer's* face, trying to infuse him with her own strength. "Help is coming. Be strong."

Please, God, do not make me watch him die as I did Seth. Save this man if it is Your will.

With her free hand she stroked his face, offering him what comfort she could. The stubble on his cheeks rasped against her fingertips, sending an unexpected shiver zipping along her nerve endings.

His sharply chiseled features were deeply tanned, but his underlying pallor gave his skin a sickly color. His hair lay dark and thick where it wasn't matted with blood. Dark brows arched finely over his pain-filled eyes.

Raising an unsteady hand to touch her face, he fixed her with a desperate gaze and whispered, "Don't leave me."

Grasping his cold fingers, she pressed them against her cheek. He might die, but he would not die alone. "I won't leave you. I promise."

"You're...so beautiful." His voice faded. His arm went limp and dropped from her grasp.

Karen tensed. His life couldn't slip away now, not when help was so close. She shook him and spoke firmly. "Listen to me. Help is coming. You must hang on."

"Hang on...to you," he mumbled.

Tears sprang to her eyes. "Stay with me. Let God be your strength. Hold fast to Him."

After several slow breaths, he said, "Yea, though I walk...through...the—"

She took up the rest of the Twenty-third Psalm for him. *"Through the valley of the shadow of death, I will fear no evil: for thou art with me; thy rod and thy staff they comfort me. Thou preparest a table before me in the presence of mine enemies: thou anointest my head with oil; my cup runneth over."*

She glanced toward the farm. Where was her father? What was taking so long? Desperately, she prayed help would come in time for the man she held.

Clearing her throat of its tear-choked tightness, she finished the psalm with a voice that shook. *"Surely*

*goodness and mercy shall follow me all the days of my
life: and I will dwell in the house of the LORD for ever."*
    Please let Your words bring him comfort, Lord.

It seemed like hours, but finally the buggy came rat-
tling to a stop beside her once more. Her father climbed
out gingerly. His left arm rested in a sling with a cast
to his shoulder.

He was dressed in dark trousers and a dark coat. His
plain clothes, long beard and black felt hat proclaimed
him a member of the Amish church. His calm demeanor
bolstered Karen's lagging spirits.

"What is this, daughter? Anna is wailing about a dead
man." Eli Imhoff pulled a bundle of blankets from the
seat. Jacob remained in the buggy, controlling the restless horse.

Looking to her father in relief, she said, "We found
him like this, Papa. He is badly hurt."

"I saw him first," Anna said, making sure everyone
understood her contribution.

Eli's eyes grew round behind his wire-rimmed
glasses. "An *Englischer?*"

"*Ja.* He is so cold. I sent Noah to the telephone to
call for help."

Eli stroked his gray-streaked beard, then nodded. "It
was the right thing to do. Let us pray he lives until the
English ambulance comes."

As they spread more covers over the man Noah came
racing back. He stopped in the lane and braced his hands
on his thighs, breathing heavily. "Is he dead yet?"

"No, and he will not die," Karen stated so firmly that
both her brothers and her father gave her odd looks.

She didn't care. She had seen too much death. She
wanted this man to live. "Surly God has not led us to
him only to snatch his life away."

"We cannot know *Gotte wille,*" her father chided.

God's will was beyond human understanding, but Karen prayed He would show His mercy to this unknown man.

"How did he get here?" Jacob asked getting down from the buggy. He handed off the reins to his younger brother. Noah didn't seem to mind. He stood at Molly's side transfixed by the sight of the stricken man.

"Perhaps he was injured on the road and walked this far before he collapsed," Eli suggested.

Squatting by the stranger's feet, Jacob shook his head. "He didn't walk. The bottoms of his socks aren't even muddy."

They all glanced at each other as the implications sank in. Someone had dumped this man and left him to die. Karen grew sick at the idea of such cruelty and tightened her hold on him.

Eli looked at his children and spoke sternly. "This is a matter for the English sheriff. It is outsider business. We must not become involved. Do all of you understand this?"

The boys and Anna nodded. Jacob stepped away and began walking along the ditch toward the highway. Eli scowled at him, but didn't call him back. A dozen yards down the road Jacob stopped and dropped to his haunches. Karen thought she heard the faint sound of chimes for a second but then nothing more.

Eli called out to Jacob. "Did you find something?"

"Tire tracks from a car, that's all." Rising, Jacob shoved both his hands in his pockets, glanced over his shoulder and then kept walking.

In the distance, Karen heard the sound of a siren approaching at last. Her father laid a hand on her shoulder. "I will go to the highway to show the English where they are needed."

When her father and Noah had driven away, Karen looked down at her stranger. His eyes were open, but his stare was blank. Cupping his cheek, she smiled at him. "Rest easy. Help is almost here."

At the sound of her voice, he focused on her face. He tried to speak, but no words came out. His breath escaped in a deep sigh, and his eyes closed once more.

She bit her lip as she tightened her hold on him. "Just a little longer. You can do it."

Within moments the sheriff's SUV and an ambulance arrived, stopping a few feet away. Her father and Noah followed them. One of the paramedics brought his gear and dropped to his knees beside Karen. "I'll take over now, miss."

She had to let them do their job, but she didn't want to let go of her stranger. She had promised him she wouldn't leave him. God had brought her to this man's side in his hour of need. A deep feeling of responsibility for him had taken hold in her heart, but she realized her job was done.

She cupped his cheek one last time. "You will be fine now."

Rising, she stepped aside praying she had spoken the truth.

Shaking out her damp, muddy skirt, Karen crossed her arms against the chill morning air. With trepidation she saw the sheriff turned his attention her way. He was intimidating, with his gun strapped to his hip and his badge glinting on the front of his leather jacket. Sheriff Nick Bradley was English, but he had family who had remained Plain. Members of Karen's church believed him to be a fair and impartial officer of the law and friendly toward the Amish.

Stopping in front of her, he pushed his tan hat up with one finger. "Tell me exactly what happened here this morning, Miss Imhoff."

He took notes as she answered his questions and then talked to each of the children separately. Karen barely listened to her siblings' accounts. Her entire attention was focused on the man being cared for by the emergency personnel.

Her fingers itched to touch the *Englischer's* face again. She wanted to reassure him, and herself, that he was going to be all right.

The sheriff followed Jacob to where he'd found the tire tracks, took pictures and placed yellow plastic markers at the site. When he finished, he approached Karen's father. "Mr. Imhoff, the children can go on to school, but I may have more questions for them later."

Papa nodded, but Karen could tell he wasn't pleased. This was outsider business. Papa wanted nothing to do with it. The children, on the other hand, shared excited looks. They would have plenty to tell their friends when they finally got to school. Within a day everyone in the community would know what had taken place on the Imhoff farm this morning.

One of the ambulance crew returned Karen's coat and then loaded their patient into the ambulance. As she slipped the wool jacket on, she felt the stranger's warmth surround her. Lifting the collar to her face, she breathed in the spicy-woodsy scent that clung to the dark wool.

His fate was out of her hands now. As the emergency vehicle drove away, she realized she would never see her *Englischer* again.

Chapter Two

John wiped the last trace of shaving lather from his neck with one of the hospital's coarse white towels. The face staring back at him remained as unfamiliar today as the new shoes on his feet.

How could a man forget what he looked like? How could he forget who he was, his own name?

Turning on the water, he rinsed the blue disposable blade. He knew how to use a razor but not where he'd purchased his last one or what brand he preferred. Things every man knew. It seemed only the personal parts of his memory were missing. It was the most frustrating part of his condition.

Traumatic amnesia his doctors called it. Those two words seemed woefully inadequate to describe the entity that had swallowed his life the way a black hole swallowed a star without letting a single ray of light escape.

He almost laughed at the absurdity of his thought. He could remember that weird trivial fact but not his own name. How ridiculous was that?

His doctors said his memory would return in time. They told him not to force it. Yet after eight days his past remained a blank slate. He was sick of hearing their reassurances.

"I'd like to put them in my shoes and see if they could take their own advice," he muttered as he put away his razor. Chances were good they'd be doing the same thing he was. Relentlessly trying to make himself remember.

Looking up, he stretched his hand toward the likeness in the mirror and forced a smile to his stiff lips. "Hello, my name is…"

Nothing.

Nothing came to mind this morning just as nothing had come to mind for the past week. The only identity he had was the one the hospital had given him. John Doe.

Staring at the mirror, he said, "Hi, I'm Andy. Hello, I'm Bill. I'm Carl. I'm David. My name is Edward."

If he did happen on the right name would he even know it? Rage and frustration ripped through him, bringing on a crushing headache that nearly took him to his knees.

"Who am I?" he shouted. His fingers ached where they gripped the porcelain lip of the sink.

His whole life was gone. He couldn't pull a single relevant detail out of the darkness in his mind.

He touched the bandage on the side of his scalp. According to the local law enforcement, he had been beaten, dumped in a ditch and left with no wallet or identification. Every effort to identify him was under way, but with no success thus far. His fingerprints and DNA weren't in the system. No one was looking for a man fitting his description. Even TV reports and newspaper articles had failed to bring in one solid lead.

Somewhere he must have a mother, a father, maybe even a wife, but the man in the mirror had no faces or names for anyone he'd known before waking up in the hospital.

"Too bad I wasn't microchipped like—"

Like who? Like what? The thought slipped away before he could fully grasp it. His head began pounding again. The pain worsened each time he tried to concentrate.

Forced to leave the past alone, he buttoned the last button on the gray flannel shirt the hospital social worker had purchased for him. The shirt was new. The one he'd been wearing couldn't be salvaged but the jeans were the ones he'd been found in. They fit well enough, although he'd lost some weight. Eating seemed so unimportant.

A knock sounded at the door to his room. He moved to sit on the edge of his bed and winced at the pain in his bruised ribs. Someone had planted a kick on two in his side after they'd split his skull. He said, "Come in."

The door swung open, revealing a tall, blond man in a sheriff's uniform. John had been expecting Nick Bradley, the officer in charge of his case.

Sheriff Bradley said, "Are you ready?"

"As ready as I can be. Thanks for giving me a lift."

John was being discharged. After a week and a day of testing and probing he'd been declared fit. Physically, he was in good shape so the hospital had no reason to keep him.

Mentally? That was a different story. Leaving this room suddenly seemed more daunting than anything he could imagine. How did he start over when he had no point to start over from?

No, that wasn't exactly true. He had one point of reference. His life started a week ago in a ditch outside the town of Hope Springs, Ohio. That was where he had to go.

"Are you sure this is what you want to do?" The sheriff clearly wasn't in favor of John's plan.

"I must have been in Hope Springs for a reason. Seeing the place might trigger something. Besides, it's all I have."

"I still think you'd be better off staying here in Millersburg, but I can see you aren't going to change your mind."

Reaching into his breast pocket, Sheriff Bradley withdrew a thick white envelope. He held it out. "My cousin Amber lives in Hope Springs. She's a nurse-midwife there. She knows about your situation. She wanted me to give you this."

"What is it?" John reached for the envelope.

"Her church took up a collection for you."

John opened the package and found himself staring at nearly a thousand dollars. Overwhelmed by the generosity of people he didn't know, he blinked hard. Tears stung the back of his eyes. He hadn't cried since—

It was there, just at the back of his mind, a feeling of grief, a feeling of overwhelming sadness. But why or for whom he had no idea. The harder he tried to concentrate on the feeling the faster it slipped away.

He forced himself to focus on the present. "Please tell your cousin how grateful I am."

"You can tell her yourself when you see Doc White to get your stitches out."

After gathering his few belongings together, John bid the nursing staff farewell and slipped into the passenger's seat of the squad car parked in front of the hospital.

Within minutes they were outside the city and cruising along a narrow ribbon of black asphalt.

The highway rose and fell over gentle hills, past manicured farms and occasional stands of thick woodlands. Looking out the window he saw herds of dairy cattle near the fences. The cows barely glanced up at their passing. A half-dozen times they came upon black buggies pulled by briskly trotting horses. Each vehicle sported a bright orange triangle on the back warning motorists it was a slow-moving vehicle.

John waited for something, anything, to look familiar. He held tight to the hope that returning to where he had been found would jog his absent memory. As they finally rolled into the neat small town of Hope Springs he was once again doomed to disappointment. Nothing looked familiar.

Sheriff Bradley pulled up in front of a Swiss-chalet-styled inn and said, "This is the only inn in town. The place is run by an Amish woman named Emma Wadler. The rooms are clean but nothing fancy."

Now that he was actually at his destination, John struggled to hide his growing fears. How would he go about searching for answers? Was he going to stand on the street corner and ask each person who walked by if he looked familiar? When the sheriff got out, John forced himself to follow.

A bell over the doorway sounded as the men walked into the building. The place was cozy, charming and decorated with beautifully carved wooden furniture. An intricately pieced, colorful quilt hung over the massive stone fireplace at one end of the lobby. A display of jams for sale sat near the front door.

Behind the counter stood a small woman in blue

Amish garb. Her red-brown hair was neatly parted down the middle and pulled back under a white bonnet. She was talking to someone inside a room behind the desk. She glanced toward the men and said, "I will be with you in a minute, gentlemen."

John watched her eyes closely for the slightest sign of recognition. There was none.

Turning her attention back to the person inside her office, she said, "I would gladly send overflow guests to your farm, cousin. It would be much better than telling them they must go to Millersburg or to Sugarcreek."

A woman replied, "We have spare rooms and as long as they don't mind living plain it will work. The extra money would be most welcome. If I can get *Dat* to agree to it, that is."

There was something pleasing about the unseen woman's voice. He enjoyed the singsong cadence. Her accent made will sound like vil and welcome sound like vellcom. It was familiar somehow.

The grandfather clock in the corner began to chime the hour. John reached into the front pocket of his jeans, but found it empty.

Confused, he looked down. Something belonged there. Something was missing.

"What can I do for you, Sheriff?"

John turned around as the inn owner began a conversation with Nick. The hidden woman came out of the office and headed for the front door. She wore a dark blue dress beneath a heavy coat. An Amish cap covered her blond hair. Slender and tall, she moved with unhurried steps and innate grace. When she happened to glance in his direction, John's breath froze in his chest. His heart began thudding wildly.

Rushing across the room, he grabbed her arm in a crushing grip. "I know you. What's my name? Who am I?"

Karen recoiled in shock when a man grabbed her arm and began shouting at her. She threw up one hand to protect herself and tried to twist out of his grasp.

"Tell me who I am," he shouted again, his face only inches from hers.

A second later, the sheriff was between her and her assailant. Pushing the man back, Sheriff Bradley said, "John, what do you think you're doing?"

"I know her. I know her face. She knows who I am," he insisted, pointing at Karen.

By this time, Emma had rounded the counter and reached Karen's side, adding another body between Karen and the angry man. "Cousin, are you all right?"

Rubbing her forearm, Karen nodded. "I'm fine."

Karen glanced at the man and recognition hit. This was her *Englischer,* the man she had discovered lying injured beside their lane. That recognition must have shown on her face.

His eyes widened with hope. "You know me, right? You know my name."

She shook her head. "*Nee.* I do not."

The sheriff spoke calmly but firmly. "John, this is Karen Imhoff. She's the one who found you."

His body went slack in the sheriff's hold. The color drained from his face as the hope in his eyes died. His look of pain and disappointment twisted her heart into a knot.

She said, "It was my little sister who spotted you lying in the weeds."

His eyes suddenly narrowed. "I was told I was unconscious when the paramedics arrived. How is it that I know your face?"

As her racing heart slowed and her fright abated, Karen took a step closer. He was alive and standing here before her. Joy gladdened her heart. He had been in her thoughts and prayers unceasingly. It took all her willpower not to reach out and touch his face.

She said, "You opened your eyes and spoke to me. You told me you were cold. I put my coat over you."

The sheriff released his grip on John. "She doesn't know anything about you. I've already questioned her and her family. There's no connection between you."

A look of resignation settled over John's features. He raised a hand to his forehead and rubbed it as if trying to rub away pain. "I'm sorry if I hurt or frightened you, Miss Imhoff. Please forgive me."

He did not remember her holding him close. Perhaps that was for the best. She had come to the aid of a stranger, nothing more. The rest, the closeness, the connection she felt with him, those things would remain in her secret daydreams.

"You are forgiven," she said quietly. What she didn't understand was why he had insisted that she tell him his own name.

The sheriff looked toward the innkeeper. "Sorry for the disturbance, Emma. This is John Doe, the man found injured near here a week ago. John has amnesia."

"What does this mean?" Karen asked, unfamiliar with the English term.

John's eyes locked with hers. Once again she felt a stirring bond with him deep in her bones. It was suddenly hard to breathe.

He said, "It means I can't remember anything that happened before I was hurt. Not even my own name, but I remember your face and the sound of your voice."

Compassion drenched Karen's heart and brought the sting of tears to her eyes. His suffering had not ended when the ambulance took him away from her.

Sheriff Bradley said, "John needs a room for a little while, Emma. He doesn't have any ID so I came to vouch for him in person."

Emma said, "I'm sorry, I don't have anything available for a week. I just rented my last room an hour ago. You know the quilt auction begins tomorrow. It runs for several days, and then there is the Sutter wedding. By next Friday I will have a room."

Clearly upset with himself, Nick said, "I'm sorry, John. I should have called ahead. They aren't normally booked up here. I know you had your heart set on staying in Hope Springs. I didn't even think about the auction being this week. I'll take you back to Millersburg. We can find a place for you there."

"We have a room to let." Karen's desire to help John overrode her normally good sense. He was a stranger lost in a strange land. He needed her help today as much as he'd needed it the day she found him.

His eyes narrowed as he stared at her. Karen bit the corner of her lip. What had she done? She should have discussed this with her father first, but she had already made the offer and couldn't withdraw it.

When she explained things her father would realize the benefits of this additional income. Especially after she had failed to get the teaching job.

Their family's income had been severely limited following her father's injury a month earlier. A farrier couldn't shoe horses with his arm in a cast. There were still medical bills that needed to be paid in addition to their everyday expenses.

She would point out all those things, but she knew he would not be pleased if she brought this man and his English trouble into their house.

She fidgeted under John's unwavering gaze. Finally, he said, "Your farm was the first place I had planned to visit when I arrived. Renting a room there makes sense."

"For a week," she stressed. "After that, Emma will have a place for you here."

"It seems you've come to my rescue once again." He held out his hand to seal the deal and gave her a crooked grin. It deepened the lines that bracketed his mouth, lending him a boyish charm.

With only a brief hesitation, she accepted his hand. Her pulse skipped a beat then pounded erratically as her small hand was swallowed by his large, warm one. It wasn't soft, it was calloused and rough like the hand of a man who worked outdoors for a living. A blush heated her cheeks, but she couldn't take her eyes off of him.

She remembered him so clearly. The shape of his brow and the stone-gray color of his eyes, even the way the stubble of his beard had felt beneath her fingers. She remembered, too, the husky sound of his voice when he had told her she was beautiful.

Something light and sweet slipped through her veins. An echo of a time when she'd been a giddy teenager smitten with a local boy. A time before she'd had to become a surrogate mother to her younger siblings and put her girlhood dreams away.

Thoughts of the children brought her back to earth with a thud. She pulled her hand away from John. This man was an outsider and thus forbidden to her. She had offered him a room to rent for a week and nothing more. Her strange fascination with him had to stop, and quickly.

Gesturing toward the door, she said, "I must get home."

He said, "I don't have any sort of transportation. May I hitch a ride with you?"

Oh, *Dat* really wasn't going to like this, but what could she do? She gave a stiff smile. "Of course."

Emma asked quietly, "Karen, are you sure about this?"

Pretending a bravery she didn't feel, Karen answered, "Yes. Goodbye, cousin, I will see you at Katie's wedding next Thursday."

Emma didn't look happy, but she nodded. "Give *Onkel* Eli my best."

John shook hands with the sheriff, who promised to check up on him soon, and then followed Karen out the door. Her nervousness increased tenfold as he fell into step beside her.

He was taller than she thought he would be. She had been called a beanpole all her life, but he stood half a head taller than she did. She felt delicate next to his big frame. It was a strange feeling. Spending the next half hour in this man's company in the close confines of her buggy might prove to be awkward.

After unlatching Molly's lead from the hitching rail, Karen was surprised when John took her elbow to help her climb in the buggy. She was used to taking care of herself and everyone else. It had been a long time since someone had wanted to take care of her.

John walked slowly around the front of the horse.

Raising a hand, he patted the mare's neck and made a soothing sound as he cast a critical eye over the animal. "She's got good conformation. She's a Standardbred, right?"

"*Ja*. You know about horses?"

"I think I do." He scratched Molly under the earpiece of her headstall. The mare tipped her head and rubbed against his hand in horsy bliss.

It seemed he could charm horses as well as foolish Amish maids. She said, "We must be going."

He nodded and climbed into the buggy beside her. Karen turned the horse and sent her trotting briskly down the street. The fast clatter of Molly's hooves matched almost exactly the rapid pounding of Karen's heart. It was going to be a long ride home.

Clucking her tongue, she slapped the reins against Molly's rump, making the mare go faster. The sooner they reached the farm, the better.

Karen's skin prickled at John's nearness. He had been in her thoughts and prayers constantly since that day. The special connection she'd felt between them had not diminished. She had wondered who he was and if he had gotten better. She'd wondered, too, if he had a wife to care for him. She had prayed he wasn't alone.

Now, he had come back to her.

He had been helpless as a babe that day, a man in need of tender care. The vibrant man beside her now was anything but helpless. What had she been thinking to invite him into her home?

He remained silent beside her as they drove out of town. Covertly, Karen glanced his way often, but he was scanning the countryside and paying her no mind. The cold, rainy weather of last week had give way to sunny days of Indian summer. The countryside was aglow with the vibrant hues of autumn. It should have been a pleasant ride. Instead, Karen felt ready to jump out of her skin.

After twenty minutes of listening only to the clip-clop of Molly's hooves and the creaking of the buggy, John spoke at last. "This isn't the way I came into Hope Springs with Sheriff Bradley. What road is this?"

She glanced at him. "It's called Pleasant View Road. Does that mean something to you?"

He shook his head. "Nothing more than it's well named. Where does it lead?"

"It makes a wide loop and goes back to Highway 39 about ten miles south of here. From there, you can go to the town of Sugarcreek or over to Millersburg."

"Why would someone like me be on this road?"

Shrugging her shoulders, Karen said, "Because you were lost?"

He barely smiled. "If I wasn't then, I am now."

Her curiosity about him couldn't be contained any longer. "The sheriff called you John Doe, but that is not your name?"

"No. John Doe is a name they give to any man who is unidentified. It's usually given to a dead body, but fortunately for me I'm still alive."

"This amnesia—will it go away?"

He stared into the distance for a long time before answering. Finally, he said, "The doctors tell me my memory may come back on its own or it may not come back at all."

"It must be awful." Her heart went out to him.

His attention swung back to her. "What can you tell me about the day you found me?"

"I was driving my younger brothers and sister to school. Normally they walk, but I had an appointment that day. I thought it would be easier just to drop them on my way."

"Did you notice anything unusual that morning?"

Giving him a look of disbelief, she asked, "You mean other than finding an unconscious man by the side of the road?"

That brought a small, lopsided grin to his face, easing the tension between them. "Yes, other than finding me in a ditch, did you notice anything that was unusual or out of place?"

"Nothing." She wanted to help him, but she couldn't. "The sheriff has already asked us these questions."

Leaning forward, he braced his elbows on his knees and clasped his hands together in front of him. "I just thought you might have remembered something new since that day. Maybe you heard the sound of a car or voices. Do you have a dog?"

"We do not."

"Do you remember hearing anything during the night?"

"*Nee,* I heard nothing unusual. I'm sorry."

He pressed his lips into a thin line and nodded in resignation. "That's okay. Are we close to your farm?"

"It's not far now. You will see the sign."

"Tell me about yourself, Karen Imhoff." He fixed her with an intense stare that brought the blood rushing to her face.

"There is not much to tell. As you can see I am Amish. My mother passed away some years ago so I am in charge of my father's house."

"What did you mean when you told the innkeeper that your lodgers would have to live plain?"

He really didn't know? Grinning, she said, "You will be wanting your money back when you find out."

"Do you give refunds?"

"*Nee,* when money goes into my pocket it does not come out easily."

"Okay, then tell me gently."

"Plain living means many things. No electricity and all that comes with it. No television, no computers, no radio."

"Wow. What did I get myself into?"

She glanced at him, but he was smiling and didn't look upset. Feeling oddly happy, she said, "We go to bed early and we get up early. My father farms and is the local farrier, but we will not put you to work shoeing horses."

"Thanks for the small favor."

"I have two brothers, Jacob is fourteen and Noah is ten. I also have a sister. Anna is eight."

His mood dimmed. "I wonder if I have brothers or sisters."

"You are welcome to some of mine," she offered, hoping to make him smile again. It worked.

"Don't you find it hard to live without electricity?"

"Why would I? People lived happily without electricity for many centuries."

"Good point. Why don't the Amish use it?"

"We are commanded by the Bible to live separate from the world. Having electricity joins us to the world in a way that is bad for us. We do not shun all modern things. Only those things that do not work to keep our families and our communities strong and close together."

"I still don't get it."

"That is because you are an *Englischer*."

"I'm a what?" He frowned.

"English. An outsider. Our word for those who are not of our faith. This is our lane."

Karen slowed the horse and turned onto the narrow road where a large white sign with a black anvil painted on it said, Horse Shoeing. Closed Wednesdays. The word Wednesdays was currently covered by a smaller plaque that said Until Further Notice.

John sat up straighter. "Where did you find me?"

"A little ways yet."

When they approached the spot, Karen drew the horse to a stop. John jumped down and walked into the knee-high winter-brown grass and shrubs along the verge of the road. The sheriff had combed the area for clues but found nothing.

Karen kept silent and waited as John made his own search. One look at his face made her realize John Doe was still a wounded man, but he was in need of more than physical care.

Chapter Three

John stared at the matted grass around his feet. No trace of the incident remained. No blood stains, no footprints, no proof that he had ever lain here.

Squatting down, he touched the grass and waited for an answer to appear. Why had he been in this place?

Had his injury been an accident or had someone deliberately tried to kill him? Had it been a robbery gone bad as the sheriff thought? No matter what the explanation, the fact remained that he'd been left here to die. The knowledge brought a sick feeling to the pit of his stomach.

Standing, he shoved his hands in his pockets and scanned the horizon. All around him lay farm fields. To the east, a wooded hill showed yellow and crimson splashes of autumn colors. A cold breeze flowed around his face. He closed his eyes and breathed deeply, hoping to trigger some hint of familiarity.

Nothing.

He searched his empty mind for some sliver of recognition and drew a blank.

He'd been so sure coming here would make him remember. This was where his old life ended. He wanted to see the scattered bits of it lying at his feet. He wanted to pick up the puzzle pieces and assemble them into something recognizable. Only there was nothing to pick up.

Now what?

He glanced toward the buggy where Karen sat. He'd been found on her land. Did she know more than she was letting on? Sitting prim and proper with her white head covering and somber clothes, it was hard to imagine she could be involved in something as ugly as an assault. But what did he know about her, anyway? Maybe coming here had been a mistake. He would proceed with caution until he knew more about her and her family.

She watched him silently. As their eyes met, he read sympathy in their depths. Turning away he bit the inside of his cheek until he tasted blood. The pain overrode the sting of unshed tears. He didn't want sympathy. He wanted answers.

John didn't know how long he stood staring into the distance. Eventually, Molly grew impatient and began pawing the ground. He glanced at Karen. She drew her coat tight under her chin. He realized the sun was going down and it was getting colder.

Walking back to the buggy, he said, "I'm sorry. I didn't mean to keep you waiting so long."

She smiled softly. "I don't mind, but I think Molly wants her grain."

"Then we should go." Walking around to the opposite side he climbed in.

"Did you remember anything?" she asked.

"No." He stared straight ahead as his biggest fear slithered from the dark corner of his mind into the forefront. What if he never remembered? What if this blankness was all he'd ever have?

No, he refused to accept that. He had family, friends, a job, a home, a car, a credit card, a bank account, something that proved he existed. His life was out there waiting for him. He wouldn't give up until he found it.

When they reached the farmyard, Karen drew the mare to a stop in front of a two-story white house. A welcoming porch with crisp white railings and wide steps graced the front. Three large birdhouses sat atop poles around the yard ringed with flowerbeds. Along one side of the house several clotheslines sagged under the weight of a dozen pairs of pants, dresses, shirts, socks and sheets all waving in the cool evening breeze.

Across a wide expanse of grass stood a large red barn and several outbuildings. In the corral, a pair of enormous caramel-colored draft horses munched on a round hay bale with a dozen smaller horses around them. Molly whinnied to announce her return. The herd replied in kind.

John swallowed hard against the pain in his chest. What did his home look like? Was someone waiting to greet him? Were they worried sick about where he was? If that was the case, why hadn't they come forward?

Something of what he was thinking must have shown on his face. Karen laid her hand on his. The warmth of her touch flooded through him.

Sympathy had prompted Karen's move. She saw and understood the struggle he was going through. "Let God be your solace, John. He understands all that you are going through. You are not alone."

John nodded, but didn't speak.

Karen turned to get out of the buggy but froze. Her stern-faced father stood before her. He looked from John to Karen and demanded, "What is the meaning of this, daughter?"

Stepping down from the buggy, she brushed the wrinkles from the front of her dress. "Papa, this is Mr. John Doe. John, this is my father, Eli Imhoff. Papa, I have rented a room to Mr. Doe."

Eli Imhoff's dark bushy eyebrows shot up in surprise. "You have, have you?"

Karen had learned the best way to handle her father was to charge straight ahead. She switched to Pennsylvania Dutch, the German dialect normally spoken in Amish homes, knowing John would not be able to understand them. "I will show him to his room and then I will speak with you about this."

"Better late than never, I'm thinking," Eli replied in the same language.

"I'm sure you'll agree this was a *goot* idea. You know we need the money. The *dawdy haus* is sitting empty. This is only for a week, and he is paying us the same amount that Emma charges her customers."

"And if I say *nee?*"

She acquiesced demurely. "Then I shall drive him back to town. Although Emma has no room for him at her inn I'm sure he can find someplace to stay."

John spoke up. "Look, if this is a problem I can make other arrangements."

Karen crossed her arms and raised one eyebrow as she waited for her father to answer.

The frown her father leveled at her said they would hold further discussions on the matter when they were alone. Looking to John, he said, "You are welcome to stay the night."

"Thank you, sir. I promise not to be any trouble."

"You are the man my daughter found on the road, *ja?*"

"I am. I want to thank you for your help that day."

"We did naught but our Christian duty," Eli said, turning away.

As her father disappeared into the house, Karen swung back to John. "Come. You will have a house to yourself. It has its own kitchen, sitting room and bedroom. It is the *dawdy haus* but my grandparents have both passed away and it is not in use. You may take your meals with us unless you enjoy cooking."

"What is a *dawdy haus?*" John asked as he pulled his small bag from behind the buggy seat.

"It means grandfather house. Among our people it is common to add a room or home onto the farmhouse so that our elderly relatives have a place to stay. Many times we have three or four generations living together under one roof. It is our way."

"Sounds like a good way to me."

She smiled at that. "I'm glad you think so."

He swept one hand in front of him. "Lead the way."

The *dawdy haus* had been built at a right angle to the main farmhouse. It was a single-story white clapboard structure with a smaller front porch. A pair of wooden chairs flanked a small table at the far end of the porch. The outside door opened into a small mudroom. A second door led directly into the kitchen.

Karen said, "We have gas lamps. Have you ever used them before?"

"I don't know."

She cringed. "I'm sorry."

"Don't be. There's no point in tiptoeing around with your questions. Either I'll remember a thing or I won't. I won't know until you ask."

Striking a match, Karen raised it to the lamp and lit it. A soft glow filled the room, pushing back the growing darkness. She glanced at John and found him watching her intently. Suddenly, it seemed as if the two of them were cocooned alone inside the light.

The lamplight highlighted the hard planes of his face. She became acutely aware of him, of his size and the brooding look in his eyes. The tension in the room seemed to thicken. His gaze roved over her face. Her palms grew sweaty as her pulse quickened. She wondered again if she had made a serious mistake in bringing him here.

Yet, she could not have left him in Hope Springs any more than she could have passed by him in the ditch without helping. There was something about John Doe that called to her.

He tried to hide his discomfort and his aloneness, but she saw it lurking in the depths of his eyes. He was afraid. She wanted to help him, wanted to ease his pain. He needed her.

The white bandage on his forehead stood out against his dark hair. She gave in to an overwhelming urge and reached out to touch his face. Her fingertips brushed against the gauze dressing. "Does it hurt?"

He turned his head aside. "It's nothing."

"You're forgetting that I saw the gash."

The muscles in his jaw tightened. "I've forgotten a lot of things."

She let her hand drop to her side. How foolish of her. He wasn't a stray puppy that needed her care. He was a grown man, and she was flirting with forbidden danger. For the first time in her life she understood how a moth could be drawn to the flame that would destroy it.

She must harden her heart against this weakness. "Let me show you the rest of the house."

He grasped her arm as she started to turn away. "I can manage. If I need anything I'll find you. Right now, I'd like to be alone. It's been a long day."

"Of course." She handed him the box of matches. "Be sure and turn off the gas lamps when you leave the house. There are kerosene lamps, too, if you need them. Supper will be ready in about an hour. You may join us at the table or I can bring something to you."

"If it's all the same, I'm not up to company and I'm not really hungry. Thank you, though, for everything."

Slowly, he withdrew his hand from her arm in a gentle caress. She rubbed at the warmth that remained. She must not confuse his gratitude with affection nor give in to her feelings of attraction. To do so would be unthinkable.

She mumbled, "It is our Christian duty to care for those in need. I will be back with linens and a pillow for you in a little while."

As she left the house, she paused on the porch to slow her racing pulse. Her family must not see her flustered.

She did not doubt that God had brought John Doe into her life again for a reason but that reason was hidden from her. Was it so that she might help this outsider? Or had John Doe been sent to test the strength of her faith? Would she pass such a test or would she fail?

John drew a deep breath as soon as Karen was gone. He couldn't seem to concentrate when she was near.

He didn't understand why. The woman wasn't a great beauty, but she had an elegant presence he found very attractive. Perhaps it was the peace in her tranquil blue eyes or the surety with which she carried herself.

She knew exactly where she belonged in her small reclusive world while he was adrift in an ever-changing sea of turmoil that sought to swallow his sanity along with his memories. Her empathy had quickly become his lifeline. One he was afraid to let go of.

"Get real. I can't hang on the apron strings of an Amish farmer's daughter."

Pushing his attraction to her to the back of his mind, he studied the small kitchen. He was surprised to see a refrigerator. On closer inspection, it turned out to be gas not electric, but it was empty and had apparently had the gas turned off. The few drawers were filled with normal kitchen utensils. The stove was wood burning.

Did he even know how to cook?

He opened a cupboard and pulled out a heavy cast-iron skillet. Hefting it in his hand, he suddenly saw it full of sizzling trout. He saw himself setting it on a trivet, hearing murmurs of appreciation, a woman's lighthearted laughter.

He spun around to face the table knowing someone sat there, but when he did—the image vanished.

"No!"

The loss was so sharp he doubled over in pain. Who was the woman with him? His mother? A sister? A wife? Where had it taken place? When? Was it a real memory or only a figment of his imagination?

He looked at the pan he held and saw only a blackened skillet. Setting it on the stovetop he rubbed his hands on his thighs. It had been a real memory, he was sure of it. But had it been a month ago or ten years ago? It held no context. It faded before he could grasp hold and examine it.

Pulling himself together, he blew out a shaky breath. Okay, it had only been a flash. But it could mean he was on the mend.

Hope—new and crisp—flooded his body. Maybe the doctors had been right and time was all he needed. He had time. He had nothing but time.

Using the matches Karen had given him, he lit a kerosene lamp sitting on the counter and began walking through the rest of the house. The wide plank floors creaked in places as he entered the sitting room containing several chairs and a small camelback sofa. None of the furniture shouted "kick back and relax." It was utilitarian at best.

Down a narrow hallway he passed a small bathroom and noted with relief the modern fixtures. At the end of the hall he opened the door to a sparsely furnished bedroom.

The narrow bed, covered with a blue striped mattress, stood against a barren white wall. A bureau sat against the opposite wall while a delicate desk graced the corner by the window. The walls were empty of any decorations. The one chair in the room was straight-backed with a cane seat.

Crossing the wooden floor, he set the lamp on the bedside table. He stared at the thin mattress, then sat down and bounced slightly. It was one shade better than his hospital bed but only two shades softer than the floor. Apparently, the Amish didn't go in for luxury.

He lay back on the bed and folded his arms behind his head to stare at the ceiling. Was his own bedroom this bare? He waited for another spark of memory, but nothing came.

The pain in his head had settled to a dull ache he'd almost grown used to. There were pain pills in his duffel bag, a prescription filled at the hospital pharmacy, but he didn't like the idea of using them. His thinking was muddled enough without narcotics. He closed his eyes and laid one arm across his face. Slowly, the tension left his body and he dozed.

A rap on the door brought him awake. He sat up surprised to see it was fully dark beyond the window outside. Karen stood in the doorway, her arms loaded with sheets, quilts and a pillow. She asked, "Did I wake you?"

"No. I was only resting." John wasn't about to make Karen feel bad after all that she'd done for him. He rose to take the linens from her. Their fresh sun-dried fragrance filled his nostrils.

Taking a step back, she folded her arms nervously. "I left you a plate of food on the table. You should eat. You need to regain your strength."

"Thanks." He expected her to hurry away, but she lingered.

"Is the house to your satisfaction?" she asked.

"It's great. Better than a four-star motel. That's a place where people can stay when they're traveling—if you didn't know." Did he sound like a fool or what?

An amused grin curved her full lips. "I know what a motel is. We do travel sometimes. I have even been to Florida to visit my great-aunt and uncle there."

"I'll bet the horse got tired trotting all that way."

Her giggle made him smile. A weight lifted from his chest.

Composing herself, Karen said, "I took the train."

It surprised him how much he enjoyed talking to her. He asked, "Can't you fly?"

"No, my arms get too tired," she answered with a straight face.

He laughed for the first time since he'd awakened in the hospital. "I don't know Amish rules."

"We can't own automobiles, but we can hire a driver to take us places that are too far for a buggy trip. With our bishop's permission, we can travel by train or by bus and even by airplane if the conditions are warranted."

"That must be tough."

"That's the point. If it is easy to get in a car and go somewhere, to a new city or a new job, then families become scattered and the bonds that bind us together and to God become frayed and broken."

"It's an interesting philosophy."

"It is our faith, not an idea. It is the way God commands us to live. How is your headache?"

"It's gone," he said in surprise.

"I thought so. You look rested. And now you must eat before your supper gets cold."

He followed her down the hall to the kitchen. A plate covered with aluminum foil sat on the table. He peeled back the cover and the mouthwatering aroma of roast chicken and vegetables rose with the steam. His stomach growled. He was hungry. "Smells good."

He hesitated, then said, "I remembered something tonight."

Her eyes brightened. "What?"

If he shared his small victory would she think he was nuts? He didn't care if she did. He was tired of being alone.

"I've cooked trout before. I know it doesn't sound like

much, but it's my first real memory. At least, I believe it was a memory."

"It is a start. We must give thanks to God."

His elation slipped a notch. Wasn't God the one who'd put him in this situation? If he were to give thanks it would have to be for remembering something important—like his name.

She said, "At least you know one more thing about yourself."

He could cook fish, he had no criminal record and he didn't crave drugs. Yeah, he was off to a roaring good start in his quest to collect personal information. Maybe tomorrow he'd find he knew how to sharpen a pencil.

Depression lowered its dark blanket over him. "Thanks for the supper."

"You are most welcome. I will expect you at our breakfast table in the morning," she stated firmly. The look in her eyes told him she was used to being the boss.

Her family would be there, people who would stare at him with pity or worse. Was he ready for that?

Not waiting for his answer, she said, "I will send Jacob to get you if you don't appear. No, I will send Noah. His endless questions will make you wish you had stayed in Hope Springs. The only way to silence him is to feed him. *Guten nacht,* John Doe."

"Good night, Karen."

The ribbons of her white bonnet fluttered over her shoulders as she spun around and headed out the door. It appeared he wouldn't be allowed to hide here in the house if she had her way.

That was okay. He wouldn't mind seeing her face across the breakfast table or at any other time. Why wasn't she married?

He reined in the thought quickly. It was none of his business. She was an attractive woman with a vibrant personality, but he was in no position to think about flexing his social skills. What if he had a wife waiting for him somewhere?

He stared at his left hand. No discernible pale band indicated he normally wore a wedding ring. It wasn't proof positive, of course. Not every married man wore a wedding band. Did he feel married?

How could he remember frying trout and not remember if he had a wife?

The creaking of a floorboard in the other room caught his attention. Was there someone in the house with him? His mouth went dry as a new fear struck.

Had someone come back to finish the job and make sure he was dead?

Chapter Four

❧

Grabbing a knife from the drawer beside the sink, John walked slowly to the doorway of the sitting room and scoped it out. It was empty.

Was he imagining things now? He started to turn away, but another sound stopped him. He focused on the sofa just as the face of a little girl peeked over the back. The moment she saw him watching she ducked down again.

Relief made him light-headed. Karen had mentioned she had a sister. It seemed one Imhoff was too curious about him to wait until morning. He said, "I see you."

"No, you don't," came her reply.

Feeling foolish, he laid the knife on the table, then he crossed the sitting room and bent over the sofa. Looking down, he saw her huddled into a little ball. "Okay, now I see you."

Wearing a dark blue dress with a white apron and a white bonnet identical to her older sister's she looked like a miniature Karen. She nodded and grinned. "*Ja*, now you see me."

Scrambling to her feet, she sidestepped to the other

end of the sofa. "You are my dead man. I saw you in the ditch. Everyone said I made it up, but I didn't."

"I was in the ditch, but I wasn't dead."

She moved around the room trailing her fingers along the furniture. "I know. God didn't want you, either. We are just alike."

He had no idea what she was talking about. "I'm not sure we are."

"It's true," she insisted. "This house belonged to my *grossmammi.*"

"I don't know what that means."

She cocked her head sideways. "Really? It means grandmother. These are her things, but God wanted her in heaven, and she had to leave her things here."

John sat on the sofa. "Do you think your grandmother will mind that I'm using them?"

She shook her head. "She liked it when people came to visit."

He said, "My name is John. What's your name?"

"Anna."

"It's nice to meet you Anna. What did you mean when you said we are the same?"

"God didn't want me to go to heaven the day my mother died. Seth, Carol and Liz got to go to Heaven with Mama, but God didn't want me. And he didn't want you. Why do you think that is?"

"I have no idea."

She came to stand in front of him. Tipping her head to one side, she said, "Papa says it is because God has something special for me to do here on earth. I don't think it's fair, do you?"

John stared at his toes in hopes that an appropriate answer would appear. None did. He wasn't up to discussing the meaning of life with this odd child. "I think maybe you should talk to your dad or Karen about it."

"Okay. Are you going to eat all that chicken?"

"I was, but I'm willing to share."

Spinning around she bounced toward the kitchen and settled in one of the chairs. He followed her and took a seat at the head of the table. Uncovering the plate, he pushed it toward her. "I'll let you choose the piece you want."

"I like the leg, but you are the guest."

"That makes it easy because I like the thigh."

He watched her bite into his supper. "Anna, can I ask you a few questions?"

She considered his request for a moment then nodded. "Okay."

"What's with the bonnets that you and your sister wear?"

Reaching up to touch her head, she asked, "You mean our prayer *kapp?*"

"Yeah, why do you wear them? I know you do because you are Amish, but why?"

She looked at him with wide eyes. "Are you joshing me?"

"No."

"It says in the Bible that I should cover my head when I pray. I should pray all the time so I wear this all the time. Sometimes I forget to pray, but Karen reminds me. Can I ask you a question?"

"Sure."

"Why were you in our ditch?"

"I don't remember what I was doing there. I don't remember anything that happened to me before you saw me. John Doe isn't even my real name. It's a name they gave me because I can't remember my own."

Her mouth dropped open. "Now you *are* joshing me?"

Shaking his head, he smiled and said, "I wish I were."

The outside door opened and a teenage boy entered. He frowned at Anna. "You should not be here."

She rolled her eyes. "Neither should you."

"She's not causing any trouble," John said in defense of his visitor.

The boy ignored him. "Come now or I will tell *Dat*."

Anna finished her chicken and licked her fingers. "This is my brother, Jacob. He says having an *Englischer* stay here will get us all in trouble with the bishop."

John looked from Anna to her brother. "Is this true? Will my being here cause trouble?"

Jacob came into the room and took Anna by the hand. Looking at John he said, "You should leave this place."

Turning around, Jacob left, taking his little sister with him.

It seemed getting to know the Imhoff family was going to be more difficult than John had anticipated.

Karen was cooking breakfast when John knocked at the door the following morning. She hadn't had to send one of the children to wake him. After bidding him enter, she turned back to the stove and smiled as she stirred the frying potatoes. John was an early riser. That was one more thing he could add to his list about himself.

She moved the skillet off the heat. "Take a seat, Mr. Doe."

He said, "Please call me John."

Noah and Anna were already at the table sitting opposite each other but Eli and Jacob had not yet come in from the milking. Anna pointed to the chair opposite her. "Sit by Noah, John."

He settled himself into the chair she indicated and looked at the boy beside him. "You must be Noah."

Karen glanced over her shoulder to see Noah fairly bursting with curiosity.

"*Ja,* I am Noah. Is it true you can't remember your name? Not even where you came from? Do you remember that you're English or did someone tell you? How did you know how to talk? If you need to know how to use a knife and fork I can show you."

Karen caught John's eye and said, "I warned you."

While John patiently answered Noah's rapid-fire questions, Karen pulled her biscuits from the oven. Dumping them into a woven basket, she set it on the table in front of everyone.

Just then the front door opened. Her father and Jacob came in. After washing up, they took their places at the table. Karen sat down opposite John. Everyone folded their hands. Silently her father gave a blessing over the meal. He signaled he had finished by clearing his throat, then giving a brief nod to Karen. She began passing food down the table.

Eli said, "*Guder mariye,* Mr. Doe."

"Good morning, sir." John took a biscuit and watched with a bemused expression as the children dived into their food. By the time the plate of scrambled eggs reached him only a tablespoon's worth remained.

Eli spoke to Karen. "William Yoder wants me to look at one of his draft horses this afternoon. His gelding has a split hoof. He wants my opinion on which treatment to try."

She asked, "Do you need me to drive you?"

Jacob perked up with interest. "Can I go with you, Papa?"

Karen's spoke quickly, "You have school today." Jacob was growing up fast, but she wasn't ready for him to take on their father's tough and sometimes dangerous profession before it was necessary.

Sitting back in his chair, Jacob said, "I don't see why I have to go to school now. Papa needs me at home to help him with the horses."

"You will be out of school soon enough," Karen said. "A few more months won't do you any harm."

Jacob made a sour face. "Ken Yoder has already left school. He is only two months older than me. I don't need any more schooling. I want to work with you, Papa. I want to be a farrier."

John said, "A farrier needs an education, too."

Karen looked at him in surprise. It was becoming clear he did know a thing or two about horses.

"What do you know about it?" Jacob scowled at their guest.

"Jacob." Eli's firm tone rebuked his son.

Bowing his head, Jacob mumbled, "Forgive me."

Spreading jam on a piping-hot biscuit, John said, "If the horse has a turned foot, a farrier needs a shoe to correct it for him. You would have to know how many degrees the foot was off true in order to make a shoe that brings it up to level. How thick does the shoe need to be to give such an angle? These things you learn in school."

Anna shook her head. "We don't learn horseshoeing in school. We learn how to read and write, how to speak English and how to do our sums."

Eli smiled at her. "And did you finish your sums last night?"

Her bright face clouded over. "No, Papa."

"And why not?" Karen asked, surprised to hear Anna had neglected her homework.

"Because I went to visit John Doe."

John said, "I would have sent her back if I had known. She kept me company while I ate."

Jacob glared at John and then spoke to Karen. "See. No *goot* can come of having him stay here."

"Hush Jacob, this is not how we treat our guests," Karen said.

Pushing back from the table, Jacob got up. "The *Englischer* will only bring trouble. You will see."

He grabbed his coat and hat and headed outside, letting the door slam behind him. Eli rose, motioning to Karen to stay seated. "I will talk to the boy."

Slipping his coat over his sling, he followed Jacob outside. Embarrassed by her brother's display, Karen glanced at John.

He gave her a tight smile and said, "I'm sorry I upset him."

"It's not you." She knew what troubled her brother and her heart ached for him.

Noah spoke around a mouthful of egg. "Jacob doesn't like the English ever since the accident."

Puzzled, John asked, "What accident?"

"The accident that killed our mother, brother and sisters," Karen explained.

"That *Englischer* was drunk. He hit their buggy doing like seventy miles an hour," Noah added dramatically.

Karen was thankful Noah had not been there that day. It had been she and Jacob who came upon the terrible carnage.

Karen reached across the table to grasp Noah and

Anna's hands. "We have forgiven him as God has asked us to do."

Nodding solemnly, Noah agreed. "We have."

Anna shook her head. "I don't think Jacob has."

Karen squeezed her hand. "We will pray Jacob finds forgiveness in his heart."

John asked, "What happened to the driver?"

Letting go of her siblings, Karen folded her hands in her lap. "He had barely a scratch."

Frowning slightly, John looked from the children to Karen. "How do you do that? How do you forgive someone who has done something so terrible?"

"It is our way," Karen replied. Closing her eyes, she sought the peace that forgiveness always brought her.

When she opened her eyes, she found John's gaze resting thoughtfully on her. Heat rose in her face. Hoping he hadn't noticed, she said, "Hurry up children, or you will be late to school."

In the resulting rush, Karen masked her nervousness by handing out lunch boxes, scarves and mittens. By the time the children were out the door, she had a better grip on her emotions.

John, on the other hand, looked ill at ease. The frown lines that creased his forehead yesterday were back.

Karen began picking up plates. "Would you like more coffee or more eggs?"

"I don't want to cause you extra work. Coffee is fine if you have it." He remained seated, elbows resting on the table.

"It's not extra work. Cooking is what I do all day long. Ask now or go hungry until lunch."

"Okay, more eggs would be great."

"Did you sleep well?" She pulled a bowl of fresh eggs from the refrigerator.

"Not bad."

She glanced his way. Something in the tone of his voice made her suspect he hadn't. "The bed was not to your liking?"

He shifted uncomfortably in his chair. "It wasn't that."

"Then what was it?"

"Anna mentioned that Jacob thinks your family might get in trouble for having me here."

Turning around, she folded her arms and stated as firmly as she could, "You were invited into this house. There is nothing wrong in that."

"Are you sure? Because I got the feeling your father wasn't happy to see me, either."

"Papa has agreed that you may stay."

It had taken some persuading, but Karen had been able to convince her father that having an outsider with them for a short period of time would not be harmful. She was sure her father didn't suspect the depths of her interest in John Doe. If he did he would never allow him to stay.

To change the subject, she asked, "How do you like your eggs?"

"Scrambled."

She smiled at him over her shoulder. "Is that a thing you remember?"

"I don't know. It's just the first thing that came to mind."

Using a fork, she whipped the eggs quickly and added them to the skillet. "What is it that you would like to do today?"

"I need to discover why I was in this area."

Wrapping the corner of her apron around the coffee-pot handle, she carried it to the table. "If the sheriff could not discover the reason, what makes you think you can?"

He waited until she had finished filling his cup. After taking a sip, he said, "I don't know if I can do better or not, but I have the most at stake. I have to try."

Karen returned the coffeepot to the stove and stirred the eggs. "It seems a simple thing. If you were on this road, then you must have been on your way to, or coming from, one of the farms along this road."

"It's a simple thing if I was on this road in the first place because I wanted to be."

She glanced at him and frowned. "What you mean?"

"The sheriff is going on the assumption that I was robbed and my car was stolen along with my wallet and any personal effects. I could've been dumped here by someone who was attempting to hide my body."

She shook her head. "There are much better places to hide a body than on our farm lane."

"That's exactly what I was thinking."

She dished the eggs onto a plate. After carrying it to the table, she got a second mug, filled it with coffee and sat down across from him. "Will you then visit every farm along this road?"

"That is the only plan I can come up with. What do you think?"

"It makes sense, but it may not be easy." She hesitated not knowing exactly how to phrase her words.

"What do you mean?"

"There are over forty farms along Pleasant View road. Most belong to Amish farmers."

"And?"

"They may not be comfortable talking to an outsider."

Picking up a spoon, he stirred his coffee slowly. After a moment he looked directly into her eyes. "Will you help me?"

She glanced out the window toward the barn. Papa would not like her getting involved. It troubled her that she was considering helping this man against her father's wishes. But she was.

John must have sensed her reluctance. He said, "If you aren't comfortable with helping me, I understand. You don't know anything about me."

Tipping her head in his direction, she arched one eyebrow. "You don't know much about you, either."

That brought a ghost of a smile to his face. "True."

Crossing her arms on the table she stared at him. "I know that you like scrambled eggs and that you don't want to cause me trouble. I will do what I can to help you, but I am afraid it may not be much."

Rising to her feet, Karen said, "Finish your breakfast. I have much work I must do today, but tomorrow I will drive you to some of our neighbors' farms."

"Are you sure we can't get started today?"

She scowled at him. "Who will bake my bread? Who will mend the clothes my brothers must wear? Who will cook lunch for my father and our evening meal? These things I must do and many more. Tomorrow, I will make time for you. Besides, you need a day of rest. I see it in your eyes."

He looked ready to protest, but finally nodded. "You're right. One more day won't make a difference. You rented me a house, you didn't sign on to be my driver."

"*Goot,* and you will rest, *ja?*"

"I'll try. Does Hope Springs have a public library?"

"Yes. It is across from the English school on Maple Street. Why?"

"I need internet access. There is a national website for missing persons called NamUs. If anyone in the country reports a man of my description missing, the information will be posted there. I know Sheriff Bradley is doing all he can, but he doesn't have much manpower to devote to my case. I must help myself."

"Tomorrow, we can go there first thing."

"No, I'd like to start questioning people first."

"As you wish. Now you must finish your breakfast and get out from under my foot so I may wash the kitchen floor."

He quickly finished his plate, swigged the rest of his coffee and carried everything to the sink. "Is there anything I can do to help?"

"*Ja.* Would you go to the barn and check on *Dat?*"

"Your dad?"

She nodded. "I'm worried about him. He is trying to do too much too soon. He broke his arm five weeks ago when a neighbor's horse kicked him. He wants to get back to work, but the doctor says no. The broken bone damaged a nerve and he has lost feeling in his hand."

"I'll be happy to check on him."

"Danki."

He eyed her intently. "And that means?"

"It means, thank you."

"How do you say, you're welcome?"

"Du bischt wilkumm."

He repeated the phrase and she was surprised by his almost perfect pronunciation. "*Goot.* Now, out, or you will find yourself with a mop in hand."

She was smiling as he walked out, but her grin

faded quickly. She had chosen to remain with her family and care for her younger brothers and sisters after their mother was killed. She had given up her chance to marry and have a family of her own because she had been needed here.

At twenty-five, she was considered an old maid by many in the community. She considered herself too old and too wise for a youthful infatuation, but that was exactly the way she felt around John.

He was handsome in his English way, but he was not Plain. So why did a smile on his face make her heart beat faster? It was wrong to think of him in such a way. To forget that would be to bring heartache to all her family. They had suffered enough already. She would not bring them more pain.

Chapter Five

Stepping off the front porch, John looked up. The morning sky hung low, gray and overcast. The wind carried a hint of rain as it scattered fallen leaves across the ground in front of his feet. Glancing over his shoulder, he watched Karen working in the kitchen through the windows. Once again he was struck by how gracefully she moved.

She wore a dark purple dress today with a black apron over it. The color accentuated her willowy frame. The ribbons of her white cap drew his attention to her slender neck, the curve of her jaw and her delicate ears.

He turned away from the sight, recognizing his interest for what it was. The attraction of a man to a lovely woman. He had no business thinking about any woman in a romantic light. Not until he'd solved the riddle of his past.

Heading toward the barn, he studied the looming structure. It was a huge, solid building, obviously well cared for. Pulling open one of the doors he entered into the dim interior. Instantly, the smells of animals assailed him along with the odors of hay, old wood and feed. He knew these smells the way he knew he was right-handed.

Off to the left was an area that served as Eli's black-smith shop. Brooms and assorted tools hung from horse-shoes attached to the bare wooden walls and overhead beams. Two steel frames suspended from the ceiling had been rigged so they could be released to swing down on either side of a fitful horse during a shoeing. An anvil sat secured to a worn workbench. Beside it was a water barrel and racks of horseshoes of different sizes. A rolling cart in the corner contained all the tools a farrier needed in their proper places.

Walking over to the shoes, John picked one up. It was too heavy. He hefted another. They should be lighter. He didn't know why, but he knew they should be.

The sound of a loud whinny greeted him. He replaced the shoes and moved toward the source. In the filtered daylight he made out a half dozen equine heads hanging over their stall doors to check out this newcomer.

He stopped at the first stall. Molly nuzzled at his shirt pocket. He scratched her head. "Sorry, I didn't know I needed to bring a treat. I'll do better tomorrow."

"Do you like horses, Mr. Doe?"

John turned to see Mr. Imhoff approaching from the back of the barn. In his free hand he held a pitchfork.

"It appears that I do," John answered.

"Is it true what my daughter says? That you have no memory of your life before you were found on our lane?"

"Yes, it's true."

"I have heard of such a thing. My father's oldest brother was kicked in the head by a horse. It was a full day before he recovered his senses."

"I have recovered my senses, just not any personal memories."

"That is a strange burden for God to give a man, but He has His reasons even if we cannot understand them."

Hiding his bitterness at God, John turned back to Molly. "Your mare has nice confirmation. Do you plan to breed her?"

"I've already had two nice colts from her." Eli began walking toward the back of the barn. John followed him to a small paddock where a black horse was trotting back and forth.

John leaned his elbows on the top rail and watched the animal with pleasure. "Hey, pretty boy. You look like you've got some get up and go," he murmured softly.

A blinding pain made him wince. He saw another black horse, rail-thin with its hip bones sticking out. The animal was covered in sores and flies. Death hovered over him.

Sucking in a quick breath, John opened his eyes. The vision was gone.

Eli didn't seem to notice anything unusual. He said, "This one's name is One-Way, and he should look fast. His sire, Willows Way, won the Hamiltonian at the Meadowlands ten years ago."

John rubbed the ache from his temple. "I'm sorry, I'm afraid that doesn't mean anything to me."

"It means his sire was a racehorse, a trotter and a *goot* one."

John looked at the Amish farmer in his dark coat, long gray beard and worn black hat. "You are raising racehorses?"

Eli smiled. "Mostly I raise and train carriage horses.

I bought my first Standardbred when I was a teenager. I was looking for a fast horse to impress my girlfriend."

"How did that work out?"

"The courtship did not, but the horse did. I got interested in the breed, began to study trade magazines and it wasn't long before I was breeding them myself. Back then I couldn't afford the stud fees of high-profile stallions. I got very *goot* at losing money at what my wife called my foolishness."

"Isn't horse racing and betting against your religion?"

"*Ja,* it is a worldly thing and thus forbidden to us."

"Okay, then I'm confused."

Eli's grin widened. "There is nothing wrong in breeding a fine horse. They are God's creatures, after all. If you can sell that horse for an honest price, there is nothing wrong with that, either. This one's brother is doing well on the racing circuit this year."

John smiled as understanding dawned. "I see. If the fine horse should win a race or two for some new owner, then the next foal from your mare will be worth even more money."

"*Ja.* It is all in the hands of God. I try to remember to keep Him first in my life for He rewards His faithful servants."

"When will you sell this fellow?"

"After the first of the year I will take him to the Winter Speed sale in Delaware, Ohio."

The place meant nothing to John.

Eli said, "My daughter has taken a keen interest in you."

John was surprised by the abrupt change of topic. "Your daughter has been very kind."

"She has a *goot* heart. It was the same with her mother." Eli's voice became wistful.

"I'm sorry for your loss. Karen told me what happened."

Eli turned to John. In a low steely voice, he said, "I would not want to see my daughter's kindness repaid with sorrow. Be careful of that, John Doe."

Taken aback, John stared at Eli. The last thing he wanted was to cause trouble for the woman who'd shown him so much kindness. He nodded solemnly. "I will, sir. I promise."

Late the following morning, Karen stopped the buggy where the lane met the highway and gave a sidelong glance at John seated beside her. He turned the collar of his coat up against the cold drizzle, but his excitement at finally getting to do something shimmered in his eyes.

"Which way would you like to go?" she asked.

"Which direction is the nearest interstate?"

She pointed north. "If you go through town and then take Yoder Road north about twenty-five miles you will reach the interstate."

"Let's go toward Hope Springs then and stop at the farms between here and the town. If I'm not from the area I most likely came in on a major highway."

Slapping the reins against Molly's rump, Karen sent the mare trotting down the blacktop. "I have one stop I need to make at the Sutters' farm. Are you certain you are not from this area?"

"No. Except that no one has reported me missing from around here. And no one has recognized me from the TV piece the local news ran on me. Do you mind if I try my hand at driving?" he asked.

Surprised by his request, she said, *"Nee,* I do not mind. Do you know how to drive a horse?"

"I think I can. I've been watching you do it." Taking the reins, he sat up straight and guided Molly down the highway.

After watching for a few minutes, Karen said, "That is *goot.* I think you've done this before."

John smiled at her. "I think you're right."

"Perhaps you are ex-Amish."

The moment the words left her mouth her heart sank like a stone. If John had taken the vows of their faith and then left the community, all would shun him. She would have to shun him.

He didn't seem to notice her concern. "The sheriff did discuss that possibility."

Dismissing the idea as unacceptable, she said, "You don't speak or understand our language. Surely you could not forget the tongue you grew up with."

He shrugged. "Who would think I could forget my own name? As far as I'm concerned anything is possible."

Racking her mind for local families with members who'd strayed, she quickly came up with several. In their tight-knit community, she was sure she knew all the young men who'd left. The only one close to John's age would have been Isaac Troyer's son who left almost ten years ago. He looked nothing like John. The others she could think of who had left the community were much younger men and a few young women.

There were at least three families who had moved into the area recently. If they had members leave the faith before coming to this church district she didn't know about them.

In less than a quarter of a mile, they reached the lane of another farm. John turned the horse onto the narrow road. Karen said, "When we get to the bishop's house, you should stay in the buggy."

"Why?"

"So that I may speak privately to Bishop Zook and ask if he can assist you."

"And if he says no?" John's tone carried a hint of annoyance.

"Bishop Zook is a wise and much-respected man. If you have his permission to speak to the members of our church it will open many doors that might otherwise be closed to you."

John relented. "All right. I'll follow your lead."

"Goot." She nodded her satisfaction.

Driving the buggy up to the front of the house, he drew the mare to a stop. Before Karen could step out, Joseph Zook walked out of the house toward her.

"Guder mariye, Karen," he called cheerfully. "What brings you here today?"

"Good morning, Bishop. I have brought someone to meet you. This is John Doe, the man who was found unconscious beside our lane."

Concern furrowed the minister's brow. "I have heard the story. I am glad to see that you are recovered, Mr. Doe."

"I'm not quite recovered, sir." John touched the bandage on the side of his head. "I have no memory of my past. I'm hoping that you can help me."

"I am sorry for your injury, but how can I help?"

"Do you recognize me? Have you ever seen me before?"

The bishop studied him intently then said, "*Nee,* I have not."

Karen could feel John's disappointment in the slump of his body beside her. She addressed the bishop. "John wishes to speak to members of our church to see if anyone knows him or knows something about him."

The bishop studied Karen intently. He switched to Pennsylvania Dutch. "You must be careful, Karen. To become involved in this outsider business is not a good thing."

She bowed her head slightly. "How can helping an injured man be a bad thing? I feel that this is what God wants me to do."

"Be sure it is God's will you are seeking, Karen, and not your own."

"I will heed your advice, Bishop."

The bishop turned his attention back to John and spoke in English. "You may speak to members of our church if they wish it also. I will pray that you find the answers you seek, young man."

Karen watched the bishop walk away. She had been warned. Her support for John must be limited and above reproach. She reached for the reins but John ignored her outstretched hand, turning the horse easily in the yard and sending her down the lane.

Karen put the bishop's warning behind her. "You have driven a buggy many times."

"Maybe I'm just a fast learner."

"Perhaps." Her spirits sank lower. How many English knew how to drive a buggy? Not many. It seemed more likely that her earlier assumption was correct. John had been raised Plain.

If he had left the church before his baptism, he would

be accepted by most of the Amish in her community. If, on the other hand, he had rejected the church after baptism he would be considered an outcast until he made a full confession before the congregation.

She glanced at him once more. How could a man confess his sins if he had no memory of them? He looked happy at the moment driving Molly along at a steady pace. The cold rain had stopped and the sun peeked out. Up ahead on the road, Henry Zook, the bishop's youngest son, was traveling to market in his farm wagon. John slowed Molly to follow behind him. When the way was clear and free of traffic, he sent Molly high stepping around the wagon.

When the mare drew level with the other horses she suddenly picked up her pace eager to get in front of them.

"You've got some speed, Molly girl," John called to the horse.

Instead of letting the mare keep her fast pace, he reined her in and grinned at Karen. "I'd love to let her go and see just how much she's got."

"Why don't you?" she asked, hoping to hear the right answer.

He shook his head. "No, she has too many miles to haul us yet. It wouldn't be kind to wear her out on a joyride."

Looking straight ahead, Karen smiled inwardly. "Whatever you have done in your past life, you care about animals. You can add it to your list of things you have discovered about yourself."

"Now if I can only locate a pencil sharpener," he added drily.

"What?" She tipped her head to stare at him in confusion.

"Never mind. Where to next?"

"Up ahead is the farm of Elam Sutter. He and some of his family moved here from Pennsylvania almost two years ago. Elam is getting married next week."

Twisting in the seat, she grasped his arm as excitement rippled though her mind. "I don't know why I didn't think of it sooner. It makes perfect sense."

"What makes perfect sense?"

"Perhaps you were coming for the wedding. Elam's fiancée, Katie Lantz, lived out in the world for several years. She knows many English. That must be it."

John tried not to get his hopes up but Karen's excitement was contagious. He asked, "Why didn't they report me as missing?"

"I don't know. Maybe they weren't sure when you would arrive. Maybe your coming was a surprise for them."

He wanted to believe her scenarios but he was growing used to disappointment. Still, his palms began to sweat. "We will see soon enough."

As they rolled into the yard, John saw four other buggies lined up beside the barn. He drew Molly to stop in front of the house.

Karen withdrew a large box from the back of the buggy. John took it from her and followed her to the front door. He was surprised when she didn't knock but went right in. The spacious kitchen was filled to overflowing with enticing smells of baking and the happy chatter of a half dozen women engaged in cleaning and polishing every surface in the house.

The oldest woman in the room came forward drying

her hands on her white apron. With a bright smile on her face, she said, "Karen, how nice to see you."

Karen said, "I've brought some of my mother's best bowls and platters for you to use at the wedding, Nettie."

"Wonderful. They will come in handy. I've forgotten how much work it takes to get ready for a wedding dinner." Nettie indicated a place for John to set his burden.

Karen said, "I have come with another errand, Nettie. Everyone, this is John Doe, the man who was found injured on our farm." Karen smiled encouragement at him.

The room grew quiet. John felt everyone's eyes on him. He scanned their faces looking for any hint of recognition. He saw nothing but blank stares. Either they had no idea who he was, or they were very good actresses. Once again his hopes slipped away. Why didn't someone know him? Why?

Looking over the group, Karen asked, "Where is Katie?"

Nettie said, "She is upstairs changing the baby."

One of the other women stepped forward. "Are you a friend of Katie's? I am Ruby, her future sister-in-law. This is my sister Mary, my sister-in-law Sally Yoder, and this is my mother, Nettie Sutter."

John nodded to them. "I'm not sure if I know Katie. I sure hope she knows me. The injury to my head robbed me of my memory. Karen thinks I may have been coming to the wedding."

Ruby and Mary exchanged puzzled glances. The two women were in their late twenties or early thirties. They were clearly related to Nettie. The women shared the same bright blue eyes, apple-red cheeks and blond hair although Nettie's was streaked with silver. They all wore plain dresses with white caps and white aprons.

The teenager, Sally, had red hair and freckles, but she wasn't smiling in welcome the way the others were. Her eyes held a frightened, guarded look. She said, "I will go get Katie."

Spinning around, she opened a door and rushed up the stairs beyond.

He waited, not taking his eyes off the stairwell. After an eternity, he heard footsteps coming down. The woman who entered the kitchen was dressed in the same Amish fashion as the others, but her hair was black as coal. She came toward him with a perplexed expression in her dark eyes. He held his breath, not daring to hope.

Stopping in front of him, she said, "Emma Wadler mentioned that she had met you at the inn, Mr. Doe. I'm sorry I can't be of any help. I don't recognize you."

He could barely swallow past the lump in his throat. A vicious headache, brought on by his frustration, sapped his strength. He managed to say, "I'm sorry we interrupted your afternoon. Thank you for your time."

Nettie spoke up, "Would you like some tea? I have the kettle on."

He shook his head, eager to escape before the pounding in his temple made him sick.

Katie said, "Elam is in his workshop. Perhaps he has met you before."

After looking at John closely, Karen said, "Come with me. I will show you the way."

He followed her outside into the fresh, cool air. Only then did he realize how hot the kitchen had been. Breathing deeply, he struggled to master the pain in his head.

"Take slow deep breaths," Karen said, standing at his side.

"I'm okay. How did you know?" If he kept his eyes closed the pain wasn't as bad.

"My mother used to get migraines. Do they happen to you often?" she asked gently.

"Two or three times since I woke up in the hospital."

She led him toward a small bench set beneath the bare gnarled branches of an apple tree. "Sit here. I will fetch Elam."

John was in no shape to argue. Leaning back against the rough bark of the tree, he let his mind go blank. Slowly, the pain receded.

"Hey, buddy, think fast."

John's eyes popped open as he threw up his hands to catch the apple being thrown at him. Only there was none. He was alone. He closed his eyes again and rebuilt the scene in his mind.

The tree overhead was lush with green leaves and heavy with fruit. Yellow apples. He was sitting on the cool grass with his back against the trunk of the tree. A hot breeze flowed over his skin, making him glad of the shade. Birds were singing nearby. An occasional raucous cry sounded from among them. He heard the drone of insects, then the pad of footsteps approaching.

Close by, a woman's voice, low and sweet said, "Here is my geils-mann loafing under a tree."

He tried to turn his head to see her face, but found himself staring at his boots, instead. The harder he tried to see her, the more rapidly the scene faded.

"John? John, this is Elam Sutter."

Opening his eyes, John saw Karen standing in front of him. Blinking hard, he looked around. The tree branches were bare. The lawn was brown and curled in winter sleep. Behind Karen, a tall, broad-shouldered man in a dark coat and black Amish hat stood regarding him intently.

Sharp bitterness lanced through John at the loss of his brief summer memory. His identity had been so close he could almost touch it and now it was gone.

How often could his mind be torn in two this way without finally ripping into pieces?

Chapter Six

Disappointment drained John's strength. The memory was gone. He couldn't get it back, but Karen and her friend were still waiting for him to speak.

He forced himself to rise and extended his hand to Elam. "I'm pleased to meet you, Mr. Sutter. I guess Karen has told you why I'm here."

Elam's grip was strong and firm. "She has. I do not know your face, John Doe. I wish I could be more help."

"Thank you. I'm sorry we interrupted your work."

The sound of the front door closing made them all look toward the house. Katie came out wrapping a black shawl around her shoulders. John happened to glance at Elam's face. The soft smile and the glow in the Amishman's eyes told John this was a love match. When Katie reached them, Elam slipped an arm around her waist to block the cold.

She said to John, "Are you sure you won't come in for a while? We have hot apple pie and coffee if you'd like."

"No, but thank you. Congratulations on your engagement."

"Danki," Katie blushed sweetly as she gazed at Elam

with adoring eyes. John wondered if a woman had ever looked at him that way.

After bidding the couple farewell, John followed Karen to the buggy. He relinquished the reins to her, knowing his headache wouldn't let him keep his mind on the road. They were getting ready to leave when Nettie came racing out of the house carrying a large basket covered with a checkered cloth.

Breathlessly, she reached them and handed the basket to Karen. "This is for you and your family. A couple of my peach pies because I know Eli likes them best. How is he doing?"

Karen accepted the basket. "He gets his cast off next week, but he must still wear a brace and sling. He is chaffing at the bit to get back to work."

"Has feeling returned to his hand?"

"Some, but he has no strength in it."

"The poor man. He's coming to the wedding, isn't he?" A faint crease of worry appeared between Nettie's brows.

"He would not miss it," Karen assured her.

Relief smoothed away Nettie's frown. "That is *goot*. And you, Mr. Doe, you are welcome to come to the wedding dinner. There will be plenty of food and there will be other English there, too," she added with a bright smile.

"Thank you. That is very kind." He tried to be non-committal. Attending the wedding of someone he barely knew seemed presumptuous.

Nettie fixed her gaze on Karen. "Tell your father…tell him I think about him often. When this wedding fuss is over you must all come for Sunday dinner."

"We will look forward to it."

John closed his eyes and rubbed his brow as Karen drove Molly back to the highway. The jolting and creaking of the buggy added nausea to his discomfort.

Karen pulled Molly to a halt when they reached the end of the Sutters' lane. "Do you still wish to go into Hope Springs?"

What he wanted was to lie down somewhere dark and quiet and let his mind travel back to that green, hot place and stay there until he saw the face of the woman who had been with him. As much as he wanted to do that, he knew he couldn't stop now. "Let's keep going. I want to see as many people as I can today."

Karen studied John with deep concern. His color was pale, his eyes sunken with pain. He looked as if he might topple out of the buggy at any second. He kept one hand pressed to his forehead in an attempt to block the light from his eyes.

When she didn't start Molly moving, he glanced at her. "What's wrong? I said let's go into town."

She let out a sigh. "*Nee,* we are going home. You have done too much today. You are in pain and you need rest."

He sat up straight to hide his weakness. "I'm fine. It's just a headache."

"Men! Always trying to show how tough they are. Anyone with eyes in their head can see you are done in. We will go home now and that is the end of it. Tomorrow will be here soon enough."

"I'll be okay," he insisted.

"*Ja.* When you have had a rest I'm sure you will be fine." Clicking her tongue, she urged Molly onto the highway and sent her trotting briskly toward their farm.

"Are you always this domineering?"

He had no idea how tough she could be, but he just might find out. "When I must tell a child what to do, *ja,* I am."

"Now you're saying I'm acting like a child?"

"A stubborn, willful child."

"I'm going to let that slide. I can see arguing with you is fruitless. When did you take over the job of raising your brothers and sister?"

"I am the eldest daughter. It is expected of me to care for the younger ones. My mother was killed four years ago if that is what you are asking?"

"You do a good job with them."

"They are *goot* children. They make the job easy."

"Even Jacob?"

"Jacob is in a hurry to be the man of the house. He wants to take over for our father until Papa is well."

"But you don't want him to do that."

She hadn't realized her fear was that transparent. "Being a farrier is a hard job. It takes strength. A man must know how to read a horse. Some of the draft horses my father works on weigh nearly a ton. A man can shoe a horse nine times without trouble and on the tenth time that horse decides he wants to kill the farrier."

"I didn't say you were wrong to worry."

Her annoyance slipped away. "I'm sorry. It's just that he is so young yet. He idolized Seth, our brother who was killed. Seth was big and strong like Papa, not slender like Jacob. Seth had the touch when it came to horses. Mamm used to say he could whisper to them and they did just as he wished. Jacob wants to be a horseman like Seth was but he is impatient."

John sat back and stared into space. "A horseman. He

wants to be a horseman, a *geils-mann*. Here is my *geils-mann* loafing under a tree."

Karen eyed him with concern. "What are you talking about?"

He focused on her face. "I had another memory flash. It was summer, and I was sitting under an apple tree. There was a woman behind me. She said, 'Here is my *geils-mann* loafing under a tree.' I heard the words clear as day."

"Who was she?" Karen asked.

"I don't know. I didn't see her face."

"How did you know what the word meant?" she asked in surprise.

"I'm not sure. I just know."

As the ramifications of his comment sank in, Karen's heart sank, too. *Geils-mann* was an Amish expression. Only someone raised speaking Pennsylvania Dutch would use the word. If John had not been raised Amish then the woman he spoke of surely had been. Karen glanced at John. Who was John Doe and who was this woman to him?

Several days later, John was outside early in the morning gathering a load of wood for his stove when he saw Nick Bradley drive into the yard. John's heart jumped into overdrive. Maybe the sheriff's investigation had turned up something new. He waited with bated breath as Nick climbed out of his SUV.

Touching the brim of his hat, Nick said, "Morning. I was in the neighborhood and thought I'd check and see how you're doing."

"I'm fine. Have you learned anything new?"

"No. I'm sorry."

John's anticipation drained away. He carried the logs to the box beside his front door and dropped them. He'd have to learn not to get his hopes up. Somehow.

Nick said, "I was hoping you might have found out something. Not that I want you to make me look bad."

"No worries. I'm still a walking blank. I've had a few flashes of memory, but nothing concrete."

"Are you writing them down?"

John paused and looked at the sheriff. "I hadn't thought of that."

"You should. Even the smallest thing you recall might help me. How's the head?" He pointed to John's bandage.

"Better."

"My cousin Amber wanted me to remind you that you need to come in to Dr. White's office and get your stitches out."

He rubbed gingerly at his dressing. The sutures had started to itch. "I know I was supposed to go in a few days ago, but I've had other things on my mind."

"I've got time to run you into Hope Springs this morning. Shall I see if they can work you in? I'm free for a while unless I get a call."

"That would be great, but how do I get back if you've got to leave?" A light dusting of snow covered the ground this morning and occasional flakes drifted down from the gray sky. John didn't want to walk five miles back to the farm in this weather.

"We have a couple of folks in town that provide taxi services to the Amish. Amber can arrange a ride if you need it." Nick made the phone call.

After a brief conversation, he closed the phone. "All set. They can see you in half an hour."

"Let me tell Miss Imhoff where I'm going. She likes to keep a tight leash on me."

Nick chuckled. "I've heard she can be a tough cookie."

The two men walked toward the main house. Nick asked, "How's it working out? You staying here."

"It's fine. The boy, Jacob, isn't thrilled, but Noah and Anna don't seem to mind. Eli is taking a wait-and-see attitude."

"And Karen?"

John glanced toward the house. "She's been very kind."

Before they reached the steps, Eli came out to greet them. His stoic face showed nothing of what he was thinking. He nodded to the sheriff. "*Goot* day to you."

"The same to you, Eli. I'm going to take John into town so Doc White can check him out. I'll see that he gets back, too. How is your arm?"

Flexing his fingers in the sling, Eli said, "It is healing."

Jacob came out of the house followed by Anna and Noah. The children hung back at the sight of the sheriff.

Nick glanced from Eli to Jacob. "I had a complaint about some Amish boys racing buggies over on Sky Road yesterday. You wouldn't know anything about that, would you?"

"*Nee*. We do not," Eli stated firmly. John caught the furtive glance Jacob shot in the sheriff's direction before looking down.

Nick nodded. "It's dangerous business racing on a public road. Gina Curtis had to put her car in the ditch to avoid hitting someone. It did a fair amount of damage to her front end. None of the buggy drivers stuck around. She wasn't hurt but she could have been."

Eli glanced at his son. "Do you know anything about this?"

"No, Papa." Jacob glared at the sheriff. If he did know something, he wasn't talking. Noah remained uncharacteristically quiet.

Eli said, "Go on to school now, children."

The kids rushed down the steps with their lunch pails in hand and headed toward the school two miles away. Several times they threw looks over their shoulders. John had the distinct feeling they did know something.

After bidding Mr. Imhoff goodbye, John climbed in the sheriff's SUV. When Nick got in and started the truck, John said, "You think Jacob was involved, don't you?"

Nick turned the vehicle around and drove out the lane. They passed the children walking. Only Anna waved.

Nick said, "Gina's description could fit ten boys in this area. I didn't expect to get a confession. Illicit buggy racing goes on amongst Amish teenagers the same way drag racing goes on among the English kids. A lot of Amish parents turn a blind eye to that kind of behavior during the *rumspringa*."

"What's that?"

"It means running-around years. Amish teens are free to experiment with things that won't be allowed once they join the church. You'll see their buggies outfitted with boom boxes, they'll have cell phones and they'll dress like regular kids when they are away from the farm. Jacob is young for that type of behavior. *Rumspringa* normally starts when the kids are about sixteen, but his dad has some fine horses."

"Yes, he does."

The sheriff looked at him sharply. "Do you know something about horses?"

"I know which end is which. I seem to know what a good Standardbred looks like. I found out I can drive a buggy and Eli's two-wheeled cart without a problem. He's been letting me use the cart to visit farms around here. The one thing I did remember was a woman's voice. She called me her *geils-mann*."

"She called you her horseman? That's interesting. Maybe we ruled out your being ex-Amish too soon. It's good to hear things are coming back to you."

John had been wondering about the young woman ever since his vision. Was she his sister, a friend, his wife? He had no way of knowing.

He turned to stare out the window. "Not enough things are coming back to me."

Karen didn't want to reveal to her father her burning curiosity about the sheriff's visit. Instead, when he came inside, she served him another cup of coffee before casually asking, "Where is the sheriff taking John?"

"To see the doctor in town."

"Oh." Relief made her knees weak. He wasn't taking him away to his old life. She sat down quickly. Even though that was what she prayed for, losing him, even for the right reason, wasn't something she wanted to face. Not yet.

Eli watched her closely. "You have taken a great liking to John Doe."

Apparently her feelings weren't as well hidden as she had hoped. She toyed with the corner of her apron. "He is so lost. I wish to help him. That is all."

Her father covered her hands with his own. "Take care, daughter. He is not one of us."

"He is one of God's children."

"Do not seek to divert me. You know exactly what I mean. Our faith makes no exceptions for those who stray outside the *Ordnung*."

"I have done nothing against the rules of the church. John will only be here a few more days." She forced herself to smile in reassurance, but her father was not fooled.

"I should have encouraged you to marry long ago, but I was so befuddled without your mother. It was selfish of me."

"Papa, I am happy caring for the little ones and keeping your house. I could not ask for more."

Sadness filled his eyes. "I would ask for more in your life. A woman should have a husband to love and shelter her. The risk of temptation would not be so great."

Karen looked down at her hands. "I am not tempted by John Doe."

"Do not forget that I am a man like all other men. I see the way he looks at you. I see the way you try not to look back at him."

She pulled her hands away from his. "I care about him. I don't deny that. When I saw him lying on the ground bleeding and wounded, I saw Seth. I could not save my brother. He died in my arms. I know his death was the will of God. Just as I know John lived by the will of God alone."

"We do not know why God brings sadness or joy into our lives. We only know all comes from His purpose for us." Eli leaned back in his chair and took a sip of coffee.

"I know that, Papa. But why has God taken away

John's memory? I believe it is because God wants to show John something he could not see before."

Eli grasped her hand again. "Karen, Karen, you cannot know this. You cannot presume to know *Gotte wille*."

She looked into his eyes so full of concern. "I'm sorry, Papa. I did not mean to upset you. Please trust me when I say you have nothing to worry about."

Leaning forward, she said earnestly, "My heart is here, with you, and with the children. Nothing could make me throw that away."

He relaxed and nodded slightly. "You have always been a *goot* daughter and strong in your faith. You see something in the *Englischer* that I do not see. You may be right. God sent John Doe into our midst for a reason. I will keep an open mind about this man."

John entered the Hope Springs Medical Clinic, a modern one-story blond brick building, with a niggling sense of dread. He'd had enough of hospitals and doctors without getting any answers in return. Inside, he checked in with the elderly receptionist and took a seat in the waiting room. He didn't have to wait long.

A young woman in a white lab coat and blue scrubs called his name. He followed her down a short hallway and took a seat on the exam-room table.

"It's nice to finally meet you, Mr. Doe. I'm Amber Bradley, Nick Bradley's cousin." She stuck a thermometer under John's tongue.

She removed it when it beeped and John said, "You're the one I need to thank for the financial help."

Wrapping a blood-pressure cuff around his arm, she said, "You're welcome, but it wasn't just me. A lot of people wanted to help."

John remained quiet until she had finished with his blood pressure. When she took the stethoscope out of her ears, he said, "I wasn't aware that I required a midwife."

She chuckled. "I am a woman with many hats. One of those being an office nurse."

The door opened and a tall, distinguished man with silver hair came in leaning heavily on a cane. "Yes, and she is proof that good help is hard to come by these days."

"Ha!" she retorted. "You just try running this office without me, Harold."

"No doubt I'll have to when you marry what's-his-name," he grumbled.

"Is that any way to talk about your grandson? Don't worry, Mr. Doe, Dr. White's bark is worse than his bite." She checked John's ears, his eyes and then his throat.

Dr. White, who had been reading John's chart, said, "You are a very interesting case, Mr. Doe."

"So I've been told." John tried not to let his bitterness show. He hated being an oddity, the freak with a damaged mind.

"I imagine you're tired of hearing that." The doctor washed his hands and pulled on a pair of latex gloves.

"Good guess."

Harold began removing the bandage from John's head. "We medical people live for cases like yours. The odd thing, the unusual diagnoses. It's like catnip to us. We want to define it, study it, understand it, cure it."

John winced as the tape pulled his hair. "I'm in favor of a cure. Tell me which pill to take."

"Amnesia following a trauma isn't unusual, but normally it involves losing a short period of time just prior to the injury. A prolonged and complete amnesia such as you have is exceedingly rare."

"Lucky me." This time John didn't disguise his sarcasm.

"Your scalp is healed nicely. How are your ribs?"

"Not bad if I take it slow."

"Good. I'm going to have Amber take out the stitches. Any headaches?"

"Sometimes."

"Bad ones?"

"They can be. I think they're getting better. Maybe I'm just getting used to them."

"Is there any particular thing that triggers them?" The doctor pulled off his gloves and picked up John's chart.

"I get these flashes, like images from a movie. I think they are memories, but I can't be sure. When that happens the pain gets intense."

"You say you think they're memories. Anything specific?"

John felt stupid sharing the few instances that he'd had. "Frying trout. A woman laughing. A sick or starving horse. A woman using an Amish word. Nothing with any context of time or place."

"The same woman?" Amber asked.

"I'm not sure. I don't see her face."

"Are these flashes becoming more frequent?" The doctor made a note on the chart.

John held still as Amber began removing his stitches. "Not that I can tell. Some days I'll have one or two, some days I won't have any."

He winced but didn't yelp as she worked on one stubborn stitch. Finally, she said, "All done. You'll just need to keep it clean and dry, but otherwise you're good to go. I understand you're staying at Eli Imhoff's place."

"Yes. That's where I was found. I've been interviewing the Amish in the area for the past several days hoping to find someone who recognizes me. I mean, I must have been in the area for a reason."

Closing the chart, Dr. White asked, "You've been going door-to-door?"

"I started with the farms closest to where I was found but I'm not having much luck. Don't get me wrong. The Amish have been forthcoming, maybe because I've had Karen Imhoff with me, but no one knows anything."

Amber and Dr. White exchanged glances. Amber said, "There might be an easier way to meet people than going to every house in the area."

John looked at her with interest. "How?"

Dr. White said, "November is the month for Amish weddings. Sometimes as many as four hundred people show up for them. Elam Sutter's wedding is this coming Thursday."

"Nettie Sutter did invite me to the supper."

"Great," Amber said, looking at Harold. "Phillip and I will be there, too."

"Oh, and I'm chopped liver now?" Harold asked, a teasing edge in his tone.

Amber smiled at John. "Dr. Harold White will also be attending the event, and he knows every soul in this county."

Harold met John's gaze and said, "Chances are almost everyone there will have already heard your story."

"How?" John asked. "They don't have radio or TV."

Amber laughed. "You would be surprised how fast news travels in a small community like this."

Harold rubbed his chin. "I'm sure the Imhoff family will be going for the entire day. Why don't you ride along with me, young man? I'll introduce you around and see if we can come up with someone who knows you."

John realized it could be his best chance to meet many of the reclusive Amish in the area. He inclined his head. "Sir, I would be delighted to accompany you."

Chapter Seven

True to his word, Nick stuck around to give John a lift from the clinic back to the farm. As the sheriff drove away, John stood in the yard staring at the farmhouse. Once again he was struck by how tidy the farmstead was. The fences were all in good repair, the barn and out-buildings had been recently painted. Everything spoke of order and neatness. Eli Imhoff was a good steward of his land.

Shoving his hands in his pockets, John wondered what kind of steward he was. Did he have lands and a home to care for? Or did he live in an apartment in a crowded city? If he could wish for a home—it would be one like this.

Instead of going into the grandfather house, John made his way to the barn and to the stalls where the horses stood dozing or munching grain. He was surprised by how comfortable he felt among them. Sometime in his life he must've worked on a ranch or farm. If only he could remember where or when.

He was petting the nose of the big draft horse when he heard a door open. Looking over his shoulder, he saw Karen coming from another part of the barn. In her hands she carried a pail brimming full of apples.

Her face brightened when she caught sight of him. "You are back. What did the doctor say?"

John moved to take the pail from her. "He said I'm doing good. Except for not remembering anything, of course."

"You will remember when God wills it."

"I wish He'd hurry up, I'm tired of living in the dark."

"I know it is a terrible burden for you."

"You must be tired of hearing me complain. What are the apples for?"

"I'm putting up applesauce."

"Need some help?"

She slanted a grin at him. "Can you pare an apple?"

Giving an exaggerated shrug, he said, "Only one way to find out."

Inside the house, John sat at the kitchen table and quickly discovered he could use a paring knife. As he cored and chopped the contents of the bucket into a large bowl he had a chance to observe Karen at work.

Every move she made was efficient. She seemed to know exactly what she needed to do when she needed to do it. The canning jars were washed and placed in a large kettle and boiled. Setting them aside after ten minutes, she put his chopped apples into a second kettle. Before long the mouthwatering aroma of cooking apples and cinnamon filled the air.

"I hope you're not going to can all of it," he said as he started cutting the last pile of apples. His stomach rumbled loudly.

She wiped her brow with the back of her hand. The

steam had given her face a rosy glow. "I am saving plenty for supper."

He tipped his head. "I think I should have a taste now in case the apples were bad. You don't want to give bad applesauce to your family."

She fisted her hands on her hips. "Of all the pieces you sampled while you were chopping, how many were sour?"

"Okay, I'm busted. I missed lunch, you know. Do you have eyes in the back of your head under that bonnet thing?"

"I don't need eyes in the back of my head. I brought in enough apples to make eight pints. I can see I'm only going to have enough to fill seven jars."

"If I promise to go get more fruit can I have a dish of those apples before you squish them?"

Karen laughed and pulled a brown ceramic bowl from the cupboard. "*Ja,* but you had better not complain if it spoils your supper."

As she heaped the bowl full of stewed apples, John quickly carved an apple skin into the shape of huge red lips and stuck it between his teeth. When Karen turned around and saw him she doubled over with laughter, nearly spilling his snack on the floor. For the first time in his new life John felt totally happy.

Later that evening, when everyone was finishing their meal, he caught Karen's eye, wiggled his brows and held up his empty plate with a wide grin. She smothered an abrupt giggle, causing her family members to stare at her. Rising quickly, she began to clear the table.

John said, "Let me help you."

Anna, also in the process of gathering up plates, gave

him a funny look. "This is woman's work." She looked at her father for confirmation. "Isn't it, Papa?"

Eli glanced at Karen and then at his boys. "A man must know how to do a woman's work if his wife needs help just as a woman must know how to do a man's work if her husband needs help."

Noah eyed the dirty dishes in disgust. "But you don't need help tonight, do you Karen?"

"*Nee,* Anna and I can manage, but thank you for your offer."

John slipped his hands in the front pockets of his jeans wishing he could spend more time with Karen but knowing it wasn't wise.

Noah said, "Come and play checkers with me, John."

Relieved, John followed the boy into the living room where Noah quickly set up the board. Eli settled himself in his favorite chair, opened his Bible and began reading. Jacob pretended interest in a book of his own, but his eyes were drawn repeatedly to the game.

Karen and Anna joined the men when they were done in the kitchen. Karen pulled a basket of mending from the cupboard in the corner, sat down beside her father and began to thread a needle. It seemed to John that she was never idle. Anna brought out a small, faceless doll to play with.

John's gaze was drawn repeatedly to where Karen sat. The lamplight gave a soft glow to her face. A gentle smile curved her lips. The white bonnet on her hair reminded him of a halo.

She was so beautiful it hurt his eyes, and he had no business admiring her.

"Your move," Noah said.

John realized he'd been staring and focused his attention on his play.

Anna came to John's elbow. "Do you want to hear the poem I'm going to recite for the school Christmas program?"

Noah shook his head. "Not again. We've heard it a million times."

"Noah, she needs the practice," Karen chided gently.

John said, "I haven't heard it. Miss Anna, I would love to hear your poem."

Flashing him a bright smile, she folded her hands and stared at a spot over his head. *"Auf einer Nacht so ehrlich in einem Land weit entfernt."*

Jacob snickered. "He doesn't understand German, Anna."

She propped her hands on her hips. "David Yoder is repeating it in English at the program so everyone will know what it means."

John sought to soothe her. "You say it just as you will at your program. When you're done, you can interpret it for me."

Her smile returned. "The first line means on a night so fair in a land far away."

"Got it. Let me hear the whole thing. I'm sure Noah will tell me if you mess up."

Noah chuckled. "You know that's right."

Anna began again. As she spoke, John caught Karen's eye. The look she gave him conveyed her approval. A warm feeling of happiness settled over him. He smiled back at her.

Eli cleared his throat. John caught the stern look he shot his daughter. Karen quickly returned to her sewing. John gave his attention back to the checkerboard.

After Anna finished her poem she went back to playing with her doll. When Noah lost his third match in a row to John, he dropped his head onto his forearms. "Jacob always wins, too."

John ruffled the boy's hair. "You almost had me on that last one."

Eli closed his Bible. "Do you play chess, Mr. Doe?"

Did he? John tried to see the pieces and the moves in his mind. He nodded. "I think so."

"Jacob has a talent for the game. Why don't you two play?"

"I'm willing." John looked at the boy. Indecision flashed across Jacob's face.

Not wanting to push the kid, John began clearing the checkers from the board. He hummed a tune softly as he stacked them inside the box. When the board was clear, he looked at Jacob. The boy's face had gone pale. He snapped his book shut. "I'm going to bed."

John watched Jacob rush out of the room and wondered what he had done to upset the youngster. He looked at Karen. She just shrugged her shoulders.

Folding up the chessboard, John handed it to Noah. Rising to his feet, he said, "I think I'll turn in, too."

Laying her mending aside, Karen said, "I will get you a lamp. It is dark out."

In the kitchen, she pulled a kerosene lamp from a cabinet. Setting it on the counter, she lifted the glass chimney and lit the wick.

John took it from her hand. "I'm sorry if I've upset your family. Maybe my staying here wasn't a good idea."

"It is only for a couple more days. We can manage."

Gazing into her luminous eyes, John found himself

wishing he could stay longer. The thought was foolish and he knew it.

Once he found out about his past, then maybe he could start thinking about a future. Until then he would be crazy to get attached to anyone, especially the lovely Amish woman standing before him.

The beautiful autumn morning of the wedding dawned cold but clear. After making sure everyone in the family was dressed in their Sunday best Karen ushered them out to the waiting buggy. Jacob had gone ahead with the bench wagon. The special enclosed wagon held the several dozen narrow wooden benches that their church district used for Sunday services.

Karen glanced toward the *dawdy haus* and saw John watching them from the porch. For the past several days he'd been making himself at home on the farm, helping her father with the horses and her with chores. Having him across from her at the supper table had become the high point of her evenings. But he would be moving to the inn tomorrow. His time with her family was almost up. There wouldn't be any more afternoons spent laughing over a pail of apples.

He lifted a hand in a brief wave. Karen glanced at her father and saw he was watching her. She didn't wave back but climbed in the buggy instead.

The trip into town was accomplished in short order. The wedding ceremony itself was to take place at the home of Naomi and Emma Wadler, both friends of the bride. When Karen and her family entered the house the bridal party was already sitting in the front row of the wooden benches.

Katie wore a new plain dress of light blue. Elam looked quite handsome in his dark coat and not the least bit nervous. Near them sat two each of Elam's sisters and brothers-in-law, their wedding attendants.

Nettie, the groom's mother, wouldn't be at the ceremony. She would be at home getting ready for the dinner. Karen and several other women would leave, once the vows were exchanged, to act as servers for the several hundred people expected to arrive that afternoon.

At exactly nine o'clock the singing began. Bishop Zook and the two ministers escorted the bride and groom to a separate room. While they were given instructions on the duties of marriage in the Council room, the congregation sang the wedding hymns.

When the bridal couple returned, the bishop began his sermon. He spoke with simple eloquence about the marriages in the Old Testament. He spoke about Adam and Eve and proceeded to the Great Flood and the virtuousness of Noah's household. He recounted the story of Isaac and Rebekah and talked about the way God works through events to bring marriage partners together.

Bishop Zook looked at the couple and said, "God had a plan for you. You found each other because you were willing to submit to His will and to His choice."

His words brought tears to Karen's eyes. She knew the struggles Katie had endured in her life away from the Amish. It was through those circumstances that God led her and her baby daughter back to the faith and into the life of Elam Sutter.

Karen couldn't help wondering how God was using John in her life. What plan did He have for each of them? Whatever it was, it could not be marriage.

It was nearly noon before the lengthy sermon was concluded and the bishop asked Katie and Elam to step forward. They clasped hands with gentle smiles at each other. The bishop placed his hand over theirs. He pronounced a blessing upon them and asked, "Are you willing to enter together into wedlock as God in the beginning ordained and commanded?"

"Yes," they both answered in firm, solemn voices.

As he asked each of them if they were confident God had chosen the person beside them to be their husband or wife, Karen's thoughts turned again to John.

Had he made a similar vow? Had he pledged to cherish and care for a woman as a Christian husband until the Lord separated them by death? Was there someone waiting and praying to see him again?

Was there a woman whose heart skipped a beat at the sight of his smile the way hers did?

John was happy for the company of the gruff doctor when they arrived at the Sutter farm. Buggies filled every free space between the house and barn and extended down the lane. The corral overflowed with horses munching hay as they waited patiently to take families home. Everywhere, groups of women in long dresses and men in dark suits with black hats stood talking in animated conversations or were working together.

One group of adults was busy washing dishes in large red plastic tubs as a trio of young women carried out trays of dirty plates and hurried back inside with the clean ones.

The doctor had been right. There had to be over two hundred people John could speak with. He worked to temper his expectations. He'd been disappointed too many times already.

When Dr. White got out of the car the men and women standing nearby greeted him cheerfully. One, a small gnomelike man with a long white beard said,

"The *goot doktor* is here. If you want free advice, step right up."

Harold clapped a hand on the old man's shoulder. "Good to see you, too, Reuben Beachy. Tell me, why did they invite an old rascal like you to this wedding?"

Reuben chuckled. "Who better to invite than a harness maker when you are getting hitched for life?"

Everyone laughed at his joke including Dr. White. Harold raised one hand and said to the group, "I will have time to hear what ails you and repeat all the gossip, but I must see the bride and groom and eat before the food is gone."

They all chuckled as Harold led the way to the house. As John entered the Sutter home, he was stunned by the transformation that had taken place inside. Wall partitions had been removed to open up all the downstairs rooms. The kitchen itself was a crush of women working.

From the front door he could see trestle tables had been lined along the kitchen walls, around three sides of the living room and even into an adjoining bedroom.

The bride and groom sat in one corner of the living room in view of everyone. Katie sat at Elam's left hand. Young women filled the tables around the couple and sat with their backs to the walls while the young men sat on the opposite side of the table facing the girls.

The tables didn't contain flowers. Rather, stalks of celery had been placed in glass jars as decoration. Candy dishes, beautiful cakes and large bowls of fruit completed the simple but festive array. John searched for Karen in the rooms but didn't see her anywhere.

Doctor White glanced at John. "Shall we start by asking the women in the kitchen if they know you?"

John's eyes were drawn to the bride and groom and

the loving looks they exchanged as they visited with their friends.

He nodded toward them. "No. This is their day. I don't want to take anything away from them. We can speak to people outside after the meal is done."

The doctor gave John a smile of approval. "All right."

A strapping Amish man with a clean-shaven face approached them. He introduced himself as Adam Troyer and asked them to follow him. He seated them at one of the bedroom tables where Amber and a tall, handsome man already faced each other.

The man with Amber rose and held out his hand. His resemblance to Harold was unmistakable. He said, "You must be John. I'm Dr. Phillip White and this old rascal is my grandfather." He clapped Harold on the shoulder.

"Who you calling old?" Harold grumbled.

"Behave," Amber warned them both with a hard look.

The men grinned at each other, but took their seats. Amber and Phillip already had their food. John and Harold didn't have to wait long. In another minute, a petite woman came in with a plate loaded with roast chicken and duck, mashed potatoes, dressing and creamed celery. She set the dish in front of Harold. John recognized her as the woman who ran the inn. She set down a second plate loaded with cookies and slices of cake.

Harold said, "Thank you, Emma. I hear the wedding was held in your home."

"*Ja,* Katie has no family here so we are her family now." She smiled at John. "Your plate is coming."

"I have it here."

John looked over his shoulder to see Karen bearing a pair of plates for him. When she set them down, his eyes grew round. "You don't expect me to eat all that, do you?"

"I do, and you will have more later. No one leaves an Amish wedding hungry."

He pushed the dessert plate toward her. "At least help me with this."

She patted her slender waist. "I ate before the wedding party arrived so that I could help serve today. I must get back to work. More guests will begin arriving shortly."

Emma said, "Why don't you take a short break? Ruby and I can handle serving for a little while. I'm sure Mr. Doe has questions about our customs. I will bring you a cup of tea."

Karen grinned. "Then I will happily cover for your break when I am done here. You may tell Adam Troyer I won't be long. I'm sure he is ready for a break, too."

Emma's flushed cheeks turned an even brighter red. She left the table without another word.

"So that's the way the wind is blowing," Harold said with a chuckle. "I wondered why Adam was always at the inn. I thought surely there couldn't be that much work for a handyman to do around the place."

Emma returned with a cup of hot tea for Karen but didn't linger. Karen took a sip, then filched a cookie from John's plate. John leaned toward her. "Should I go wish the bride and groom happy before I eat?"

Karen shook her head. "No congratulations are given at an Amish wedding. It is taken for granted that Elam and Katie have found the partner chosen by God for them. We have no divorce so marriage is forever. Today is a happy but serious day."

In the living room, a young man with curly brown hair rose to his feet and spoke in Pennsylvania Dutch.

Dr. White said, "The first round of eating is almost over. It's time for the singing to start."

John sent Karen an inquisitive glance. "The first round of eating?"

"*Ja,* we will start the wedding supper in an hour or so. Many of the older guests will leave soon, but the young people will stay. There will be much visiting and even games out in the barn."

Around the tables, guests were bringing out their songbooks. The curly-headed young man, in a beautiful voice, started the hymn, and soon all joined in except the bride and groom. There was no accompanying music, just a moving blend of dozens of voices.

Karen asked, "Do you recognize the melody or the words?"

Was that worry he saw in her eyes? Why would she be concerned if he knew the song? He shook his head. "No, it's not familiar."

She seemed to relax. At least she gave him a half smile before joining in the hymn. Her sweet alto was pleasing to his ear. Once again he felt a deep pull of attraction toward Karen, something he couldn't put his finger on but something he wanted to hold on to. Each day he spent with her those feelings deepened.

He counted her among his very few friends. He wasn't sure she would appreciate how often he thought of her not as a friend but as a woman.

When the first song was done, a young woman stood to announce a second song. She then led the congregation. Her voice, pure and light as sunshine, flowed around the room. He listened more closely. There was something deeply familiar in her voice. Had he heard her before?

Chapter Eight

When the song ended, John touched Karen's arm and gestured toward the singer. "Who is that woman?"

"That is Sarah Wyse, why?"

"She has a beautiful voice. Could I have heard her before?"

"Where?"

"I have no idea. Does she live near you?"

"Not far. She lives just at the edge of Hope Springs. Her husband ran a harness shop. He passed away three years ago from cancer. She works in the fabric store now."

"It's strange. I just think I've heard her voice before."

"I will see if she will talk to you when the singing is done." Karen stayed for one more hymn and then returned to her duties serving the guests.

When John had eaten his fill, he excused himself from the table and walked outside. Uncertain of how to introduce himself to the Amish and uncomfortable at being an outsider at a wedding feast, he stood alone on the porch gathering his courage. The door opened and Nettie bustled out with a large pan full of dishes.

Catching sight of him, she stopped and settled her load on one hip. "Have you had enough to eat, Mr. Doe?"

"More than enough. Thank you. Why are you working? Shouldn't you be inside enjoying your son's wedding day?"

"The parents of the bride and groom receive no special treatment on this day. It is my job to supervise the kitchen and make sure everything runs smoothly. That is my gift to my son and my new daughter. And you, Mr. Doe, you wish to speak to some of our guests, do you not?"

"I thought I did but I didn't realize I would feel so awkward about it."

She looked over to the men gathered near the barn. "Do not feel awkward. Let me get someone to take you around and introduce you."

Waving her hand toward them, she called to Eli Imhoff. "Eli, come here."

He crossed the yard with quick steps. "What do you need, Nettie?"

John couldn't help but notice the soft look that passed between them or how the color bloomed in Nettie's cheeks. She said, "John wishes to be introduced to some of our guests. I have not the time. Can you escort him for me?"

Eli nodded. "It was my intention to do so."

As Nettie carried her pan to the washing tubs, Eli followed her with his eyes. John said, "She has been very kind."

"*Ja,* she is a *goot* woman."

The door to the house opened. Several Amish couples came out followed by Harold. The elderly doctor pulled a roll of antacid tablets from his pocket. "I knew

I was going to need these. The food is always so good but so rich."

He offered some to John and Eli. John declined but Eli accepted them. Dr. White said, "How is the arm, Eli?"

"Old bones heal slow."

"Tell me about it." Harold rubbed his thigh.

Eli jerked his head toward the barn. "Let us see if any one recognizes John Doe."

Harold said, "Amber and Karen are asking around inside. I thought the women would be more comfortable talking to them."

John followed the men through the maze of buggies to the barn. Inside, youngsters were engaged in games and chatting in groups. He caught sight of Jacob and several of his friends looking down from the hayloft. He was surprised to see the young men were much older than Jacob. The boy's friends were staring at John with outright curiosity and snickering.

Eli asked for everyone's attention, speaking English out of deference to John and Harold. He briefly explained John's situation and asked if anyone knew him or had seen him before. John scanned the faces of the young men and women looking for signs of recognition. The only one he knew was the freckle-faced redheaded young woman he'd met several days before.

Sally, that was her name. He smiled and nodded to her. Her eyes widened. She spoke to her friends and then hurried past him back toward the house.

He followed Eli and Harold from group to group speaking to elderly couples, young parents with children and teenagers that had paired off and were enjoying the social event. Each time he met with expressions of compassion but no concrete information.

Giving up for the moment, John excused himself from the older man and returned to the house. Something in Sally's expression stayed with him. He wanted a chance to talk to her in private but didn't know how that would be possible. He was about to open the door when Karen came out with Sarah Wyse, the singer, by her side.

Karen stopped in surprise when she saw John in front of her. "We were just coming to find you. John, this is Sarah Wyse."

The way his eyes roved over Sarah's face sent a prickle of envy through Karen. Immediately, she chided herself for allowing such emotion to taint the day. Sarah was pretty. The young men had flocked around her when she and Karen had been in school together, but none of that had gone to Sarah's head. She remained a devout member of the church in spite of all the heartache in her life.

John said, "It's nice to meet you, Mrs. Wyse. I wanted to compliment you on your beautiful singing voice."

Sarah glanced from Karen back to John. "Compliments are not needed. All gifts come from God. We do not seek honors or to stand apart from each other."

"I'm sorry," John said, "I did not mean to offend you."

"No offense was taken. Karen says you have some questions for me."

The three of them moved to the end of the porch so they weren't blocking the flow of traffic in and out of the house. John said, "I don't know how to say this, but your voice sounds familiar to me. Is there any way I could have heard you singing before?"

"Not unless you have heard me as one of many voices praising God in song during our church services."

He heaved a tired sigh. "I was afraid you were going to say that."

"I wish I could be more help. I will inquire about you when people come to my shop. We have townspeople, Amish and tourists in."

John said, "I'll ask the sheriff to send over one of the photographs he had taken of me."

The women exchanged glances, then Karen said, "Sarah would not be able to show it. We consider photographs of people to be graven images. They are forbidden."

"I'm sorry. I didn't know." He looked embarrassed.

Karen couldn't help herself. She poked his shoulder. "Oh, John, you don't know your name, you don't know about the Amish and photographs, what do you know?"

"Karen!" Sarah looked aghast.

John looked shocked for a full second then he threw back his head and laughed. "I know if I go back in the house someone is going to try and make me eat more. I'm still stuffed to the gills."

Relieved to see him more comfortable, Karen said, "Then you had best go walk up an appetite because supper will get under way in about an hour."

Sarah said, "Mr. Doe, I can't use a photograph but if someone were to sketch your face I could use that."

Nodding Karen said, "That is a *goot* idea. Sally Yoder has a fine hand with pencils. Perhaps she could draw his picture."

John asked, "Is she the one with red hair and freckles?"

"Ja." Karen looked around. "I saw her a few moments ago."

Sarah said, "I saw her go upstairs with Katie and

the baby. I will ask her if she would do a sketch of you. Provided her parents do not object. If she may, I will let you know."

"I appreciate your help, Sarah. Thank you. And even if compliments are not permitted, I still say you sing like an angel."

Her smile turned sad. "You should have heard my sister sing. She is the one with the voice of an angel."

John waited until Sarah disappeared into the house then he turned his attention to Karen. "What did she mean about her sister?"

"Sarah has a twin sister. Bethany left here a month after Sarah's husband died. She wrote Sarah a letter telling her she had to go away but gave no other explanation. No one has heard from her in three years. Most think she ran away with an *Englischer*. It broke Sarah's heart."

"I see. Well, I should let you get back to work."

Karen didn't want to leave him. She wanted to stay and find some way to make him laugh again. The sound made her heart light. It made her want to laugh out loud with him.

With a start, she realized what was happening. She was getting in over her head. When had she started to care so deeply for John?

Perhaps the moment she saw him lying in the ditch. Embarrassed by the flood of feelings she couldn't control she took a step back. "*Ja,* I must go."

He raised his hand but let it drop quickly to his side. "I guess I'll see you when you get home."

"It will be very late. We will have much cleaning up to do here."

"I don't mind staying up." He smiled softly at her and left the porch to rejoin the men standing by Harold's car.

* * *

Late that evening, John sat outside on the *dawdy haus* porch with his feet propped up on the rail and his hands shoved deep in the pockets of his coat. The cold night air was a reminder that winter would come roaring in soon.

What was he doing? He was waiting to get in trouble, that's what.

The lights in the main house had been off for hours. The Imhoffs were normally early to bed and early to rise, but Karen had not yet returned from the wedding supper. Was she visiting with the women or was there a man in her life? Some tall, sturdy Amish farmer who would give her a dozen children and a lifetime of hard work?

John wanted to hope that was true, but even more he hoped it wasn't.

The clatter of horse hooves on the lane finally announced her return. John rose to his feet but hesitated. What right did he have to engage Karen's affections? The answer was abundantly clear. He had no business seeking time alone with her.

Even as his thoughts formed, his feet were moving toward the barn where she was unhitching the buggy. She saw him coming. She stood waiting, not speaking. He knew words would only sound artificial. Instead, he began unharnessing the horse, happy to be doing a simple thing for her.

Working in silence, they soon completed the task and led Molly to her stall. Karen lit a lantern so he could see to brush the mare down. He made quick work of it while Karen forked hay into the stall. When the mare was settled, they closed her stall door, put out the lantern and walked side-by-side out of the barn.

At the porch steps they paused by unspoken consent. Karen sat down, drawing her coat tighter. John sat beside her staring up into the night sky. A million twinkling stars decorated the black heavens with breath-taking beauty.

She pointed over the barn. "Look, there is a falling star. You should make a wish."

Hunching his shoulders, he shook his head. "I don't believe in wishing."

"Why not?"

He gazed at her intently. "What good does it do to want a thing you cannot have?"

She drew the edges of her coat closer together. "When we say we wish the rain would stop, or we wish the sun would shine, or we wish you could remember, are these wishes not simply little prayers?"

"I guess they are."

"Don't you believe in the power of prayer?"

"Anna told me once that you remind her to pray. Are you trying to remind me now?"

"It is something we all need to do."

He leaned back and braced his elbows on the step behind him. "I don't remember how to pray. If I ever knew."

"But you did. The day I found you, you began the Twenty-third Psalm. I've prayed it with you."

"You did? I wish I could remember that." He drank in the beauty of her face in the starlight, gathering in every detail to save in his memory. This night was one he never wanted to forget.

He leaned toward her. Uncertainty clouded her eyes and she looked away.

He drew a deep breath and leaned his head back. "I don't remember the stars looking this beautiful."

"Perhaps you lived in a city where the stars could not be seen."

"Maybe." John shook his head. "I don't know, they just don't seem right."

She looked up. "What could be wrong with the wondrous night sky God has given us? I see nothing wrong with the stars. What do you mean?"

"I don't know. I look up and I think something is missing."

"The moon is not yet up. Perhaps that is what's missing."

He watched her intently. "Maybe the stars look wrong because they pale in comparison to your eyes."

"Please don't." She dropped her gaze to stare at the ground.

"I'm sorry." He'd meant every word, but he was sorry to cause her any distress.

"You're forgiven."

"I'm not sure I want to be forgiven for telling you what a beautiful person you are. I don't mean just beautiful on the outside, although you are. I mean you're beautiful on the inside."

She raised her gaze to his. "You told me that once before. That I was beautiful. The day I found you. Before the ambulance came."

"Did you believe me then?"

"I did," she answered quietly.

"And do you believe me now?" He held his breath waiting for her answer.

"This is foolishness." She surged to her feet and started to go inside but he caught her arm.

"Please don't go. We'll talk about something else.

We'll pretend we're two old friends having a pleasant visit. You are my only friend, you know."

She studied his face. "I know I am now, but you have other friends who are looking for you. You are not a man who cuts himself off from others. They will find you."

"And what if they don't? What if no one is looking for me? What if I'll always be alone?" He couldn't stop the quiver in his voice. The fear and the loneliness bottled up inside rose to choke him.

She reached out to cup his face. "Do not give up hope."

Closing his eyes he covered her hands with his own and pressed them against his face, feeling the warmth and the strength and the compassion in her touch. Unbidden, a tear slipped from the corner of his eye.

Suddenly her arms were around him and she was holding him tight. "Be not afraid, John Doe, for God is with you. You are never alone."

Wrapping his arms around her, he leaned into her strength. She comforted him as if he were a child, murmuring soft sounds of reassurance. He tried to choke back his tears, but it was no use.

Chapter Nine

Karen held John tightly, her heart aching for him. All she had wanted from the moment she first saw him was to help him. She couldn't imagine the suffering he had endured and was still enduring. He was in so much pain, but she didn't know how to help.

He clung to her like a drowning man. His shoulders shook with muffled sobs. Offering him what comfort she could, she stroked his hair and whispered, "It will be okay."

But would it be? She had faith in God's plan for his life, but she knew that didn't mean his life would be easy. Her own family was proof of that, but God had not abandoned them. He gave them strength and hope. Without her faith, it would have been impossible for her to go on.

John regained his composure before she was ready to let him go. Stepping away from her, he wiped his eyes on his sleeves. "I'm sorry."

"Don't be, John. You have the right to grieve."

"I didn't mean to fall apart like that."

"Are you sure you're okay?" She was shocked at how

much she wanted to be needed by him. Shocked by how much she wanted to hold him and to be held by him.

He shoved his hands in his pockets and avoided making eye contact. "The doctors warned me that I might have a meltdown. Stress, you know. I guess I should have warned you, but I didn't expect to start blubbering like a baby."

Stepping back, he said, "Don't let me keep you up any later, Karen. You've had a long day. I'll be fine."

"Many times I have found my burdens too heavy to bear. Tears help sometimes and so do prayers. Pray for strength, John."

"I'll try. Thanks. For everything." He turned away and entered the grandfather house as if he couldn't wait to get away.

Karen climbed the steps slowly and entered her kitchen. Inside, she closed the door and leaned against it, crossing her arms tightly.

Her collar was damp from John's tears. She could still smell the faint scent of the soap he used, still feel his lingering warmth on her skin. Never in her life had she been drawn to a man the way she was drawn to John.

In a stunning moment of clarity she realized her feelings had progressed far beyond wanting to help him. The emotions filling her heart and mind were those a woman saved for the man she was to marry.

Tears pricked at the back of her eyes. She blinked hard to hold them at bay.

It was wrong. Wrong to feel so much for someone not of her faith. How did it happen? How could she have been blind to the changes in her own heart?

She knew right from wrong. She recognized her need

to be with John, to be held in his arms, to touch his face, those things were wrong.

In her mind she knew it—but her heart would not agree.

Any relationship between them was doomed. She knew that, but did John? Had she inadvertently set him up for more disappointment? She couldn't bear the thought of hurting him more than he was already hurting.

"What am I going to do?" she whispered in the darkness.

To step outside the *Ordnung,* the rules of her faith, was to invite heartache for her and her entire family. She had others to think of. Her father had been through so much pain already. She could not add to his overburdened shoulders the shame of having a daughter shunned.

Straightening, she moved across the room and up the stairs, listening to the familiar creak of each tread, hoping not to wake anyone. After reaching her room, she got ready for bed and lay beneath the heavy quilt her mother had stitched. Somehow, she had to find a way to harden her heart against the temptation she faced. John would leave tomorrow afternoon when Emma had room for him at the inn. Until he was gone, Karen would guard her heart closely. No one must know how she felt.

Closing her eyes, she prayed for strength. It was a long time before she fell asleep.

John sat at the desk in his room listening to the hushed stillness of the night. Like a hamster in a wheel, his brain ran around and around the problems he faced, without generating any answers.

His breakdown tonight scared him more than he wanted to admit. Was the stress unhinging his mind? Could he face the fact that he might never remember his life from before?

It had been nearly three weeks since Karen found him. He had visited Amish and English farms all along Pleasant View Road. He'd spoken to dozens of families, and yet he was no closer to the answers he needed. No one knew who he was. How could he not be missed? Why wasn't someone looking for him?

A chilling thought brought his overworked brain to a screeching halt. Maybe no one cared enough about him to wonder where he was.

What kind of man had he been? What kind of man wasn't missed by anyone?

Panic rushed through him until he recalled Karen's voice telling him he should pray for strength. He wanted to have faith in God's goodness, but that was easier said than done.

He bowed his head, resting it on his folded hands, and spoke the words in his heart. "God, I'm floundering here. I've got no idea what You want from me. Karen says I need Your help and I believe her. She is the one good thing You've done for me.

"I can't face this alone. You know I want answers. If I get them or not, well, that's up to You. Just give me the strength to accept whatever comes and keep me from going insane."

Raising his head, he drew a deep cleansing breath. Nothing had changed except for one small fact. Whatever happened, he didn't have to face it alone.

The chill in the air soon drove him under the covers. Lying in bed, he knew he needed a new plan. The money he had wouldn't last much longer. He could afford another week, maybe two at the inn in Hope Springs when he left here, but then what?

One more unanswerable question. He wanted to scream with frustration. Rolling to his side, he resolved to stop worrying about the future and have faith.

He slept fitfully the rest of the night. It was still dark outside when he gave up. Dressing in the chilly room he chided himself for not banking the fire the previous night. The stove was stone cold when he checked it and the wood box was empty.

Pausing on the front porch, he glanced at the main house. All the windows were still dark, even the ones upstairs. He wasn't sure which one was Karen's bedroom but he knew she would be up soon.

How would she treat him after seeing him break down last night? Would she think less of him? Did she see him as weak, now? Her opinion mattered. Maybe more than it should.

After carrying in an armload of wood, John set to work rebuilding the fire. When he had a small blaze going, he closed the firebox door and straightened, noticing his ribs didn't protest the movement. Physically, he was healing.

Mentally? Not so much. He needed something to do. Something to keep him busy besides endlessly turning over every rock in his mind looking for his memory.

A sudden idea occurred to him. Karen's father needed help with the chores. Horses were something John seemed to know about. He glanced out the window toward the barn. He was up, he might as well lend Eli a hand.

He was in the barn thirty minutes later when Jacob and Noah came in yawning and with lagging steps.

"Morning," John called cheerfully. He finished shoveling out the last stall, then laid his pitchfork and shovel on top of the heaping wheelbarrow.

"What do you think you're doing?" Jacob demanded.

"Mucking out the stalls." John started toward the rear of the barn.

Noah grinned and fell into step beside John. "Yippee. Now I don't have to do it."

Jacob chided Noah in Pennsylvania Dutch. John understood the tone if not the actual words.

Noah's grin turned to a scowl. "I'm going to help Jacob with the milking."

Looking over Noah's head, John said, "I have one more stall to do. If you want to show me how to milk a cow I could help with that, too."

"We do not need your help, English." Jacob took his younger brother by the sleeve and pulled him toward the dairy cows patiently waiting by their stanchions.

After dumping his wheelbarrow load, John returned to the last stall. Slipping a halter on One-Way's head, John led him out to the small paddock and turned him loose. Snorting and prancing, One-Way showed his appreciation of the open space by bucking his way around the enclosure.

Smiling at the animal's high spirits, John said, "Work off a little of that ginger and maybe we'll try some training later."

One-Way trotted to the fence. Stretching his neck over the top boards, he playfully nipped at John's sleeve, then took off like a rocket.

"I don't care what you think of the plan," John shouted

after him. "There's a harness in your future. You'd better get used to the idea."

Chuckling to himself, John finished cleaning One-Way's stall. After making sure all of the horses had hay, grain and freshwater, he brought the young Standard-bred back in. Locking the stall door, John leaned on it admiring the horse.

Behind him, he heard Anna say, "There you are, John Doe. Have you forgotten where the house is?"

Stifling his amusement, John crouched in front of her. "I'm so glad you found me. I thought I was going to have to stay out here with the horses all day. Which way do I go?"

Anna shook her head as she grasped his hand. "Come, I will show you. Breakfast is ready."

"Thank you." Rising, he let the child lead the way, but stopped when he saw Eli watching them.

Anna said, "I found him, Papa. He forgot where the house was."

Eli's lips twitched. "Thank you, Anna. Run along and tell Karen we are coming."

"Hurry up 'cause I'm hungry." She headed toward the house at a run.

Eli moved to the nearest stall where a pretty brown mare with a white star greeted him. "Noah tells me you did his chores."

"I hope you don't mind. I felt the need to work. I've loafed long enough."

"Work is *goot* for a man's body and soul."

"It felt good. It felt right."

Eli turned away from his inspection of John's work and began walking toward the house. "What are your plans now?"

John fell into step beside him. "I've talked to just about everyone in the community and I've come up empty. I guess I need to find work and a place to live now. I'm not giving up hope. I'm just being practical."

Eli combed his fingers through his beard. "A job will not be easy to come by this time of year. What kind of work were you thinking of doing?"

"All I seem to know is horses."

"I see. How would you break a green horse to harness?"

John answered without thinking. "You don't break a horse. You train it."

Eli eyed John critically. "That is true. How would you go about training that bay mare with the white star?"

"The first thing I'd do is get her used to having a blanket thrown over her. Then I'd work up to a partial and finally a full harness," he replied almost by rote. Each step closer to the house and to Karen increased John's dread. His palms grew sweaty.

Eli said, "That is what I would do, too."

They reached the front porch and climbed the steps. John pulled open the door. Eli went in while John hesitated on the doorstep.

What would he say to Karen? How would she treat him? He rubbed his damp palms on the sides of his jeans.

Suddenly, she was standing in front of him. She held a pan of cinnamon bread with the corners of her apron. "Close the door, John Doe. You're letting the cold air in," she scolded. "And don't forget to wipe your feet."

Noah and Anna, already seated at the table, snickered into their hands.

Whirling around, she scowled at them and placed the pan on the kitchen table before moving back to the stove.

John relaxed a little. Okay, good. Apparently she wasn't going to walk on eggshells around him. He wiped his feet, washed his hands at the sink and took his place at the table. A moment later she took her place opposite him. Everyone bowed their heads for silent prayer.

When they were finished, Karen looked at John and said, "Pass the butter, please."

No lingering glance, no pitying look, just pass the butter, as if nothing had happened. He appreciated her effort to put him at ease.

Everyone started eating. As usual, there was very little conversation at the table. Mealtime was for eating. John had learned that talk revolved mainly around what chores needed to be done and plans for the upcoming events such as the horse auction.

When the meal was finished, Anna helped Karen clear the table. Eli retreated to the sitting room to read his paper while Jacob and Noah finished getting ready for school. John remained at the table nursing his cup of coffee.

Anna gathered the tableware slowly, casting several speculative glances at John. Finally he asked, "What is it, Anna?"

"If I invite you to our school Christmas program, will you be able to remember that?"

He rubbed his hand over his chin. "I think if I write it down I'll be able to remember. When is it?"

"It's on December twenty-fourth."

"Christmas Eve, I'm sure I won't forget that. Have you been a good girl this year? Do you think Santa Claus will bring you presents?"

Anna laid a comforting hand on John's arm. "There is no Santa Claus. Did you forget that, too?"

Karen rinsed a plate and set it in the drain board. "We do not believe in such things, John. For us, Christmas is a time to remember the birth of Christ."

"You don't exchange gifts?" he asked.

"Little things only on the day after Christmas," Karen said. "It is a time to visit with family and friends."

"Last year I got new mittens," Anna added with a bright smile.

He wished he could remember a Christmas past. Would it ever end, these constant reminders that he was an incomplete man?

Karen saw the change come over John's face. Before she could think of something to say he shot to his feet and said, "Have a good day at school, Anna. I won't forget about your Christmas program."

He lifted his coat from the hook by the door and was gone a second later. Karen wanted to run after him but she didn't. He would have to come to grips with his missing memories in his own fashion.

Smiling at Anna, Karen said, "Go get ready for school."

Before long she had all the children out the door. That first minute of blessed silence afterward was always the best part of her day. She finished wiping down the counters and the table and had just started sweeping the floor when her father came in from the sitting room.

"Where is John?" Eli asked.

She didn't look up from her sweeping. "I don't know. He left about five minutes before the children."

"I'm thinking of letting him stay on a little longer."

Karen looked up in surprise. "You are?"

"*Ja*." Eli stared at her.

She started sweeping again. "If he stays it will make more work for me, but we could use the extra money."

"He seems to know a lot about horses." Eli slipped into his coat and pulled it over his sling.

Moving a chair, she swept under the table. She couldn't believe her father was considering this. "Perhaps he could be some help to you. Until your arm heals."

"Maybe."

Karen swept her pile of dirt into the dustpan without looking up. "He may not want to stay."

"Why do you think that?"

She straightened to meet her father's gaze. "Plain living is hard for the English. He may want to live where he can have television, a phone or a computer."

"I've not heard him complain about living plain, have you?"

"*Nee,* but he often goes into Hope Springs to use the computer at the library."

"Well, if he wishes it, he may stay. I will tell him." Eli opened the door and went out.

Karen backed up until she located a chair, then she sat down abruptly.

Would John stay?

Did she want him to stay?

The simple, frightening answer was yes, she did. With sudden clarity she saw exactly what she must do.

John stuffed the last of his meager possessions into his duffel bag. He started to close the top when he heard Eli call his name. He answered, "I'm in the bedroom."

Eli appeared in the doorway. "John Doe, I have a proposition for you."

"What kind of proposition?"

"I've been thinking. If you want, you could stay here until you find a job."

"Stay here?" John wasn't sure he'd heard correctly.

Eli winced and adjusted his sling. "I could use help getting the horses ready to sell. A horse that is trained to harness will bring more money than one that is not."

John buckled his bag. "Jacob can help you with that."

"Jacob must go to school, and he is already doing many more of the chores that I cannot do."

"What if I can't actually train a horse? I mean, I only feel like I know how."

"We can work together. My arm is broken but my voice works. I will tell you what to do and you do it?"

John was so very tempted to say yes. This family had opened their home to him. He was comfortable here. Karen was here.

That was why he should go.

"Think it over," Eli suggested before John could say anything.

Eli turned to leave but John stopped him with a question. "Have you told Karen about this?"

Chapter Ten

Eli gave John a sharp look. "*Ja*, I told Karen I would offer to let you stay on."

"And she was okay with it?"

"She offered no objection. Why?"

Was that because she felt sorry for him or because she liked having him around? He wished he could ask her. "I don't want to make more work for your daughter."

Eli cracked a wide smile. "She did say you would make extra work, but she also said we can use the money."

John ran a hand through his hair. "Depend on Karen to tell the truth."

"She speaks her mind. It is a thing she learned from her mother."

John quickly made up his own mind. He walked toward Eli and held out his hand. "I will stay on one condition. If I'm going to be working for you I expect to pay less for rent."

Eli's smile widened. "We had best agree on this before Karen gets wind of it."

"Before I get wind of what?" Her voice came from down the hall.

John braced himself to face her and pretend he wasn't thrilled to be spending more time near her. He had nowhere to go. He apparently had no one who cared about him. So why shouldn't he find some measure of happiness in the new life he'd been given?

"Looks like you aren't getting rid of me just yet," he called out.

She appeared in the doorway beside her father, her face serene and composed. "Then strip the sheets from the bed while I get clean ones and hurry up. I don't have all day."

Spinning on her heels, she took off down the hall and John heard the front door slam. He looked at Eli. "Are you sure she doesn't object to my staying?"

"I would bundle up the sheets and have them ready for her if I were you." Chuckling, Eli hooked his thumb under his suspender.

Feeling bemused, John stripped the bed. When Karen returned with the clean sheets neatly folded in a laundry basket John held the wadded ones under his arm.

She bustled in, put the basket on the bed and pulled the sheets out of it. "Put the dirty ones in here." She indicated the basket with a nod.

Eli said, "Since you are going to stay, John Doe, I will turn on the refrigerator for you. It can be tricky to get started."

As Eli headed for the kitchen, John stuffed his armload of linens in the basket then lifted it off the mattress so Karen could get to work. With a few flicks of her wrists, she spread the crisp white linen over the mattress and smoothed away the wrinkles.

As she was tucking in the far side, John set the laundry basket on the desk, turned the desk chair around and straddled it. Crossing his arms over the ladder-back, he rested his chin on his forearms. "Was this your idea? Not that I'm complaining, I'm just curious."

She shook out the second sheet and let it settle over the bed. "It was not my idea."

Disappointment pricked him but he refused to show it. "You're okay with it, right?"

"Of course." She wouldn't meet his gaze. Instead, she kept her eyes on the task she was performing.

"It won't be forever. Once I find a job I'll be able to get a place of my own." He knew he was being overly optimistic but he didn't want her caring out of pity.

Stuffing the pillow into the case, she shook it down. "What kind of work will you do?"

"Whatever it takes. I don't have much choice. I have to make my own way now."

She paused, clutching the pillow tight to her chest. "I wish you well, John Doe."

Was that a quiver he heard in her voice? He said, "Someday I will repay all that you have done for me."

Turning to face him, she shook her head. "*Nee,* you owe me nothing. I will do everything I can to help you find a job."

Was she hinting that she wanted him to move on? "Any suggestions where I should start?"

"The newspaper."

"Right. I can see the ad now. Wanted: Man with amnesia for high-paying job."

Throwing the pillow on the bed, Karen propped her hands on her hips and scowled at him. "With that attitude you will end up begging on street corners."

Taken aback, he said, "I was joking."

She kept her voice low as she glanced toward the door to make sure Eli wasn't outside. "Finding a livelihood is no joking matter. You must be serious, you must work harder and smarter than anyone else and prove you can do the job."

John held up both hands in a gesture of surrender. "Okay, I will."

"If you go around feeling sorry for yourself then your life will be filled with pity and not with the blessings God has bestowed upon you."

Anger welled up inside him. "Excuse me for not feeling blessed at the moment."

She took a step toward him. "Well, you should feel blessed. You are alive. You are strong. You have a roof over your head and food to eat. If you whine about the things you do not have then you are ungrateful for all you have."

Why was she trying to rile him? He said, "I have all these things because of the charity of others. I did not earn it."

She folded her arms and raised her eyebrow. "And that is not a blessing?"

Rising from the chair, he turned to the window. Bracing his arms on the sill he stared outside. "I don't want to be grateful to others. I need to be in charge of my own life."

She moved to stand close behind him. "Then pride is your sin, John Doe. The Amish live humble lives. We accept that we are nothing without God."

John's anger drained away. He understood better than most what being *nothing* felt like. Looking over his shoulder at Karen, he asked, "Do you think that's why God is doing this to me? To humble me? What kind of person was I to deserve this?"

Karen bit her lip, drawing his attention to her mouth. He wanted to kiss her, wanted to hold her and feel her arms around him. As much as her compassion meant to him that wasn't what he longed for. He wanted more.

He wanted her to care about him as a man, not as an emotional cripple in need of charity.

She looked down and fixed her gaze on her clenched hands. "We cannot know God's plan for us. It is beyond human understanding. We can only accept what trials come to us secure in the knowledge that God is with us always. He sent His only son to die for our sins. He does not abandon us. We lean on His mercy and grace so that we may not stumble on the righteous path He sets before us."

"I wish I had your faith, Karen. I wish I believed in mercy and grace."

She did look at him then. "You have only to open your heart to God, John. All the rest will follow."

The soft expression in her eyes gave him hope. She did care for him, he was sure of it.

"How can I doubt God's goodness when He brought me to you." He reached for her as he stepped closer.

She took a quick step away. "John, we can't—I can't. How do I say this? There must be no closeness between us."

Her retreat cut him like a blade. Lowering his hand, he closed his eyes and pressed his lips into a thin, painful line. Finally, he drew a deep breath and nodded. "I understand. I'm sorry if I offended you with unwelcome attention."

"There is nothing to forgive. I am your friend."

How could such simple words sound so lame?

What had he expected? She was a devout Amish woman. She would never consider stepping outside the boundaries of her faith with someone like him. She offered her friendship. He would be content with that. It was more than he deserved.

At the sound of Eli's footsteps coming down the hall, John quickly composed himself. He fashioned a reassuring smile for her. "I couldn't find a better friend if I searched the world over," he said, meaning every word.

Karen blinked hard to hold back her tears. They would have to wait until later, when she was alone and no one could hear her sobs. They would be her punishment for wounding John. In spite of his words, she knew she had wounded him.

At every turn she had sought to guard him from harm, to ease his way, to be the one person he could turn to. Her foolish need to be his rescuer had led to this affection for her. How could it be otherwise? Perhaps in her heart she even wanted such affection, but it wasn't right for either of them.

She had to let John find his own path and his own strength. The only way to do that was to push him out into the world.

"Your refrigerator is working now," Eli announced from the doorway.

John slipped the chair in place under the desk. The sudden silence seemed to radiate guilt. Karen quickly picked up the laundry basket and walked out the door without looking back. She had never felt so ashamed of her own weakness.

That night she prayed for strength and the courage

to harden her heart against the attraction she felt for John. Confused and frightened, she knew only God's help could save her from her own foolishness.

If John recovered his memory she could let him go knowing he had people and a home waiting for him. But while he was still lost and alone, she couldn't turn her back on him. She couldn't.

On Sunday morning she accompanied her family to church services and prayed earnestly for strength and guidance. The saving grace of the weekend was having the children underfoot to minimize the risk of finding herself alone with John.

On Sunday afternoon, Sarah Wyse arrived with Sally Yoder to sketch a picture of John. Sally seemed oddly ill at ease. As John posed for his portrait, he tried to engage her in conversation, but he received only the briefest of replies in return.

When Sally was done, John thanked her, then left the room saying he had work to do. Sally began to put away her materials.

Karen picked up the sketch. "This is *goot* work, Sally. God has given you a wondrous talent. I know John is grateful for your help."

"I must do all I can to aid him." When Sally looked up Karen was surprised to see her eyes glistening with unshed tears.

"Sally, do you know who John is?"

Glancing from Sarah to Karen, Sally shook her head. "I don't. I wish I did, but I don't." Before Karen could question her further, Sally grabbed her sketchbook and hurried outside.

Karen and Sarah exchanged puzzled looks. Sarah

said, "She is young and she has a tender heart. This out-sider's injury and burdens touch us all."

Nodding, Karen let the subject drop unwilling to dis-cuss her own feelings for John.

Sarah gathered her cloak and gloves. "I promise to have copies of this made and post them around town. Perhaps it will bring someone forward, but I hope John isn't holding his breath."

Karen knew she would be holding hers. She no longer prayed that someone would recognize him. These days, she prayed only to keep her heart and her faith intact.

During the next week the first heavy snowfall of winter arrived, coating the fields and farms in a flaw-less, glittering white blanket. Winter was tightening its grip on the Ohio countryside as Christmas loomed only weeks away.

In spite of her determination to stifle her affection for John, her eyes were drawn constantly to wherever he was. When she was in the kitchen, she kept watch on the corrals beside the barn where John, under the di-rection of her father, began training the little bay mare named Jenny and One-Way, her father's great hope for their financial recovery.

To Karen's surprise, her father appeared to enjoy working with John. She often heard them deep in con-versations about horse care and training methods and occasionally saw them laughing together. If John had been Amish she would have been thrilled to see the rela-tionship growing between the two. But he wasn't Amish and no matter how much Eli liked him, he would never accept him as a suitor for Karen.

Anna and Noah had been delighted when they learned John would be staying. Jacob kept his opinion to himself, but it was easy for Karen to see he was upset. Especially after he learned Eli was letting John train the horses. Karen would have been happier if Jacob had expressed his unhappiness in words. Instead, he became withdrawn and secretive.

On Monday morning, Karen came down early to start breakfast and caught Jacob sneaking into the house just before dawn. Staring at his disheveled clothes, she asked, "Jacob, what have you been doing?"

"Nothing." He avoided looking at her and hurried up to his room.

Amish teenagers, especially boys, were expected to rebel against the strict rules they were raised with. She held her tongue, but decided to keep a closer watch on her brother. He was growing up too fast for her liking.

As the days passed, Karen began to relax. There had been no repeat of her closeness with John. Perhaps his initial attraction to her had worn off. She could only hope so. In spite of her prayers her feelings had only grown stronger.

John went out daily to visit other farms and to look for work. She knew he stopped frequently in Hope Springs to check the missing-persons website he'd told her about. In a way, it was hard to watch him go out into the world without her help, but she knew it was what he needed to do.

In the evenings, the family gathered in the sitting room after supper. Tonight, as had become the norm, Noah and John were engaged in a board game. Eli and Jacob were reading while Anna played with her doll on the windowsill.

Karen worked on her seemingly endless pile of mending as she covertly watched John. He seemed so at home

among them. He was good with the little ones, especially
Noah. John would make a fine father someday.

At that thought, she turned her mind elsewhere. Down
that path lay only heartache. Glancing at Anna, Karen
frowned. The child had both hands pressed against the
frosty windowpane. As Karen watched, Anna glanced
over her shoulder, then crept up behind Noah and put
her hands on the back of his neck.

"Ach!" He jerked away, and she broke into loud giggles.

"'Sis kald heit." Anna extended her hands toward
John.

He pulled away in mock terror. "What does that
mean?"

Noah shivered as he rubbed the back of his neck.
"She said, 'It is cold today,' but what she means is she's
a sneaky jerk."

"Noah," Eli chided. "Do not call your sister names.
Anna, do not trouble your brother."

The siblings made sour faces at each other when Eli
returned to his reading.

"What is this in Pennsylvania Dutch?" John patted
his head.

"Your *kobb*," Noah replied.

"And this?" John pulled up a lock of hair.

"Hoah," Anna answered quickly.

John repeated the word then held up his hand. "What
do you call this?"

"Hand," Noah said before Anna could.

John shook his head at the boy. "No, come on. What's
the Amish word for hand?"

Noah and Anna fell into a fit of giggles. Even Eli gave
a little chuckle. John glanced at Karen, a questioning

look on his face. She stifled her mirth at his confusion. "The Amish word for hand *is* hand, John."

He began laughing, too. "At least I don't have to learn all new words to learn Amish. That should make it easier. Give me another that's the same."

"English." Jacob's tone made the word sound like an insult as he rose and walked out of the room.

Anna shook her head. "It's *Englisch*. That one's close but it's not the same. Fox, that's the same."

Eli laid down his book. "Bushel."

"Blind," Karen said, racking her brain for more identical words.

"Land," Anna supplied one more.

"What I need is a teacher." John was looking at Karen when he said it. She caught a glimpse of longing in his eyes, but he looked away so quickly she knew he was trying to hide it from her.

Sadness crept into her chest. They were both struggling to mask their true feelings. How long could they keep up this charade?

Anna said, "I will be your *teetshah*. You can use my schoolbooks."

John smiled at Anna, but Karen saw the effort it took. Her heart broke for him all over again.

On a Sunday morning nearly a month after his arrival at the farm John watched the Imhoff family leave for church from the window of the grandfather house kitchen. For a moment he was tempted to go with them, but he wasn't sure an English person would be welcome.

He had learned from Anna, his new and devoted teacher of all things Amish, that the Amish had no church buildings. They held their services in the homes of members rotating the services from house to house every other week.

He'd also learned the Imhoffs wouldn't be back until early afternoon as a meal always followed the services. As far as he was concerned, that left him with far too much time on his hands. He didn't like being alone.

Had he always been that way? Or was it a new condition brought on by his trauma?

Picking up his Bible, he read for an hour, absorbing the words and trying to see how they applied to his own life. For a while his restless spirit was calmed, but eventually he closed the book and started looking for something else to do.

His options were limited. On Sunday the library in Hope Springs would be closed. He'd already made several trips into town to check the NamUs website, but he hadn't found anyone looking for a man of his description. The stories in the news and on the website about loved ones who'd vanished without a trace were as depressing as not finding information about himself. How could so many people disappear? How could he be one of them?

Slipping into his coat, he bundled up against the cold and headed out to the barn. He'd been unable to find work yet and so had spent more time training the horses than they really needed but it was something he enjoyed.

When he opened the door, a gray tomcat, one of the dozen or so that kept the rodent population under control, sat in the center aisle licking his paw. Music started playing. John heard the tinkling sounds of a waltz as if it were coming from a music box.

A sharp pain stabbed his temple. He squeezed his eyes shut. Suddenly, he was in a sunlit room with a large window. A white cat lay curled on a window-seat cushion in a patch of sunlight. As John watched, the animal stood, stretched with lazy feline grace, then jumped to the floor. Once there, it padded over to sit beside the front door. John heard a key in the lock. He sucked in a breath knowing the door was about to open. Blind dread filled his mind.

A loud whinny erased the scene.

John found himself staring at the empty center aisle of the Imhoff barn. The music was gone. He stumbled forward until he reached One-Way's stall. There, he leaned against the door drawing in harsh gulps of air to fill his starving lungs.

"Are you okay?" The tentative question came from overhead. John looked up to see Jacob staring at him from the hayloft. He heard the sound of footsteps moving away, but he couldn't see anyone else.

"Not really." Closing his eyes, John willed his racing heart to slow. The searing pain in his head died away bit by bit.

"What's the matter with you?"

John's first thought was to say nothing, but he stopped himself. Why lie to the boy? He began massaging his temples with his fingertips. "Sometimes I get memory flashes. When I do it hurts."

Jacob looked skeptical. "Did you remember who you are?"

"I never remember anything that will help me. I know this is weird, but did you hear music just now?"

Jacob sat on the edge of the opening and let his feet dangle, sending a shower of straw onto John's head. "What did you remember?"

Brushing the straw from his hair, John said, "I remembered a white cat sitting in the window. I remember the sound of a music box. Nothing that helps me figure out who I am. I'm beginning to wonder if I'll ever know."

Hearing a noise, John looked up to see Jacob lower himself from the hayloft floor. He hung for a second by his hands then dropped lightly down beside John. Jacob adjusted his black hat and said, "You should go back to the English world where you belong."

As Jacob turned and sauntered toward the door, John caught a whiff of cigarette smoke. "Who else was up there with you?"

Jacob didn't reply. It seemed he wasn't about to rat on his friends.

John yelled after him, "Why aren't you at church?"

"Why aren't you?" came Jacob's reply. He walked out of the barn without looking back.

John muttered to himself, "Because I don't know if I belong in church. I don't know where God wants me."

Opening One-Way's stall, John snapped a lead to his halter and went to lead the young horse outside to the exercise corral. As he passed by Molly's stall, he glanced in. The mare stood in the corner, her head drooping and flecks of foam speckling her chest.

Tying up One-Way, John stepped into the stall with Molly. She still bore the sweaty marks of her harness. It was odd because the family had used a different horse to pull the buggy that morning.

John glanced in the direction Jacob had gone. The boy shouldn't have left Molly in this condition. Annoyed with the thoughtless teenager, John quickly curried the mare and walked her until she was cooled down completely.

When he was finished, he took One-Way out to the exercise pen and turned the horse loose. Folding his arms on the top rail, John watched the young horse pacing proudly around the ring.

It had been more than a month since John's injury. Five full weeks without answers. He'd spent day after day searching his mind for things that were not there. Karen believed God had brought him here for a purpose. What purpose? The question circled his mind the way the horse circled the paddock.

John shoved his hands in the pockets of his coat. In spite of his occasional flashbacks, his hopes of recovery faded with each passing day. He had to face the facts. What if he never recovered his memory, never found his past?

What if God had a reason for making him forget that past? What if his former life had been so terrible that he couldn't face it? Perhaps his amnesia was a blessing and not a curse.

Could he accept that? Right now, right this minute, could he decide to stop searching?

Hadn't he already found everything he needed here? This was a place where he could make a new life. As wild as it once seemed, he could have an Amish life.

Was this what God had in mind for him? Was that why He'd brought Karen into John's life? To show him a devout, simple way to live with God at the center of everything?

John chewed the corner of his bottom lip. He was happy here. He felt he belonged here. Should he be asking for more than that?

In the beginning he'd prayed for any crumb of information about himself. Now, he knew giving up his past was the only way he could fashion a life Karen could find acceptable. Was he willing to do that?

Chapter Eleven

Seated among the women on one of the narrow wooden benches at the preaching service, Karen glanced across the aisle, looking for her brother. Her father and Noah were seated among the men but she couldn't see Jacob. Once again her heart grew troubled as her worry about him intensified. He had come ahead bringing the bench wagon to the Beachy farm, but Karen had not seen him since they arrived.

At the front of the room the bishop began speaking. Forced to give up her search she turned her attention to the preacher. Bishop Zook, in a solemn voice, announced the banns of Adam Troyer and Emma Wadler. The wedding was to take place the Thursday before Christmas.

There were quite a few soft murmurs of surprise from the congregation. Emma had long been considered an old maid in their community. At thirty-three she was still single but God had seen fit to bring the right man into her life. Karen had suspected as much but hadn't known for sure. Amish couples frequently dated and planned their engagements in secret.

Although Karen was happy for her cousin, she

couldn't help the twinge of envy that marred her joy. Chiding herself for the selfish thought, Karen decided she should take it as a sign that someday God could bring the right man into her life when the children were grown and able to manage without her.

The Sunday service lasted nearly three hours. Afterward, as the men set up tables and the women began unpacking the food for the meal, Karen and Anna followed the crowd of young people into the barn. They would have to wait their turn to eat. The elders would be served first.

Anna took off to play with several of her school friends. Looking around, Karen spied Emma and Adam being congratulated. Beyond the pair she caught sight of Jacob at last. She breathed a sigh of relief until she saw he was with a group of older boys.

They were all fast boys, known to be troublemakers and a worry to their parents. Karen wasn't happy to see Jacob so comfortable among them. The ringleader was Henry Zook, the bishop's youngest son, a young man who should know better.

Karen joined the group around Emma and Adam and spent a pleasant half hour listening to Adam's family tease him about giving up his bachelor ways.

Later, on their way home in the early afternoon Karen noticed her father had become unusually quiet. He'd had his cast removed the day before, but he still wore his arm in a sling. Checking on her siblings, Karen saw Anna and Noah were dozing in the backseat. Jacob followed behind them with the bench wagon.

Karen said, "Is something wrong, Papa? Is your arm hurting?"

"What?" He sat up straight. Karen could've sworn he looked guilty about something.

"I asked if your arm was bothering you?"

"*Nee,* it is fine. Did you know that Emma and Adam Troyer planned to marry?"

Karen smiled. "I knew something was up between them. I'm sure they will be happy. They have both waited a long time to find the right person."

"A man is blessed indeed to find a woman who will make his house a home. I pray God grants them many children." He fell silent again. Karen couldn't shake the feeling that something was troubling him.

"You had best tell me now, Papa. You know I will find out." Had he learned something about John? Was he trying to tell her that John would be leaving?

His eyes grew round as saucers. "What do you mean?"

"You have something on your mind. I see the signs. Whatever it is, do not be afraid to tell me."

He nodded, then said slowly, "*Ja,* you will find out."

"And you are afraid I'll be upset? I won't, Papa."

"Very well. I have asked Nettie Sutter to marry me and she has accepted my offer."

Karen stared at him in blank astonishment. Whatever she had been expecting, it was not this. "You're getting married?"

Exactly where did that leave her?

The words seemed to rush out of him. "I have wanted to ask her for many months. Then I broke my arm and lost the feeling in my hand. I knew I couldn't ask her to marry a man unable to support her or his own children. But God has seen fit to heal me and I thank Him for that. Today, when I heard the bishop publish the banns for Emma I felt it was the right time to approach Nettie. She said yes. She will make a *goot* stepmother. She is a devout woman. The children already know and like her."

"*Ja,* she is a *goot* woman." Karen's mind reeled. Nettie would become the woman of the house. She would run the home as she saw fit and Eli would support her decisions. Karen would have to step aside and give up the reins of control.

She would go from being the woman of the house back to being an unmarried daughter. In her community she was already seen as an old maid with few marriage prospects. All of her friends had married by twenty. Most had several children by the age of twenty-four.

"You are taking this very well." Her father smiled in relief and patted her knee.

"I want you to be happy, Papa."

"*Danki.* We have decided to wait until next fall. Nettie wants her children who live in Pennsylvania to be able to attend and one of her daughters there is expecting soon. I'm telling you this because I want you to start going to the singings again. You must look about for a husband of your own, Karen. Who knows, perhaps there will be more than one wedding in the family."

A husband of her own. As her father's words sank in, one name slipped into Karen's mind. John Doe.

Quickly, she dismissed the thought. Even without her responsibilities to the children and her father, she had made a vow before God and the community to uphold the ways of the Amish faith. Her first responsibility was always to God.

John was an outsider and forbidden. No matter how much she liked him she could never forget that fact.

* * *

Anna pursed her lips as she stared at John. "What is *haus?*"

John held back his grin. The kid was so serious. "House."

"Haus-dach?" Anna snapped quickly.

House something. He racked his brain until the answer popped into his head. "House roof."

"Goot. What is *natt?"*

"That is… Don't tell me. That is wet." Proud of himself, he smiled broadly.

"Nee. Wet is *nass. Natt* is north."

"North, *natt.* Wet, *nass.* Got it." Learning a new language wasn't easy. Especially when Karen was nearby to distract him.

"Handkerchief?"

His shoulders slumped. "You're making this too hard, Anna."

"We did this one yesterday." She gave him *that look.* The one that reminded him so much of Karen when one of the children stepped out of line.

He took his best guess. "Handkerchief is shoeduck."

"No, it's *shnubbe-duch,"* Anna corrected in her most serious voice.

"Oh, come on. I was close."

Glancing to where Karen stood at the sink listening, John caught her smile at his wheedling. He didn't know what was more adorable, Anna as the benevolent and determined teacher or Karen as his amused and supportive audience.

For the past three days when Anna arrived home from school she quickly finished her chores and set up her classroom at the kitchen table. She called John in from work when she was ready. Their interchanges had become the highlight of his afternoons.

Anna said, "Now we're going to work on colors. What color is Karen's dress?"

He leaned back in his chair happy for the opportunity to study Karen openly. "That's difficult to say. Your sister's dress is sort of sea-foam green. Her apron is black, but her hair is honey-gold. Her lips are ruby-red and her eyes are the same beautiful sky-blue that you have, Anna."

Karen continued peeling potatoes. "And John is trying to avoid answering the question because he doesn't know the Amish word for green."

Busted. "Sadly, that is exactly what I'm trying to do. Anna, can we do the colors tomorrow? I have to go into town this afternoon. I've got a job interview."

Karen looked at him in surprise. "A job interview? Where?"

"Your father made arrangements with Reuben Beachy to give me a try. If I can do the job he'll take me on as an apprentice."

"The harness maker? That sounds like a fine job."

Without a driver's license or a social security card John was limited to where he could apply for work. The Amish carried neither of those trappings of the outside world. "Any job is a good thing because I need to be able to support myself. Your father has kindly loaned me the farm wagon to drive."

"Why don't you take the buggy?" Karen offered.

"Your *daed* is using it." John glanced at Anna to see if he'd gotten the word for father correct. She grinned and gave him a thumbs-up.

A puzzled expression appeared on Karen's features. "Where has Papa gone?"

"To see Nettie Sutter," Anna answered. "He's sweet on her."

"No kidding?" John looked to Karen for confirmation.

She nodded. "Anna, can you get me a jar of peaches from the cellar?"

When the child was out of the room, Karen turned to John. "My father and Nettie are to be married next fall. Please don't say anything to the children yet. He hasn't told them."

"Sure. Are you okay with your father getting remarried?"

Her chin came up. "Why wouldn't I be?"

"Won't it make some big changes for you?"

"I will have more help in the kitchen. I won't mind that." She didn't sound enthusiastic.

"What things will you mind?" he asked gently.

Laying her knife aside, she bowed her head. "I have raised them like my own children. Anna can barely remember our mother. Now I must step aside and let another woman take my place. How do I do that?"

Rising from the table, John walked to where she stood and rested his hands on her shoulders. "You have always done what is best for the children. You will continue to do that."

She tipped her head to the side and laid her cheek against his fingers. "You are right. The children must come first."

John's gesture of comfort quickly changed into something deeper. His need to hold her threatened to destroy his self-control. He could feel her slender collarbones beneath his hands, the softness of her cheek against his knuckles. His body ached with the effort it took not to slip his arms around her and pull her against him.

"Danki," she breathed the word out and he knew she treasured his touch as much as he treasured her nearness.

The cellar door banged opened and Anna raced into the room with a jar of peaches in her hand. "Is one enough, sister?" she asked, setting the quart container on the table.

John quickly dropped his hands and stepped away, hoping the child hadn't noticed.

"Ja, one is fine." Karen picked up her knife and began peeling potatoes again.

John took hold of the jar. "Let me open this for you."

"I can manage," Karen turned to take it from him, but he shifted away.

"I've got it." He gritted his teeth as he tried to twist the lid and break the seal. It didn't budge.

"I have a jar opener if you need it," Karen offered, a smile twitching at the corner of her adorable lips.

"No." He grunted as he battled the tightest lid ever to grace a jar of produce. Karen folded her arms and waited. Anna giggled.

He held it below his waist to try a new angle. That did the trick. The ring gave way, he popped off the seal and in triumph, held the jar aloft. It slipped from his hand, struck the corner of the table and shattered, spilling peaches, glass shards and juice down his pant legs and across the floor boards.

In the ensuring stunned silence, Anna sighed and said, "I'll go get another jar, but John can't open this one."

Feeling his face heat to flaming red, he said to Karen, "I'm so sorry."

"Don't worry." Karen struggled to keep from laughing but lost the battle. Her delightful giggle gladdened his heart.

Suddenly, he was laughing, too. He spread his hands wide. "I got it open. What more do you want?"

She regained a modicum of composure, but giggles continued to slip out. "I didn't want them on the floor, John."

He looked down and saw a peach half had landed on the toe of his shoe. He raised his foot toward Karen. "This one is still good."

She broke into laughter and turned her face away. "Yuck."

Plucking the peach from his soaking shoe, he said, "Yuck. After my great display of strength all you can say is yuck? I'll show you yuck."

He made as if to press the fruit to her face. She squealed and ducked away, slipping around to the other side of the table.

"John, you wouldn't."

"Don't tempt me, woman." He advanced slowly. He was between her and the doorway. There was nowhere for her to run. That didn't stop her from trying. She darted past him, but he caught her and backed her into the wall. With her laughter still ringing in his ears, he touched the peach to the tip of her nose.

"John!" She rubbed her nose vigorously on her sleeve. The laughter died in his throat as he realized he had her exactly where he wanted her. In his arms. Close to his heart.

She met his gaze and the smile faded from her face,

too. Her lips were so close. All he had to do was bend down a little. When he did, she turned her face away. With her arms braced against his chest, she said, "Please, don't."

She might as well have asked him to stop breathing. But for her—he would do even that.

Karen heard the sound of Anna's footsteps coming up the stairs over the drumming of her pulse. Staring into John's eyes, Karen saw the same intense longing there that was racing through her blood. Her heart yearned to answer his unspoken request, but she could not.

His expression went carefully blank. Dropping his arms from around her, he stepped back and said, "I'll help clean up."

Anna came into the room and set the second jar on the cabinet. "I'm not going to fetch another one."

Karen moved away from John, keeping her gaze averted but she could feel him watching her every move. "I can manage. John, you need to get changed for your job interview unless you want to go smelling like peaches."

He looked down at his pants. "These are my only jeans."

Anna's mouth opened in shock. "You've been wearing the same pair of jeans every day for a month?"

He was quick to defend himself. "Hey, I wash them. They dry pretty quick in front of the fire but they won't get dry before I have to see Mr. Beachy today."

"I have some clothes you can borrow." Karen's thundering heart slowed painfully. She couldn't take much more of this.

Anna said, "Papa's clothes will be too big on him."

"I know. I have some of Seth's things in a cedar chest. I think they will fit. I'll go get them."

"If you're sure you don't mind." John watched her closely. He always sought to make sure she was okay. She admired that about him.

"I do not mind, John Doe, but I thank you for your concern. It is *goot* that some use can be made of them."

He spread his arms wide. "Okay. I will take care of this while you do that."

His eagerness to help was another thing she found endearing about him. Quickly she climbed the stairs to the attic and opened a large flat trunk in the center of the room. The clothes lay where she had put them the day after the funerals. Her mother's dresses and shoes and her songbook lay on top. Beneath it her sisters' aprons, handkerchiefs and *kapps* were neatly folded. To one side was Seth's dark suit and his black hat stuffed with paper to keep its shape.

Karen sank to her knees beside the trunk. She hadn't been up here in over a year. As much as she loved and missed the members of her family, life went on.

Pulling Seth's clothes from the trunk, Karen closed the lid and walked down the stairs. John and Anna were emptying the last of the broken glass into the trash can. The floor had been swept and washed.

Forcing a smile to her face, Karen approached John and handed him the bundle. "Try these on, I think they might fit."

"Thank you." He accepted the clothes from her.

"It's *danki,* John," Anna corrected.

"Danki, teetshah." He bowed in her direction and she beamed.

When he went out the door Karen clung to the soft

glow he left behind. Never in her wildest dream had she thought she would fall for an outsider. In spite of all her resolutions and prayers, she was falling hard for John Doe.

John changed into the plain clothes with mixed feelings. Once again Karen had come to his rescue. Was it possible his affection for her was nothing more than misguided gratitude? She had been there for him at every turn.

No, he didn't believe it. Maybe he didn't remember what loving someone felt like, but being near Karen felt like love.

The trousers were a little big at the waist and the cuffs fell over the top of his shoes. They would need to be shortened, but they would do for today. The shirt was a better fit. He searched for belt loops and found none. He clipped on the suspenders and raised them over his shoulders but they didn't feel right. In his mind old men wore suspenders.

Maybe it just felt odd wearing another man's clothes.

After pulling on the jacket John stared at the black felt hat lying on the table. The hat was the crowning touch. It, more than anything else, would make him appear Amish. Should he wear it? What would Karen think? Would she like him better in plain clothing?

Sighing, he hung the hat on a wooden peg by the front door. He didn't want to pretend he was something he wasn't.

Stepping outside the grandfather house John brushed at the creases in the coat. Summoning his courage he walked to the main house front door and entered. Karen was rolling out pie dough on the kitchen counter. She

turned around to study him with a flour-covered rolling pin in one hand. There was a smudge of flour on
her cheek. His hand itched to brush it away but he knew
such attention would be unwelcome. Anna was nowhere
in sight.

"What's the verdict?" Spreading his arms wide, he
turned around slowly.

"You look Plain, John Doe."

Dropping his arms, he tucked his hands in the pockets of his trousers. "Who knows, maybe I am. Would
that make a difference to you?"

She turned back to the table and resumed rolling the
dough. "I don't think you are Amish. You don't know
the language, you don't know our ways."

He took a step closer, not understanding why he
needed to push the issue. "But if I were Amish, would
that make things right between us?"

She paused. "*Nee.* It would not."

"Why?"

Facing him, a gentle expression filled her eyes. "You
cling to me because you know no one else."

Was she right? Hadn't that very thought crossed his
mind only a few minutes before? He refused to accept
it. "You make me sound like a child, Karen. I'm not."

"Give yourself more time, John. Your answers may
yet come to you."

"Okay, that's fair. But you should know something.
How I feel about you isn't going to change no matter
what I discover about myself."

Spinning on his heels, he headed out the door. He had
a job interview to get to. He had to start building some
kind of life for himself. He wasn't clinging to Karen

because she was the only woman in his life. He had to prove that to her.

He would get a place of his own, live in the community, make friends among them. Eventually, he would become one of them.

Was such a thing possible? He wasn't sure.

If it was, he would do it. Then Karen would see his feelings were genuine.

He was crossing toward the barn when the sound of a car reached him. As he watched, Sheriff Bradley drove into the snow-covered yard.

Chapter Twelve

The tires of the sheriff's SUV crunched loudly on the crisp snow as he pulled to a stop beside John. Opening the vehicle door, Nick stepped out. "Afternoon, John."

John dipped his head. "Sheriff. What brings you out here?"

"Not good news I'm afraid. I wanted to let you know we got a report back from the FBI on your DNA and fingerprints. You're not in their system."

John's last bit of hope crumpled like a wadded piece of paper. He was no better and no worse off than he'd been five minutes ago. He still had a plan. He still needed to get to his job interview. "Thanks for the update, Nick."

"I'm sorry it wasn't better news."

John's gaze was drawn to the house. "I guess that means I'm stuck here."

"My offer of a place to stay in Millersburg still stands, John. I think you'd be better off in town."

"I appreciate that, but I'm doing okay."

"On an Amish farm? Look, I've got nothing against the Amish, I've got family who are Amish, but why cut yourself off from contact with the outside world? I mean, who knows, maybe you'll see something on the six-o'clock news that sparks a memory about a place or someone you know. You're insulated here, John. That may make remembering even harder."

"Maybe, maybe not." John crossed his arms over his chest.

"Suit yourself, but you might want to be asking yourself why you're hiding out here."

Staring at his boots, John pushed a clump of snow aside with his toe. "For one thing, someone tried to kill me. You haven't a clue who that was. I think I'm safer here than I would be on the streets of a city."

"You're probably right about that."

Looking at the sheriff, John said, "Thanks for your concern. If anything new comes up you know where to find me."

"All right. I just wanted you to know that I'm not giving up. I'm going to keep digging."

"I'm not giving up hope either, but there comes a point when I have to move on. I've read dozens of stories about people who've been missing for decades. I've even read about people like me. People who never recover their memory. I have to prepare myself for that possibility."

To his surprise, John got the job with Reuben Beachy at the harness shop. His success had more to do with Reuben's outright curiosity about John's condition than John's skill with the tools of a harness maker's trade.

The spry, elderly Amishman whistled or hummed continually while he worked on his large pedal-operated sewing machine. John's job was to take orders over the phone and from customers as well as cutting lengths of leather or synthetic biothane into the sizes his boss needed.

Reuben, as it turned out, had been making harnesses for more than sixty years. He made gear for everything from mini to draft-size horses. Recently, he had added leather dog collars and leashes to his inventory. Most of those he sold to dealers out of state.

Chuckling, Reuben confided to John on his first day at work, "A product with 'Amish Made' guarantees it is of *goot* quality and 'green' because we make it without the use of electricity. The English like that now. Once we were seen as backward people, but now they think we are on to something. It always makes me laugh."

It wasn't the only thing that made Reuben laugh. Every day he regaled John with witty comments and funny stories. Having seen the more serious side of the Amish, John was happy to see that humor had a place in the tight-knit community. By the end of his first week at work, John realized he had made a genuine friend.

Leaving a customer at the front counter, John entered the work area and approached the oversize sewing machine where the gnomelike bearded man toiled. "Reuben, David Miller is here to pick up a new harness he ordered."

Reuben stopped pedaling. "Would that be Pudgy Dave Miller or Smokey Dave Miller?"

"I've got no idea. How would I tell?" The man was a lean muscular farmer.

Ruben cackled. "Ach, we have so many people with the same names around here that we need nicknames to tell them apart. Pudgy Dave has blond hair. He isn't pudgy now, but he sure was when he was a boy."

"Then it must be Smokey Dave out front because his hair is brown."

Rubin rose from his seat and moved to where several large boxes were stacked on a bench. Selecting one, he handed it to John. "This should be it."

"Are you going to tell me how Smokey Dave got his name?"

"His house caught on fire. They saved the place, but he got a nickname real quick."

"I guess that makes sense." John took the box to the waiting customer, collected the money then turned over the closed sign.

Reuben was putting away his supplies when John returned to the room. As he was clearing away the leather scraps, Reuben said, "My mother's name was Miriam. What was your mother called?"

John waited for something to pop into his mind but nothing did. Finally, he shrugged. "I don't know. I don't remember."

"Which way is Texas from here?"

"Southwest," John answered without hesitation.

"Ever been there?"

"I don't know. Are we going to play Twenty Questions every night when we close up?"

"This is a strange illness you have, John Doe."

"No kidding."

"I know a good faith healer if you want to try one. I know you English don't set much store by that kind of thing, but Elmer Hertzler has a way with herbs."

"I'm coming to accept the fact that I may not remember more than snatches of my previous life."

"If that is what God wills, it is good that you should accept it."

"Reuben, what does it take to become Amish?"

Chuckling, Reuben winked. "An Amish *mamm* and *daed.*"

"All joking aside, can an outsider join the Amish church?"

"It has been done, but not by many. The ones I know who have tried have all left within a few months."

That wasn't what John wanted to hear.

Reuben sensed his disappointment. "If you admire our devotion to God, John Doe, be more devout in your own life. You don't need a black hat for that. If you think our plain, frugal ways are good, become plain and frugal in your life. We do not live fairy-tale lives as the English make us sound."

"I know that. I'm trying to be devout. I'm living plain, but I believe the Amish faith is the life for me."

Reuben stroked his long gray beard. "You are serious."

"I am. I think God placed me here for a reason."

Suddenly, Reuben started chuckling again. "You mean you've fallen for an Amish girl. That's the usual reason a man starts asking questions about our religion."

John felt searing heat rush to his face. "That may be part of it, but it's not the only reason I'm interested in learning more about the Amish faith."

Reuben wagged a finger at him. "Just remember, Adam had it pretty good in Eden until he started listening to a woman."

"They can't be all bad. You're married."

"*Ja,* three times. I maybe should have quit at two." He began chuckling again. "Don't tell my Martha I said that."

John smiled. "I won't. Three times? I thought the Amish weren't allowed to divorce and remarry."

"We are not. My first wife died in childbirth a year after our wedding. My second wife took sick and died from cancer. That was a hard time for me. Martha lost her husband to a stroke about the same time. Two years later we wed. I thought we had a lot in common, but it seems we didn't. If you are serious about becoming one of us you will need to learn the language and live among us for a time."

"For how long?"

"The English, always in a rush. Until you are accepted as one of us. It make take a year or it may take five years."

John quelled his need to rush forward into this new life. He wanted, needed, to belong somewhere. "Anna Imhoff is teaching me the language."

"Good. I can help with that, too. You should speak to Bishop Zook. He is the man who could help guide you."

John hesitated. Would it cause trouble for Karen if her bishop knew an outsider was interested in courting her? It wasn't that they had done anything wrong, but with John living on her farm it could give that impression. "Thanks, Reuben. I'll think on it."

"Pray about it, John Doe. God's wisdom is far beyond our own understanding. Now come, it's payday for you." Reuben led the way to the cash drawer and began counting out John's wages for the week.

Happy to have money that he'd earned himself, John pocketed the bills. After hitching one of Eli's horses to his borrowed cart, John swung by the grocery store on his way home. Leaving his horse at one of the hitching rails at the front of the store, John noticed Molly dozing at the next rail down.

Inside the store, he quickly spied Karen. Now that he left early for work each day and spent his free time working with Eli's horses, John saw her only at breakfast and for an hour or so in the evenings after supper. Normally her family surrounded her but today it appeared that she was alone.

Taking a cart from the line by the doorway he pushed it in her direction. Her eyes brightened when she caught sight of him.

He counted out several bills and offered them to her. "You're just the person I wanted to see. I'd like you to take this."

She placed two sacks of sugar in her cart. "What is that for?"

"You do all my cooking. I feel I should contribute more than just my rent."

"Especially after you got my father to lower it?" she suggested.

"Okay, yes."

"Very well." She extended her hand.

He made a sad face at his money. "Goodbye, hard-earned cash. When you go into Karen's pocket I know I'll not see you again."

She struggled not to smile at his teasing. Snatching the money from him, she said, "*Ja,* when money goes into my pocket it does not come out easily."

"So I've heard."

"Are you liking your new job?"

"I do. Reuben is a fine man to work for. It tickles him that I can't remember things. He's worse than Anna and Noah combined, with all his questions."

Karen chuckled. "I see you are wearing your plain clothes." She had given John several pairs of shortened pants as well as a couple of shirts. They went a long way toward stretching his meager wardrobe. He no longer had to spend the evenings wrapped in a quilt at home while his jeans dried over a chair in front of the stove.

John leaned on his cart as Karen piled several large bags of flour in her cart followed by two big cans of shortening. He said, "Reuben's going to help me with my Amish, too. Don't tell Anna. I want her to think I'm improving because of her teaching."

A slight smile curved Karen's lips. "I won't breathe a word."

It was nice talking about ordinary things, walking beside Karen, doing a simple thing like shopping. "Anna's really excited about her Christmas program. She keeps asking me if I remember that I said I would come."

"It is the one time that Amish children are encouraged to perform. Although we strive to remain humble before God and the world, you will see many proud parents and grandparents in the audience. And you will enjoy the entire program as most of it is in English."

"That's a relief. My Pennsylvania Dutch isn't progressing very fast."

"*Nee*. Do not disparage yourself. You are doing well."

She had noticed. His spirits lightened. "I was wondering what kind of Christmas presents would be appropriate for me to get the children?"

"Only little things."

"Define little things for me because an iPod is a little thing and I'm pretty sure that's not what you're thinking of."

"Colored pencils for Anna. A board game for Noah. Things like that. Homemade gifts are best."

John couldn't think of any simple thing he could make or buy that would be appropriate to give Karen. Perhaps Reuben could give him some ideas.

He said, "Okay, that's a start. Tell me what an Amish Christmas is like. Will you get a tree or decorate?"

"*Nee,* we do not allow ourselves to be distracted from the meaning of the day by such commercial things. We put up some greenery in the house, but Christmas Day is for reflecting about our Lord's birth. We will have family and friends over or we will travel to visit others. We do much visiting this time of year."

He hadn't considered he might be spending Christmas alone. The thought was utterly depressing. He strived to sound casual when he asked, "What are your plans for this year?"

"Nettie, Elam and Katie will have dinner with us on Christmas Day. Some of our cousins are coming, too. It will be fun. On second Christmas we will be traveling to visit some of my mother's family in Pennsylvania for a few days."

"What's second Christmas?"

"The twenty-sixth. It's when we exchange gifts. Goodness, I have so much baking to get done before then." She perked up and pushed her cart down the aisle.

John drew back to let another shopper past, then he stepped up beside Karen again. She was comparing the prices of poppy-seed filling on two brands. John asked, "What kind of gift would your father like?"

"Save your money, John," she chided. "You do not need to get gifts for our family."

"Yes...*ja,* I do."

She pressed her hand to her lips to hold back a giggle without success.

"What?" he demanded.

"It seems funny that you want to be like us."

"Your family, the Amish lifestyle, it's really all I know."

Sadness clouded her bright eyes. "A hen may sit on a duck's egg until it hatches, but the baby will still be a duckling and not a chick."

"I'm not a hapless egg. I have a choice about how I want to live my life. God has given me that. I don't know what I was in the past, but I know what I want in my future."

"And what is that?" she asked quietly.

"You."

As she stared at him in openmouthed shock, he smiled at her then rounded the corner of the aisle, picked up the things he'd stopped for and went to check out.

That evening Karen kept her composure through supper and the rest of the evening, but when John announced he was going to turn in she made an excuse to follow him a few minutes later.

He waited for her outside. She raised her shawl over her hair against the chill night air. A sliver of moon low in the west illuminated the nighttime farm. The combination of moonlight on snow gave her just enough light to see John's face.

Suddenly, she was beset with doubts. Had she misunderstood him earlier today? She had been so shocked by his words that she hadn't been able to demand an explanation. The moonlit setting and her racing heart were making it difficult to broach the subject.

"Is there something you need, Karen?"

The hint of humor in his voice pushed aside her reservations. If he had been toying with her she wasn't amused. "You can't make a statement like you did in the store and then walk away without an explanation."

"You mean when I said I wanted you in my future? I truly meant that."

There it was again, that softness in his tone that made her knees weak and sent the blood humming through her veins. She folded her arms tightly across her chest and walked away from the house. John fell into step beside her.

A dozen thoughts warred inside her brain. She cared for John so much, but her love of God and her family could not be brushed aside easily. She hardened her heart against the hurt she was about to cause him.

He was close beside her, but not touching her. They left the yard and walked side by side down the lane. The snow-covered fields reflected the moonlight with a gray-white glow. Overhead, the stars sparkled in the inky blackness. The whole world lay hushed except for the crunch of their footsteps on the frosty snow.

Finally, she said, "What you want is not possible, John."

"Because I am not Amish?"

"Yes."

"What if I became Amish? What if I joined your faith? Would there be a chance for us, then?"

"Why would you do this?"

"Because God brought me to this place for a reason. All around me are simple hardworking people who devote every day to the glory of God. Surly you don't think I'm here by chance?"

"I do not."

"You and your family have shown me that religion isn't about Sunday services. It's about doing what God has instructed us to do in the Bible. I'm serious, Karen. I want to embrace a new life. I can do that here. It feels right. If you are the woman who can help me do that, then I will be doubly blessed."

She stopped and faced him. His gaze, intense and piercing, never wavered. Was it possible he could join her faith? It wouldn't be easy. What if he did manage to do it and then his memory came back to him? Would he want to stay? There was no way to be certain.

"What are you asking of me, John?"

"For now, acceptance is all I ask."

No promises, no bold talk of overpowering love. She pondered what he asked and realized it was something she could do. "All right. I accept that you have a strong desire to learn about my faith and to become one of us."

"Thank you. How do you think your family will feel about it?"

After a second, she shook her head. "Skeptical."

"I can always trust you to tell me the truth."

Karen knew that wasn't true. If it were, she would be telling him how firmly he was planted in her heart and mind and how much she longed to find a way to be with him in every sense. Yet a prickle of doubt about his motives could not be silenced by her own desires.

It had only been a month and a half since she found him on the road. It was too soon. It was too soon to know her own heart and too soon for him to know his.

He tipped his head toward the house. "We should get back. I don't want you to get sick, with Christmas less than three weeks away."

"*Ja,* I have much to do." And much to think about.

* * *

On Saturday, John went out to continue working with the horses. He was surprised but happy to find Jacob waiting inside the barn to help him. John was grateful for a chance to spend some one-on-one time with the lad.

Together they continued training Jenny and One-Way. By now, both young horses accepted their harnesses without a problem and could be hitched and unhitched from a cart and driven short distances. The young filly proved more temperamental than the colt, but both of them were progressing well.

After putting One-Way through his paces out on a narrow dirt-packed road that circled the inside of the pasture, John drove him back to the barn where Jacob waited to take Jenny out next. John drew the colt to a halt and looked at Jacob. "What do you think about taking this fellow out on the highway?"

Looking pleased to have his opinion consulted, Jacob said, "He's spent plenty of time tethered near the road to get used to traffic. It doesn't seem to bother him anymore. *Ja,* I think he is ready."

John offered the reins. "Would you mind driving him? You've got more experience and more skill than I do. I've worn him out this morning. I think he'll behave, but I'd like to ride along to see how he does."

Jacob's slender chest puffed out at the compliment. He quickly climbed into the two-wheeled cart beside John and turned the horse around. John jumped out to open the gate and close it behind them, then resumed his seat.

In the front yard a buggy sat in front of the barn. Through the open door John saw Eli wearing a heavy leather apron as he examined the hoof of a palomino pony. Reuben Beachy stood beside Eli watching him work. He caught sight of John and waved. John waved back, happy to know he had at least one friend outside of the Imhoff family.

John asked Jacob, "When did your father start shoeing horses again?"

"He announced last night that he thought his arm was strong enough to try it."

"I'm glad for him."

"*Ja,* he has missed it."

"Do you plan to be a farrier, too?"

"Maybe. I'm strong enough." Jacob scowled at John, daring him to disagree.

"I think a man can do anything he puts his mind to. It isn't always about being the strongest."

"Karen thinks I can't do it," Jacob admitted.

"Karen worries about you, that's all. She will come around if that is what you really want to do."

"Maybe." The boy's tone carried a heavy dose of doubt. Before John could explore the subject further, they reached the highway. Since it was Saturday, John knew there would be less traffic on the road, but he still wasn't sure how One-Way would handle the new situation.

The horse took to the roadway as if he'd been doing it all his life. Even a passing car didn't disturb him.

John said, "It seems he has inherited his mother's calm nature as well as his father's speed. It's a good combination. Someone is going to be very happy with this colt."

Jacob urged the horse to pick up his pace. "I'd love to see how fast he can go."

John laid a hand on the boy's arm. "Me, too, but this isn't the time or place for it."

The boy shot John a sour look but pulled the horse back. After two miles, John said, "I think this is good. Let's take him home."

As they slowed to turn around, an open buggy drawn by a high-stepping trotter came down the road, and One-Way whinnied a greeting. The Amish teenager driving the other vehicle drew to a halt.

"*Guder mariye,* Jacob," he called out.

"Hello, Henry." Jacob replied brightly. It was easy to read the hero-worship on his face.

John recognized the young man as one of Bishop Zook's sons. He'd seen Jacob hanging out with him and several older boys at the wedding and in town after school.

"Is this Eli's racehorse I've been hearing about?" Henry cast a critical eye over the colt.

"*Ja,* it is." Jacob couldn't disguise the pride in his voice.

Henry turned his attention to John. "Are you the *dummkopf*—the *Englischer* who can't remember his own name?

Chapter Thirteen

The teenager's mocking tone caught John completely by surprise. He'd met with nothing but sympathy and kindness among the Amish. He was unprepared for ridicule.

Henry's smile turned snide. "Your horse doesn't look all that fast, Jacob. I think my Dobby could beat him running on three legs."

Jacob rose to the challenge. "I don't think so."

"Too bad we can't find out." With a laugh, Henry slapped his lines hard on the back of his sweaty horse and headed down the road at a breakneck pace.

John said, "Your friend isn't a very good judge of horseflesh." He wasn't kind, either.

Urging One-Way toward home, Jacob said, "Henry was just kidding."

John didn't believe that for a minute. "Is Henry a good friend of yours?"

"Sure. I'm his buddy."

"He seems quite a bit older than you."

"Henry is eighteen, but he doesn't mind if I hang out with him. He knows how to have fun. He has a swell radio in his buggy."

"I thought listening to the radio was frowned upon as worldly."

"Just because a bunch of old geezers don't like modern music that doesn't make it wrong. Besides, we are in our *rumspringa*. We get to do those kinds of things."

"Aren't you too young for your *rumspringa?*"

"Henry says I'm not."

"He likes to race, doesn't he?"

"Sometimes." John could feel Jacob's retreat.

The whole situation didn't sit well with John, but what could he do? He was finally making some headway in getting to know Jacob. If he told Karen or Eli his vague suspicions that Jacob was involved in illicit buggy racing he would be guilty of betraying the boy's confidences.

What choice did that leave him? The only thing he could do was keep a watchful eye on Jacob.

On Sunday morning John joined the family in the buggy as they were getting ready to leave for church services. He looked forward to the day although it was barely six o'clock. The service would be at the home of a family some fifteen miles away. Eli had gone ahead with the bench wagon a half hour earlier.

John squeezed into the backseat between Noah and Jacob. Karen rode up front with Anna. When they were on their way, John found the courage to ask, "What can I expect today?"

"To be bored stiff," Jacob answered under his breath.

A sharp look from Karen proved he'd been overheard. She said, "Worship begins at about eight o'clock and it usually lasts until after eleven. Women are seated in one area, and men in another."

"Three hours on a backless bench?" John winced. What had he gotten himself into?

Karen continued. "Hymns are sung from the *Ausbund,* a special hymnal used by us. The songs were written by martyrs for our faith over four hundred years ago."

"So, no English songs I can sing along with?"

"*Nee.* There will be two preachers along with Bishop Zook at the service. They will take turns preaching. The first sermon begins about eight-thirty. It will be in Pennsylvania Dutch. Scriptures are read in High German. Did you bring your English Bible so you can follow along?"

He patted his coat pocket. "Yes, I did."

The trip was long and tiring, and everyone was glad to get out when they finally arrived at the service site. A group of men in charge of unhitching the buggies and taking the horses into the barn quickly went to work to settle Molly after her long trip.

John felt awkward joining the men as they began to file into the house, but Eli was there already and Reuben came over to quickly make John feel welcome. A long row of black hats lined the porch wall. John added his to the end and took a moment to wonder how he would find it again out of the seventy or so hanging there.

Noah tugged John's coat. "Don't worry, I'll poke you if you start to fall asleep."

"Gee, thanks."

The benches were as hard as John feared, but when the hymns began he was mesmerized by the simple beauty and power of the singing. There was no organ or musical instrument of any kind. The profoundly moving and mournful sound was created by more than a hundred people packed into the lower rooms of the house.

He couldn't follow the preaching, but he read and studied the passages Eli pointed out to him. In his own way he felt connected to the outpouring of faith around him.

After an hour, he felt Noah slump against him. Looking down, he saw the boy had nodded off. He wasn't the only one. At least one of the very elderly men who had been given household chairs to sit in was snoring softly. John nudged Noah who quickly sat up straight, but no one bothered the elder in the corner.

When the meeting came to an end, John closed his book, feeling refreshed in mind and body. Had he felt like this before during a church service? Had he known this closeness to God and lost it?

He glanced across the room and caught sight of Karen. Had he known this special closeness with a woman and forgotten it?

"Our program is tonight. It's tonight. It's tonight. I can't wait. I can't wait." Anna's excitement had been growing by leaps and bounds over the past days. Tonight was finally Christmas Eve and her school program was only an hour away.

Anna hopped around the kitchen table repeating her refrain until Karen finally had enough.

"Silence, little sister."

Anna immediately stopped chanting but continued to bounce. Karen tried not to smile and took pity on her. She remembered well her own anticipation for the biggest night of the school year.

"Why don't you go see if John is back," Karen suggested hoping for a moment of peace and quiet to finish her preparations. There were fresh cookies cooling on the rack that would have to be packed for the trip and her peanut brittle was nearly done. She couldn't stop stirring for fear it would scorch.

But peace and quiet was not to be hers. Before Anna reached the front door, it opened and John stepped into the room.

Anna grabbed his hand. "*Frehlicher-Grischtdaag,* John. I knew you wouldn't forget."

"Merry Christmas to you, too. It's your big night. How could I forget that? Reuben had us close the shop early so I could get home in time to go with you."

He was wearing his plain clothes and her brother's hat. Karen's heart expanded with happiness. Knowing that John was seeking God and a place in her community warmed her inside and out. If only she dare believe such a thing was possible.

She glanced at the clock. It was a few minutes after one o'clock in the afternoon. "Anna, go tell your father it's time to get ready."

The child rocketed out of the house without bothering to put on her coat. John chuckled. "She's ready to pop with excitement."

"She is. Noah is almost as bad. The children spend weeks, even months, making preparations for their Christmas program. They'll sing songs, read poems, as if you hadn't already learned that from Anna, and they will have a play about the meaning of Christmas. It's a big deal for them."

"It sounds like a lot of fun. What can I do to help you get ready?"

"Stack those cookies in these plastic containers and don't snitch. They are for the children's teacher." She motioned with her hand toward the container.

"You never let me have any fun. How do you know they are any good? I should test them." He popped one in his mouth.

"John!"

"They're fine," he mumbled around his full mouth. He packed the box to the brim and then snapped the lid in place. "Is there anything else I can test for you?"

Karen shook her head and returned to stirring her candy but her lighthearted mood persisted. He could always make her smile.

"Are you sure it's okay for me to come to this program?" he asked.

"*Ja,* there will be many English visitors. Lots of our families work for non-Amish businesses and have non-Amish friends. We welcome them to share the joy of Christ's birth."

Noah and Jacob came through the front door. Noah shook off his hat. "It's snowing again. Papa says we should take the sleigh."

Anna came in behind them wrapped in her father's big coat. "We're going to have a sleigh ride!"

Eli, smiling indulgently at his littlest daughter, closed the door behind her.

Only Karen looked upset at the prospect. "Really, Papa? Can't we take the buggy? It will be so much warmer."

"*Nee,* the snow is piling up fast. You won't think it's warmer if you must walk home and leave the buggy stuck in a drift."

"Very well. Jacob, Noah, get the lap robes from the chest upstairs. Everyone else, go get dressed or we will be late."

Everyone departed. Only John remained in the

kitchen. Karen began carefully pouring her hot peanut-brittle candy over the nuts arranged on wax paper in a long pan.

"Are you sure I can't test that for you?" John's voice tickled her ear. He stood close behind her. Suddenly, her hands began to shake. Quickly, he grasped the pan handle enclosing her fingers beneath his own to help steady it. "Careful."

Trying to ignore the rush of emotions singing through her heart, she said, "There is nothing for you to test here. It's too hot."

"But I have a sweet tooth."

"Your sweet tooth will have to wait."

"Can't. This will have to tide me over." He planted a quick kiss on her cheek.

She should scold him, but the words died in her throat. Instead, she cast a sly grin his way. "Go harness Benny to the sleigh and be quick about it."

"Yes, ma'am." He winked at her as he went out the door.

Returning to her work, Karen began humming her favorite Christmas song.

John didn't waste any time getting the big draft horse hitched. Within ten minutes he was waiting outside the front door for the rest of the family. For some reason he was almost as excited as Anna. A sleigh ride with Karen beside him was his idea of the perfect romantic Christmas Eve.

Anna was the first one out of the house. She quickly claimed her spot in the front seat. Noah scrambled up beside her with the lap robes in his arms. John gave over the reins and took his place in the back. Noah handed several robes to John then spread one over himself and Anna. Wiggles and giggles was the only way John could think to describe Anna's demeanor.

Karen and Eli came next carrying boxes filled with treats that they stowed on the floor. "Everyone be careful not to step on these," Karen cautioned with a pointed look in John's direction.

Eli took his place up front and that left Karen standing beside the sleigh with no choice but to sit next to John. He smiled broadly and patted the seat.

After casting a quick glance at her father, she got in. John spread the robe over her and said in a low voice, "Don't worry. I won't let you freeze."

"Jacob! Come on," Anna shouted, causing the patient horse to toss his head.

Jacob came out the door letting it slam shut behind him. He had been trying to act as if the program was no big deal, but John could see he was excited, too. The teenager piled in the backseat with them.

After a second or two of getting settled, Jacob said, "Scoot over, Karen, and give me some room."

John grinned. *Thank you, Jacob.*

Wishing he could give the boy a pat on the back, John lifted his arm to make more room for Karen and laid it along the back of the seat. She moved closer, but remained stiff as a chunk of wood beside him. As much as he wanted to slip his arm around her shoulder, he knew it would only make her more uncomfortable.

"Ready, everyone?" Eli asked. Five confirmations rang out. Eli slapped the lines and the big horse took off down the snow-covered lane.

Sleigh bells jingled merrily in time with Benny's footfalls. The runners hissed along over the snow as big flakes continued to float down. They stuck to the hats of the men turning their brims white before long.

As Anna and Noah tried to catch snowflakes on their tongues between giggles, John leaned down to see Karen's face. "Are you warm enough?"

She nodded, but her face looked rosy and cold. John took off his woolen scarf and wrapped it around her head to cover her mouth and nose. "

"Thank you," she murmured.

"My pleasure. It's a perfect day, isn't it?"

The thick snow obscured the horizon and made the farm seem like the inside of a snow globe. The fields lay hidden under a thick blanket of white. Cedar tree branches drooped beneath their load of the white stuff. A hushed stillness filled the air broken only by the jingle of the harness bells. It was a picture-perfect moment in time.

The school lay only two miles from the farm. For John, they reached their destination all too soon. As they drew close they saw a dozen buggies and sleighs parked along the south side of the white wooden school building. All the horses had their faces close to the wall to keep them sheltered from the wind.

As everyone scrambled out of the sleigh, John offered Karen his hand to help her out. When she took it, he gave her an affectionate squeeze. She graced him with a shy smile in return.

Inside the building, the place was already crowded with people. Student desks had been pushed out of the way to make room for benches down the center facing a small stage at the front of the room. Swags of fragrant cedar boughs decorated the windowsills and colorful paper chains ran from each corner to a light fixture in the center of the ceiling. Pegs along one wall held coats and hats while a table on the opposite wall bore trays of cookies and candies.

An atmosphere of joy, goodwill and anticipation permeated the air. Everywhere John looked there were welcoming smiles. The Imhoff children hurried to join their classmates behind a large screen off to one side of the stage. Eli, John and Karen found seats in the center.

For the next hour the little school became suspended in time. John saw parents and grandparents, aunts and uncles, friends and neighbors focused not on the problems of the world or their own lives, but on the stage where children preformed their assigned roles, not perfectly, but beautifully nonetheless.

Together the community shook with shared laughter and sighed with quiet joy as the reason for the season was retold not by preachers but by eager young voices. When the last song began, Jacob had a small solo. To John's surprise, the boy had a beautiful voice, by far the best in the group. His rendition of "Silent Night" was enough to bring tears to many eyes.

After the performance ended, Reuben Beachy came from the back of the school carrying a large sack. He didn't wear a red suit, but his beard was white and his eyes held a distinct twinkle as he preformed the role of Father Christmas and passed out small gifts to the children.

Anna was delighted with her gift, a wooden puzzle. The little girl beside her unwrapped a book. Although she tried to hide it, it was clear she wasn't as pleased with her gift. Noticing her friend's unhappiness, Anna offered to swap gifts.

John glanced at Karen. She had seen her little sister's unselfish act, and he knew she was pleased by it.

Later, when everyone had a plate of treats, Anna squeezed in between Karen and John. He said, "You did very well, Miss Anna. Your poem was perfection."

"Danki." Her excited high was fading.

"It was very nice of you to change gifts with your friend," Karen added.

Anna shrugged. "Mary already has that book. I don't."

"It was a *goot* thing anyway." Karen slipped her arm around the child and gave her a hug.

It was dark by the time the festivities wound down and families began leaving. John brushed the accumulated snow from the sleigh's seats while Eli lit the lanterns on the sides. Benny stood quietly, one hip cocked and a dusting of snow across his back.

John stepped back inside to tell Karen they were ready. Scanning the room, he saw her with a group of young women. Two of them held babies on their hips. Karen raised a hand to smooth the blond curls of a little boy. As she did, her gaze met John's across the room. In that moment, he knew exactly what he wanted.

He wanted Karen to have the life she was meant to live and he wanted to be a part of it. He wanted to spend every Christmas with her for the rest of his life.

"Is it time to go home? I'm tired." Anna, sitting at her desk, could barely keep her eyes open.

"Yes, it's time to go home." He picked her up and she draped herself over his shoulder. Karen joined them a minute later.

In the sleigh, Noah and Jacob sat up front with their father leaving John to settle in with Anna across his lap and Karen seated beside him. The snow had stopped and a pale moon slipped in and out of the clouds as the horse made its way home. Snuggled beneath a blanket with Karen at his side, John marveled at the beauty of the winter night and the beauty of the woman next to him.

When they pulled up in front of the house, John handed Anna over to Eli, who carried her inside. The boys took the horse to the barn leaving John standing on the porch steps with Karen.

He said, "I had a wonderful time. Thank you for inviting me."

"I'm glad." She didn't seem eager to get in out of the cold.

"I had no idea an Amish Christmas could be so much fun." Or that it would clearly show him his heart's desire.

She said, "We are just getting started, John. Tomorrow we will have many guests for dinner. We will have games to play and stories to share."

He stepped closer. She fell silent but didn't move away. Reaching out, he cupped her cheek. "Merry Christmas, Karen."

"Merry Christmas to you, John." Her voice was a soft whisper in the night.

Slowly, he lowered his lips to hers and kissed her.

Chapter Fourteen

Karen knew she should turn away from John, but she couldn't make her body obey. His mouth closed over hers with incredible softness, a featherlight touch that wasn't enough.

She raised her face to him, and he deepened the kiss. A profound joy clutched her heart and stole her breath. This was the moment she had been waiting a lifetime to experience.

Her arms crept up to circle his neck and she drew him closer still. The sweet softness of his lips moved across her cheek, touched her eyelid and then her brow as if claiming every part of her. When he pulled away, Karen knew he owned a piece of her soul forever. She would never be the same.

His eyes roved across her face. "I love you, Karen. If I have to spend a lifetime proving it to you, I will."

Looking up at his beloved face, she whispered, "I do not doubt it for I love you, too."

Slipping his arms around her, he pulled her close. She leaned against his chest, feeling his strength and his tenderness as he held her. Nothing had ever felt this right and yet she knew it was wrong.

With his cheek resting against her hair, he said, "You've taken the despair from my heart and replaced it with something wonderful. I belong here. I belong with you."

"I wish with all my heart that you might stay among us," she answered.

"I will stay. I'll do whatever it takes to become Amish. I don't know what my old life held. I may never know, but God brought me to you. I trust in Him. I believe this love and this faith is His will. It is His gift to me, and I will be thankful all the days of my life."

She wanted to believe as he did but the reality of their situation was far from simple. "John, to become Amish is not an easy thing. What if your old life comes back to you and you must leave us?"

"What if it doesn't?" he countered. "I can't live in limbo forever. I need to belong somewhere. I need to make a life for myself. I want that life to be with you."

She understood his desire to forge his own way but was it too soon? When would the time be right? Six months? A year? What right did she have to tell him to wait? He was certain of his love and of God's plan for him.

Selfish or not, it was the same plan Karen prayed John would follow for she wanted him in her life as much as she'd ever wanted anything.

The sound of the barn door opening signaled the boys were returning. Reluctantly, she stepped out of John's embrace. "I must go in."

He nodded. *"Guten nacht, meim glay hotsli."*

His little heart. She liked the sound of that. "Good night to you, too, John."

She entered the house and climbed the staircase with measured steps that belied the happiness inside her. Pushing aside her doubts, she relived the moment in his arms. With one kiss John had made this the most wonderful Christmas ever. He loved her.

Karen's happiness carried her through Christmas morning with a smile that wouldn't fade. The snow had stopped and the sun shone bright above a glittering world. Glancing out the window, Karen thought if someone could see inside her heart it must look the same.

Surely there was a sparkling and beautiful wonderland where an ordinary heart had resided only the day before. If not for a small dark cloud of doubt and worry that hovered in the background it would be perfect.

After a morning spent in respectful prayer, the entire family pitched in to get ready for the Christmas feast. When Nettie, Elam and Katie arrived, Anna quickly took over the care of baby Rachel. Less than an hour later, Eli's brother, Carl, and his family arrived, disgorging eight more cousins along with Aunt Jean from the bulging buggy. Soon the house was filled with the smell of baking meats and pies and happy voices.

As the women took over the kitchen, the men took over the sitting room. Karen glanced frequently through the doorway wondering if John felt uncomfortable among her family, but she need not have worried. Once, when she checked on him, he caught her eye and winked then proceeded to jump several of her father's checkers to the hoots of the onlookers.

Noah grinned at everyone. "I told you he is a *goot* player."

It wasn't until the guests left in the late afternoon that Karen tried to steal a few minutes alone with John. Her father and brothers had gone out to start the evening chores. John made to follow then, but Karen quickly asked him to help her put away the extra table leaves.

When her family was out of sight, John swooped in for a quick kiss. It was too brief as far as Karen was concerned, but she recognized his restraint and admired him for it. Part of her longed to bask in the glow of his love and believe everything would work out for them. Another part of her knew her happiness could shatter at any moment. She had spent her life listening to her practical side, but just for today she silenced those doubts and gave thanks to God for the precious gift of a Christmas day spent with the man she loved.

He said, "I'm going to miss you tomorrow."

"We'll only be gone three days. Besides, Papa is leaving Jacob in charge of the farm while we're gone so you'll have him to keep you company."

"Jacob's a nice kid, but I'd much rather spend time with you."

She cupped his cheek. "I will be back before you know it."

John covered Karen's hand with his own. The happiness that bubbled through him was almost impossible to contain. He wanted to shout from the rooftops that he loved Karen Imhoff and she loved him. He thrust aside the tiny voice in the back of his mind that said he was rushing things.

He said, "I don't know how Amish couples managed to keep their feelings a secret. I'm pretty sure people will take one look at my face and know I'm in love with you."

"If they suspect, they won't say anything. It's a private matter for young couples, but we are expected to conduct ourselves modestly."

"All right, I'll behave but I wish you weren't leaving."

"It's only for a little while."

"It already feels like forever."

She hesitated, then said, "While we are gone…"

"What?"

"Nothing, I'm being silly."

"No, tell me." He would do anything she asked.

"Keep an eye on Jacob for me. He has been hanging out with a group of older boys. I don't think they are a good influence on him."

"I'll do my best. Don't worry."

She smiled then, a wonderful soft smile that melted his heart. "I won't."

The following morning, John saw them off in their hired car. Anna and Noah were excited as ever. Eli looked uncomfortable at the prospect of a car trip as he gave Jacob final instructions about the livestock. Karen just looked adorable.

As the car drove out of sight, John turned to Jacob. "Would you like some help with the horses this morning?"

"*Nee.* I can handle it."

"I don't doubt it for a minute, but Reuben's shop is closed today so I'm free."

"I don't need your help."

Why was the boy so touchy? Perhaps he had the impression that John didn't trust him to do the work right. "If you don't need me I may go to the library in Hope Springs for a while."

He hadn't checked the NamUs website for more than

a week. He no longer expected to find anything, but he couldn't give up his faint hope just yet.

Shortly before noon, John took the farm cart and one of the draft horses and traveled the five miles into Hope Springs. At the library, he checked the missing-persons website and found nothing new that related to him. The vague sense of dread that had accompanied him into the building slipped away.

For weeks he had feared he'd never find out about his past, but that had changed. Now, he worried he'd discover something that would take him away from the life he was building. Away from Karen.

On the trip home, John caught sight of a buggy leaving the Imhoff lane and heading away from town. He was almost sure the horse pulling the buggy was One-Way. Had Jacob decided to give the colt a little more road time?

Karen's concerns and his own gut feeling made him decide to follow the boy. Benny was no match for One-Way's pace and John soon fell farther behind.

When he crested the hill south of the farm the buggy was nowhere in sight. John drew Benny to a stop. Where had Jacob gone? Had he turned into one of the farm-steads? Suddenly, Benny looked east and whinnied. Buggy tracks led into a seldom-used side road.

Giving Benny his head, John let the big fellow lumber down the narrow lane. As they rounded a curve, John saw a dozen young men and buggies lined up at the side of the road. Ahead of them, two buggies sat side by side. An Amish boy with a red cloth in his hand stood in the middle of the lane. With a shout, he brought down his flag. The two buggies sprang forward, as the horses raced neck and neck down the narrow road. One of them was One-Way with Jacob in the carriage.

John watched in horror as the buggies rounded a sharp turn, sideswiped each other and locked wheels. The next instant, he saw the wheels of Jacob's carriage catch the edge of the snow-filled ditch.

The sudden drop broke the vehicles apart. As the other driver raced on, Jacob made the mistake of trying to swing back into the center of the road. He lost control. The black buggy flipped over onto its side dragging the horse off its feet.

John jumped down from his cart and raced toward Jacob, running past the other boys who were frozen with shock. He watched in helpless fear as One-Way floundered in the snow, tangling himself in the traces. Reaching the animal, John began speaking soothing words. He worked quickly to untangle the horse. John didn't dare let go of the horse for fear the animal would injure itself or Jacob if he had fallen under the buggy. He had to keep One-Way still. He called out, "Jacob, are you all right? Answer me."

Two Amish teenagers finally raced up to help. After making sure the boys had a good hold on the horse, John said, "Unhitch him and keep him quiet."

Making his way back to the cab, John peered inside. Jacob lay crumpled on the floor. Fear stole the breath from John's lungs. He climbed through the front windshield to reach the boy. "Jacob, can you hear me?"

Please, Lord, let this child be okay. Do not break Karen's heart with another loss.

Reaching Jacob, John felt for his pulse and was relieved to find it steady and strong. "Jacob," he called softly. "Are you hurt?"

Jacob eyes fluttered open. "I don't think so," he answered in a shaky voice.

"Just lie still." John laid a hand on his shoulder to prevent him from rising.

It didn't do any good. Jacob pushed his hand aside and pulled himself into a sitting position. "What about Henry? Was he hurt?"

John shook his head as he searched Jacob's arms and legs for any obvious fracture. "He didn't tip over."

Jacob struggled to stand up. "What about One-Way?"

Hearing the panic in the boy's voice, John knew he was more concerned about the horse than about himself. "I don't know. I wanted to make sure you hadn't broken your foolish neck."

"I'm okay. Please, check on One-Way."

"Your friends are with him. Let's get you out of here first." The two of them climbed out of the buggy.

Before Jacob could rush to check on his horse John gave him a more thorough once-over. Taking the boy's chin in his hand, he tipped his head to the side. Blood trickled from a gash above his eyebrow, giving him a gruesome appearance.

John said, "You're gonna need stitches. Are you dizzy? Can you tell me how many fingers I'm holding up?"

"Two," Jacob answered correctly.

"Do you hurt anywhere?"

"My head aches, but it isn't bad."

John studied the boy's face and decided he was telling the truth. "Let's see if One-Way fared as well."

As they approached the colt, it became clear that One-Way was injured. The horse was limping heavily on his right front leg.

Jacob abruptly sat on the snowy roadway. "I have ruined my father."

John approached the young horse, speaking softly. He ran his hand down the animal's leg, assessing the damage. "It's starting to swell. It may only be a sprain, but a horse this young can easily fracture a bone. We need the vet to take a look at him."

A tall, slender boy with glasses spoke up. "My *dat* has a phone in the barn. I'll call the vet."

John nodded and the boy took off. As he did, the other carriage came back and John recognized Henry Zook driving it. His cocky attitude had evaporated. "Jacob, are you hurt?"

Rocking himself in the road, Jacob said, "Why did I do it? Why did I let you goad me into racing? I've ruined my father's best horse."

Henry climbed out of his buggy and came to squat beside Jacob. "I'm so sorry. I never meant for this to happen."

John said, "Henry, stay with Jacob. The rest of you come and help me." The young men followed John and lined up beside the fallen buggy. Together they heaved it upright on the road. The damage looked minimal in spite of the rough landing.

Returning to Jacob's side, John said, "We need the vet to look at One-Way and Jacob needs to see a doctor. Can one of you take him into town?"

"I will," Henry said quickly.

"I'm not going anywhere until One-Way has been taken care of."

John was quick to disagree. "You're going to the doctor. Your sister will kill me if she finds out I let the horse be seen first."

John approached the horse again and ran his hand down the injured foreleg. Already he could feel the heat in it. Looking at the boys, he pointed to one of them. "Let me have your scarf."

The young man yanked it off his neck and held it out. John packed it with snow and wrapped it around the horse's leg to control the swelling.

"Papa will be so upset with me. What are you going to tell him?" Jacob pinned John with a wide-eyed gaze.

"I will not lie to him, Jacob. You are the one who must tell him there was an accident."

John looked over to the rest of the boys. "This kind of racing must stop. You can see now how dangerous it is. I will accept your word that this kind of thing will never happen again. If I hear about *any* of you racing, I *will* speak to everyone's father and the sheriff."

The young men, looking sheepish and relieved, all agreed there would be no more impromptu contests. After sending Jacob off to see Dr. White, John waited with One-Way until the vet arrived.

That evening, John finished icing One-Way's leg and was securing an elastic bandage when he realized someone was watching him. Looking up, he saw Jacob standing outside the stall. The boy sported a small dressing over his eye and a look of doom on his face.

John patted the horse's neck. "He's doing well. With some rest and therapy the vet thinks he'll be fine in time for the sale. How's the head?"

"I needed five stitches."

John stepped outside the stall and latched the door securely. It was a hard way for the boy to learn a lesson but it could have been so much worse.

"Do you like it here?" Jacob asked suddenly.

"Of course I do. I love working with the horses. I love the way your family has welcomed me in. I love…" John stopped, realizing how close he'd just come to revealing his secret.

"You love my sister."

Turning away, John gathered up his supplies. "I'm fond of all of you."

"I did not like you when you first came."

"No kidding? I never would've guessed," John replied, not bothering to hide his grin.

There was no answering humor in Jacob's face. "The day we found you I knew someone had robbed you and dumped you on our road."

The boy's serious tone set off alarm bells in John's head. He asked, "How did you know that?"

"You had no shoes on but your socks were clean and you had no wallet."

"The sheriff came to the same conclusion." John moved to fork hay into the stalls. A sense of dread uncurled inside him.

After a long pause, Jacob said, "I found something not far from where you were laying. I thought you would think whoever robbed you took it."

John stopped his work. His heart hammered hard enough to jump out of his chest. "What did you find?"

Jacob opened his hand and held it toward John. "I took it. I'm sorry. When you came here and couldn't remember anything, I thought it would not matter that I had kept it. Later, I was afraid to give it back because the sheriff might think I had done this thing to you."

John took several unsteady steps toward the boy and lifted a gold pocket watch from his hand. The cover was finely engraved with the figure of a running horse. John recognized the weight and feel of it in his hand.

When he flipped it open he saw it was an elaborate timepiece that included a stopwatch. Chimes began to play a tune. It was the same tune he'd heard that day in the barn. He looked at Jacob. "You've had this all along?"

Jacob couldn't meet his gaze. He stared at his feet and nodded. "I liked the music. Papa would never let me keep such a fancy thing."

Turning the watch over, John saw it was engraved. His legs gave way. Falling back against the stall door, he slid to the ground. Here was his answer.

He read the words aloud. "To Aaron from Jonathan. Happy birthday, pal."

"I'm sorry," Jacob whispered.

A horrible buzzing filled John's head. He struggled to catch his breath. He could barely wrap his mind around this discovery. "My name is Aaron and I have a friend named Jonathan."

John pressed a hand to his mouth as the implications and possibilities swirled in his mind. He had a name. He had a friend.

He opened the cover and the tune began to play again. It was a waltz. He closed his eyes.

A woman, dancing and swirling, crossed a hardwood floor on bare feet. Her red skirt billowed around her shapely legs as she danced to the tune being played by the watch. Her long blond hair flowed like silk down her back. She stopped suddenly and held out both hands. Clear as day John saw the gold band on her left hand. She smiled. "Dance with me, Aaron."

Pain shot through John's skull. Tears filled his eyes

but he didn't know why he was crying. He didn't want to know.

Snapping the watch shut, he pressed his hands to his temples. He didn't want to remember any more.

Chapter Fifteen

Karen stepped out of the car and stretched her stiff muscles, grateful to finally be home. She'd only been away a few days but it felt like a lifetime. While she had enjoyed every minute of her visit with her maternal grandparents, aunts, uncles and cousins, she had missed John terribly. Excitement at the prospect of their private reunion skittered across her skin.

Would he kiss her again?

Jacob stood waiting for them on the front porch. His hat was pulled low on his forehead. Karen waved at him, but he didn't wave back. He stared at his boots as he addressed Eli. "Papa, I must speak with you in private."

That didn't sound good. Karen and Eli exchanged worried glances. What had happened? She said, "Go on, Papa, I will take care of the car."

As Jacob and Eli went inside the house, Karen paid the driver, took their suitcases from the trunk and herded the younger children toward the house. Noah hefted one of the larger suitcases and struggled toward the steps with it. Anna carried her own but she still wore the same unhappy pout that had appeared shortly after they left their grandmother's home.

Karen asked, "What is the matter, little sister? Aren't you glad to be home?"

"Yes, but I don't want Christmas to be over."

Smiling indulgently, Karen patted her shoulder. "All things must come to an end, even good things."

"I know." Anna shuffled her feet.

Noah stopped and draped an arm across her small shoulders. "Christmas is over, but we can look forward to the horse sale tomorrow."

Giving him a skeptical glance, Anna asked, "Is it really fun? I've never gone with Papa before."

Noah threw up his hands. "Yes, it's fun. You'll see lots of new people and pretty horses. There will be tents set up and they sell all kinds of neat things. Papa will buy us ice cream and good things to eat."

"He will?" She perked up.

"You'll see. It's more fun than market day."

Mollified, Anna followed her brother into the house, begging for more information. "Will I get to choose any flavor of ice cream I want?"

Inside the kitchen, Karen pulled off her black bonnet and hung it along with her heavy coat on one of the pegs beside the door. Disappointment dimmed her happiness. John wasn't waiting for her.

Surely he'd heard the car drive in. Perhaps he wasn't home from work yet. She didn't know if Reuben had his shop open or not. Many Amish closed their businesses and spent the days after Christmas traveling to visit family. Reuben had enough grandchildren that he could easily visit throughout the month of January and not see them all.

Karen tried to console herself with the fact that she would see John soon enough. He rarely missed a meal.

Taking down her apron, she tied it on and began making preparations for supper. She could hear the muted tones of Jacob talking to her father in the living room but she couldn't make out what was being said. Did it involve John? Was that why he wasn't here?

A sudden thought made her freeze. Had John remembered who he was? Had he gone back to his old life?

She wrestled that ever-present fear to the back of her mind where she kept it caged. John wouldn't have left without waiting for her to return. He wouldn't go without saying goodbye. He loved her and she loved him.

She clung to that knowledge in the face of all reason. God had brought John to her. They were meant for each other.

A few minutes later, Jacob came out of the sitting room and she caught a glimpse of his face without his hat on. A bandage and a bruise marred his forehead.

Crossing to him, she grasped his chin and turned his head toward the kitchen window for more light. "What happened to you?"

"I had a carriage accident. I got a couple of stitches, that's all."

Eli had followed Jacob into the kitchen. "The boy and I have discussed this."

"Is John okay? Was he involved?" she demanded.

"John's fine," Jacob answered without looking at her.

"Where is he?" Karen sensed her brother wasn't telling her everything.

"He's working in the barn. I should go help him finish." Jacob made a quick exit, leaving Karen to stare after him.

She turned to her father. "What's going on?"

"Jacob got in some trouble while we were gone. He has told me everything. We will not mention it again." Eli donned his hat and coat and left the house.

Far from feeling reassured, Karen returned to her work with more questions than answers running around in her mind. Perhaps John felt responsible for Jacob's accident and that was the reason he hadn't come to welcome her home. She had asked him to keep an eye on her brother, but she had no illusions about Jacob. If he wanted to seek out trouble, he would find it even with a watchdog.

Jacob and Eli returned a half hour later, but there was still no sign of John. She couldn't help but feel disappointed. Why was John avoiding her?

When supper was almost ready, Karen called Noah in from the living room and said, "Go tell John that supper is ready."

Noah donned his coat and hat and hurried out the door. When he came back a few minutes later, she asked, "Did you find him?"

"*Ja.* He says he is not hungry, but I am," Noah answered as he hung up his coat.

Something was definitely wrong. Karen felt it in her bones.

Supper seemed to last forever, but finally her father rose from the table and retired to the sitting room. Karen made quick work of the cleanup with Anna's help. After wrapping some leftovers in foil, she donned her coat and walked over to the *dawdy haus.*

Stepping inside the front door, she paused to wipe her feet on the braided rug just as John came out of the living room. He held a Bible in his hand. The happy welcome she had hoped to see was missing in his eyes.

Suddenly feeling awkward and uncertain, she held out the plate. "I brought something in case you get hungry later."

"That wasn't necessary."

She gathered her courage as she set the plate on the counter. Gripping her hands together, she faced him. "What's wrong, John?"

He couldn't meet her gaze. "I need to apologize for my behavior on Christmas. I shouldn't have taken advantage of your kindness."

Fear uncoiled inside her, making her pulse pound. "How did you take advantage of me?"

"I shouldn't have kissed you. It won't happen again."

Her heart sank. She took a step closer. "Don't say that."

He closed his eyes. "I need you to leave now, Karen."

"I don't understand. Why won't you talk to me? Why won't you look at me?"

"I had another memory flash while you were gone."

Suddenly, Karen thought she understood. "You remembered her?"

He nodded.

Although she knew she didn't want to hear his answer, she asked. "Who is she?"

"I think she is my wife."

_No, no, no!_

Karen's mind screamed the denial, but she managed to keep her voice calm. "You think she is, but you don't know for certain?"

"No."

"If you have a wife, why isn't she searching for you?"

Karen would have turned the world upside down to find him.

He shook his head. "I don't know."

She had to find some other explanation. She and John were meant for each other. She had known it the first moment she saw his face even though she had tried to deny it.

Stepping close, she laid her hand on his cheek. "You could not kiss me with such tenderness if you had a wife. You are not that kind of man, John. Tell me what you have remembered."

John captured Karen's fingers against his cheek and held them tight as he gazed into her eyes. He wanted to believe she was right. He wanted to believe with all his heart and soul that they were meant to be together, but the evidence was becoming overwhelming.

He whispered, "Let me show you something."

He led her into the sitting room where the watch lay on a table by the sofa. He'd been staring at it for hours. He said, "Jacob found this near me the day I was dumped on your lane."

"It's a watch. Is it yours?" She looked at him in confusion.

"Read the inscription."

Picking it up, she turned it over. "To Aaron from Jonathan. Happy birthday, pal."

Her eyes brightened. "Is your name Aaron?"

"I think so."

"I will have trouble getting used to it, but it is a good name. Why does this make you sad? You have longed to know your own name all these weeks."

He sat down on the sofa. "The watch plays music

when it's opened. When I heard the tune, I remembered a woman dancing, holding out her hands and asking me to dance with her. She wore a wedding ring."

Karen laid the watch back on the table and shook her head. "That is not proof you are married."

"What else can it mean?"

She crossed her arms and took a step back. "I don't know, but it is not proof. You had no ring on your hand."

"It could have been stolen." He gazed at his fingers trying to see some evidence that he'd once worn a wedding band.

"What will you do now?" she asked softly. He heard the fear underlying her voice. He knew exactly how she felt.

"I'll take the watch to the sheriff and see if he can trace where it was made or purchased. It's an expensive piece, probably custom-made."

Her chin came up. "It's too late to do anything tonight and Papa will need your help at the sale tomorrow."

She was making excuses and he knew it. She was trying to prolong the inevitable.

So, what would one more day hurt? He deserved one last day of happiness with her and her family, didn't he? Wasn't that why he hadn't gone to the sheriff already? The answers he sought wouldn't change in twenty-four hours. After tomorrow he would resume his search and pray it didn't take him away from the woman he loved.

Glancing at Karen's lovely face in the lamplight he honestly didn't know if he had the courage to leave her.

What could possibly exist in his past that was better than what he'd found in Hope Springs? He'd found peace, happiness and love. He'd discovered a new and simple faith that felt as if he'd lived it forever.

One more day with her. It was all he might have.

He said, "I reckon I can wait until after the sale."

She smiled, but it was forced. "*Goot.* We will have a wonderful time tomorrow. Get some rest. We must leave very early."

She turned away quickly but not before he saw the tears in her eyes. The sight cut his heart to the quick. More than anything, he didn't want to be the cause of her suffering. He'd been foolish to confess his love when he didn't know if he was free. Now, he had hurt both of them.

After Karen left John tried to follow her advice, but sleep never came. The thing he'd longed for had become the thing he dreaded.

What lesson was God trying to teach him?

Just before dawn, a large white pickup pulling a blue-and-white horse trailer rolled to a stop in front of the Imhoff barn. The driver, a young Mennonite from Sugarcreek, helped John and Eli load and secure the horses. When they were ready to leave, Eli and Jacob climbed in the front seat of the extended cab with the driver, leaving John, Karen, Anna and Noah to squeeze into the backseat.

Anna and Noah kept up a running excited chatter. John was glad because it covered the awkward silence that stretched between him and Karen. He had hoped for one more day of happiness, but there was a pall over the day that couldn't be ignored. He tried to be cheerful for the sake of the children, but each time he met Karen's eyes he knew she was suffering as he was.

The trip took almost two hours. As they pulled into the fairgrounds where the sale was to be held, John saw dozens of Amish buggies along with numerous horse vans, cars and pickup trucks sharing the parking lot. Large numbers of people were already milling about or clustered in front of the tents selling coffee and hot chocolate.

Inside the main building the bleachers were filling quickly as the auctioneer in a booth behind the show ring tested his audio equipment. Long rows of stalls on one side of the enormous building held nearly a hundred horses.

A second long aisle had been set aside for vendors where corn dogs and ice-cream stands shared space with harness makers and nutritional horse-feed specialists. An old-time county fair atmosphere prevailed everywhere John looked. He and Eli settled the horses in their assigned stalls. Cowboys, Amish men and businessmen all filed past looking over the animals going on sale.

Once the auction got under way, John stayed with Eli while Karen took the children for their promised treats. One-Way had made a full recovery. He was the eleventh horse to enter the ring. When the big colt trotted into the ring and the auctioneer read off his information, including the facts that he was already trained to harness and was a full brother to a stakes winner, John saw a number of English pull out their cell phones. The bidding started low but quickly rose until Eli was grinning from ear to ear.

When the gavel went down on the final price, Eli slapped John on the back. "It is all in God's hands. He rewards His faithful servants. I can't wait to tell Karen. She'll not have to worry about money this year. Where is she?" Eli and John both stood to examine the onlookers crowding around the show ring.

John shook his head. "I don't see her."

"We'll have better luck finding them if we split up. You look by the food tents, I'll check outside and we can meet back here in fifteen minutes."

John left the bleachers eager to find Karen and share the good news of One-Way's sale. Knowing his work with the colt had benefited Karen in some small way lessened the pain he had been feeling.

He left the building to check some of the tents set up outside. The day was cold but not unpleasant and groups of visitors were checking out trailers and horse-care equipment for sale along the south side of the building.

The noise from a loudspeaker drew John's attention to the fairground grandstands across the roadway. A bugle blared forth the stirring notes of the Call to Post.

A parade of harness horses pulling two-wheeled carts began circling the oval track. The noise from the crowd in the stands grew louder. A race was about to get under way.

The colorful silks of the jockeys flashed in the sunlight as they positioned their horses behind a slow-moving truck with wide gates mounted on the back to keep the horses even. John's pulse began pounding in his ears. His breath came in ragged gasps.

He knew this. He'd seen races like this his whole life. Bit by bit, memories of childhood events tumbled out of the fog that had hidden them. In his mind, he saw himself carrying a bucket of feed toward the stalls. He heard his father's voice calling his name, saw his father dressed in yellow-and-white silks with a racing helmet under his arm walking toward him.

Exhilaration flooded John's body. All his answers

were there at the racetrack. He started forward, but stopped when he felt a hand touch his arm.

Karen caught up with John. "Papa found me and gave me the good news. It is a happy day for us thanks to you."

The moment John turned to her, Karen read the truth in his eyes. Her heart stumbled painfully.

He said, "I remember. Karen, I know who I am!"

She tried to speak, but no words passed the lump in her throat.

Excitement poured from him. "My name is Jonathan. Jonathon Dresher. I remember going to a racetrack like that one with my father. He worked there. He was a driver. Karen, I remember him. His name was Carl Dresher. He had the most amazing laugh. He was always laughing at things I did."

The joy suddenly left John's eyes. Karen knew he was looking inward and not at her. He said, "My dad is dead. He died when I was fifteen. My mother—I can't remember her at all. She died when I was little. It was just Dad and I."

"What about your wife?" Karen asked. She didn't dare breathe waiting for his answer.

"Who?"

"The woman you saw dancing."

Confusion flashed in his eyes followed quickly by sorrow. "The woman I kept seeing was Bethany, Aaron's wife. Aaron was my best friend. I loved him like a brother and his wife like a sister. Bethany was Sarah Wyse's sister. That's why I came to Hope Springs, to see Sarah…"

He pressed his fingers to his forehead. "They're both

gone. They died in a car accident the day after I gave Aaron the watch."

"I'm so sorry." Karen laid a hand on his arm in a gesture of comfort.

As if speaking to himself, softly he said, "Everyone I love is dead. No wonder I didn't want to remember. The waltz was Bethany's favorite song. I had the watch made to remind Aaron what a lucky man he was to have found his soul mate."

John turned away to stare at the racetrack. Bowing his head, he wiped his eyes with the back of his hand.

He was grieving for his family and his friends. He'd found them and lost them again all in the space of a few moments. Karen grieved with him and for him—and for herself.

He knew who he was. He knew where he belonged, among the English who raced horses, not among the Amish and their buggies. Would he leave her now? How could she bear it? How would she find the strength to go on without him?

She summoned the most difficult smile of her life. "I'm glad your memory has returned, Jonathan Dresher."

He continued to stare across the road. "So much is still jumbled in my head. I work with a racehorse rescue foundation, but I can't seem to remember who they are or how to reach them."

He gripped her hand and started to pull her along. "I need to go over there and see if I can remember more. I need a phone to call Sheriff Bradley."

Karen held back. He realized what she was doing and stopped. Giving her a puzzled look, he said, "Come with me."

"*Nee,* I cannot. That is a worldly place. An Amish woman can have no business in a place of gambling."

He stepped close to her. "I don't know what else I'll discover about myself, Karen, but I know I want you at my side. Always."

He didn't mean just for today. Karen suddenly faced the hardest decision of her life. Now that he had discovered his past, he was sure to want to go back to his old life. Could she go with the man she loved into the English world?

Her father was about to remarry. Nettie would make a fine stepmother to the children. Karen wouldn't have to take care of them any longer, but leaving with Jonathan would eventually cut her off from them forever.

Her family would be shamed by her behavior. They would have to shun her. First it would only be her father and the adults of her church, but as Jacob and Noah and finally Anna reached adulthood and took their vows she wouldn't be able to visit with them, or see them marry and raise families of their own.

Could she give up all that for John? She closed her eyes unable to face either future.

He cupped her face between his hands. "I don't want to be where you are not. You've given me everything. You gave me faith and family and love when I had nothing."

"John… Jonathan, I love you so much. You know that, don't you?"

He smiled softly, the warmth of his love shown in his eyes. "I had a sneaking suspicion."

"If you love me you will go now. You will find what you need to know, but I cannot go with you into the world."

A new pain filled his eyes, one she could not bear to look upon. Turning her face away, she said, "I have made a vow to remain true to my faith. I could give up my home and even my family for you, but I cannot turn my back on God."

Jonathan's grip on her fingers tightened. "God will go with us if we keep Him in our hearts. You taught me this."

She laid her hand on his chest. She could feel the thud of his heart beneath her fingers. "Then perhaps that was the reason God brought you into my life."

"I can't do it without you, Karen. I need your strength. You make me whole."

She withdrew her hand and took a step back. "God makes you whole. Go back into the world, Jonathan Dresher. Remember me kindly for I will never forget you."

"I'll come back to you. I promise."

"If God wills it." Turning away, she walked quickly to where her father stood as tears blurred her vision.

She could not look back at Jonathan. If she did she would run to his arms and leave all that she was behind.

Chapter Sixteen

He had his life back.

Jonathan Dresher stood on the steps of the police station in downtown Millersburg breathing in the cold January air. He'd regained almost all of his memory over the past two days but it didn't feel real.

Jonathan knew where he had been going before the incident in Hope Springs. He knew what kind of work he did. He knew what kind of friends he had. What he didn't know was what he was going to do now.

Two months ago he would've given anything to know the things he had remembered during the past forty-eight hours. Back then he had no idea that finding his past would cost him the most important thing in his life. The only woman he'd ever loved.

He stared down at the plain Amish boots he still wore. Karen was safe in her Amish community. She had chosen not to come with him into his English world. He understood that. He respected her decision, but that didn't stop the deep ache in his heart.

He had his life back, so why was he standing on these

snow-covered steps wishing he were in the snug house on Eli Imhoff's farm?

Because that's where Karen was.

He could see her making supper, talking about a new horse with Jacob, helping Anna with her arithmetic, discussing the Bible with Eli and Bishop Zook, fending off the endless questions of Noah.

Jonathan closed his eyes and held tight to his memory of Christmas Eve and the sweetness of Karen's kiss. Then he locked the memory away for later. Someday, he would take it out and relive that beautiful evening. For now, the pain of his loss was too sharp, too fresh.

Pulling the watch from his pocket he opened the lid and listened to the music. Aaron and Bethany had died together in the car crash. They would never know the pain of being separated. He was thankful for that.

He could see Bethany plainly now. He could hear her laughter, see the love in her eyes when she looked at Aaron. He could hear her beautiful voice raised in song. The memories no longer brought Jonathan pain, only a gentle sadness.

Perhaps one day he would be able to think about Karen without pain, too. He had promised to come back to her, but he hadn't known the kind of commitments he faced in his professional life. He closed the watch, shutting off the sweet sounds of the chimes.

Jonathan had taken over the reins of Aaron's racehorse rescue foundation branch in New Zealand after his friend's death. Once a top prize-winning harness race driver, Aaron had used his substantial earnings to start an organization that cared for injured, abused and abandoned Standardbreds, first in the United States and then later in New Zealand.

A racehorse that wasn't winning often became a liability for those shoddy owners who cared more for money than their animals. It was now Jonathan's duty to see that his friend's work of protecting those horses was carried on.

Would Karen understand? Would she approve of what he did? He didn't see a way he could join the Amish faith and still do his job, which required hours of fund-raising, computer use and business travel. Even though he longed for the simple life and faith the Amish shared, he was destined to remain in the English world.

Sheriff Nick Bradley came out of the building and stopped beside Jonathan. The sheriff settled his trooper hat on his blond hair. "I spent a lot of sleepless nights trying to figure out your story, but I never came close to this. An American, living in New Zealand, comes to Hope Springs to find the Amish family of a dead friend and gets mugged for his trouble."

Jonathan gave him a wry smile. "Sounds like a spiel for a bad movie, doesn't it? There were clues in the things I remembered but I couldn't put them together. I once told Karen there was something missing in the night sky. It was the Southern Cross, a constellation that Bethany said proved God was watching over her life down under."

Nick said, "It sure explains why no one locally could identify you."

"My company wasn't expecting me back until after the first of the year, but I'm sure they're wondering why I haven't been in contact."

"What are your plans now?"

Jonathan shook his head. "There are so many things I need to do. I need to get a new driver's license and a new passport. I need to get access to my bank accounts and rent another car, but first I need to see Sarah Wyse and tell her what happened to her sister. I'm dreading that."

After Aaron and Bethany's deaths, Jonathan had returned to the United States to try and find Bethany's family. He had little to go on, only her maiden name and the name of the town where she grew up. It had been a daunting task, but one he felt he had to complete for her. She often spoke fondly about her sister, Sarah.

Although Bethany deeply regretted leaving her Amish family she knew they would never accept her marriage to Aaron. In her mind, leaving without telling them why spared them the shame of knowing she had left her faith. It was a view Jonathan didn't share and intended to rectify.

He glanced at Nick. "Could you give me a lift to Sarah Wyse's shop?"

"Sure. You know for a guy who didn't have a clue about himself for months you don't seem very excited about getting your memory back."

"There are things I wish I hadn't remembered."

Nick laid a hand on Jonathan's shoulder. "Everyone's life contains moments they would rather forget. I know mine does. It's how we find the faith and strength to face those things that define who we are. Come on, I'll drive you into Hope Springs."

Leaving the outskirts of Millersburg behind, Nick glanced from the road to Jonathan as the SUV rolled past snow-covered fields and farms. He said, "We're still looking for the men who attacked you, but you need to realize we don't have much to go on."

"I'm sorry that I can't remember their faces."

"Knowing what kind of car they stole may help us

trace it and we'll check for any activity on your stolen credit cards."

"I imagine the car has been chopped up and sold for parts by now."

"That's quite likely the case. I want you to show me the exact place you were attacked in Hope Springs if you can. It's a long shot, but there might still be physical evidence at the scene. However, unless your witness comes forward with more information for us, finding them is a long shot."

"I understand."

Nick hesitated, then said, "I hope you don't hold it against Sally Yoder that she didn't report the assault. It isn't the Amish way. They forgive such crimes rather than report them. It makes the Amish seem like easy prey to unscrupulous men."

"I don't blame her. I'm just glad that I gave her a chance to get away from the men attacking her. I didn't plan on having my head cracked with a tire iron. Besides, even if she had come forward, she didn't know who I was. She couldn't help identify me."

"Are you *sure* it was Sally?"

Jonathan closed his eyes, trying to relive those moments. The woman had passed close beneath a streetlight across from him. Her open buggy had allowed him a good look at her pretty, freckled face framed by a dark bonnet. "I think Sally was the woman I saw that night, but truthfully, it was her behavior when we met that makes me all but certain it was her."

"Is there anything else you remember about that night?"

"I pulled into the filling station at the edge of town but it was closed for the night. I was putting some air in my rear tire when an Amish girl driving an open buggy passed me. I remember thinking it was late for a young woman to be out, but Bethany had told me about some of her escapades during her *rumspringa* so I didn't think anything else about it."

He recalled clearly the day Bethany had discovered Aaron and himself loafing beneath the apple tree. She had often called Aaron her *geils-mann* with a smile that made it an endearment. That day Jonathan felt a sharp stab of jealousy. They were so in love. Bethany had given up everything to be with Aaron. Jonathan wondered if he would ever know that kind of love.

As she joined the men beneath the tree that lazy summer day, Bethany enchanted them with stories of her Amish life.

Perhaps that was why he felt at home so quickly with Karen and her family, and why it felt so right loving Karen. In his heart he knew there was no one else for him.

Nick asked, "Then what happened after you saw Sally go past?"

"We've already gone over this."

"Humor me. The smallest remembered detail can crack a case. Just tell me again. When did you first see the truck they were driving?"

"I don't remember seeing the truck until it pulled in front of her buggy forcing her to stop. A man got out of the truck and tried to pull her out of the buggy. When I heard her scream I ran toward them yelling something. I think that was the first time he saw me because I'd been squatting down beside my car."

"And you can't remember anything about the truck? The color, the make?"

"It was dark. I was focused on reaching a woman in trouble."

"It's okay. I understand."

"The man trying to pull her out of the buggy let go of her arm and spun to face me. I saw her whip her horse and make a break for it. That's when a second man got out of the truck. He made a grab for her bridle, but she shot past him and got away."

"Thanks to you."

"I didn't do that much. Anyway, at that point, I realized I was facing two lunatics with nothing but my car keys in my hand. I bolted for my car. I guess I didn't make it because that's the last thing I remember. Do you have any idea why they dumped my body on Eli Imhoff's lane?"

"My guess? It was a warning to frighten their Amish victim into keeping her mouth shut."

"I don't understand."

"The Amish are tight-lipped with outsiders, but the news of you being found traveled like wildfire through the community. The blacksmith sign at the end of Eli's lane would have told them it was an Amish farm even if they weren't familiar with the area."

"Are you going to question Sally?"

"I have to. I don't want the same thing to happen to another woman—one who might not be so lucky." Nick's determination to see justice done reverberated in his tone. Jonathan knew Nick would do everything in his power to protect the people in his district and solve this crime.

A short while later they had reached the outskirts of Hope Springs and Nick pulled to a stop in front of the Needles and Pins fabric shop. Jonathan knew his purpose for coming to Hope Springs was about to be realized. After he spoke to Sarah Wyse, he had no reason to remain in the United States. He could go home.

Home was a small apartment above the stables at the farm Aaron and Bethany had owned, but it wasn't where his heart lay. His heart would remain in Hope Springs with a bossy, devout Amish woman named Karen Imhoff.

Nick asked, "Do you want me to come in with you when you talk to Sarah? I've had some experience breaking this kind of news to people."

"No thanks. I need to do this myself." Jonathan took a moment to pray silently.

Please God, give me the right words to say. Let me bring Your comfort and blessing to this woman in her hour of sorrow.

Nick said, "Sarah is a strong woman. Stronger than you know. It will be hard for her to hear her sister is gone, but it's better to know the truth."

"The Amish are strong, aren't they? Their faith is overwhelming in the face of every hardship. I admire them deeply."

Nick laid a hand on Jonathan's arm. "Many of them admire you, too. You'll always be welcome in Hope Springs, Jonathan Dresher."

Karen moved through her days like a woman in mourning. Every corner of the house, every spot in the barn and on the farm carried some memory of her time with John.

Jonathan, she corrected herself. He'd had his life restored. He would be back at his job and with his friends by now.

With sad irony she realized that now she was the one who wanted to forget. She wanted to erase the pain of losing the man she had loved with all her heart.

He had written her one letter in the weeks since he'd recovered his memory. It had been a lengthy missive about his life and what happened before they met. He had signed it, "All my love, John."

She kept it under her pillow and took it out each night. It still brought tears to her eyes but she would never discard it. It was all she had of him.

On the second Sunday following Jonathan's departure, she went through the motions of getting ready for church. She put on her best dress and packed food for the dinner afterward. She went through the familiar motions of living because she didn't know how to do anything else.

Everyone in her family seemed to understand. They made no demands on her time. Instead, they looked after themselves better than they ever had before. Nettie came frequently to lend a hand with the household chores that would soon be hers.

Now, when Karen needed to be needed the most, her family was proving they could do without her.

The trip to William Fisher's farm for services was long and cold and they arrived with only a few minutes to spare. Karen and her family quickly filed into the house and took their places on the wooden benches, men on one side, women on the other. She kept her head down and focused on her hymnbook and prayed for the strength she needed to get through one more day.

Anna tugged on Karen's sleeve and whispered. "Look, there is John."

Karen's head snapped up. She scanned the room

around her. Anna pointed to the back row of the men's benches.

It *was* John. Karen's heart hammered in her ears so loudly she thought she might faint. She pressed her hand to her mouth to hold back a gasp.

He was dressed in plain clothes and seated between Reuben Beachy and Elam Sutter. When he caught sight of her, he winked.

She turned back to face the preacher. He had winked at her in church. Jonathan Dresher had come back to Hope Springs. Why? Did she dare hope that he was back for good?

As the singing started, Karen added her voice to the others in humble prayer and gratitude for the Lord's blessing, but her mind was turning like a windmill in a gale. When the song was finished, she endured the longest preaching service of her life.

The minute the final amen sounded, Karen shot to her feet and waited impatiently for the crowd to get out the doors. Outside, she lost no time in locating Jonathan. He was standing by her father and Jacob. The three of them were laughing and smiling like it was any other day. Eli caught sight of her. "Karen, look who has returned."

Jonathan's gray eyes filled with deep emotion when his gaze fell upon her. He said, "Hello."

Karen's voice had fled. She could only stare. The foolish hope that he had come back for her bloomed in her heart.

Anna launched herself at Jonathan and threw her arms around his waist. "John, I knew you wouldn't forget me."

He swung her up to his shoulder and she wrapped her

arms around his neck. Smiling at Karen, he said, "I find all the Imhoff women are...*unforgettable*."

"We've missed you so much." Anna said the words Karen wanted to say but couldn't.

"I've missed you, too." Setting the child down, he cupped the back of her head and dropped a kiss on her bonnet. She clung to his hand, looking up with adoration shining in her eyes.

Noah, hopping with impatience, began peppering Jonathan with questions. "Did you go all the way to New Zealand and back already? Did you fly in a plane? Did you know the sheriff caught the men who beat you up? They'd been stealing a whole bunch of stuff from Amish people."

"Yes, yes and yes, I knew they'd been arrested." Jonathan answered Noah, but his eyes never left Karen.

Realization dawned on her and the foolish hope in her heart withered. He'd come back because of the arrest, not because of her. He would be needed at the trial.

She found her voice at last. "How long are you going to be staying? You must come and have supper with us while you are here."

"I'm going to be staying for a long, long time. As long as God and you will let me."

She blinked hard. What was he saying?

Several of the men who knew him had come up to greet him. Among the handshakes and well-wishes of Jonathan's friends, Karen found herself crowded backward.

"Are you moving here?" Jacob sounded as confused as Karen felt.

Jonathan nodded. "*Ja.* The organization I work for is leasing a small farm not far away. Our need for more stable space in this part of the country is growing because of the recent changes in U.S. horse-slaughter laws."

Several of the local men nodded. One said, "We have heard of this. Broken-down racehorses used to be sold for meat, but now they can't be unless they are shipped out of the country."

Jonathan nodded. "That's right. More of them are being abandoned now than ever. We will take them in, retrain them for riding or pulling buggies and find them proper homes."

"You will need good harnesses for these horses." Reuben Beachy's eyes lit up at the prospect of new business.

"I will. I'll need hay and grain and repair work done on the stables."

"You will need a good farrier, too," Eli added.

"That I will," Jonathan agreed. Looking down at Anna, he said, "I will need my Amish tutor again and I will need to study the Amish ways so that one day I may take the vows of your faith."

A murmur of surprise rippled through the group. Karen's breath froze in her throat as tears sprang to her eyes. He was planning to join her faith. He had declared it in front of everyone.

"After that, I'll need a wife." He looked over the crowd to where Karen was standing.

Anna shouted, "I'll marry you."

Everyone laughed at that, everyone but Karen. Stepping between the men, she grabbed Jonathan's sleeve and pulled him toward the Fishers' greenhouse without a word to anyone.

Inside the plastic enclosure, surrounded by the smell of earth and new plants, she turned to Jonathan and crossed her arms to keep from hugging him. "Is it true?"

He smiled at her tenderly. "Yes. In time, I will marry you, Karen Imhoff. Never doubt it."

Her heart melted with joy. She threw her arms around him holding him as tight as she could. She never wanted to let go again. "Oh, I've missed you so much."

She felt his lips on her forehead. "I've missed you, too, darling."

Holding her away from him, he looked into her eyes. "The moment I reached New Zealand I realized I couldn't stay there. I belong here. With you. With your people. I'm never leaving again."

He pulled her close once more. She returned his embrace with such joy in her heart that she thought she might die of it.

"I dreamed of this," she whispered.

"Wake up, my little heart. I'm not a dream. I'm a flesh-and-blood man who loves the most wonderful woman in the world."

"*Nee,* I will not open my eyes. You will be gone."

"I won't, but I do see one problem with our courtship. Ah, make that three problems."

She looked up to find him smiling. He nodded behind her. Noah, Anna and Jacob had their faces cupped against the plastic walls trying to see in. Karen grinned at Jonathan. "I'm sure they will not object to our courtship as they know you plan to become Amish."

He planted a quick kiss on her lips. "I wasn't thinking about an objection. I thought Amish couples kept their courting a secret. I don't think that's going to happen for us."

She patted his cheek. "I can live with that. Can you?"

He drew her close once more. "As long as I know you

will be mine, I can live with anything. God has blessed me, Karen. I will praise Him always."

"He has blessed us both."

Smiling tenderly at her, he said, "I'd like a Christmas wedding."

She smiled back. "I think we can arrange that."

She lifted her face for Jonathan's kiss and gave thanks as her long-hidden love bloomed like a beautiful rose.

* * * * *

FAMILY BLESSINGS

Anna Schmidt

For those who nurture the children—woman or man.

Remember ye not the former things,
neither consider the things of old.
Behold, I will do a new thing;
now it shall spring forth; shall ye not know it?
I will even make a way in the wilderness,
and rivers in the desert.
—*Isaiah* 43:18–19

Chapter One

Celery Fields, Florida,
Autumn 1932

Pleasant Obermeier dropped small dollops of batter into the oil sizzling over the wood-fired stove and expertly rolled each doughnut around in the oil until it was golden-brown before rescuing each and laying it on a towel to drain. Over the years that she had been the baker in her father's bakery in the tiny Amish community of Celery Fields, she must have made thousands of these small sweet confections. Like the loaves of egg and rye bread that she had already baked that morning, her apple cider doughnuts had remained a staple of the business in spite of the hard times that had spread across the country.

It occurred to her that little had changed about her daily routine in spite of the major changes that had taken place in her life these past three years. She still rose every morning at four and was at her work by five. Even so, her father, Gunther, still arrived before she did and had the fires stoked and ready to receive the morning's wares. The two of them had followed a similar routine since Pleasant was no more than a girl of fifteen. Now a woman of thirty-two—middle-aged by some standards—she had already been married and widowed and had taken on responsibilities she could never have imagined a few years earlier.

Three years earlier she had married Merle Obermeier, a man ten years her senior. Then after Merle had died in a tragic accident two summers ago she had taken on responsibility for raising four children from his first marriage as well as responsibility for the large house and farm that he had left behind. But in spite of all of that, she had refused to give up her role as the local baker. There was something very comforting in the routine of the bakery. It was the one place where she could be alone with her thoughts. Even the few customers she was called upon to serve when her father was off making a delivery, or otherwise engaged as he was this morning, did not interrupt her revelry for long.

The bell over the shop door jangled and Pleasant hurried to dip up the last of the doughnuts and drop them onto the towel. "Coming," she called out in the Dutch-German dialect common to the community as she quickly rolled the still-warm doughnuts in sugar and set them on a cake plate. Before carrying the plate with her to the front of the shop, she automatically reached up to straighten the traditional starched white prayer *kapp* that covered her hair and smooth the front of her black bibbed apron.

But when she reached the swinging half door that separated the kitchen from the shop, she stopped. Her customer was a man—Amish by his dress—but someone she had not seen before. Celery Fields did not see many strangers. Their customers were mostly the local village residents and the farmers who raised celery in the fields that stretched out beyond the community. Occasionally, someone from the outside world—the *Englisch* world as the Amish called it—would stop as they passed through on their way to nearby Sarasota. But this was no outsider. This man was Amish.

She pasted on a smile. *"Guten morgen."*

He turned and she found herself looking straight up and into a pair of deep-set hazel eyes accented at the corners by the creases of a thousand smiles. Her earlier feeling of contentment was gone in an instant. Pleasant was wary of strangers—especially handsome male strangers. She had fought a lifelong battle against a streak of romanticism that for a woman like her was sheer folly. Tall, good-looking men like this one were not for her, regardless of how engaging their smile might be. She had long ago faced the fact that she was not only a member of a plain society—the Amish—but also that the face that looked back at her in her brief encounters with her reflection in a storefront glass was plain as well.

The cake plate teetered dangerously as the pyramid of doughnuts shifted and a few of the confections tumbled from the plate to the top of the counter. To make matters worse, both she and the stranger reached to rescue them at the exact same moment. His smile turned to laughter as their fingers brushed. But then their eyes met and his smile faded. He withdrew his hand as if it had been scalded. Certain that it was her expression of horror that had sobered him, Pleasant hurried to restore order. He was, after all, a customer.

"Clumsy," she murmured as she rescued two doughnuts that had made it to the floor and discarded them.

When she stood up again, he had picked up the single doughnut still on the counter and seemed unsure of what to do with it. She held out a trash bin and after a moment's consideration he popped it into his mouth. Then he closed his eyes and savored the warm sweetness of it. "So you are the baker," he said.

Unnerved, she set the plate on top of the counter and covered it with a glass cake cover. "How may I help you, Herr...."

"Troyer," he said. "Jeremiah Troyer. I am Bishop Troyer's great-nephew." He smiled at her as if he expected this to be welcome news. He did have a most engaging smile.

"Are you and Frau Troyer visiting the bishop then?" she asked politely, refusing to permit his charming smile to disarm her while she gathered background information and was clear about what he wanted.

"I've just moved here," he replied. "And I am not married, Fraulein Goodloe."

"I am Frau Obermeier," she corrected. "My husband passed away two summers ago." She forced herself to meet his gaze. "Welcome to our community, Herr Troyer."

"I'm sorry for your loss," he said. "Is your father here?"

"Not at the moment. May I be of some help?"

He seemed to consider this and then plunged in to tell her his story. "Perhaps your father mentioned that I intend to open an ice cream shop," he explained. "I've also taken a position with the Sarasota Ice Company and bought the property next door." He waited for her to speak and when she said nothing, he continued, "I might have use for some of his wares in my ice cream shop, and when I spoke with your father last night..."

"You want to sell our baked goods right next door

to us?" Pleasant's polite smile faded. In many ways Pleasant was a far better business manager than Gunther Goodloe had ever been. Gunther tended to be soft-hearted when it came to delayed payments or supplies not delivered as promised. Pleasant had no such problems. And when it came to the prospect of a competitor moving in on them, she...

The smile flashed again. "Actually, Frau Obermeier, I need cones for my ice cream and I was hoping that your father might help me concoct a recipe that would make my cones different from those of any potential competitors. But he assures me that you are the expert when it comes to baking."

"Ice cream cones," she murmured, fully understanding his interest now. This was business. Well, it would certainly be a change from the basic breads and rolls she turned out day after day. "How many were you thinking of ordering?"

Jeremiah laughed and the sound was like music in the otherwise subdued surroundings. Oh, he was a charmer, this one.

"Why, Frau Obermeier, we are not talking of a single order here. Once we come upon the perfect recipe, I shall need a steady supply of them."

Pleasant saw Merle's sister, Hilda, approaching the bakery. Her heavyset sister-in-law huffed her way up the three shallow steps that led from the street to the door and entered. "Pleasant," she said, addressing Pleasant but looking at the stranger. "I don't believe I've had the pleasure. I am Mrs. Obermeier's sister-in-law, Hilda Yoder."

"I am Jeremiah Troyer and I'm pleased to meet you, Frau Yoder. Your husband owns the dry goods store?"

"Yes, that's right." In spite of the fact that Hilda often

made a point of reminding others that pride was viewed as a sin by people of their Amish faith, she couldn't help preening a bit to have her husband known.

"I was coming to call on him next," Jeremiah reported. "And since Herr Goodloe is not here at the moment, perhaps I should stop back later this afternoon."

"That might be best," Hilda said before Pleasant could answer.

Jeremiah put on his stiff-brimmed summer straw hat and tipped it slightly toward Hilda and then Pleasant. "Give my regards to your father, Frau Obermeier," he said. "And please accept my deepest sympathies to both you ladies for the loss of your husband and brother," he added before leaving the shop and heading across the way to Yoder's Dry Goods.

Pleasant did not realize how closely she was watching him until Hilda lightly touched her arm and cleared her throat. "What are those boys up to now?"

Through the open front door Pleasant could see Merle's five-year-old twins—Will and Henry—wrestling with each other in the dusty street. "They'll spoil their clothes," Hilda chided, but Pleasant only laughed.

"Oh, they're just playing, Hilda. Clothes can be washed, you know."

"Of course, you would think that," Hilda replied stiffly, making it clear that in her view, Pleasant knew nothing about properly raising children—especially a pair of rambunctious five-year-olds. "It just seems to me with all you have to do at the bakery, you are certainly busy enough without adding extra loads of laundry to your chores." She clicked her tongue against the roof of her mouth. "I understand that Gunther intends to do business with the bishop's great-nephew and apparently it somehow involves you—some foolishness about needing you to make ice cream cones."

Before Pleasant could think of any appropriate response to her sister-in-law's comment, Hilda had left the shop, carefully skirting her way around the boys as she returned to the dry goods store.

"Boys, stop that," Pleasant called to the twins who rolled to a sitting position and blinked innocently up at her.

"Yes, Mama," they chorused.

Pleasant felt the familiar tug at her heart to hear any of Merle's children call her "Mama" without even thinking about it. That triumph—especially with Rolf and Bettina, the older two—had required a good deal of patience on her part and she treasured each and every use of the title. Always shy and withdrawn, even somewhat sickly while their father was alive, the two older children had blossomed under Pleasant's care. Rolf and Bettina never missed school and were often seen taking care of some chore or another around the large house. The twins—only toddlers when their mother died—had accepted her without question from the day she moved into the house.

Her heart melted as it always did in the presence of the identical boys. "Come here," she said, stooping down and holding out her arms to receive them. Giggling, they ran to her, colliding with her at the same moment so that they nearly knocked her off balance. "Look at the two of you," she fussed as she tucked their shirts into matching homespun trousers and slicked down identical cowlicks with fingers she wet on her tongue. "Now please try to stay clean," she pleaded as they scampered away.

It was at times like these that thoughts of Merle

sprang to mind unbidden. He had had such a difficult youth as he often reminded her when he thought she was being too soft with the children. His own father had shamed the family by running away with his wife's sister when Merle was only a little older than Rolf was now. Merle had been forced to leave school and take a job in addition to managing the small family farm in order to support his mother and siblings. Knowing his painful past made the fact that Merle would never see how well his own children had turned out all the more poignant. And yet, she realized, that in the year she had been married to him, never had she witnessed a moment of such unconcealed love between Merle and any of his children as she had just enjoyed with the twins. Merle Obermeier had been a bitter man and in a year of marriage she had made little progress toward softening his ways.

She was about to close the shop's front door to prevent the dust from the street from blowing in when she saw Jeremiah Troyer exit the dry goods store and wave to her. She waited until he was in front of the bakery and then asked, "Did you need something more, Herr Troyer?"

"I came back to give you this," Jeremiah said, his tone easy and calm as he held out a folded piece of paper to Pleasant. "It's one of the recipes used by someone I knew back in Ohio. I'd like to consider something similar to this for the cones," he told her. "It's important to set one's product apart from that of the competition."

"You had an ice cream business in Ohio then?" she asked as she stepped onto the front stoop and accepted the recipe.

"Not exactly. You see, Frau Obermeier, as a boy I was ill with rheumatic fever, and my uncle—my father's eldest brother—thought it best that I take a job in town since I was too weak to work in the fields. The only person hiring was Peter Osgood, the pharmacist. He bought the cream and eggs for making the ice cream he served in the soda shop in the front of his drugstore from our farm. One day he mentioned that he was looking for a young man to help make the ice cream." Jeremiah shrugged. "I was already making the delivery of eggs and cream. It stood to reason that I might as well stay to do the work, and so I was hired. I was there for ten years."

Pleasant fingered the rough thick paper he'd handed her for a moment. His childhood held some similarities to that of Merle's thin and awkward eldest son, Rolf. "Mr. Osgood knows you have his recipes?"

Jeremiah laughed. "I didn't steal them. He handed them to me himself at the train station when he came to see me off and wish me well. In fact, you may have the opportunity to meet him one day. He's promised to come for a visit."

"And your father did not mind that you…"

A shadow of deep sadness flitted across his handsome features. "My father died when I was thirteen. My brothers and sisters and I were raised by our uncle."

"I see." Another thing that he and Rolf had in common. She looked up at him.

"And that's probably a good deal more than you need or want to know of my childhood," he said with a wry smile.

Pleasant pocketed the recipe and turned to open the bakery door. "I'll give this to my father when he returns and let him know that you stopped by." For reasons she didn't fully understand, she hesitated. "Good day, Herr Troyer," she said softly.

"And to you," he replied and he headed down the steps and on to the empty building he'd purchased to turn into an ice cream shop.

Almost as soon as Pleasant had entered the bakery, Hilda was back, her brow knitted into a frown of disapproval. "What was that paper he gave you?" she asked as she ran one finger over the display case and clucked her tongue at the dust she found there.

"A recipe for me to give Papa," Pleasant replied. "And now if you'll excuse me, Hilda, I have…"

"That man is trouble," Hilda muttered as she followed Pleasant into the kitchen. "He has this habit of laughing and smiling far too easily. In these hard times what does he find to be so happy about? You'll want to stay clear of him."

Pleasant decided to ignore this last remark. Ever since Merle's death, Hilda seemed to have assumed the need to speak for him. Pleasant could almost hear her late husband issuing the same warning to keep her distance. It occurred to her that Merle would not have liked Jeremiah Troyer. Pleasant could not say how she knew that or what the basis for Merle's dislike might have been. But she knew beyond a doubt that he would have offered her the same warning that his sister offered now. And as Hilda prattled on about the foolishness of even thinking of opening an ice cream shop in the middle of a depression, Pleasant could not help but think that perhaps she would be wise to take heed of such signs.

Amish communities around the country had long ago established the habit of holding their biweekly Sunday services in private homes or barns around the district. In fact, many districts were composed of no more than twenty-six households, making sure that each family would host services at least once during the year. In Celery Fields, they still had a way to go to reach twenty-six families. The community was still growing and for the second time that year, the service was to be held at Pleasant's house. The simple wooden benches stored on a special wagon and moved from house to house as the services did had arrived on Saturday and now stood lined up in the two large front rooms of the house.

In the two years that had followed her husband's death, Pleasant had made a number of changes that most everyone in the small community applauded. For one thing, the citizens of Celery Fields no longer dreaded gathering in the house that Merle had always kept cloistered and shuttered even in the stifling summer heat. On the day of Merle's funeral, friends and neighbors had arrived to find the windows and doors of the house thrown open, exposing the somber and shadowy interior of the house to the light. Pleasant had stood together with Merle's four children on the wide front porch, greeting each new arrival. Further, when time came for setting up the benches—usually all crowded into the small front room at Merle's insistence—Pleasant had suggested spreading them into the adjoining dining room and giving people more room.

Then there was the matter of how she had handled the children—three boys and one girl. It was well-known that she had married Merle more because he was her one chance at ever finding a husband than because of any deep love for the man. For his part, Merle had made it clear that he had chosen her for equally practical reasons. She had managed her father's house after the deaths of her mother and her father's second wife. She had practically raised her two half sisters, and even now she continued to help her father in the family's bakery business. Merle had needed a mother for his four children and someone to manage the impressive house he'd built on the edge of the acres of celery fields he farmed. Theirs had been more of a business arrangement than a marriage. And that had suited them both.

Pleasant thought on all of these matters as she listened to the service, trying hard to keep her focus on the children and the responsibilities God had given her rather than the broad back of Jeremiah Troyer seated just two rows in front of her. When the service finally ended she hurried off to make sure that her oldest son, Rolf, had put out hay for the horses waiting to take the churchgoers home later, and then headed around the side of the house toward the kitchen.

On her way, she was struck by what a truly beautiful day God had given them. She took a minute to pause and close her eyes as she drew in a breath of the sweet warm October air. She could smell the herbs thriving in flowerbeds she'd planted herself all around the perimeter of the house. She almost felt as if she could smell the sun itself as the warmth of its rays bathed her face. She silently offered up a prayer of thanks for all of the blessings that God had seen fit to bestow on her as well as a plea for forgiveness for all the times she had complained about the life she'd been given. If she opened her eyes and turned away from the house and the bounty of its herbs and flowers, she knew that she would find herself looking out to the fields that stretched out for acres beyond the house. Merle's legacy for his children that had once thrived lay fallow now, the furrows parched and cracked. Still, the land and house were paid for so she thanked God that she and the children had food and shelter and, in these hard times, she felt truly blessed.

In the kitchen Hilda and several women were working in an easy and familiar rhythm. While the men reset the benches, the women prepared platters of fried chicken, mixed up a variety of salads and cut up pies still warm from the morning's baking. Pleasant joined her good friend, Hannah Harnisher, to help slice the heavy loaves of bread she'd baked the day before and lined up on one counter.

Hannah had once been married to Pleasant's brother, but after he died she had married Levi Harnisher. The couple had met a few years earlier after Hannah's son had run away with the circus—a circus then owned by Levi. Pleasant and Gunther had gone with Hannah to Wisconsin to retrieve the boy and the journey had forged a lifelong friendship between the two women—one they had not shared before that journey.

Pleasant had been different in those days. Life had dealt her a number of disappointments early on—her mother's death, her father's remarriage bringing two new siblings into the household. And then her brother had married the beautiful Hannah and the two of them had been so very happy. In those days, Pleasant had viewed each event as further evidence that she had been abandoned by those she loved. Then she had gone to Wisconsin with Hannah and along the way had gotten to know a group of women—circus folk—changing her outlook forever. With these new and unlikely friends she had discovered humor in the face of hardship and kindness in the face of the prejudice that is born of ignorance.

"Who was that man Gunther was sitting with?" Hannah asked.

"That's Bishop Troyer's great-nephew from Ohio."

"He's visiting then?"

"No, apparently he's come here to go into business." She could see that several other women—especially those who lived some distance from town and were eager to learn more about the handsome stranger they'd seen for the first time that morning—had leaned in closer to hear what she was saying. "An ice cream shop," she added, setting off a chain reaction of whispers as the news was repeated from one group to the next. The women were soon occupied speculating about the addition of an ice cream parlor and whether or not that was a good thing or something far too frivolous for an Amish community.

"Yes," Hilda added, "it seems that the bishop's nephew—great-nephew that is—has purchased the empty building next to the bakery and the storehouse behind."

As this new bit of information set off a wave of speculation among the others about whether or not the newcomer would also live in the building, Pleasant moved closer to Hannah and lowered her voice. "He has asked me—well, Father, really—to provide him with the baked cones he will use to serve his ice cream," she confided. "He expects to be in need of a steady supply."

Hannah's eyebrows lifted. "You'll be working even longer hours then. Hilda certainly won't approve of that."

"Well, what can I do? In these times, business has slowed to such a state that we almost never sell more than the basics. This is an order that we can't afford to decline and frankly, it will be nice to work on something besides rye bread and rolls."

"Perhaps Greta could…"

Pleasant laughed at the very idea that her youngest

half sister might be any help at all. "Greta? That girl is a dreamer and it's all she can do to attend to the few chores she's responsible for at home. She would forget to check the ovens and no doubt burn the cones to a crisp," she said, but there was a fondness in her tone that spoke volumes. "And Lydia has all she can manage with the school."

Hannah pressed her hands over her apron. "I suppose I could help some," she said. "At least for a while."

Pleasant saw how her friend caressed the flatness of her stomach under her apron. "Oh, Hannah, you're expecting another child?"

Hannah's smile was radiant—more radiant than it had been even on the day when she had married Levi or the day when she had delivered twins—a boy and a girl, now three years old and the image of their mother. She nodded then put her finger to her lips. "Shhh. I'm fairly certain and I don't want anyone to know until I have the chance to tell Levi."

Pleasant could not have been more touched that Hannah was trusting her with this wonderful secret. It was a mark of just how much their friendship had grown.

"Caleb is going to soon feel outnumbered by little ones," she teased. Caleb was Pleasant's nephew—the boy who had run away with Levi's circus. Now as a teenager he was of an age to make one of the most important decisions of his young life. In the Amish faith—as in any Anabaptist group—baptism was an act of joining the church and as such was not performed until the person was of an age to be able to understand the covenant he or she was making with God. To prepare a young person for such a decision, parents often looked the other way while their teenagers took some time to explore the ways of the outside world. That time was called *Rumspringa* or "the season for running around." Of course, in some ways, Caleb had done that when he ran away with Levi's circus.

Hannah did not smile as Pleasant might have expected. Instead, she sighed. "I do worry about how he will feel about another baby in the house. After all, I remember what you said about your feelings after Gunther remarried and then Lydia and Greta came along. What if he decides to run away again?"

"Caleb will be fine," Pleasant assured her. "It's not the same at all."

Hannah's smile showed her relief. "I certainly have you to inspire me. The way you came into this house and made a true home for Merle's children. They love you as if you were their real mother, you know."

Pleasant waved away the compliment. "That was God's will. And God will show you and Levi the way as well."

Hannah squeezed her hand. "Thank you, Pleasant." She finished slicing the last loaf of bread, then added, "Bishop Troyer's great-nephew seems quite…nice. Is he…does he have a family?"

Pleasant knew the look her friend was giving her. It fairly shouted Hannah's idea that perhaps there might be a potential for romance for Pleasant here. "He is single and I'm sure there will be any number of our younger unattached women who will be happy to learn that."

Hannah watched Pleasant take ears of corn from a large pot and stack them on a platter. "It's been two years, Pleasant."

"You know my feelings on this matter," Pleasant reminded her.

"But why not at least open your heart to the possibility?"

"I have been married, Hannah."

"But have you ever truly been in love?"

Pleasant looked at Hannah for a long moment. Hannah had been twice blessed with true love—first with Pleasant's brother and then again with Levi. But other women—women like Pleasant—were called to other things. "Shh," she whispered and nodded toward one of the other women who had moved in closer to hear their conversation.

Then Hannah picked up two platters of sliced bread. "You'll bring the corn?"

Out in the side yard the men had just set the last of the benches for serving the meal. Hilda organized a parade of women, each carrying some platter, bowl or pitcher and headed across the yard. Pleasant looked at the stacked ears of sweet corn on the platter, but found herself remembering the plate of doughnuts and the ones that had fallen, and the touch of his hand.

And the way he had looked at her. Had he felt what she felt, if only for an instant?

She pushed the back door open with her hip, and although she heard the music of Jeremiah's laughter, she battled the temptation to glance his way. She refused to surrender to an old maid's fantasy that a man like that could ever be interested in one so plain.

Chapter Two

On Monday morning, after attending services with his great-uncle and aunt, Jeremiah stood at the front window of his shop. Along the unpaved road that stretched before him lay acres of celery fields on one side and a line of boxy houses—some of them little more than wooden shacks but every one of them pristine—on the other. At the far end of the street stood the large white house where services had been held. The home of the baker.

There was no reason that he could define about why he had been drawn to her like a moth to light. In the brief encounters he had had with her, he had noticed something in her eyes—a sadness and resignation that this was the life she'd been given and she needed to make the best of it. Jeremiah understood that feeling. He'd dealt with it from the day his father had died and he and his mother and siblings had moved in with his uncle. Watching Pleasant as she stood a little apart and observed the gathering of church members standing around her yard after services, he had wanted to tell her that things could change. She could change them. It was a feeling he'd had before when meeting people for the first time, but never more intensely than he did in meeting Pleasant Obermeier.

Jeremiah shook off the thought and continued his survey of his new community. At his end of the street a town center of sorts had cropped up. There was a small wooden shack that served as the community wash house where the migrant workers who came to plant and later harvest the fields could wash themselves and their clothing. Next to that was a larger building that housed the local hardware store, and next to that was a building made of cement blocks and surrounded by a hodgepodge of machinery and parts. Next door to his property stood Gunther Goodloe's bakery. Yoder's Dry Goods occupied the largest storefront and the Yoders' modest house stood behind the store.

He lifted his face to the sun and thought that the small community in Ohio on the shores of Lake Erie that he'd left the day after his uncle's funeral seemed very far away. After years of living in the shuttered and isolated world that his uncle had fabricated as a proper Amish family household, he had sold his share of the family farm to his younger brother, packed his belongings and announced his intention to move to Florida and start fresh.

And the moment he stepped off the train at the base of Main Street in Sarasota and heard the rustle of palm branches high above him as he gazed out on the calm waters of the bay, he knew he'd made the right decision. He had gone immediately to the home of his great-uncle John who was his uncle's opposite in every way. Where Jeremiah's uncle had been a stern, unforgiving man, John was a jovial and kind soul who, along with his wife, Mildred, welcomed Jeremiah with open arms.

He told them of his business plans and to his delight John had not only been enthusiastic about the idea, he had offered his financial support as well. In addition to serving as the community's beloved bishop, John had a furniture-making business that had attracted the attention of several wealthy businessmen and their wives in Sarasota. He had done very well for himself and Jeremiah respected the support and counsel his great-uncle could provide.

He explained to John how the advent of the chemical compound called Freon had made refrigeration commonplace in *Englisch* homes, but obviously because the Amish continued to avoid electricity and other modern conveniences, a source of ice to run their iceboxes and preserve their meats was essential.

"There's an ice packinghouse in Sarasota," John had told Jeremiah. "I know the owner and could speak to him on your behalf. After all, you'll be needing a paying job until you can get this ice cream business up and running."

Within a week of his arrival Jeremiah had accepted a job with the ice company and had finalized the purchase of the building next to the bakery as well as the small barn that came with it where he could set up his business and live in back of the shop. The ice packinghouse would, of course, be his main source of income, but he was looking forward to getting the ice cream shop up and running. Already his great-aunt Mildred had helped him furnish his living quarters with the essentials for getting settled.

"You need to concentrate on establishing yourself," she had insisted when he thanked her for everything she was doing for him. "You'd do well to focus your attention on your paying job first. An ice cream shop in these times…well, I don't know." Mildred was a sweet and gentle woman but had made it clear that she and John both questioned anything that smacked of frivolity. They were plain people—simple not only in their faith but in their daily routine as well.

"I believe there's a place for such a business even in these times, maybe especially in these times," Jeremiah replied.

"Your Uncle Benjamin taught you to make ice cream?" Mildred asked, her surprise evident as she laid out a handmade quilt on his single bed.

"In a manner of speaking. He was certainly responsible for my learning." He thought about the years spent working with Mr. Osgood. In addition to learning the business, his times at the shop had been some of the happiest of his life. The Osgoods had provided him with the encouragement and love that was often missing from his uncle's house. Indeed, the only person who had come to see him off at the train station was Mr. Osgood. The pharmacist had pressed an envelope into his hands. "An investment," he'd said.

Inside the envelope had been the recipes for all of Osgood's various ice cream concoctions and five crisp one-hundred-dollar bills. Jeremiah had arrived in Sarasota feeling like a rich man in every way.

Shaking off the memory, Jeremiah turned back to his work and finished taping the large sign that Mildred had made for him against the window. *Troyer's Creamery and Confection Shop—Opening Soon.* Then he stepped outside to make sure the sign was straight and saw a woman coming out of Yoder's Dry Goods. She looked vaguely familiar but with the sun behind her, he couldn't be sure. He shaded his eyes with one hand and waited for her to come nearer. After all, Peter Osgood had taught him that the best way to build a business was to befriend as many people in the community as possible.

But then he saw that it was the baker's daughter. *Pleasant,* he thought and in looks she was all of that and far more. Her hair—what he could see of it under the starched white *kapp*—was the pale gold of freshly cut hay. At their first meeting it had surprised him that in sharp contrast to her fair skin and hair, her eyes were the color of the dark chocolate he used in making his ice cream. She moved with a natural grace worthy of royalty—or at least how he had always imagined titled people moving. And yet there was purpose in her step. She was carrying a satchel in each hand filled to the brim, her shoulders perfectly balanced by the weight of them.

Her expression was passive as she fixed her eyes on her destination—the bakery—and covered the ground necessary to reach it in long purposeful strides. She wore a solid blue ankle-length dress with the usual black apron and short cotton cape covering most of it. Most surprising of all, she was barefoot.

She was almost even with his shop before she saw him standing on the small wooden porch watching her.

"*Guten morgen,* Frau Obermeier," he said easily, falling into the German-Dutch dialect of their shared heritage.

"*Guten morgen,*" she replied but she kept walking. No time for visiting apparently, not even a moment.

"May I help you with those?" Jeremiah asked as he stepped off the porch and fell into step beside her. "They look quite heavy."

"I'm fine," she replied. "But thank you."

He bounded up the steps that led to the bakery entrance and opened the door for her. A bell jangled but no one came out to greet them or relieve her of her burden.

"Danke," she murmured as she entered the shop and headed immediately for the back room.

Everything about her posture, her failure to meet his eyes or smile, her single-mindedness about the contents of the satchels told Jeremiah that he should simply close the door of the bakery and go back to his own shop. Instead, he followed her into the large and spotless kitchen that held the lingering scent of yeast.

"Did you have the opportunity to look at the recipe I left with you on Saturday?"

"I did," she replied as she bustled around the kitchen putting things away.

Jeremiah decided to make himself useful by unpacking the satchels for her and handing her items such as cans of baking powder and bottles of vanilla. He did not miss the way she hesitated at first to take the items he held out to her. And then to his surprise she almost snatched them from him as if he might decide to run off with them. And not once did she look directly at him.

"We could go over it now if you have a few minutes," he said. "The recipe," he added when she glanced back at him over one shoulder.

"I have shown it to my father. He'll be here later. You can discuss it with him then."

"But you are the baker, are you not?"

"Yes, but…"

"Then I would like to discuss it directly with you." He had removed his straw hat and laid it on the long worktable that dominated the center of the room.

Still not looking directly at him she folded the cloth satchels and stored them in a basket under the table then began transferring a series of large flat pans, each covered with a cloth, to the table. The string ties of her *kapp* swung to and fro with the motion of her actions. She handed him his hat and went back to the side counter for another tray. It was clear that this was a process she had repeated hundreds—perhaps even thousands—of times. When she removed the cloths he saw that they held unbaked loaves of bread—rye from the looks of them.

"Frau Obermeier?"

"When my father returns, then we can discuss your order, Herr Troyer. Until then, I have bread to bake."

Jeremiah saw a series of hooks on the wall near the doorway that led to the front of the bakery and made use of one of them to hang his hat. Then he rolled back the long sleeves of his shirt.

Her eyes—definitely one of her best features—went wide with what Jeremiah could only interpret as shock. "What are you doing?" she demanded.

"I thought that as long as you wish me to wait until your father arrives that I could help you."

"Oh, so now you are a baker as well?"

Out of any other woman's mouth the words might have sounded teasing, even flirtatious. After all, Jeremiah was not blind to the fact that from the time he reached eighteen years and suddenly filled out the gaunt body that his earlier illness had left behind, he had attracted female admiration. His easy smile and determination to be everything his uncle was not had always resonated with females of all ages. But when Pleasant Obermeier spoke these words, they were no less than a condemnation.

Hoping to disarm her, he chuckled. "I'm afraid you would need to teach me that, Frau Obermeier. I had only thought I might move the trays to the ovens when you are ready."

"Thank you, but no. I can manage." She turned her back to him as she checked the heat coming from the large wood-fired ovens. "I'll let my father know that you wish to speak with him," she said.

"And you," he added as he retrieved his hat. "As the baker, you must have an opinion."

Her back still to him, he saw her shoulders slump slightly as if he had finally defeated her—or perhaps simply tried her patience beyond her ability to be polite. "Herr Troyer…"

"Jeremiah," he interrupted.

She turned to face him. "Herr Troyer," she repeated emphatically. "This is my father's business. If he asks me to be at this meeting, then I will be there. Until he makes that decision, I bid you a good day."

He had been dismissed. With nothing more to say, Jeremiah put his hat on and left the shop. But then the streak of impishness that had gotten him in trouble numerous times throughout his youth blossomed. He waited until a count of ten and then re-entered the shop, the bell announcing the arrival of a customer. He filled the time it took Pleasant to clatter a tray of breads into the oven and call out, "Coming," by considering the sparse but luscious selection of baked goods displayed in the shop's cases.

There were apple dumplings, whoopee pies that leaked their vanilla cream filling from between the chocolate cake sandwich like mortar from a freshly set brick wall, and the most mouthwatering-looking lemon squares that Jeremiah had ever seen.

The woman he assumed was responsible for all this

temptation emerged from the back room with a welcoming smile that faded the moment she saw him. "Did you forget something, Herr Troyer?"

"I'd like a dozen of these, half dozen of those, and if you could add in a loaf of that rye bread you're baking."

"It won't be ready for…"

"I realize that. I thought perhaps you might be so kind as to drop it off on your way home later today. I'm right next door."

Pressing her lips together in a thin line of disapproval that did nothing to add to her appearance, Pleasant started filling his order. She packed two boxes, tied them with string and set them on top of the bakery case. When she had finished, he noticed that the small display of pastries he'd admired was almost completely gone.

"Will that be all?" she asked.

"I seem to have wiped out most of your…"

"I can always bake more," she said. "Would you like anything else?"

Jeremiah pretended to consider that question by looking around the shop. He plucked a bag of day-old rolls from a small table near the door and added it to the pile. "How much do I owe?"

When she punched in the amounts on the heavy brass cash register he thought she might actually bend the keys with the force of her strokes. He watched the numbers tally in the small window on top of the register and just before she hit the total key, he reached across the counter and stopped her by touching the back of her hand. "Did you add in the rye bread?"

"You can pay my father for that when he delivers it later today. At Goodloe's Bakery we make it a habit not to take payment until we are certain we can deliver what has been ordered."

"Meaning?"

"I might burn the bread," she said. "Or it might not have risen properly." She hit the key to total the sale and the cash register drawer sprang open. "Anything is possible," she added. "I might drop it on the floor or…"

The color that flooded her cheeks suddenly told him that they were sharing the memory of when she had dropped the doughnuts. He smiled and handed her the money. Without meeting his look she made change, slammed the cash drawer shut and dropped the coins into his outstretched hand. "Good day, sir," she said as she presented him with his parcels.

"And a pleasant day to you, Pleasant," he said as he accepted his order and headed for the door. Then he paused and sniffed the air. "I can see that I found a premiere location for my shop as well as my home if every morning I'm to be awakened by such wonderful smells."

Finally, the thin line of her mouth softened as her lips parted but she did not go so far as to actually smile. Pity, Jeremiah thought. Her smile was lovely.

Outside he found that he was in an even better mood than he had been upon first awakening that morning. Yes, he was going to enjoy life in Florida. It was impossible not to be in a good mood when practically every day was filled with sunshine. He closed his eyes and thanked God for the many blessings he had already found by moving to Celery Fields.

In spite of her determination not to surrender to her curiosity about Jeremiah Troyer, Pleasant edged toward the front window of the bakery and peeked out through the muslin café curtains to see where he might go next. To her surprise he was standing almost directly in front of the bakery, his eyes closed and his face raised to the sky above.

Was he praying? In the middle of the street?

And then with no warning, he opened his eyes and raised his hand in greeting to the Hadwells who owned the hardware store. He set the bag with the day-old bread and the larger box that held an assortment of pastries on the porch of his shop and carried the smaller box— the one that held six apple cider doughnuts—over to the hardware store.

He offered a doughnut to Mr. and Mrs. Hadwell and then called out to Harvey Miller who ran the machine shop to come and join them. Within ten minutes they had each taken a seat on one of the many nail barrels that lined the porch to enjoy the doughnuts. Gertrude Hadwell brought out tin cups and a pot of coffee and served the men. Jeremiah had his back to her but Pleasant could tell by his gestures and the rapt interest on the faces of the others that he was telling them some story.

"A tall tale, no doubt," she huffed as she dropped the curtain back into place and returned to the kitchen. The man had a way of taking over whatever space he might occupy. One might expect that of someone like Levi Harnisher, for example. Levi had once owned one of the largest and most successful circus companies in the country. And Pleasant would never forget the day he had walked right into this very bakery while she and Hannah were working and announced that he had sold the circus in order to return to his Amish roots and court Hannah.

Never in her life did Pleasant think she had ever witnessed anything so romantic as that. The love that shown in Hannah's eyes as she looked at Levi and his love for her that was reflected there was nothing short of breathtaking. And the memory of that devotion naturally brought to mind her relationship with Merle. Of course, she and Merle were very different from Hannah and Levi, who were romantics by nature. To the contrary, both she and Merle understood and respected the hard realities of life.

Jeremiah Troyer is a romantic, she thought and bit her lip as she focused all of her attention on rolling out crusts for pies instead of dwelling on the handsome newcomer who was to be their neighbor—and perhaps business associate. *Neighbor and business associate,* Pleasant sternly reminded herself, *and nothing more.*

If there was one lesson she had learned, it was that men were rarely as they presented themselves to others. Or perhaps it was that she was a poor judge of the male species. After all, she had foolishly thought that a young man from Wisconsin was flirting with her, calling at the bakery day after day just to see her. More to the point, the man she had thought Merle was before they married and the man he had turned out to be were not at all the same.

Hannah and others had tried to warn her, but she had insisted that they simply did not understand people like Merle and her—serious people who were devoted to their work and who understood the hard realities of life. But even she was not prepared for day in and night out of living with a man who saw little good in anyone or anything—including her and his own children.

The shop bell jangled and Pleasant sighed heavily as she wiped her hands on her apron and headed to the front of the store. "Did you need more doughnuts, Herr

Troyer?" she asked as she stepped past the curtain separating the kitchen from the shop and saw Hilda standing there with all four of Pleasant's children.

"Pleasant, you must do something with this girl," her sister-in-law said as she pushed Bettina forward. "I am quite at my wit's end."

Chapter Three

"Bettina, are you all right? Has something happened?" Pleasant asked, coming around the counter and kneeling next to her daughter whose face was awash in silent tears.

"I didn't know they had wandered off," the girl said in a whisper as Pleasant wiped away her tears with the hem of her apron.

"Shhh," Pleasant murmured. "It's all right."

"It is not all right," Hilda thundered. "For it was your idea to give the child responsibility for making sure the twins are properly brought to my house before she and Rolf leave for school."

On weekdays, when the bakery was busiest, the twins stayed with Hilda who had seven children of her own. On Saturdays, they spent their day at the bakery with Pleasant while Rolf and Bettina took care of chores at home.

"I wanted to get the wash hung before…" Bettina began.

Pleasant stood up so that she was eye to eye with Hilda. Merle's sister had first watched over the children after their mother's death, taking them in so that Merle could tend his celery fields. And even after Merle and Pleasant married, she had continued to insist that the children spend their days at her home, persuading Merle that it was asking too much of them to accept Pleasant right away. But when Pleasant had accepted this arrangement without question and gone back to helping her father in the bakery, Hilda had done a complete about-face, complaining to Merle that Pleasant was ignoring the children, not to mention her duties as his wife and the keeper of his house.

Pleasant kept one hand around Bettina's shoulder as she tried to assure herself that only fear and panic would make Hilda speak so sharply in front of the children. "Hilda," she said quietly, "the children are all safe. She's only a girl and…"

"At her age their father was already working a paying job. At his age…" Hilda gestured toward Rolf. "He was…"

Pleasant touched her sister-in-law's arm. "Hilda, please," she murmured and was relieved when the woman swallowed whatever else she had been about to say.

Meanwhile, the twins had eased away from the drama and worked their way behind the counter where they had opened the sliding door of the bakery case and were helping themselves to some of the sweets that Jeremiah had not purchased. Bettina tugged on Pleasant's skirt and nodded toward the boys.

"Stop that this instant," Pleasant demanded as she moved quickly around the counter and picked up one twin under each arm like sacks of flour.

When she failed to take away the pastry each boy

clutched, Hilda snorted. "You do them no favors by indulging them," she huffed as Pleasant deposited both boys closer to the door.

"Tell your Aunt Hilda that you're sorry for causing her worry and then apologize to your sister as well," Pleasant instructed.

"Sorry," Henry muttered even as he stuffed the last of his pastry into his mouth.

Pleasant grabbed an empty lard bucket she kept under the counter to collect waste and shoved it under Henry's chin. "Spit it out," she said in a voice that brooked no argument. The boy did as he was told and then burst into tears. Within seconds his twin had joined in the chorus and the racket they made was deafening.

Hilda threw up her hands. "Do you see what you've done?" she demanded and Pleasant prepared to defend her action until she saw that her sister-in-law had addressed this remark to Bettina.

Pleasant realized that if she didn't do something at once, her father—or worse—any customer who came in was going to find the shop crowded with crying children. "Let's all just calm down and have a nice glass of milk in the kitchen," she suggested just as the bell above the door jangled.

"Ah, Frau Yoder," Jeremiah Troyer said, ignoring the chaos of the overwrought children. "I thought that was you I saw coming down the road before."

Beyond caring why Jeremiah Troyer had invaded the bakery for a third time that morning, Pleasant seized the opportunity to herd all four children into the kitchen. She noticed that all sign of tears and protests had abated the minute Jeremiah entered the bakery. The children seemed quite fascinated by him.

"Sit there and be quiet," Pleasant said, indicating a long bench that ran along one wall. She was glad to see that even the twins seemed to recognize the limits of her patience. While she poured four glasses of milk and handed one to each child, she tried in vain to overhear the conversation taking place in the shop. Then she heard the opening and closing of the outer door and a moment later, Jeremiah stepped into the kitchen.

"May I have a word with Rolf, Frau Obermeier?" he asked.

"What about?" Pleasant asked.

Jeremiah gave her that maddening smile of his and tousled Rolf's hair. "With your permission, Frau Yoder has suggested that he might be a candidate to help out at the ice cream shop."

Rolf's eyes widened with a mixture of such surprise, unadulterated joy and pleading that Pleasant's heart sank. This was the most difficult part of being a parent. She was going to have to say no.

"I don't believe that would be a good idea," she said.

Rolf's face fell but he said nothing. Jeremiah's smile tightened. "I see. Perhaps this is not the right time." He glanced at Bettina and the twins and seemed to focus on their tear-stained faces. "Forgive me for the intrusion, ma'am. We can discuss the matter later." He nodded to the children and headed for the door.

"Wait a minute," Pleasant said, hurrying after him.

He had opened the door and the bell was still vibrating when she caught up to him. "I know you mean well, Herr Troyer, but..."

"Are the children all right?"

Pleasant blinked up at him. "Yes, of course they are." *Why would he think otherwise?* She saw a flicker of doubt cross his expression and felt her defenses go on alert. "Herr Troyer, please understand that Rolf has his schooling and chores at home and…"

"As do many other children." The implication that other boys Rolf's age were working or learning a trade was clear.

"The children are my responsibility," Pleasant said tightly. "I will decide when the time is right that they should take on more than they must already manage."

Jeremiah looked away for an instant, out the leaded glass of the bakery door. "Of course, you know best, but if I may offer an observation as someone who was once smaller and not nearly as strong as others my age?" He seemed to wait a beat for her to grant permission and when she said nothing, he continued, "Do not deny the boy the opportunity to find his place in the world."

"He is only twelve," Pleasant protested. "Besides, he will one day have his father's farm to manage and…"

"I am not speaking of his life as an adult. I am speaking of his life now—the things that will surely shape the man he will one day become. There is a tempest building in that boy. A growing view of the world and those around him as unfair. He is fast approaching a crossroads where he will either accept his size as a challenge to be met or he will surrender himself to the belief that he has been unjustly punished."

Pleasant thought of Hannah's son Caleb and how he had run away. Everything there had turned out for the best, but Rolf was different. Small and quiet—too quiet, she had often thought. And Merle had been especially hard on the boy.

"Why are you really reluctant to have your son work

for me?" Jeremiah asked. "Or perhaps it is not just me? Perhaps you are reluctant to let him go?"

She looked up at him as if truly seeing him for the first time. His dark wavy hair was the color of chestnuts. His eyes were the gold-and-green hazel of autumn leaves in his native Ohio and they held no hint of reproach, only curiosity. His expression was gentle and reflected only a deep interest in her reply.

I am afraid, she thought and knew it for the truth she would not speak aloud. "I will think on what you have said," she replied. "I respect that you have seen in Rolf perhaps some of your own youth, but I would remind you that he is not you—nor your son."

"Nein," Jeremiah whispered, glancing away again. "A friend then? Could we—you and your children and I—not be friends?" He arched a quizzical eyebrow and the corners of his mouth quirked into a half smile.

"Neighbors," she corrected.

He grinned and put on his hat. "It's a beginning," he said. "Good day, Pleasant."

"Good day," she replied without bothering to correct his familiarity. She watched him hop off the end of the porch closest to his shop and thought, *And perhaps in time, friends.*

There had been one reason and one reason only that Jeremiah had gone to the bakery for a third time in the same morning. He had been sitting outside the hardware store sharing doughnuts with the Hadwells when Mrs. Hadwell had noticed Hilda herding Pleasant's children down the street. The girl was in tears and the three boys lagged behind her and their aunt, looking distraught.

Mrs. Hadwell had cleared her throat, drawing her

husband's attention and then she nodded toward the little parade passing their store. Roger Hadwell glanced up and then turned back to the conversation he and Jeremiah had been having about remodeling Jeremiah's shop. But Jeremiah knew that look. He'd seen similar glances pass between neighbors and friends of his family his whole life. Louder than a shout it was a look that warned, "This is none of our business. Stay out of it."

And to his surprise, Jeremiah found it easier to comply with that unspoken warning than to call out to Hilda Yoder and ask if there was a problem. To his shame he lowered his eyes until Hilda had passed by on her way to the bakery, her fingers clutching the thin upper arm of Pleasant's daughter. But the scene stayed with him even as he headed back to his own shop and even after he forced himself to focus on the plans for remodeling the space. And when he heard one of the children cry out, he could stand it no more and headed for the bakery.

With no real plan in mind, he was a bit taken aback when he passed the bakery window and saw Pleasant thrust a bucket under the nose of one of the younger boys. Perhaps the child was ill. Perhaps he had misread the entire situation. He entered the bakery, closing the door with an extra force that he knew would cause the bell to jangle loudly. It worked. Everyone turned to him. Instinctively, he focused his smile on Hilda Yoder who scowled at the interruption while Pleasant said something about milk and took advantage of his arrival to take the children into the back room.

"What is it now, Herr Troyer?" Hilda snapped.

Jeremiah had no idea what he should say. He racked his brain for some reason why he might have needed to have dealings with the woman.

"I saw you come down the street earlier and then it occurred to me that you might be just the person to give me some advice." He suspected that giving advice was Hilda's stock in trade and when her scowl shifted from irritation to suspicion, he was pretty sure that he had guessed correctly.

"What sort of advice?"

Jeremiah chuckled. "I may know how to manage a business and make a decent ice cream, but when it comes to decorating the premises…" He shrugged. "I am quite at a loss." He could practically see the wheels turning in Hilda's brain and hurried on to press his advantage. "Clearly, I'm going to need tables and chairs and a serving counter and…"

Hilda nodded, her small light eyes flitting back and forth as if typing up a list. "Have you colors in mind?"

Jeremiah shrugged.

Hilda huffed out a sigh that, when translated, meant, "Men are hopeless," and set to work ticking off what he was going to need. "The place is a mess. You'll need cleaning supplies and then paint—a lemon-yellow I would think. Stop by the store this afternoon and I'll have Herr Yoder pull together those initial supplies. In the meantime, you can order tables and chairs and the counter from Josef Bontrager. He's an excellent carpenter."

"Frau Yoder, you are a blessing in disguise. How will I ever thank you?"

"You can pay your bills in cash and at the time of delivery," she informed him without a trace of humor.

"Of course. Thank you. I'll be by right after lunch if that's convenient."

Hilda nodded and headed for the door. She appeared

to have forgotten all about the business that had brought her and the children here in the first place.

"I'll need a helper," Jeremiah said as he hurried to open the door for her. "Perhaps you know of a young boy who…"

"My older boys all work in the celery fields," she said, making the assumption that her sons would be at the top of Jeremiah's list. She glanced toward the kitchen. "Perhaps Rolf—he's too small for field work."

"Another excellent suggestion. Thank you," Jeremiah said as he ushered her out and closed the door behind her.

It had been a stroke of genius or more likely God's divine guidance that had made him ask her advice on a helper. The one thing he understood was that Hilda Yoder took great pride in seeing herself as invaluable to others when it came to handling their affairs. He did not consider what he might do if she were to suggest that he hire one of her seven children. But as things turned out that should have been the least of his concerns. He had been totally unprepared for Pleasant Obermeier to reject his offer. He had seen the dead and baked fields behind her house. Surely she could use the money the boy could bring home.

He stood for a moment looking down the road at the large white-washed house with its tin roof and wrap-around porch where she had lived with her late husband and where she now lived with his four children. He glanced back at the bakery where, according to his great-aunt Mildred, she had spent a good portion of her life helping her father run the business even after she had married Merle Obermeier.

Jeremiah had lived most of his life in a house where dreams were frowned upon and only hard work was respected. And until he had gone to work for Peter Osgood, he had followed that regimen, burying his dreams in order to try and please his uncle. Now he could not help but wonder what dreams Pleasant had put aside in order to care for first her widowed father and then her half sisters and finally the widower and his four motherless children.

He remembered how, after his father had died, his own mother had abdicated the raising of the children to her brother-in-law. That was to be expected for Jeremiah's father—a kind but timid man—had always bowed to his older brother's wishes as well. How many times had Jeremiah wished that his mother would stand with him when he tried to challenge his uncle's rigidity?

Oh, Pleasant, he thought, *do not make the mistake my mother made.*

But it was hardly his concern, he reminded himself. He had a job to attend to as well as a business to get up and running. His fascination with the baker and her children was nothing more than that—idle curiosity, and as his uncle had reminded him more than once and emphasized with the back of his hand, idle thoughts were the devil's workshop.

Chapter Four

Pleasant had underestimated the amount of time she would have to devote to creating the ice cream cone recipe. In spite of the fact that the bakery's business had dwindled to the basics—breads, rolls and the occasional pie or dozen cookies—she was still busy from dawn to well after dusk. Merle's house was a large one and required constant cleaning to keep it presentable. With four growing children there was a great deal of washing and ironing to be done on top of the cooking she did at home and the upkeep of the kitchen garden she relied upon for fresh produce to feed herself and the children.

Then there was the celery farm itself. Over the years, Merle had acquired a great deal of land—land that needed to be plowed and planted and harvested. Land that this past spring had barely produced a saleable crop and that now in the fall was nowhere near ready to be planted. After her husband's death, Pleasant had turned the management of the farm over to her brother-in-law. Hilda's husband, Moses, was a shy, quiet man—nothing like Hilda. But he had a head for business and managed the farm as well as his dry goods store with an expertise that set Pleasant's mind at ease. Still, he would not make a decision without first consulting with her and Rolf. For as she explained to Jeremiah, the farm was Rolf's future, in spite of his father's doubts that he would ever amount to anything as a farmer or businessman. She worried about Rolf. Merle's constant badgering of the boy had taken its toll, and of all the children, he had been the hardest to bring closer. Whenever she tried to show her appreciation for some chore he had done without being asked or commented on his high marks in school, his dark eyes flickered with doubt and distrust.

It had been a week since Jeremiah Troyer had stopped at the bakery and asked to interview the boy for a job in his ice cream shop and Pleasant had been unable to forget the look that had crossed Rolf's face when she'd turned down the offer. Just before he'd lowered his eyes to study his bare feet, she had seen a look of such disappointment come over his features and there had been a flicker of something else. For one instant he had looked so much like his father.

Memories of the rage that had sometimes hardened Merle's gaze came to mind now as Pleasant rolled out dough and plaited it into braids for the egg bread she was making. She paused, her flour-covered hands frozen for an instant as the thought hit her. What if Jeremiah had been right? What if Rolf turned out to be as bitter and resentful as his father had been? Could such things be passed from father to son like the color of eyes or hair? Or was it possible that circumstances might guide the boy in that direction? Certainly Merle's resentment had begun early in life and in spite of his success in business and the love he had shared with his first wife, he had remained until the day of his death a man who looked at the world with hostility and ill will.

"Well, not Rolf," Pleasant huffed as she returned to her task. "Not my son."

But how to set the boy on a different path?

She wiped her forehead with the back of one hand and blew out a breath of weariness and frustration. *How, indeed, heavenly Father?*

She walked to the open back door of the bakery, hoping to catch a breeze before she had to face the hot ovens again. Next door she saw Jeremiah Troyer replacing a wooden column that supported the extended roof of his shop. She thought about the Sunday when he had easily lifted two of the heavy wooden benches used for church services—one under each arm. She continued to observe him as he fitted the column in place and anchored it, drawing one long nail after another from between his lips and pounding them in until the column was locked in place.

Who would teach Rolf such things? Her father? Perhaps. But he was getting on in years. He tended to leave the heavy chores to the carpenter, Josef Bontrager, who was always willing to help because it gave him an excuse to see Greta. She thought about the way Jeremiah's ready smile and easy laughter were so different from Merle's personality. Might it be enough to simply expose Rolf to this different breed of man? To let him see that not all men were like his father had been? That there were other ways he might decide to go?

Without realizing that she had done so, Pleasant opened the screen door and stepped outside. Jeremiah gave the porch post a final test for steadiness and turned when he heard the squeak of the screen door. The hammer he'd used in one hand, he raised the other hand to his hat and tipped his head in her direction. "Pleasant." He acknowledged her with a quizzical smile as he squinted against the morning sun. "Was there something I could do for you?"

Flustered to find herself outside and engaged in this exchange with him, Pleasant reverted to her usual defense. She thinned her lips and frowned. "Not at all," she replied. "The ovens give off such heat. I just needed a breath of fresh air."

Jeremiah nodded and turned back to his work. He set down the hammer and picked up a broom. Meticulously, he rounded up the wood shavings and sawdust left from shaping the porch column to match its mate.

"You know if you'd like, Rolf could paint that column for you when he comes home from school later," she called.

Jeremiah stacked his hands on the tip of the broom handle and leaned his chin on them as he studied her. "That would be appreciated," he said.

Pleasant nodded and turned to go back inside the bakery's kitchen. *It's a start,* she thought.

"I could still use an assistant," Jeremiah called and her step faltered. "Maybe we could see how painting the porch post works out and then…"

"My offer is simply that of a neighbor wishing to help another neighbor," Pleasant said stiffly.

"Got that part," Jeremiah said, moving closer, twirling the broom handle through his fingers and grinning. "But you'll soon learn that I don't give up easily, Pleasant."

It was the second time he had used her given name that morning. It was as if he were testing her. She smiled sweetly, the way she had seen her half sister Greta smile when she was determined to have her way. "And in time you will learn, Herr Troyer, that I do not make decisions lightly and I will always do what I think is best for my children."

She turned to leave but realized that he was propping the broom against the wall and intended to follow her inside.

"How's the cone recipe coming?" he asked as he held the door for her and then followed her into the kitchen.

"I expect to have some samples for you to try by the end of the week," she said. "They would best be tested with ice cream since the flavors will have to mingle."

He nodded and took a seat on one of the stools that Gunther kept in the kitchen.

Make yourself at home, she thought, exasperated by his assumption that his presence was welcome.

"How about this? You let me know as soon as you have something that you think might work and I'll make up three different flavors so we can try the various combinations. We can have a tasting party."

She opened her mouth to refuse, but then thought, *Why not?* It would be a special treat for the children. "All right," she replied, placing the braided egg loaves on pans.

His silence was unusual so she glanced up and saw him studying her, a half frown on his forehead and a half smile on his lips. "You do surprise me, Pleasant," he said and then the smile won and blossomed into a full-fledged grin. "End of the week then."

And the man actually winked at her as he pushed himself to his feet and left her standing there, a pan of unbaked egg bread half in and half out of the oven.

Jeremiah sat at his desk and watched the Obermeier boy painting the porch column. He was meticulous in the work, going back over a section that did not meet his standards for perfection. Jeremiah remembered his own painstaking attention to detail in the years he'd spent living with his father's brother. For him it had come from knowing that if he failed to do a job to the exacting standards his uncle had set for him, he would have to do it again or worse, he would be punished.

Had Rolf's father been a man like Jeremiah's uncle? Did that explain the boy's reticence?

"Maybe the kid's just shy," Jeremiah muttered as he pushed his chair away from the desk. He had to stop seeing his uncle in every adult and himself in every quiet child. He took down his hat from the wooden peg near the door and went outside. "Good job," he said.

Rolf stepped away for a moment and surveyed his work. "Missed a spot," he muttered and bent to cover it before turning his attention to the next side of the square column.

"How's school?" Jeremiah sat on the edge of the porch.

"Gut." Rolf lapsed naturally into the Pennsylvania Dutch that Jeremiah assumed was most often spoken at home.

"What are you studying?"

Sticking with his native tongue, Rolf listed the subjects. "Arithmetic, history, geography."

"Your classes are conducted in English?" Jeremiah assumed this might be the case since it was a common way to prepare young people for dealing with those outside the Amish community.

"Ja."

"Does your mother use English at home?"

The paintbrush faltered for a moment. "My stepmother does—yes."

Jeremiah considered the correction. Did it mean that Rolf resented Pleasant or simply that he felt a loyalty to his own mother? "I was about your age when my father died. Tougher on you, I expect, losing both your parents."

This time, Rolf looked at him as if trying to decide where this conversation might be headed. "Mama is good to us," he murmured, his tone slightly defensive.

Jeremiah let the silence settle around them for a long moment. "Do you like ice cream, Rolf?"

"Ja."

"Me, too. I've been working on a new flavor. How about tasting it for me and telling me what you think?"

Rolf continued his long brush strokes. "I should ask permission first."

Jeremiah covered a smile by glancing away toward the bakery. "That's probably best. Your sister's helping out at the bakery, is she?"

Rolf nodded. "After school she watches my brothers until Mama gets everything ready for tomorrow's baking, then we all go home together."

"Well, then the way I see it we've got ourselves a bunch of tasters. You finish up there and go get your mama and sister and brothers while I go get dishes and spoons and the ice cream."

"You want me to bring them over here?" The kid's eyes widened.

"Well, sure. I mean that's where the ice cream is."

Rolf's hand shook slightly as he returned to his painting, now going over an area he'd covered adequately.

"Or I could go over and get the others while you clean up here. Looks to me like you've finished." Without waiting for the boy's reply he headed for the kitchen entrance to the bakery.

Through the open door he could hear the lively chatter of the twins and the clatter of the large metal pans and bowls that Pleasant used for making the breads and rolls she baked each morning. As he got closer, he could hear the low murmur of voices—Pleasant's and the girl's. Bettina, he reminded himself.

"Hello?" he called as much to give fair warning of his approach as to deliver a greeting.

Two pairs of small feet padded across the bakery floor at a run while everything else went silent.

"Well, hello there," he said when the twins lined up at the door and stared out at him. "Is your mother here?"

"Is there a problem, Herr Troyer?" Pleasant glanced anxiously past him to where Rolf was cleaning the paintbrush.

Now why would she automatically assume that? Jeremiah thought. "Actually, I've come to ask another favor."

She waited, wiping her hands on the dish towel she held while the twins glanced from him to her and back to him.

"If we can be of help," Pleasant said, "we're more than…"

"I have this new flavor of ice cream I've concocted— vanilla with bits of mango mixed in. I wondered if you and the children might taste it for me and give me your honest opinion."

The twins did not wait for her reply, but opened the screen door and burst out onto the back porch of the bakery seemingly ready to follow him anywhere as long as he held to his promise of ice cream.

"Boys," Pleasant chided, then turned her attention

back to Jeremiah. "I thought we had agreed on the end of the week. There is no possible way that I will have anything ready by..."

"You'd be doing me a great favor," Jeremiah continued as if her protests had nothing to do with the topic at hand. "While you're developing the cone recipe, don't forget that I need to be working on special flavors for the ice cream. We can't just offer the standard flavors, after all. Besides, I tend to be far too lenient when it comes to my own tastes for flavors."

Bettina had joined Pleasant on the porch and she was smiling up at him. "What other flavors have you invented, Herr Troyer?" she asked.

Jeremiah removed his hat and scratched his head for a moment. "Well, let's see now, there was the time I thought maybe there might be a market for frog's leg chocolate."

All three children giggled and miracle of miracles, he was pretty sure that Pleasant was fighting a smile.

"You made that up," Bettina said.

"You're right. I did. But I actually did think about adding prunes to vanilla once." He made a face that had the twins convulsing with laughter. "So you see I'm not always the best judge when it comes to these things."

"I wouldn't want to spoil the children's supper," Pleasant hedged.

Jeremiah shrugged. "My guess is that you were planning to give them dessert with supper?"

"Well, yes, but..."

"So what if they have dessert first?"

Her mouth worked as she tried to find an answer to this unorthodox logic. "I...without the promise of..."

"They might not finish their peas and carrots?" Jeremiah guessed and Pleasant nodded. He frowned as he studied each child in turn. "Rolf, come over here a minute, would you?"

The boy's bare feet sent puffs of sandy dust flying as he ran across the dry dirt yard. "Yes, sir?"

"Am I to understand that sometimes you children have to be coaxed to finish your vegetables?"

Rolf and Bettina nodded. The twins studied the ground. Jeremiah sighed.

"So you see, Herr Troyer, ice cream at this hour…"

All four children looked up at her, their eyes wide with protest as they realized they were about to lose this opportunity. "But Mama, if we promised?" Bettina pleaded.

Pleasant folded her arms across her chest and studied each child. "No. There have just been too many times…"

Jeremiah was almost as disappointed as the children were. He didn't know why it meant so much to him but it did. "Your mother is right," he began.

"Unless," Pleasant interrupted, "Herr Troyer would agree to come for supper and bring some of his ice cream along for dessert."

The children whooped with delight at what they clearly considered an acceptable solution.

Pleasant was watching him though. "You do like vegetables, do you not, Herr Troyer?"

"What kind?" he asked and hoped the answer would be green beans or perhaps carrots.

"Brussels sprouts," Pleasant replied and he knew that the look of disgust that had flickered over his face for an instant was exactly what made her smile. "May we expect you at five-thirty then?"

Chapter Five

Have I completely lost my mind? Pleasant thought as Jeremiah walked back to his shop, whistling a nameless tune. But she put the thought aside as the children clamored around her.

"Ice cream! Ice cream!" the twins chanted as they marched up and down the small porch.

"He said I did fine work," Rolf reported shyly, his eyes still following Jeremiah until the shopkeeper disappeared inside his back door.

"I don't think he likes Brussels sprouts though," Bettina mused. "Did you see the look on his face? Maybe we should have the beans, after all."

"We're having the sprouts," Pleasant said. "And speaking of supper, we need to get home. Boys, stop that marching and go along home with your sister. Rolf, would you stay and help me finish closing up for the day?"

"Yes, Mama," all four children chorused and then they grinned up at her, their eyes shining with anticipation.

"And stop at your grandfather's, Bettina. Ask him and Greta and Lydia to join us for supper."

Bettina squealed and held hands with the twins as the three of them ran down the dusty road. "It's like a party," Pleasant heard her say.

"Would you like to see the job I did for Herr Troyer?" Rolf asked as he helped Pleasant finish putting away the pans and bowls and scrub the counters.

Pleasant saw the worried look the boy gave her. His father had always insisted on inspecting any task assigned to the boy and more often than not he had found something not quite to his liking.

"You said that Herr Troyer was pleased with the work," she reminded him.

"I know but Papa…"

"Your papa taught you well, Rolf," Pleasant hurried to reassure him. "I can see from here that you did a fine job. If I didn't know which was the newer post I wouldn't be able to tell the new from the old. Now let's finish up here and get home or our company will be there ahead of us."

It was an exaggeration, of course, but it made Rolf smile and the boy seemed unusually relaxed later as the two of them walked past the other shops and then the celery fields and other homes to the end of the road.

"I like Herr Troyer," Rolf murmured when they had almost reached their house. "He's sort of like Herr Harnisher, Caleb's father."

The two men were nothing alike—at least outwardly. Levi was a good man but he tended to be quiet and reserved while Jeremiah Troyer seemed to delight in getting to know people of all ages and backgrounds. But Rolf had a point. The two men did share a nature that invited others—even children and strangers—to open their hearts to them, share confidences and let down their guard of the normal Amish tendency toward reserve.

Of course, her view of the ice cream maker was that he was a business associate of her father's—nothing more. All right. He was also a neighbor and member of the congregation, but nothing more than that. Still, he had made Rolf glow with a pride of accomplishment that in spite of the Amish tendency to frown on such self-satisfaction, pleased her. Besides, until he was fully baptized and had joined the faith, Rolf was not yet truly Amish. He had been born of Amish parents but as a child he was not yet fully a member of the faith so a little pride was not a bad thing, she decided.

"Rolf, perhaps from time to time you could help Herr Troyer as he gets ready to open his shop. There's a great deal to do I expect and after all…"

Rolf was looking up at her, his expression one of disbelief. "Do you mean it?" His voice quavered as if he didn't dare give voice to his hope.

"Helping a newcomer to our community is what our people do as a matter of course, Rolf."

The smile that split his face was his father's smile—a smile she and the children had rarely seen. But she had only a second to bask in its radiance before the child threw his arms around her waist and hugged her, his hat sailing unheeded onto the ground. "Oh, thank you, Mama," he said, his voice muffled against her apron.

She smoothed his hair and relished the warmth of his thin arms clutching her. "You'll still have to manage your chores here and your schoolwork," she reminded him. "And you're to take no payment. These are good deeds—neighbor helping neighbor. Do you understand?"

"Yes, Mama." He looked up at her. "May I tell Bettina?"

"You may tell her that I have given permission for you to help Herr Troyer from time to time if he asks. This is not a job, Rolf."

He had rescued his hat and dashed away almost before the last word left her lips and she watched him go, running into the house, calling out for his sister. *At last,* she thought, realizing that she had finally broken through to the last and most reticent of Merle's children. And she had Jeremiah Troyer to thank for it.

It was pretty obvious that Pleasant had given him an extra large helping of the sprouts, Jeremiah thought as she handed him his plate. Her father sat at the head of the table, slicing a pot roast that smelled as good as it looked. He would place a slab on a plate from the stack in front of him and then pass it to Pleasant who would add potatoes and the dreaded green vegetable.

"Bread, Herr Troyer?" Bettina asked with a sweet smile. "Sometimes it helps take away the taste," she confided in a low whisper when Pleasant's attention was drawn to the twins who were busy jostling one another for more room at the crowded table.

Pleasant's half sisters, Greta and Lydia, sat across from Jeremiah, eyeing him under the fan of their pale lashes. Rolf sat to one side of him and Bettina to the other. And once everyone was served Pleasant took her place opposite her father at the far end of the table.

"Shall we pray?" Gunther asked and in unison every head bowed and silence filled the room. Even the twins were quiet.

"Amen," Gunther intoned after a long moment and the

room erupted into the sounds of flatware on china, the twins' chatter and water from a pitcher splashing into the empty glass that Gunther had just drained. "How are things coming along?" he asked, directing the question at Jeremiah.

"At the shop? Fine. Good."

"How about your job at the ice plant?"

"That's worked out better than I could have hoped," Jeremiah said. "My employers are especially pleased with the number of orders for block ice that I've gotten from people living here in Celery Fields. That business had fallen off considerably once the *Englisch* started using refrigerators instead of iceboxes."

Gunther nodded. "*Ja.* Better to buy from one of our own even if you are working for an *Englisch* company."

"And the cones?" Jeremiah asked and Gunther looked down the table at his eldest daughter.

"I…that is…" Pleasant's cheeks turned a most becoming shade of pink as every person at the table paused in midbite and looked her way. With an almost visible effort she composed herself and turned her attention to Jeremiah. "I apologize, Herr Troyer. We've had some extra orders at the bakery this week and…"

Gunther frowned. "When's your opening?" he asked Jeremiah.

"I haven't set a date yet. I was hoping to be open by the first of November."

"Less than a week," Gunther said to Pleasant.

"Plenty of time," Jeremiah assured her and turned his attention to Lydia. "Fraulein Goodloe, I understand you are the schoolteacher for the community's children."

"Yes," she replied with a shy smile. "I am blessed to have been chosen."

Her sister Greta glanced at him and when Jeremiah smiled at her she almost choked on the food she was chewing.

Perhaps it would be safer if he concentrated on his own plate, empty now except for the pile of Brussels sprouts and the round roll that Bettina had urged him to try. He picked up his knife and fork and cut into a sprout, put half of it in his mouth and then followed that with a bite of the roll and chewed.

He was aware that Bettina was watching him and when he swallowed and repeated the process she whispered, "Told you so."

"More pot roast, Jeremiah," Gunther boomed.

"Thank you but, no. I have more than enough to finish here and I want to save room for ice cream."

The twins started to speak up but Pleasant silenced them by pointing out the untouched vegetables on their plates. "Only those who clean their plates get ice cream," she reminded them.

Jeremiah couldn't help feeling a little sorry for the boys. On the other hand, they only had two sprouts each to finish while he was still facing half a dozen. He squared his shoulders and picked up his fork. Slicing each sprout in half, he wolfed them down, chasing them from his mouth with the rest of the roll and gulps of cold water until there were only two left.

He glanced at the twins who immediately saw the challenge he was sending them. Pleasant had sliced their food into bite-sized pieces. Henry nudged Will and both boys grinned at Jeremiah and the race to finish first was on. Everyone except Gunther seemed to have caught on to the game. Rolf and Bettina sat forward, silently cheering their brothers to victory. Lydia and Greta glanced uneasily from Jeremiah to Pleasant, apparently waiting for her to say something. Instead, she slowly finished the last of her supper, as if unaware that anything was amiss. But Jeremiah saw her ease a bite of the vegetable that had been hidden under some gravy forward on Henry's plate lest he miss it. The boys won and their victory was crowned by Gunther's deep belch—the Amish man's compliment to his wife or daughter for a good meal.

Pleasant stood and began removing plates that had been wiped so clean Jeremiah thought they would need only a minimum of scrubbing. Lydia, Greta and Bettina helped, making short work of clearing the table. Pleasant took small clear plates from an open shelf and handed them to Bettina. "We have Herr Troyer's ice cream and your favorite pie, Papa."

"Ah, shoo-fly pie." Gunther sighed patting his ample stomach.

"We can have both?" Henry asked.

"Ice cream *and* pie?" Will chorused.

"A taste of ice cream," Pleasant replied not looking at Jeremiah. "Remember, we are only giving our opinion to Herr Troyer."

The twins nodded solemnly and waited for their sister to serve each person a dessert of a slice of still-warm, shoo-fly pie topped with a small mound of mango ice cream. Will shoveled the ice cream into his mouth then looked at Henry for his opinion.

"Well?" Jeremiah asked.

"I'm going to need another taste," Henry announced.

"Me, too," Will said.

"I agree. Seems to me if we're to have any hope of coming out even between the pie and the ice cream we're all going to need more," Gunther said passing his plate forward.

Jeremiah took some ice cream and pie onto his fork and tasted it. He savored the mix of flavors. The cool subtle vanilla with the sweet bits of mango mingled with the molasses, cinnamon, nutmeg and ginger of the pie filling. "This is it," he murmured, taking a second bite and imagining the flavors mixed with chocolate ice cream or butter pecan or... "This is the cone we need. Shoo-fly cones," he announced.

It was ludicrous, of course, Pleasant thought later as she washed the last of the dessert plates and paid little attention to her half sisters chattering on about the handsome—and eligible—Jeremiah Troyer. The unique flavor of shoo-fly pie came from the pie filling, not the crust. How did he expect her to turn a pudding-like filling into something sturdy enough to hold ice cream? And yet the challenge had been there in the way his eyes had sought hers across the table.

But this was no game such as the one he had played with the twins to finish their vegetables. This was a business challenge, one that could mean the difference between a substantial increase in business for the bakery and none at all if Jeremiah decided to go elsewhere. She paused in her washing to gaze out the kitchen window. Although the sun had set, she knew that she was facing the fields—the empty barren fields, the fields that would not only yield little if any produce but would surely yield even less income.

The drought that was choking much of the country had not spared Florida and this season's crops had been sparse indeed even for those who had been wise enough to plan for such contingencies. After the disastrous spring harvest, Moses Yoder had warned her that after paying the field hands there would be little left from the sale of the crops. Then over the unusually hot summer months, strong westerly winds combined with the drought to blow away a good portion of the soil. In fact, dust was so thick in the air that most people in the community had taken to keeping their windows closed in spite of the heat. It was either that or dust furnishings and wash floors daily. Others had managed to eke out a small harvest, but not Pleasant.

"Do you think he left a girlfriend back in Ohio?" Greta asked and it took a moment before Pleasant realized that the question had been directed at her.

"Who?"

Greta rolled her eyes. "Herr Troyer. Who have we been talking about since he and Papa left?"

"I have no idea," Pleasant replied. *And I have no time for girlish fantasies.*

"Are you truly going to try and create a shoo-fly ice cream cone?" the more practical Lydia asked as she took the stack of dessert plates from Pleasant and placed them back on the shelf.

"Of course," she snapped impatiently, exhausted by all the many problems she faced. But then she softened her tone and smiled at her half sister, the schoolmarm. "After all, that's the assignment."

Lydia gave her an uncertain smile. "You've taken on so much since Merle died, Pleasant. You need some help."

"She needs a husband," Greta said with all the certainty of one who was enough of a romantic to believe that any problem could be solved through marriage to the right man.

"Greta!" Lydia admonished, her voice a warning.

"I had a husband," Pleasant reminded Greta, whose mouth had formed a perfect circle with the realization of what she'd just said.

"Oh, sister, I am so sorry."

Pleasant accepted the apology with a wave of her hand. "It's late and the evening was an interesting one. Your mind is on other matters."

Greta grinned, her good spirits restored. "Like Jeremiah Troyer?" She sighed. "Did you see his eyes?"

Lydia heaved a sigh of resignation and wrapped her arm around her younger sister. "Herr Troyer is too old for you, Greta, so stop daydreaming about his eyes. Besides, what would Josef Bontrager say if he could hear you now?"

"Oh, I'm just having a little fun. Anyone could see that the only one of us Herr Troyer was looking at tonight was Pleasant," she added with a mischievous smile.

Pleasant laughed. "Go home both of you. It's late and I still have work to do."

Long into the night she sat at the kitchen table scribbling notes as she tried to come up with the formula for creating a crisp cookie cone from a recipe for pie filling. When the rooster crowed at four, she startled awake and realized she'd fallen asleep at the table. She stretched and then pumped water into the kitchen sink to splash on her sleep-laden eyelids. She stirred the embers of the fire in the wood stove and set a pot of barley oats on top to simmer.

Bettina would finish making breakfast for her brothers, wash the dishes and get the twins to Hilda's on her way to school. Meanwhile, Rolf would milk the cow, feed the chickens, collect the eggs and deliver them to the bakery on his way to school. As Pleasant let herself out of the house and started down the road to the silent and dark bakery, she thanked God for the blessing of these children. They might not be hers by birth, but they were hers by circumstance and not a dawn passed that she didn't plead with God to show her the way to guide them properly.

The eastern sky showed only a glimmer of the day to come as Pleasant passed the dry goods store. She glanced up and saw a dark figure sitting on the front stoop of the bakery. She hesitated. It was not uncommon these days for homeless transients to find their way to the village and plead for food or money. Most were harmless, but she'd heard some disturbing stories.

She kept her distance and called out to the man. "Hello? May I help you, sir?"

The man started and she realized he'd been dozing. He stood, stretched and then started walking her way. "I had a thought about those shoo-fly cones," Jeremiah Troyer said and Pleasant let out a relieved breath that she hadn't realized she'd been holding.

"It's you? At this hour?"

He was close enough for her to see his grin in the left-over light of the moon and stars that had still filled the predawn sky. "Couldn't sleep," he admitted as he fell into step with her and followed her around to the back door of the bakery. "Do you want to hear my idea?"

Do I have a choice? she thought as she tallied the number of loaves she still needed to get baked and ready for Gunther to deliver in just a few hours to the Sarasota grocer he'd contracted with. "Of course," she replied as she prepared to stack wood from the supply outside the back door into the skirt of her apron.

"Let me do that," Jeremiah said relieving her of the two logs she'd already gathered.

She held the door open for him. "Just stack them in the wood box next to…"

He was still standing outside the door. "You don't lock the door?"

"No," she replied. "Papa believes that if someone wants in, a locked door won't matter."

"But what if someone were waiting?"

"Someone was," she reminded him. "This morning."

"You know what I mean," he grumbled as he dumped the load of wood into the wood box and then turned his attention to poking the fire that Gunther had already started for her.

"What's this idea of yours?" she asked, realizing that if she was to get her regular orders filled she would first need to deal with Jeremiah.

He looked back over his shoulder at her, his face lit by the flames of the fire. "What if instead of adding the molasses and spices to the dough of the cones, we made up a kind of filling and dipped the cones into it before adding the ice cream?" His smile faltered when she did not immediately respond. "Well, what do you think?" He stood and shut the iron door to the stove and dusted off his hands.

"I think you would end up with a soggy, sticky mess," she replied matter-of-factly as she uncovered a mound of dough she'd left to rise overnight and pounded her fist into its center.

"Oh," he said. "Well, what if…" He seemed at a loss

to finish the thought. "You're sure it wouldn't work? A kind of a syrup?"

In the shadows of the kitchen it was hard to see his expression now that he had moved away from the fire, but the disappointment in his voice spoke volumes. Pleasant felt a twinge of sympathy for the man. After all, he had clearly been up most of the night just as she had. "You've only just come up with this idea of shoo-fly cones, Herr Troyer. Perhaps it's not too much to expect that it may take a day or so to perfect it?"

He stood next to the worktable and drummed his fingers on its surface. "Patience has never been one of my virtues, I'm afraid." He glanced around. "Should I light some lamps?"

"No need to waste the kerosene. It will be light soon, Herr Troyer, and the work I'm doing does not require light." *Although perhaps being alone with a man in the shadows does,* she thought and was about to reconsider his offer when he let out a sigh that could be translated as nothing but exasperation.

"Look, Pleasant, I guess I can understand the Herr Troyer business when we're in public or with your children, but when it's just the two of us and we're working toward the same end wouldn't given names be…easier?"

"I just…"

"Try it—Jer-e-mi-ah." He sounded out each syllable as if teaching her a new language.

To her surprise and consternation she felt a bubble of laughter tickle her throat. "Jer-e-mi-ah," she repeated in an exaggeration of his instruction and she was very glad that he could not see her smile.

"Excellent," he announced. "Now try it in a sentence."

She stopped kneading the dough. "This is foolishness," she said. "I have work to do."

"This is foolishness, Jer-e-mi-ah," he repeated. "I have work to do, Jer-e-mi-ah."

"You are trying my patience, Jer-e-mi-ah," she chanted and pounded the dough with fresh enthusiasm. She heard the clink of harness and the muffled hoofbeats of a horse outside. "That will be Rolf come to bring the milk and eggs," she said as she wiped her hands on a flour sack towel and headed for the back door.

"Should I hide in the wood box, Pleasant?"

"Don't be silly. You'd ruin your clothes. Hide under the table there."

She went out to help Rolf, but not before she distinctly heard him murmur, "Well now who would have thought that Pleasant Obermeier has a most pleasant sense of humor?"

Chapter Six

Pleasant went about her regular chores at the bakery almost without thought. Her mind was now fully occupied in coming up with a workable recipe for the cones. While she waited for the loaves of bread and the few pies and pastries she kept in the front display case to bake, she played with some scraps of leftover dough. First she wadded them into a smooth ball and then rolling the ball flat as she tried to decide how thick a cone might need to be. Then she turned her attention to the real issue—how to incorporate the ingredients that made a shoo-fly pie so rich and sweet into the dough.

She took a bit of ginger, cinnamon, nutmeg and cloves, and ground them into a fine powder using a mortar and pestle. The fragrance of the combined spices filled the air and she savored their rich exotic scent. No perfume devised by man could ever compete with that. She mixed dark brown sugar in with the spices and set them aside. Then she picked up the jug of dark molasses and studied it as if the answer to her quandary might be found in simply holding the container.

"How's it coming?"

She had been so engrossed in thought that she'd failed to hear Jeremiah's step on the porch outside the kitchen door. "Slowly," she admitted.

Apparently, he saw that as his invitation to come inside. He considered the ingredients lined up on the worktable. Pleasant scraped up the dough and kneaded it back into a ball. "Let me show you something," she said as she rolled out the dough, then lifted an edge. "Do you think that's thick enough or too thick?"

"Looks just right to me."

"Good. Then the problem becomes how to take the dough, the spices and the molasses and put them together."

"May I?" Jeremiah reached for the bowl of powdered spices and when Pleasant nodded, he sprinkled a small amount across the surface of the dough. "Will that work once you bake it?"

"I think so, but let's see," Pleasant said as she slid the pastry dough onto a pan and placed it in the hot oven. "There's still the problem of the molasses," she reminded him.

"Do we really need molasses?"

"If you want to advertise the cones as 'shoo-fly' cones you do," Pleasant said. "Molasses is the heart of any recipe for shoo-fly pie."

"*We* do, Pleasant. This is a joint venture—a partnership."

The aroma of the spices was enhanced by baking as Pleasant checked the oven to be sure the pastry did not burn.

"Is it done?" Jeremiah asked, coming closer to peer into the oven.

"Yes." She tried not to think about how disconcerting it was to have him so close to her. His actions were perfectly innocent—he was excited about the prospect of coming up with a recipe that worked. It had nothing to do with any desire he might entertain to be closer to her.

She removed the pan from the oven and carried it to the worktable. "Let it cool," she admonished when he reached to break off a piece and then juggled it from hand to hand like a hot potato.

He grinned and popped it into his mouth. "Mmm," he murmured, eyes closed and a smile on his lips. "That's delicious."

Pleasant broke off a small bite and blew on it before putting it on her tongue. He was right. The spices and brown sugar had added something special to the bland taste of the pie dough. "We still need the molasses," she said.

Jeremiah's smile widened to a grin. "Yes, *we* do," he said. "But it's a good start. I'll leave you to it. Let me know if you come up with anything you need me to taste." He took his hat from the peg by the door and headed back across the yard to his own shop.

Pleasant picked up the rest of the pastry and nibbled at it as she watched him go. Greta was right about one thing. Jeremiah Troyer was one handsome man.

It was later that night, long after the bakery and other businesses had closed for the day, that Jeremiah came up with the answer. It happened when he was painting the last of the shop's walls and accidentally dropped a scrap of cardboard into the bucket of paint. He fished it out and held it for a moment, letting the excess paint drip off it. It reminded him of what Pleasant had said about his idea of dipping the cones in molasses.

"A soggy sticky mess," he muttered to himself as he carefully deposited the sodden cardboard in the dustbin. He continued painting and thinking about the molasses. And then it hit him and he was so excited to share the idea with Pleasant that he set his paintbrush to soak in a jar of turpentine, grabbed his hat and left for her house at a jog.

The house was dark except for a single amber light in an upstairs window. He glanced at the sky, pitch black and clouded over. All the way back down the street, not a light shone from any house. It was late. He looked back at Pleasant's house. The upstairs light was out now. Dejected, he turned to go but then heard the unmistakable squeak of a screen door opening and closing and followed the sound around to the back of the house.

"Pleasant?" he called in a whisper.

"Who's there?" Her voice held no fear, only curiosity. She was silhouetted by a single lamp in the kitchen as she dumped out a pan of water over the porch railing.

"It's me—Jeremiah. Sorry to bother you so late and all, but I had this idea."

No answer but she did not move away from the door.

"About the molasses," he continued. "What if we mixed a little into the batter? Not so much as to make it impossible for the dough to harden after baking, but..."

A dog barked and a horse snorted in the neighboring yard. Pleasant glanced toward the sound and then took a step back into the house. "It's late, Herr Troyer. Surely this can wait."

He sighed and advanced a step closer. "It's Jeremiah, remember? And yes, it can wait but I won't get any sleep and I doubt you will either thinking about the possibility, wondering if maybe..."

"All right," she said impatiently, still glancing around as if fearing to be caught at something illegal. "I'll try mixing up some samples tonight and let you know in the morning. That's the best I can offer, Jeremiah." This last was delivered in a whisper that pleaded with him to understand the position he was putting her in and pleased him enormously with her inclusion of his given name.

"Fair enough," he whispered back. "Thank you, Pleasant. See you in the morning."

Recognizing that trying to sleep would be an exercise in futility, Jeremiah spent the rest of the night completing the painting and scrubbing the wood floor of his shop. By four in the morning he had placed the half dozen iron-legged round tables and matching chairs around the shop's freshly stained counter and unpacked and washed the sundae dishes and tall soda glasses that would line the glass shelves behind it.

The sky in the east had just turned a paler shade of charcoal when he went outside and took up his position on the front stoop of the bakery. And only minutes later he saw her coming down the dusty road. She was carrying something—a tray, he thought and pushed himself to his feet to go and meet her.

"Well?" he asked when they were not three yards apart.

"I have some samples," she said and handed him the tray. Then to his surprise she just kept walking to the bakery.

"Wait. Aren't we going to try them?"

"I have tried them, Jeremiah, and I have other orders to fill. You'll let me know what you think."

He caught up with her, balancing the small tray with

the dish towel spread over its contents. "What did you think?"

"It doesn't matter what I think. You are the customer here. It only matters if you are satisfied."

"But…"

"I have work to do, Jeremiah, and as you predicted I did not get much sleep last night, so please, let me get to it." She did not wait for his response, but instead walked up the front steps of the bakery and went inside closing the glass-paneled door firmly behind her.

Jeremiah took the tray to his shop and set it on the counter. When he removed the cover he found five triangular cookies. He picked one up and broke off a small piece, taking note of its rich deep brown color and the unmistakable scent of cinnamon as he bit into it. In quick succession he performed the same ritual with the other four samples. Some were paler in color—a golden tan flecked with darker bits of the spices in one case—and others were even darker than the first sample. The thing they all had in common was that they were delicious, and while he could distinguish subtle differences in them, he could not possibly choose one over the other.

He saw Rolf driving the wagon loaded with eggs and milk from the farm to the bakery, his sister and the twins riding with him this morning. *"Guten morgen,"* he called as he exited his shop, bringing the tray of cookies with him. "I wonder if I could trouble you children to help me with a small problem."

Rolf and Bettina exchanged a glance. As usual Bettina spoke for the two of them. "We have school and the twins are late for Auntie Hilda's and…"

"This will only take a minute," he promised as he

handed Bettina the tray. "Would you and your brothers taste each of these and tell me which one you prefer?"

Bettina broke off small pieces and passed them around to her three brothers. Each child accepted the bite, chewed it thoughtfully and then waited for the next sample.

"This one," Bettina said pointing to the rich dark brown sample.

"Me, too," the twins chorused.

"And you, Rolf?" Jeremiah asked.

"I like them all," he admitted. "But if you're going to make ice cream cones with one of them, then that one."

Jeremiah grinned. "It's unanimous then. Let's go and tell your mother so she can start baking and I can change that sign to post an actual date for the grand opening."

The idea for using her recipe for molasses cookies as the foundation for making the cones had struck Pleasant just after three that morning. Why hadn't she thought of it before? She tried different ways of incorporating the spices into the recipe until she had found what she considered to be as close to the taste of shoo-fly pie filling in a cookie form that could be achieved. When Jeremiah entered the bakery, the children trailing behind him, and held up the darkest of the cookies she'd given him to sample, she could not help but smile.

"This one," he announced. "It's unanimous."

All four children nodded.

"Go on with you," she fussed, shooing the children out the door. "You'll be late for school and your Aunt Hilda will wonder what's keeping the twins."

"But we won't tell her," Bettina said with a conspiratorial glance at Jeremiah. "No one must know about the shoo-fly cones until the grand opening. Isn't that right, Herr Troyer?"

"That's right. It's a secret," he added, focusing his attention on the twins. "Remember?"

Solemnly the twins nodded, then giggled as their sister led them from the bakery.

"I'll unload the milk and eggs," Rolf mumbled.

"I'll give you a hand," Jeremiah said, following the boy out to the street. "Wouldn't want to make you late for school," he added with a glance back at Pleasant.

Relieved and pleased—in spite of her lack of sleep—to have finally given Jeremiah the product he needed, Pleasant turned her attention to her regular baking. Almost by rote she took up the mound of dough she'd left to rise overnight and began dividing it into smaller lumps. From outside she could hear the metallic drumbeat of the milk canisters being moved from the wagon to the back stoop and the occasional jingle of harness as the horse impatiently stamped a hoof or shook off an annoying fly. Rolf and Jeremiah were talking, but in such low tones that she could not make out the words. She heard Jeremiah laugh and it made her smile. It occurred to her that he would be a good parent—kind and patient. *Not like Merle was,* she thought and shook it off as disloyal.

After a moment, she heard the clop of the horse's hooves moving around the side of the building. She sighed. Rolf had gotten so caught up in his conversation with Jeremiah that he had forgotten to bring in the eggs.

"Wait," she called, running to the back door and pushing open the screen just as the wagon disappeared. "The eggs," she explained when Jeremiah looked up at her.

"These eggs?" he asked, holding up the wooden crate that they used to transport the eggs from the henhouse to the bakery every morning. He grinned. "I told the boy to get on to school. After all, I wouldn't want to be responsible for making him have to explain himself to your sister. She strikes me as a no-nonsense, and no-excuses, teacher."

"Lydia is an excellent teacher," Pleasant replied, unable to keep the shadow of defensiveness from her tone. She couldn't help wondering if in time, Jeremiah Troyer would come to understand that life here was difficult and people were quite serious about their work.

"I'm sure she is and as such she would find it hard to believe an excuse such as 'Sorry I'm late, Fraulein. I had to taste some ice cream cone samples.'" His voice had risen to a ridiculous falsetto with the excuse.

Pleasant fought a smile and held the door for him to carry in the egg crate. "Just set it there," she said, motioning to a side counter. "Thank you for helping Rolf with the delivery. He takes his studies very seriously and really hates being late—for anything."

"A good quality." She could feel his eyes on her as if he were studying her. "You're a good mother, Pleasant."

"They are good children."

"You and your husband had no children together?" He sucked in a breath and added, "I apologize. That is not my business."

She focused on filling the row of tin loaf pans lined up like toy soldiers along the edge of the long worktable. "It's all right. No, we were not blessed. We were married only a short time before his accident."

"My great-uncle John said he was kicked by a horse?"

"Yes."

"I'm sorry for your loss. It must be hard for you and the children."

"Yes."

"My mother…after my father died…she…his death was very hard on her," he said. "I don't think she was strong enough to manage the way you seem to have done."

"Your family went to live with your father's brother?"

Jeremiah nodded and she did not miss the way his normally amiable features hardened in a way that reminded her of Merle's face whenever he thought of something unpleasant. "My uncle." He bit off each syllable as if the words left a bad taste in his mouth. He turned his attention to studying the contents of the shelves that lined the kitchen walls. An uncomfortable silence settled over the room like the fine flour dust that covered every surface.

"May I ask you a question?" Pleasant ventured.

"Of course."

"Why have you never married?" She felt the heat rise to her cheeks. She must be overtired to ask such a thing and wished with all her being that she could take back the words. It was the kind of thing Greta would ask, although her younger half-sister would do so with a flirtatious lilt to her voice.

But Jeremiah seemed unmoved by the personal nature of her question. He chuckled and shrugged. "Some men are not meant to settle down."

"You're very good with children," she said.

"I like children. They give me hope for a better future for all of us." He smiled. "Young Rolf, for example. And Bettina. She will be an exceptional young woman." He pushed himself away from the counter where he had been leaning and watching her work. "By the way, I asked Rolf to come by the shop after school. I have some work to be done—washing the front window and such. Is that all right?"

"Did he agree?"

"Not really. He said we'd have to ask you first. So I'm asking."

"It's all right as long as he is home before dusk to take care of his chores there." Pleasant cracked an egg and shifted the halves back and forth until the white had run into a small dish. She set the yolk in a second dish then dampened a pastry brush with the egg white and brushed the tops of the loaves of uncooked bread. She was aware that Jeremiah was watching her and her hand shook. "Was there something else?"

"Well, yeah. I mean, don't you want to talk about the next steps for making the cones? Now that we have the recipe we have to figure out how best to create the actual product."

"I thought that I would…"

"Do you have a waffle iron?" He glanced around the shelves of the kitchen as if searching for the instrument.

"Yes, at home," she replied.

"Peter Osgood had this way of making cones on a waffle iron and then rolling them into a cone just at the right moment."

"That sounds like a lot of work," Pleasant said as she set the tin loaf pans into the oven and then wiped away drops of perspiration from her temples with the back of one hand. "How many cones will you need for your grand opening?"

He shrugged. "How many folks live here—I mean, in the Amish district?"

"Counting children? Around a hundred and twenty."

She watched as he mentally calculated the need. "A gross then just to be on the safe side."

She tried not to show her surprise. "You know best, of course," she murmured.

"But you don't agree?"

"It's just that with hard times and all, even the people here have had to watch pennies. I don't think you can really count on every single person buying ice cream from you on your opening day."

His eyes twinkled when she might have expected a frown. "But what if the ice cream were free?"

"Free? You cannot do business by giving away your wares, Jeremiah."

He chuckled. "Ah, Pleasant, once they have a taste of my ice cream and your shoo-fly cones? Why, we'll have regular customers for as long as we're in business." He picked up the last piece of her samples and studied it for a moment. "Do you think you could make a smaller version? A size just large enough to hold about a heaping tablespoon of ice cream?"

"I suppose, but why…"

"If we did smaller cones, people could sample more than one flavor of ice cream. We could do a survey and see which flavor was the most popular, and then…"

He glanced at her and then popped the last bit of the sample cookie into his mouth. "I see that you remain unconvinced, but mark my words, come the grand opening and you're going to be making me a gross of cones every week just to satisfy the people living here in Celery Fields, Pleasant." He grinned at her. "And that doesn't begin to count the *Englisch,* who will come once I hand out samples to the guys down at the ice plant."

"Speaking of which, shouldn't you be on your way to work by now?"

Jeremiah headed for the door, then paused to tip two fingers to his hat in a mock salute. "One gross," he repeated as he left the bakery. "You'll be convinced I'm right once you see them line up for ice cream," he called.

Pleasant was convinced of only one thing—as she had suspected all along, Jeremiah Troyer was a dreamer.

Chapter Seven

The grand opening of Troyer's Creamery and Confection Shop took place on a Saturday afternoon in early November when most of the community's residents traditionally gathered in town to do their marketing and other shopping for the coming week. And as he had predicted, the line for free samples of Jeremiah's ice cream stretched out the door and down the street past Yoder's Dry Goods and the hardware store nearly to Pleasant's house. The weather was perfect—sunny without a hint of the usual humidity so typical of Florida. A perfect day for ice cream.

Everyone—even Hilda Yoder—seemed to agree that Jeremiah had planned the perfect opening for his new business. "It's all so very exciting," Hilda gushed when she peeked into the back door of the bakery.

And it certainly sounded that way. Pleasant could hear children racing up and down the street squealing with delight over their favorite flavor. And outside the steamed-up kitchen windows and open doors, she caught glimpses of adults laughing and visiting as they licked ice cream from the tiny cones that Pleasant had created for the occasion.

Of course, Pleasant was so busy in the bakery kitchen turning out batch after batch of regular-size cones that she had to rely on the reports of her half sisters and the children. Lydia and Greta had been recruited by Gunther to help with the baking. They also carried trays of still-warm cones from the bakery to the creamery and then returned with empty trays that they set to refilling. Bettina stirred batch after batch of the batter while the twins sat with their grandfather and tallied up the number of outgoing cones on the hand-operated adding machine he kept on his desk in one corner of the kitchen.

From time to time Pleasant was aware of Jeremiah's laughter wafting between the two shops as he stood at the makeshift counter he'd set up on his shop's front stoop and scooped up ice cream for his customers. He had recruited Rolf to help him and assigned Hannah's son Caleb the task of making sure that no child got into line for a second sample ahead of someone who had not yet been served. And after less than two hours, Jeremiah had sent word that he was going to need more regular-size cones. It seemed that after tasting a sample, people were insisting on buying a full-size cone filled with their favorite flavor and Jeremiah was clearly determined not to disappoint anyone.

In spite of her exhaustion, Pleasant did not mind the ongoing work. She felt as if she were helping to create something that had nothing to do with waffle cones. She was working with Jeremiah and her family to offer the people of Celery Fields a kind of a reprieve from the months of poor crops and hard times that had plagued the small community for over a year now. Jeremiah Troyer had given the people of Celery Fields a great deal more than ice cream. At least for this one afternoon, he had given them a glimpse of better times to come. He had dished up hope.

"Jeremiah says we can stop now," Greta announced as she clattered an empty metal tray onto the table and collapsed on a bench. "He's completely run out of ice cream." There was a rumble of excited chatter from outside and Greta was instantly on her feet grabbing Bettina's hand. "Come on. He's going to announce the winning flavor."

Gunther and the twins hurried after Greta and Bettina, leaving a long tail of adding machine paper curled across the desk. "Are you coming?" Pleasant's father asked but she noticed that he did not wait for her reply.

She walked to the front of the bakery and stood in the open doorway. The crowd had clustered together in front of the creamery and Jeremiah was standing in the midst of them, his smile rivaling the sun for brightness. He held up his hands calling for quiet.

"Thank you, my friends," he said as the chattering throng grew quiet and mothers hushed their small children. "You have made me feel welcomed from the day I arrived, but never more so than today. The flavor you have chosen as the most popular today is…" A hush fell over the crowd. "Plain old vanilla," Jeremiah announced and those gathered around him broke into applause. "I feel so blessed," he continued once the crowd had quieted again. "I would like to ask my great-uncle Bishop Troyer if he would lead us all in a prayer of thanksgiving." He made room for John to join him and as every head bowed, Jeremiah looked over to where Pleasant was standing. And just before she bowed her head, Pleasant had the oddest feeling that everyone else had melted away and there was only Jeremiah—and her.

Forgive me, she prayed silently, shocked at her romantic foolishness. She forced her attention away from the memory of Jeremiah's gaze meeting her own. The half smile that had not quite blossomed across his handsome features. The question that seemed written in his expression. But try as she might to take in the words of thanksgiving that the bishop was offering, she could not seem to keep herself from peeking out beneath lowered lashes. She told herself it was only to confirm her silly imaginings. She saw that Jeremiah had bowed his head as well, but his eyes remained fixed on her.

The success of the opening of the creamery and confectionary had been far beyond anything Jeremiah had imagined. The people had come, drawn no doubt by the promise of free samples. But then they had returned, counting out their pennies to pay for a second cone of ice cream, sharing this larger treat with sweethearts or spouses or grandparents. For every full-size cone he sold, Jeremiah gave away another free sample. He had barely had time to look up but was aware that Pleasant kept a steady supply of freshly baked—and still warm— cones coming his way. Right up until he scraped the last scoop of ice cream from the bottom of the container, Rolf was handing him one cone after another.

"That's it," he said as he filled the last of the small sample cones and handed it to a little girl, a miniature of her mother in a dark cotton dress, a black apron and a stiff white *kapp* that hid most of her brilliant red hair. He turned his attention to Greta. "Go tell your sister that she can stop for today. We are out of ice cream."

Greta took off at a run while Rolf solemnly set about
to clean the ice cream scoops and the pails that had held
the various flavors. From the porch of Yoder's store, Jeremiah heard a groan as the little girl announced that she
had just been given the very last cone. He stepped forward prepared to apologize, but then the crowd had let
out a cheer and toasted him with raised half-eaten shoo-
fly cones. He could not recall a time in his life when he
had felt such happiness and he wondered for one brief
moment if indeed his success here would have finally
been enough to convince his uncle that he was not the
failure the older man had always labeled him.

He shook off the thought and scanned the crowd. He
saw his great-uncle and called him forward, but it was
not the community's bishop that he'd wanted most to
share this day with. It was the woman who had helped
to make it all possible. It was Pleasant Obermeier. In her
quiet efficient way, she had delivered everything he had
asked of her—the unique recipe that would set his business apart, the cones perfectly formed and to whatever
scale he required, and a steady supply of them. All without complaint or excuse. She was a remarkable woman
and he wanted to thank her but she was nowhere among
the men, women and children who crowded around his
shop.

Jeremiah frowned and then a movement at the entrance to the bakery caught his eye. She was leaning
against the doorjamb, her arms folded into her apron,
a bemused smile on her face as she observed a scene
that had to be unlike anything she'd ever witnessed in
the community before. Suddenly, the distance between
them seemed far too great and he wanted to go to her,

to tell her what her help had meant to him, to share this moment with her.

She looked over at him and he felt for a moment as if she had understood, but then she frowned and bowed her head, shaking it slightly as if admonishing herself for some wrongdoing. He wondered what this woman could ever do wrong. He thought about the way that she was raising four children—none of them her own. He recalled the way Gunther was practically incapable of making a decision without uttering the words, "We'll see what Pleasant thinks." He thought about the Hadwells and the way they had hinted that Merle Obermeier had been a difficult man.

He felt a bond to Pleasant that had nothing to do with ice cream cones. He marveled at her strength, her boundless energy, her courage to face whatever God might bring her way. As a boy he had often wished that his own mother might take a stand in favor of her children and against the tyranny with which his uncle had reigned. He bowed his head in shame. His mother had done her best to maintain peace in a house that broiled with constant turmoil.

John Troyer took his position as bishop seriously and when asked to pray, he tended to drone on for some time. Most people had grown used to it and kept their heads bowed but in spite of the invitation he had extended for his great-uncle to offer a prayer, Jeremiah seemed incapable of keeping his attention focused on the words. Instead, he kept his head lowered but looked at Pleasant. She was not a beauty in the usual sense. She was too tall, too thin and far too earnest. But, oh, on those rare occasions when she smiled, how it lit her features.

Her deep brown eyes sparkled and there was the hint of a dimple in the left corner of her mouth.

She caught him watching her and he looked away, turning his attention from her to the sorry state of his boots as he felt the heat of embarrassment rise to his cheeks. He had to take care, he reminded himself. More than once he had shown interest in a woman for her work ethic or her talent for quilting or cooking and his interest had been misinterpreted. It would not do for a woman like Pleasant—a woman who by all reports had a disappointing history in matters of the heart—to think that his interest was in any way…romantic.

"Amen," the crowd murmured in unison and then broke into smaller groups as they made their way back down the main street toward their buggies and wagons. "Amen," Jeremiah whispered, then turned to give John the traditional one-pump handshake Amish men shared. "Thank you."

"Thank you," John replied. "I'm not sure you understand how much this day has meant to the people of this community. It's been a long time since they were able to enjoy such an afternoon. God has blessed us all."

"I should go and settle my account with Gunther," Jeremiah said, nodding toward Pleasant's father who had returned to the bakery and was now holding a long streamer of paper. "Looks like I might have quite a tally there."

John laughed. "You'll join us for services tomorrow and Sunday dinner? We're meeting at Levi Harnisher's farm."

"I will," Jeremiah agreed. "Have a good evening, Uncle."

"And you."

Jeremiah watched his great-uncle head for home and realized that he was postponing the inevitable. He needed to go to the bakery and meet with Gunther and he still had not properly thanked Pleasant for what she had done to make the day such a success. He'd seen a wild orchid blooming in the tree behind the creamery, but such a gift would be far too open to misinterpretation— by her and anyone who might witness him giving it to her. No, a simple thank you was all that was called for.

He walked to the bakery planting each footstep in the soft sand of the street as if to break stride might cause him to lose his nerve and return to his own shop. "Herr Goodloe," he called out as he reached the steps leading up to the bakery entrance. "I expect you have a bill to present."

Gunther was grinning widely. "Indeed I do and you may just regret giving away all that free ice cream."

Jeremiah smiled and held out his hand. "Let's see the damage," he said. The count of full-size cones had reached several dozen and the smaller sample cones came to more than a gross.

Jeremiah let out a long low whistle and Gunther chuckled. "Told you," he said, then he sobered. "Thank you, Jeremiah. I won't pretend we can't use the money. It's a blessing in so many ways."

"I thought that the bakery was still…"

Gunther shook his head and glanced toward the door, then lowered his voice. "It's the farmers that are suffering. Those that joined the cooperative in the first place will be all right—they'll struggle but they'll make it."

"And Pleasant?"

Gunther looked away. "Moses Yoder tells me that with the mucklands pretty much dried up, the crops will suffer. The other farms—those that are part of the co-operative—have the advantage of the drainage system built a few years back. But Merle was one stubborn man when it came to having anything to do with outsiders." He sighed heavily. "Unless we have an unusually wet month, there's not much sense in Pleasant trying to plant a winter crop."

"I had no idea," Jeremiah said and felt ashamed of the triumph he'd been feeling over his own good fortune. "What can I do to help?"

Gunther shook his head. "We'll get past this. Pleasant knows she and the kids always have a place with me and they own the house and land free and clear, although certainly there's no market for selling a house or land these days. But she's stubborn. Her mother was the same." He smiled at the memory, then he grasped Jeremiah's hand. "The kids know nothing though and they had a hard enough time of things when their father was alive. I know Rolf is helping out some at your place, but..."

"I wouldn't discuss such a thing with the boy—or anyone," Jeremiah assured the older man.

Gunther smiled with relief. He was something of a talker and Jeremiah expected that he regretted having revealed so much.

"Now then," Jeremiah said, "shall we settle this account?"

Gunther grinned and led the way into the bakery's kitchen. Pleasant busied herself directing her half sisters and Bettina in cleaning up from the day's baking and preparing the kitchen for a fresh start come Monday morning. She glanced at him and nodded but said nothing as Jeremiah followed Gunther to his desk in the corner and took a seat.

"Check my figures," Gunther advised as he pushed a paper filled with penciled calculations across the desk to Jeremiah.

"Looks fine," Jeremiah replied, barely glancing at the paper. His mind was still reeling with the notion that while he had been pushing her to come up with a recipe for ice cream cones, she had been facing serious problems of her own and never said a word. Oh, once or twice she had alluded to the need to attend to her own business, but he had assumed she meant getting the standard bakery orders filled. It had never occurred to him that she might be talking about the huge tract of land her late husband had acquired and left for her to manage with Moses Yoder's help. No wonder half the time the woman looked as if she could use a good night's sleep.

He opened the small tin box that he'd used as the cash box for the opening and counted out the money he owed Gunther. "I'll be closed tomorrow, of course, and I think Monday as well." He laughed. "It will take some time to make more ice cream and I'll have to work on that between my shifts at the ice plant and making my regular deliveries. If you could deliver half the week's order of cones on Tuesday and then the rest on Friday, that ought to work out fine."

"Ja," Gunther replied as he stashed the money in a worn cloth bag and placed it in a desk drawer that he locked.

"Will that be all right, Pleasant?" Jeremiah asked.

She glanced up from scrubbing the last of the pots. "Of course," she replied, the words clipped and impatient as if he had expressed some doubt in her ability to deliver the goods.

Jeremiah could not help but wonder what had happened in the woman's past to make her so defensive, so quick to assume that she was being questioned. She turned her attention back to her work, quietly instructing Bettina in how best to dry the large container without dripping water all over the floor. Where her tone with him had been abrupt and defensive, he noticed that when she spoke to the girl her voice was soft and gentle and she was quick to give Bettina a smile when she followed instructions to the letter.

Gunther pushed his chair away from the desk and stood up. "It was a good day for the ice cream business," he noted as he offered Jeremiah a handshake.

Jeremiah stood as well and accepted Gunther's hand, knowing that what went unspoken was the fact that the two of them had just launched a kind of partnership that was sure to benefit both their businesses. "And the bakery business," he added with a smile.

He was reluctant to leave until he had thanked Pleasant properly for all her help. Yet at the same time he didn't want to embarrass her by doing so in front of her father, half sisters and the children. He decided it might be best to write her a note and leave it for her to find on Monday when she came to open the bakery for the day. "Have a good evening," he said, including everyone in his leave-taking. "I'll see you all at services tomorrow?"

"Yes. At Levi's farm," Gunther said as he walked with Jeremiah to the door.

Jeremiah glanced back toward the sink, but Pleasant was focused—as always it seemed—on her work.

Men, Pleasant thought as she scrubbed a nonexistent stain from the sink. Her father and Jeremiah had congratulated one another as if the success of the day had been entirely their doing. She was well aware that jealousy was unworthy of her and she would surely regret the uncharitable feelings she entertained at this moment, but really. Did it not occur to either one of them that she and Bettina and Lydia and Greta had contributed to the day's triumph? Certainly if they had failed to keep up with Jeremiah's constant need for more cones, he could have found an alternative. After all, she had seen the glass sundae dishes and soda glasses that lined the shelves in his shop. But still, for the sake of the others, the man surely could have given some sign that he recognized their efforts.

Pride goeth before a fall, she chastised herself. The arrangement to make ice cream cones was a business collaboration between her father and Jeremiah. Simple as that. She was the baker in her father's business. Period.

But she could not erase the memory of how Jeremiah's eyes had lit up the day she presented him with the sample cookies. She could not forget how he had come to her house—not her father's—in the dead of night because he had come up with an idea for making the cones. And she had thought often about the hunched lonely figure sitting on the step of the bakery in the predawn darkness waiting for her to deliver the news of whether or not she had been successful.

"Mama?"

Pleasant looked over her shoulder at Bettina standing with Rolf and the twins. It was clear that they had asked something and were waiting for her reply.

"I'm sorry," she said, drying her hands on a damp dish towel. She smiled at them. "Are you four ready for some supper or have you completely spoiled your appetites with ice cream?"

"Aunt Hilda and Uncle Moses have asked us to come for supper," Bettina reminded her.

The invitation had gone completely out of Pleasant's head. "I promised to bring dessert," she murmured.

"It's all right," Bettina assured her. "I boxed up the last dozen sugar cookies earlier so they wouldn't get sold as everything else did."

Rolf glanced at the clock on the wall behind them. Hilda—like her brother Merle—did not like for anyone to be late.

"We'll have to hurry then," Pleasant said, smoothing back the twins' hair and scrubbing their faces with the damp dish towel. "Where's your Grandpa Gunther?"

"He's outside talking to some people. He said we should go on and he would make sure everything was closed up."

Pleasant nodded. She knew that this meant her father would collect the money that Jeremiah had given him and that he'd locked away for safekeeping in the desk. He wouldn't leave it in the bakery overnight. Times were too uncertain to trust that some vagrant might not come looking for food and decide to see if there was any cash on the premises while he was at it.

"All right, then we'd best hurry." She held hands with the twins and followed Rolf and Bettina out the door and up the street to the home of Moses and Hilda Yoder. The house was not as large as Merle's house, but in many ways it was far more welcoming. The Yoder children were all playing in the yard when they arrived and Pleasant sent her four children to join them while she took the box of cookies and walked around the side of the house and into Hilda's kitchen.

"I'm sorry we're late," she apologized, even though

they had made it with minutes to spare. "It took longer than I thought to…"

"Moses needs to see you in the front room," Hilda said without preamble. "Supper can wait."

Pleasant set the box of cookies on the sideboard and walked down the short passageway that led from the kitchen past the stairway to the front of the house. Moses Yoder was seated in the overstuffed chair near the fireplace. When he saw Pleasant, he set aside the newspaper he'd been reading and rose to greet her. "Come sit here," he invited, indicating Hilda's rocking chair opposite him.

His tone and demeanor gave Pleasant every indication that he was about to deliver news she didn't want to hear.

"It's the farm," she said as she collapsed wearily into the rocking chair and faced him.

"Yes. I'm sorry, Pleasant, but I see no possibility that we can salvage it. Perhaps if Merle had been willing to join the cooperative, there would be some way…"

"I understand," she assured him and set the chair to rocking as she stared blankly out the front window. Outside, she could hear Merle's children laughing and squealing as they played a game of hide-and-seek with their cousins. She had done the one thing that would mark her as a failure in Merle's eyes more than anything else. She had failed to protect the farm that had been the mark of his success as a husband and father. The land that he had preached to Rolf would one day be his. The legacy that even as she laid her husband to rest, Pleasant had promised him she would protect.

Moses cleared his throat. "The drought can't last forever," he said, although what comfort this might offer Pleasant she couldn't fathom. "And you own the property free and clear."

She glanced at him and saw his misery. "Moses, you have done what you could and I am grateful for that. Please don't blame yourself. This is God's will and while it may be difficult for us to understand now, in time…"

"What I'm saying, Pleasant, is that perhaps in a year or so, the land will have value. Until then you have the house and you have the community."

She understood that he was telling her that her neighbors would help out. If there were repairs to be done, they would help. It was their way. "If we have a wet winter, then perhaps…"

Moses shook his head. "Even so, it will take more than one season before the soil is revived enough to support crops of any sort, Pleasant."

She nodded. "Thankfully, our needs are small," she whispered even as she thought of the four growing children. But she forced a smile as she met Moses's gaze. "We'll be fine. Thank you again, Moses."

"We are here for you, Pleasant," he told her. "You know that. The entire community."

"I do and I thank God for that blessing." She stood up and he did as well. "I should help Hilda," she said and fled from the room before her brother-in-law could see the tears that had already begun leaking down her cheeks.

Chapter Eight

At services the following morning, Pleasant felt as if she were literally dragging herself along. At supper the night before, Hilda and Moses had exchanged several meaningful glances, but had blessedly allowed the chatter of the children to dominate the conversation. And she was grateful to them for that. It certainly was not Hilda's habit to be so respectful and on reflection, it made Pleasant think that her loss was far more devastating than she had yet realized.

Exhausted as she had been after a day filled with endless baking, she had stayed up long after the children were asleep going over and over her household accounts. She had taken away what little remained of the money that in the past had flowed into her accounts from the sale of the crops. Before the drought that had been a sizeable sum, but over the past year it had dwindled significantly. She had never taken anything from the bakery. That was her father's business and it had provided for her before her marriage to Merle, but after that, her husband had provided whatever she or the children might need. And after his death, the legacy he had left behind had continued to fill their needs.

But now the resources for bringing cash into the household had dried up with the land that stretched uselessly beyond her back door for acres and acres. It was worthless now according to Moses, unlikely to come back to life any time in the foreseeable future. The bakery was barely bringing in enough to cover the cost of supplies and provide for Gunther and her half sisters. Of course, with the business that Jeremiah was bringing them there was always the possibility that the two families could pool their resources and make do. But Jeremiah Troyer was a dreamer and the likelihood that he would need the steady supply of cones he had ordered was remote at best.

Yes, the grand opening had gone well beyond anything she might have imagined, but that was one day and the reality of the times told her that it could not possibly last.

Pleasant went over and over the numbers and in the end came up with the same result. She and the children would become dependent on others—their charity, their hand-me-downs, their pity. *I hate this,* she had thought miserably as she laid her head on her folded arms and fell asleep.

She had awakened at her usual hour on Sunday, her back stiff from sitting in the hard kitchen chair all night. She had made breakfast for the children and supervised their preparations for attending services. For herself, she had taken only a cup of strong black coffee. If they were going to have to cut back then she was determined to make sure that the children had plenty to eat. By the time Rolf had driven them to the Harnisher farm in the buggy, they were already late and Pleasant was feeling jittery and out of sorts and hardly in the mood to consider what God might need of her in the days to come. For it was their way, she sternly reminded herself as she climbed down from the buggy and herded the children across the yard, to come to worship in a spirit of understanding how they might best serve God—not how He might remove their burden.

One lesson that Jeremiah had learned growing up in a small community was that even pious people could not resist the temptation of gossip. So when he arrived for services at the Harnisher farm the next morning, he wasn't surprised to see people gathered in small groups, their heads inclined toward one another, their combined whispers sounding like the hum of bees as he parked his buggy and walked across the yard. What confused him was that their conversation seemed to focus on something serious rather than the retelling of the grand opening of his shop a day earlier as he might have expected. Even the children seemed subdued as if they had gleaned from their parents and other adults the need to speak only in whispers and to sit quietly together rather than running about.

Fearing that some tragedy had befallen one of the church members, he went inside the modest home looking for his uncle. Along the way he realized that he was scanning the faces of the similarly garbed women looking for Pleasant. There was no sign of her. Had she taken ill? Or perhaps it was the children. He quickened his step moving down the hallway from the rear entrance of the house to the front.

"Guten morgen," Levi Harnisher greeted him.

Jeremiah had met the Harnisher family when he and Levi had discussed arrangements for Levi to provide the cream that Jeremiah would need to make his ice cream. Levi had laughingly told him that he had tried his hand at raising the celery and other produce that others had raised with great success. "Then my Hannah—and several others—suggested that with my background in handling animals for the circus it might be wiser to concentrate on raising horses. Later, I added the dairy herd. How can I help you?"

Jeremiah had felt an immediate bond with the man and took no time at all to lay out his need for a steady supply of fresh cream.

"That I can do," Levi had assured him and they had settled on the deal with a simple handshake.

And because Jeremiah trusted Levi not to think he was prying but simply concerned, he asked the question that was uppermost in his mind. "Has something happened to Mrs. Obermeier?"

Levi raised his eyebrows and Jeremiah realized that it was indeed odd for him to be inquiring about the widow so directly.

"It's just that folks seem to be abuzz about something and I thought I heard her name mentioned and I noticed she's not here for services."

His explanation seemed to satisfy Levi who was nodding as he glanced toward the lane that led from the main road to his farm. "She's with my wife." He nodded toward a closed door down a short hall. "She had some bad news yesterday." He hesitated, then added, "It's the farm. Her late husband refused to join the Palmer cooperative. He was a stubborn man."

"But surely her late husband made some provision—
if not for her than for the children."

"It's a long story, but several years ago the Palmer
family of Chicago came here for the winter and bought
a large tract of the muckland that borders the land that
Merle bought a few years later. The Palmers put in miles
of canals for drainage purposes and started selling pieces
of the land off to individual farmers with the understanding that those farmers would join the Palmer Farms
Growers Association."

"Sounds like a good deal."

Levi glanced toward the room where his wife, Hannah, had emerged and was signaling to him. "It was a
good deal and for those who took it, the arrangement
was a lifesaver. But Merle was one stubborn man and
determined to go it alone. And for a number of years he
did all right for himself, but he never put in the canals
and drainage that might have saved his land during these
hard times." He shook his head. "Excuse me, Jeremiah.
My wife needs my help."

Out in the yard church members had divided by gen-
der. The women filed in through the back door while
the men entered from the front. Separately they took
their places on the hard wooden benches that had been
unloaded from the wagon used to transport them from
home to home and set up in the Harnisher's front room.
Jeremiah lingered near the front hallway watching for
Pleasant until he heard the congregation start to sing the
opening hymn. He had the urge to walk down the hall
to see for himself that she was all right. But that would
only embarrass her and provide fresh fodder for the community's rumor mill.

He took his place at the end of the second row of

benches closest to the front door. As the hymn ended and
John and the preacher entered the room, he thought he
heard the creak of a door opening and closing. A minute
later he saw Pleasant lead the twins to a place in the last
row of benches. Bettina and Rolf had already squeezed
in on benches occupied by older girls and older boys,
respectively. Jeremiah slid over to make room for Gunther, who sat down next to him with a heavy sigh and
a weary smile.

By tradition, Amish services ran for three hours, but
on this particular Sunday the service seemed intermi-
nable to Jeremiah. He had trouble concentrating on the
sermons—the first being something about loving your
neighbor while the main sermon delivered by his great-
uncle John was on the topic of accepting that God would
provide—in hard times and good. He couldn't help wondering if that promise was bringing Pleasant any comfort at all.

But his main problem with concentrating on the service was that he was overcome with guilt. How many
times over the past weeks had he gone to the bakery—or
even her farmhouse—thinking only of what he needed?
When had he ever stopped to think about the responsibilities she had taken on in raising her late husband's
four children by another woman? Had he once considered what she might be facing because of the drought
and the crops that had failed?

Not once, he thought as he hung his head and studied
the polished planks of the Harnisher's floor. He owed
her far more than the note of thanks he had placed on
the bakery door that morning. He owed her an apology.

Having settled on a plan, Jeremiah was restless for the
remainder of the service. So much so that twice others

glanced his way and he realized that he was impatiently tapping one foot. He stilled his foot with an apologetic glance at those next to him and forced his concentration to the sermon.

As soon as the service ended, the women—Pleasant with them—headed off to the kitchen to lay out the communal meal they would all share. Older children took charge of their younger siblings while the men set up the benches for the meal. Because some of the benches would be stacked double to form tables, there would not be enough seating for everyone and so they would eat in two shifts. All of this happened without the need for instruction. It was a ritual the congregation had performed for countless Sundays over the years.

Jeremiah helped set the tables and seating all the while keeping an eye out for Pleasant. His need to see her and apologize was nearly overpowering. And yet he knew that to go to the kitchen, to ask to speak with her in front of others, would be the worst possible thing he might do. It would not only embarrass Pleasant, it would raise questions about what kind of man he was. After all, he was still something of a stranger in Celery Fields and Amish communities throughout the country differed widely in what traditions and interpretations of the unwritten laws of the faith—the Orndung—dictated. Something that might hardly raise an eyebrow back in Ohio might be grounds for real concern here in Florida. Either way, he was fairly sure that a single man taking an unmarried—even widowed—woman aside for a private conversation would definitely not be in the realm of proper behavior.

So when he saw Pleasant Obermeier emerge from the kitchen carrying a large bowl of potato salad, he headed in the opposite direction and forced himself to keep his distance for the remainder of the meal.

Pleasant had endured the genial chatter of the other women trying to disguise their pity. She was well aware that everyone knew what had kept her awake most of the night and made her late for services. She was also aware that this was their way of being sympathetic and supportive. She saw it in their eyes filled with the questions they would not ask. What would she do now? Could she find a buyer for the land or perhaps the house?

"If only Merle had…" one woman began in a hushed voice.

"Perhaps the Palmers," another woman whispered.

But Moses had told her that the land was useless for growing anything and what would the wealthy Chicago family want with a house that was already badly in need of painting and repair?

"We should have a frolic," Hannah announced as a silence fell over the food preparations and everyone seemed at a loss for some way to show Pleasant their concern. "Tomorrow at Pleasant's house?"

The other women hesitated, glancing uncertainly at Pleasant. A frolic was what Amish women called an occasion when they gathered at one of the group's houses and spent the entire day cleaning or cooking or quilting or sometimes all three. The shared work and opportunity to socialize gave the occasion its name.

"The bakery," Pleasant gently reminded her friend.

"Oh, the bakery can last one day without you," Hannah insisted. "Besides, you've always said yourself that Mondays are slow and after the grand opening of the creamery yesterday, I doubt anyone has the money to buy extra baked goods."

"I'll say," Hilda Yoder exclaimed. "I told my brood that if they wanted ice cream then they were facing vinegar pie for a month."

Several women nodded and all eyes returned to Pleasant. She saw Hannah's suggestion for what it was—a way for the women to do something for her without it seeming like charity. "I suppose," she said slowly, "I do have laundry that piled up what with spending so much extra time at the bakery and all." And then she smiled for the first time since hearing Moses's report. "And Papa suggested I needed to get some rest. A day away from the bakery might be just the medicine I need."

The women smiled and were soon engaged in plans for the gathering. Before long, they had come up with a list of things they would do that went well beyond washing and ironing, and would take much longer than a day's hours to accomplish.

"Well, what we don't finish at Pleasant's we can simply move to my house or Hilda's or someone else's," Hannah said. "Our Monday frolic," she announced. "It could become a regular thing."

Pleasant laughed and shook her head. "I think that husband of yours has influenced you to think in the same grand scale of things that he used when he owned the circus, Hannah."

Her friend blushed as she did whenever Levi was mentioned, even after all this time. Pleasant could not help but wonder if any of the other women gathered around her had experienced such a depth of pure devotion that Hannah shared with Levi. Was that unusual, she couldn't help wondering. Or was the cold silence that she had shared with Merle more the norm? Or more likely most marriages fell somewhere in between. It hardly mattered since she was now widowed and unlikely to ever marry again—at least not for love.

You didn't marry for love when you married Merle, she reminded herself. No, she had married for companionship and security. A companionship that had never blossomed and a security that was now as fragile as the fine dust blowing off the dried up fields that surrounded her home.

"Excuse me," she murmured, still struggling with the overwhelming burden that the news about the farm had thrust upon her. "I need to check on the twins," she added, picking up a bowl of potato salad as she hurried from the room.

The men glanced up from their conversation as she set the bowl on a makeshift table, but then looked immediately away. She supposed that they were also talking about her. She looked around for the children and saw that Bettina was sitting on the porch surrounded by the twins and other small children, telling them a story. She would make a wonderful teacher one day. She looked for Rolf and saw him with Hannah's son Caleb and some other boys out near the barn.

And then she saw Jeremiah. He was walking out toward the barn. She saw how Rolf's face brightened when he saw Jeremiah coming his way. The time that Rolf had spent helping Jeremiah had been good for the boy. Perhaps she had made a mistake in not accepting Jeremiah's offer to hire the boy for regular chores. At least then she would be able to count on Rolf's continued exposure to the businessman's good influence. And now that the creamery was officially opened, the likelihood that he would be stopping by the bakery or farmhouse to talk about cone recipes was remote.

She would miss that. As exasperated as she had sometimes been with him, his visits had always left her feeling a little lighter, a little more hopeful. Perhaps she would speak with Rolf, assure herself that he could manage his schoolwork, the chores at home and help out at the creamery. After all, work with Jeremiah would teach the boy a trade and now that the farm was for all intents and purposes not the future that Merle had imagined for his eldest child, Rolf would need to find some way to earn his living.

Bettina could teach until she married and Rolf could go into business—perhaps take over the bakery, she thought and silently thanked God for showing her a path that just might lead to a secure future for Rolf and Bettina. The twins had time. She breathed in the warm air and felt better. They would be all right. With God's help she would find a way for her children to be safe and none the wiser of the calamity that had befallen them.

Having decided on a plan, she joined the other mothers in gathering the children and helping the little ones fill their plates, then refilling the serving dishes so that the adults could eat. In the familiarity of routine, the afternoon passed and soon her father was driving them back to the farm.

As soon as he called for the horse to stop in the yard, the children scampered out of the buggy and ran off to change out of their good clothes.

"Pleasant," Gunther said as she climbed down from the buggy, "you can always move in with me," he murmured, his eyes looking straight ahead instead of at her.

"I know that, Papa, but we're going to be all right," she assured him.

He flicked a glance at her and then his mouth tightened as he resumed his gaze into space. "The bakery does a steady business. Perhaps…"

The bakery business had suffered along with every other business in Celery Fields. The standing orders from restaurants and small grocers in nearby Sarasota that had been the mainstay of their business had dwindled to only half what they had been a few years earlier. Without Lydia's small stipend as the community's teacher, Pleasant knew that her father and half sisters would be struggling to make ends meet. "These are hard times, Papa," she said. "But we've seen them before and we no doubt will see them again."

He nodded.

"The thing is before hard times can come again we must have some better times," she said, reminding him of what he had so often told her mother. "Otherwise, it's just hard times all the time." She reached up and placed her hand over his leathery skin. "We're going to be fine, Papa. All of us." And even as she spoke the words she felt an unexplainable comfort in hearing herself voice them.

On Monday, Jeremiah had decided that he would wait until after Rolf made his morning delivery to the bakery and the children were off to school before he went over to speak with Pleasant. He wasn't due at the ice plant until later that morning and he had rehearsed his speech several times, changing the words when he thought he was perhaps being too forward or showing that he might have listened to gossip about her.

He'd been up since before dawn but there had been no sign of her. Then he heard the familiar rumble of the wagon's wheels and went to the window. Gunther and Rolf unloaded the milk and eggs and carried them inside the bakery while Bettina held the reins and waited patiently in the wagon. There was no sign of the twins or of Pleasant. Perhaps the boys were ill, although they had certainly seemed fine after services.

He saw Rolf exit the bakery, nodding at some instruction that Gunther had offered, and then the boy climbed into the wagon with his sister and headed back to the farm. Jeremiah knew the routine. Most days Bettina would have taken her younger siblings to the Yoder house while Rolf delivered the milk and eggs. Then the two of them would return the wagon and then walk to the small wooden building behind Hadwell's hardware that served the community as its one-room schoolhouse.

Jeremiah collected his hat and strolled over to the bakery's kitchen door. As he passed a window, he saw Gunther sitting at his desk going over some orders.

"*Guten morgen,* Gunther," he called from outside the screen door using the Dutch-German that the older man seemed to prefer.

"Come in, Jeremiah," the older man boomed.

"Is everything all right?" Jeremiah asked. "I saw Rolf and Bettina earlier but not the twins. Are they ill?" It seemed best not to ask about Pleasant directly although in his heart that was the question uppermost.

Gunther smiled. "*Nein.* The women are having a frolic at Pleasant's today and she kept the twins with her since Hilda Yoder will be there and probably bringing her youngest three as well."

Jeremiah felt a mixture of relief and disappointment.

Relief that she was all right and disappointment that he would have to wait yet another day to see her and apologize for being so insensitive in the past. Gunther was rambling on and Jeremiah forced himself to pay attention.

"...expect the boy will be stopping by after school today. Unless, of course, you've changed your mind." He eyed Jeremiah, one gray bushy eyebrow arched.

"Changed my mind about...?"

"The job. Taking Rolf on as a helper in your business."

"I thought that Pleasant was not in favor of that idea."

Gunther shrugged then leaned in closer. "She would never want me to say so, but I gather that with the farm a loss and all, she's looking for some way to give the boy training that might stand him in good stead down the road. He's twelve now and the years go by fast. She understands that he's going to need a trade to make his way."

"I see."

"I told her he could work for me here, but she won't hear of it. Says he needs to work for somebody who isn't family. I reminded her that I'm not family except through marriage and really not even then when you consider that...."

"She wants Rolf to work for me?"

"Rolf wants to work for you," Gunther corrected. "She's just decided to give the idea her blessing."

Jeremiah's respect for Pleasant knew no bounds. No doubt her late husband had planned that his eldest son would take over the farm one day. No doubt Merle Obermeier had thought he was setting his son up for life when he bought the land and built the house. No doubt he'd envisioned one day when Rolf and his wife would manage the farm while he and Pleasant moved into a smaller dwelling next to the larger farmhouse to live out their later years.

But from what he'd been able to gather from Levi Harnisher and the comments of others the previous day, that wasn't going to happen. It would take years before the land could be brought to the point where it might yield crops again and in the meantime, Pleasant had already begun to consider how the future needed to change for Merle's children. "Have the boy stop by the creamery after school," Jeremiah said. "We'll see what we can work out."

Gunther nodded. "He's a good lad. A hard worker and bright."

"Then I'm certain that we can come to some arrangement that will suit," Jeremiah said. "You're sure that Pleasant approves?"

"Told me about it herself," Gunther replied. "Talked to the boy as well."

"All right then. As long as Pleasant is in favor."

Gunther shrugged. "What choice does she have?"

Rolf appeared at Jeremiah's back door later that afternoon. The boy kept his eyes on his shoes from the moment Jeremiah led him to the front of the shop and invited him to sit opposite him at one of the half dozen small round tables. "I understand that you would be interested in working for me, Rolf."

"Yes, sir," he murmured and it came out as more of a guess as to what might be the appropriate response than with any assurance.

Jeremiah leaned back in his chair, rocking it on its

back legs as he studied this boy who reminded him so much of himself at the same age. "You understand that there are conditions?"

"Yes, sir."

"You will be at the shop every Saturday morning at seven and weekdays as soon as you are finished with school…"

"I could skip school," Rolf ventured, hoping to please.

"No, sir. If things work out I expect that you will be working the cash register from time to time and I want you to know your figures."

"Yes, sir," Rolf replied, his eyes growing wide at the very idea that Jeremiah might entrust such a duty to him.

"If you are late, then I will dock you two hours pay."

"Yes, sir."

"At first you can wear your everyday clothes. You'll be mostly working in the back, churning the ice cream, washing dishes and the like."

"Yes, sir."

Jeremiah could not help but notice that with every response the boy sat a little straighter, spoke with more conviction and met his eyes more directly.

"Later—assuming business picks up—I'll need you serving customers and you'll need to make sure that you and your clothes are absolutely clean—especially your hands and under your fingernails."

"Yes, sir," the boy said and Jeremiah would not have been surprised if Rolf had snapped to attention and saluted him.

"Then we have a bargain?" He offered Rolf a handshake.

Rolf grinned and pumped Jeremiah's hand once. "Thank you, sir."

Jeremiah stood and Rolf scrambled to his feet as well. "Tomorrow after school and Saturday at seven o'clock sharp," he reminded him.

"Yes, sir." It was clear that Rolf was anxious to leave and share the good news with others.

"Rolf?"

"Sir?"

"Don't you want to know what the position pays?"

Rolf blushed slightly. "I forgot," he murmured.

Jeremiah named an hourly figure that made the boy look up at him in total disbelief. "Will that be agreeable?"

"Yes, sir."

"And if things work out, then on Saturdays you may take your choice of any leftover ice cream and share it with your family. I like to start the week fresh," Jeremiah explained.

Rolf looked as if he was about to explode with all the news he now had to share with his family. "That would be fine, sir," he managed, edging toward the door.

"Good. I'll see you after school tomorrow then."

Jeremiah couldn't help chuckling to himself as he watched Rolf run the entire distance from the ice cream shop to the farmhouse. He imagined him bursting into the house fairly exploding to share his news. He imagined Pleasant's delight and wished that he could witness the way her smile would surely ease the small lines of worry between her eyes—at least for a little while.

But certainly there was no smile in evidence when she appeared at his door not twenty minutes later.

"Exactly what do you think you're doing, Herr Troyer?" she demanded.

Chapter Nine

The very fact that Pleasant had made the trek from her house to the creamery, through town for everyone to observe with not a single thought for the way this would set tongues wagging once again, was clear evidence of how upset she was with Jeremiah. She did not break stride even when Moses Yoder called out a greeting. Nor did she so much as glance at the bakery where her father was closing up for the day.

She marched straight onto the front stoop of the creamery and pounded on the frosted glass of the front door, setting the closed sign that hung on a hook to rocking. She had not asked for his charity. No, she had sent Rolf to apply for a position that had been offered.

She knocked again.

The door opened and he stood there all six feet and more of him with his broad shoulders and that maddening smile that seemed a permanent part of his expression.

"Pleasant," he said, his eyes lighting with surprise and pleasure. "I…"

She brushed past him. "Please close the door," she

said and took the moment that it took him to do so to try and compose herself. She laced her fingers together and held her hands stiffly in front of her waist.

"You're upset," Jeremiah said and she almost laughed at the understatement.

"My family neither needs nor wants your charity," she burst out, forgetting everything she had planned to say, the calmness with which she had planned to say it.

"I don't understand." He pulled out a chair and offered it to her.

She ignored the gesture. Instead, she began to pace. "I don't know what you heard yesterday at the Harnishers. I have to believe that your intentions are only good, but you have overstepped."

"Your son applied for a vacancy at my shop. It is my understanding that he did so with your full approval. I interviewed the boy, found him up to the job and offered it to him. What exactly is the problem?"

"And you pay all of your employees so well?" She did not wait for an answer. "He is a boy who will run errands for you and do other chores—chores for which if they were his farm chores he would not expect to be paid. Even if he performed such tasks for a neighbor and the neighbor gave him a reward it would be a token— nothing more."

"This is not a household chore or neighborly errand. I have offered Rolf a job, Pleasant, with regular hours and regular duties. I have made that perfectly clear to the boy. He will work hard for the wages he earns and he has been told that if he fails to live up to the conditions I have set for the position, his pay will be docked. Again, what exactly is the problem?"

She felt confused. His words made sense and yet…

"Would it help if I were to start the boy at a lower wage until he proves himself?"

"No—yes—I don't know," she said and sank down into the chair he had pulled out for her.

He took the opportunity to take a chair opposite her and rest his elbows on the table leaning closer. "What's this all about really, Pleasant?" he asked and his voice had lost all of the businesslike tone with which he'd been presenting his arguments.

She studied her hands for a long moment not daring to look at him, not wanting to see the expression of concern that she knew softened his eyes. "I...tell me what you heard yesterday," she murmured.

"When I arrived I heard some snatches of conversation—about you and the farm. I asked Levi Harnisher what was going on and if you were all right. He told me about your late husband's refusal to join the Palmer family's cooperative and how he had not dug the canals that would help keep the land fertile in times of sustained drought. That's it."

"My husband always thought—never thought that it would get so bad. 'It's Florida,' he used to remind me. 'The rains will come,' he would say." She picked bits of dough from under her fingernail. "He was so wrong," she whispered and did not notice the tear that plopped onto the back of her hand.

But Jeremiah noticed. He pulled a clean white handkerchief from the pocket of his homespun trousers and laid it on the table between them.

"Thank you," she whispered as she picked it up and dabbed at her eyes.

"I wanted to apologize to you, Pleasant," Jeremiah said.

"No need."

"Not for this business about hiring Rolf. I need the help and I honestly had no idea of what a proper wage would be so I offered him what Peter Osgood paid me."

"What then?" she asked and looked up at him.

"Ever since I arrived I have been single-minded about setting up my business. It was selfish of me to consider only my needs and give no thought at all to what you might be facing. So when Gunther mentioned that you had given Rolf permission to apply for a position as my helper, I thought I had found a way to repay you without insulting you for all the work you did to make my grand opening a success." He smiled. "Guess I messed that up. But I want you to understand that I have always had every intention of hiring a boy and your son had shown traits that seemed to make him the perfect candidate for the job."

"I do understand that and I need for you to understand that I had my reasons for reconsidering your original offer to Rolf," she admitted. "I'm—we're—grateful for the opportunity."

"It seems to me that there's no real harm done here. I need help. Rolf seems eager to learn a trade. You're protecting his future by trying to prepare him for something other than farming."

He was making so much sense that Pleasant was having trouble remembering why she had been so upset in the first place. "Pride," she murmured.

"Excuse me?"

She stood up. "I let my pride get in the way," she said. "Thank you, Jeremiah. Rolf tells me that he's to report for his first day of work after school tomorrow." She moved toward the door and he reached around her to open it for her and walked with her out to the street. Across the way at Yoder's Dry Goods a figure moved away from the window and Pleasant sighed wearily.

"Now it is I who must apologize, Jeremiah," she said. "It seems that my impulsive action in coming here without the buffer of my father or the children could cause you some problems." She glanced toward Yoder's.

He smiled. "Do I look worried?"

"No, but perhaps you should be. After all, the people of Celery Fields are your prospective customers."

"Let me take care of that, Pleasant. It seems to me that you have more than enough on your mind at the moment. Get some rest."

His last words had been uttered as gently as a caress and on her way home, Pleasant couldn't help thinking that she felt more hopeful than she had earlier. Earlier, she had been torn between instantly understanding what the money that Jeremiah had offered would mean for them as a family, and her determination that she was the one responsible for providing what her children needed. But Jeremiah would hire a boy whether or not that boy was Rolf. He needed the help and because it was a job that carried certain responsibilities, it was only fair for the boy he hired to be paid. "He is thinking of his business—his needs, not yours," she told herself. And by the time she arrived at the farmhouse she had convinced herself that Jeremiah Troyer was not a man who offered charity. He was a businessman who would do what it took to be successful in a business that was by anyone's measure risky. Still, he would be a good influence on Rolf.

At supper all four children were unusually quiet—even the twins. *Little wonder,* Pleasant thought. The way she had stormed out of the house without a word almost before Rolf could finish delivering his news. She saw Bettina and Rolf exchange a look and then glance her way.

"Well," she said, forcing a brightness to her tone, "it would seem that we have something to celebrate tonight, but first let us bow our heads in silent prayer remembering to thank God for the many blessings he has shown our little family." She folded her hands in her lap and the children did the same. The twins squeezed their eyes closed but Pleasant saw Bettina glance at Rolf. Rolf only shrugged in reply.

"Amen," Pleasant murmured. She started to dish up meat and potatoes onto the stack of plates in front of her. She passed the first two to Bettina who cut up the meat for her younger brothers and then placed the plates in front of them. "Herr Troyer tells me you are to start work after school tomorrow," she said, handing Rolf his plate.

"I don't have to," he said, "if you've changed your mind, I mean."

"Nonsense. You have taken a position and you will do your best." She handed Bettina her plate and then placed meat and potatoes on her own while Bettina passed around the side dishes—green beans and sliced tomatoes and the day-old bread that had not sold at the bakery. "Has he described your duties to you?"

"He said at first I would be working in the back, churning the ice cream and washing the dishes from sundaes and sodas he makes out front."

Bettina snickered.

"What's so funny?" Rolf challenged.

"You washing dishes," Bettina managed between giggles.

Pleasant smiled. "She has a point, Rolf. Getting you to wash or dry a dish here at home is what I believe you once referred to as 'women's work?'"

Rolf smiled sheepishly. "Papa used to say that. I just picked it up from him."

"Well, perhaps tonight after supper you might want to help your sister with the dishes. You might learn something."

Rolf's eyes widened with protest and Bettina grinned. "Happy to have your help," she said.

For the rest of the meal they talked about Rolf's new job and how he would manage that along with his schoolwork and chores around the farm. And by the time the children went to bed, Pleasant was certain that allowing Rolf to take the job at the creamery had been the best possible decision. Not only had it helped to build Rolf's self-confidence, it had also affected the other children. As the brother and sister were doing the dishes, Pleasant overheard Bettina assure Rolf that she would help him with his chores at home. Later, as she settled the twins in for the night, Will had announced that he and Henry were perfectly capable of collecting the eggs every morning.

"How about the two of you feed the chickens while Rolf collects the eggs?" Pleasant suggested. "Of course, that means that you two sleepyheads must be up with the sun and dressed and ready without Bettina having to scold you. Can you do that?"

The tow-headed boys nodded solemnly, and Pleasant gathered them to her, hugging them both and thanking God once more for the blessing of these children giving her life meaning and purpose. It was not all she had ever wanted, but she knew now that the children were all she would ever need.

Over the next several weeks, Jeremiah could not seem to get Pleasant's farm out of his mind. The tragedy of such a large tract of land lying fallow and useless stayed with him. The sight of those empty fields that she faced at the start and end of every day had to be a constant and painful reminder of what she had lost—the secure future that her late husband had planned for her and the children. According to local gossip, Merle Obermeier had been a stern man but a good provider. He had been deeply in love with his first wife, the mother of his children. And he had married Pleasant to provide those children with the nurturing that, by all accounts, he was incapable of providing.

"If you ask me," his great-aunt Mildred revealed one day when she stopped by the creamery to bring him cloths she'd made for the tables, "every time Merle looked at those children he saw their mother and it broke his heart. In time he had no heart left—not for loving those precious little ones and certainly not for loving another woman."

"But Pleasant was in love with him," Jeremiah assumed.

Mildred shrugged. "Not at all. Let's just say that for the two of them it was a marriage of convenience. And that's all I'm going to say on that matter, Jeremiah. You've driven me to gossip and I won't have it."

"I apologize," Jeremiah told her. "You're right. It's the boy." Rolf had been working at the creamery for nearly a month by then.

"He's not working out?" Mildred asked sympathetically.

"On the contrary. He does his work perfectly and he's quick to learn any new task. But if I stop him to make a suggestion or even to urge him to take his time, he reacts as if..."

"You might scold him? Or perhaps even raise your hand to him?" Mildred nodded as if such a reaction were perfectly understandable.

"Exactly, and yet I've given him no cause to believe that I would ever...."

Mildred sighed. "You don't have to, Jeremiah. His father was a strict disciplinarian, especially to Rolf and his sister." She shook her head. "One thing's certain—those little ones were blessed the day Pleasant came into that house." She smoothed the last cloth into place and surveyed her work. "There. Makes the place look more inviting," she said.

"It does indeed," Jeremiah said. "*Danke, Tante* Millie."

"Come by for supper tonight. The bishop has invited the Palmer brothers to dine with us."

"The owners of the cooperative?"

"That's them. Every few months or so the bishop likes to have them over just to catch up on what they might be planning next." She winked. "Forewarned is forearmed is your great-uncle's motto," she said and waved as she left the shop.

The encounter had netted him a cache of questions—about Merle Obermeier, about Rolf's relationship with his father, about what business move the highly successful Palmer family might make next. As the bishop, John Troyer was the unofficial head of the Amish community and Jeremiah could see the wisdom of staying in touch with their *Englisch* neighbors, especially when those neighbors were part of a dynasty that had built fortunes in Chicago and now along the Gulf Coast of Florida.

But as things turned out, Jeremiah didn't have to wait for supper at his great-uncle's home. For that very afternoon two men—clearly outsiders—walked through his front door and ordered ice cream cones with double scoops of vanilla for one and chocolate for the other.

They were dressed in the kind of business suits that outsiders favored—coat with lapels and buttons, vest draped with a pocket watch chain for one and plain for the other, trousers that hung with a sharp crease marking the length of each leg. Their starched white shirts accented the subtle color and pattern of their silk ties.

"How's business?" one of them asked when Jeremiah delivered their cones to the table by the window where they had taken seats.

"Gut," Jeremiah replied. "Good."

"Do you have a minute?" One of the men pulled over a third chair indicating that Jeremiah should join them. "Allow me to introduce myself," he added. "I am Potter Palmer and this is my brother, Honore. We represent the Palmer Farm Growers Association. Many of your neighbors here are members."

"Ja. I am familiar with the cooperative." Jeremiah waited a beat then added. "I am Jeremiah Troyer."

"Good ice cream," Honore said.

"Danke."

"I believe you also work at the ice plant in Sarasota?" Potter asked.

An innate instinct to protect his business made Jeremiah instantly suspicious. "How can I help you gentlemen?" he asked, meeting their gaze directly.

Potter's smile reflected an element of respect. "How familiar are you with the process involved in growing and harvesting celery, sir?"

"Not very. But then I am not a farmer."

Honore chuckled. "Neither are we. We—like you—are businessmen. It is the balance sheet that is of most interest to us. Am I right?"

Jeremiah leaned back in his chair and waited for more.

Potter Palmer continued to work on his ice cream as he explained the situation. "When the celery crop is harvested, it is imperative that the produce be cooled almost immediately, as soon as the stalks leave the ground if possible. We have the equipment to manage that, of course, but for our Amish members there is some hesitation to make use of our methods because it involves the use of electricity. They would rather sacrifice yield than go against your traditions."

"And in these times," Honore added as he polished off the last bite of his cone and wiped his fingers on his napkin, "yield is already compromised."

"I understand," Jeremiah said, although he certainly did not understand what this might have to do with him.

"Are we to understand that in addition to your position at the ice plant and your shop here in Celery Fields, you also have a delivery business serving your Amish neighbors with blocks of ice?"

"*Ja.* Yes, sir. I buy the ice from the plant and then sell it. People of our faith do not believe in electricity and we must rely on block ice to preserve our food."

The brothers glanced at one another. "We would like

to discuss a somewhat similar business arrangement with you, sir," Honore said as he pulled a paper from an inner pocket of his suit jacket and handed it to Jeremiah. "This is our order for the delivery of ice for the cooperative."

"For those members of the Amish tradition," Potter corrected. "It is a standing order as you can see for as long as you can meet our needs and assuming we can negotiate a fair price for your product and services."

Jeremiah studied the paper. It was an order that could secure his business for years to come. "Why come to me?" he asked. "Would I not be taking business from my employer?"

"On the contrary, the ice company would benefit. Several of our Amish members resist dealing with outsiders and their crops can suffer in the process. But they would accept our processing standards if you delivered the ice—one of their own."

"How have you chosen me?" Jeremiah asked and saw a hint of respect for his caution flicker across the brothers' features.

"Levi Harmon..."

"Harnisher," Potter corrected his brother. "When we first met Levi, he was a highly successful owner of a circus and his name then was Harmon. Apparently, when he decided to return to his heritage, he took back the family name. But I'm afraid Levi will always be Harmon to us."

"You know Levi?"

The brothers laughed. "We've known him for years," Honore said. "Believe it or not, we used to attend the same parties and charity events. Of course, that was before."

"He's a good man and has an excellent head for business," Potter said. "We value his opinion. He was the one who suggested you and that we would only be increasing our standing with our Amish members by finding a way that they could feel they were doing business with one of their own." He arched an eyebrow. "The question is—are you interested?"

Jeremiah looked up at the brothers. He had heard their story. The heirs to a massive fortune built on shrewd business deals made by their ancestors in Chicago were not particularly interested in endearing themselves to their Amish members unless there was a profit in the bargain for them. He smiled.

"Yes, I am definitely interested, but I must speak directly with my employer at the ice company. I want to make very sure that they are all right with this arrangement."

The brothers exchanged a look and Potter reached for a gold fountain pen that he carried in his breast pocket.

But instead of accepting the pen, Jeremiah folded the paper they had laid out for him. "I just need a day or two to fully consider the arrangement and whether or not I can provide the service you need." He saw by the look they exchanged now that he had surprised them and that, as he had suspected, they had underestimated him.

He stood up. "I'll have an answer for you by Thursday if that is agreeable."

The brothers stood as well and Honore reached for his wallet.

"Please, gentlemen," Jeremiah said, "accept your first of what I hope will be many servings of Troyer's ice cream with my compliments."

Honore smiled and put away his wallet. "You make a good product, sir. And that cone—unusual flavor there."

"Shoo-fly," Jeremiah said.

"Pardon?"

"The flavor in the cone is based on a recipe for shoo-fly pie. The woman who runs the bakery next door created the recipe."

Potter glanced out the window to the bakery. "Merle Obermeier's widow?"

"Yes." Jeremiah felt himself instantly on guard again as the brothers once again communicated with one another by a glance rather than actual words. "Do you know her?" he asked, hoping to translate that veiled glance.

"Knew her husband," Honore said.

"Briefly," Potter added and frowned as if the memory were an unpleasant one. But then he gathered himself and extended his hand. "Thursday then," he said in a more jovial tone as his brother laid an engraved business card on the table. "Thank you for the ice cream."

"Yes," Honore added. "I'm going to tell my wife that perhaps for her next social event your shoo-fly cones and ice cream might be a unique dessert."

Jeremiah escorted the two businessmen to the door. Outside, he saw that Pleasant was out sweeping the constant film of sand from the bakery's porch and steps. She glanced over briefly but showed no curiosity about the outsiders coming out of his shop or in the car that pulled around from the side of Hadwell's hardware and idled in front of the creamery until both men got in. He saw a figure move away from the window of the dry goods store and knew that probably Hilda Yoder had also observed the visit.

Roger Hadwell had no such need to hide his curiosity. He strolled across the street and stood next to Jeremiah watching the car drive away leaving a trail of dust that would make Pleasant's sweeping an exercise in futility.

"The Palmers?"

"Ja."

Jeremiah was thinking about the way the Palmer brothers had glanced at each other when they mentioned Merle's name. He wondered if they thought that he—like Obermeier—would refuse to work with them. He wondered if his hesitancy might cost him an opportunity.

"What did they want?" Roger asked.

Jeremiah fingered the paper he still held in one hand. "Ice cream," he replied as the dust settled and once again the road through Celery Fields was deserted.

Chapter Ten

In spite of the need to watch every penny, Pleasant was determined that the children's anticipation of the Christmas season would not be dampened. On Christmas Day, they would spend their time fasting and praying together and reading from the Bible. But on the day after Christmas—or Second Christmas as it was known—they would visit family and friends and share a day of feasting and gift giving.

When Merle had been alive she had made the mistake of showing him the cards that her friends from the circus had sent. These outsiders did not know that the Amish did not believe in such an exchange of greetings, but to Pleasant it was the gesture that counted. Merle had been shocked that she had even opened the cards and had quickly taken them from her and thrown them into the fire. But after his death she had kept the cards and opened them with the children on Second Christmas, regaling them with stories of her adventure with the circus.

Merle had also not allowed the exchange of gifts within their family and had barely tolerated Gunther's insistence on giving the children some small token when

the two families gathered on the second day for dinner.
But a year after Merle's death, when they had been on
their way home from sharing supper at Gunther's, Bettina had sighed and said, "I wish we could exchange
gifts, Mama. It would be such fun to draw names and
plan what to give."

And that night as she tucked the children in, Pleasant had handed each of them a paper with another sibling's name on it. "Shhh," she had cautioned. "You have
a whole year now to plan your gift, but you cannot tell."
Her gift that year had been knowing that after she had
gone back downstairs, all four children had slipped out
of their beds and gathered in Bettina's small bedroom
to whisper and giggle over this new tradition. And she
suspected that long before morning dawned at least the
older two had figured out who had which name.

But perhaps the highlight of the season was the annual program presented to the entire community by the
children. Traditionally, such programs were held in the
schoolhouse and attended by the parents of the children
enrolled in the school. Lydia had assigned each child in
her classes a part to play and the excitement among the
children was palpable. Rolf was to be the narrator of
the reenactment of the story of the birth of Jesus while
Bettina was to recite a poem for the occasion and both
children were determined to do their very best. Every
evening just after supper, Bettina recited her poem for
Pleasant, and Rolf silently read through the Scripture
passages he would read as his classmates reenacted the
story.

It was on such an evening on the day before the pageant that Bettina's rehearsal was interrupted by a knock
at the door. Pleasant glanced at the clock on the man-

tel—now decorated with fresh greens—and wondered who might be calling at seven o'clock on a weekday evening. "Who's there?" she asked before opening the door, mindful of the stories that persisted of the occasional vagrant or transient going from house to house and sometimes even robbing those homes if they were desperate enough.

"Pleasant? It's me—Jeremiah."

As seemed to be her habit these days any time she saw Jeremiah or heard his voice or the sound of his laughter, her heart leaped. And being a natural worrier, her second thought was that something had happened—someone fallen ill or a fire perhaps. She opened the door as the children gathered around her. "What's happened?" she asked as she pulled the children closer.

"Happened?" He looked perplexed and actually glanced around as if he thought he might have missed something. "Why, nothing."

Relieved but at the same time irritated with him for calling at such an hour, she did not move away from the door to let him in. "Then why have you come?"

He smiled. "And greetings of the season to you as well," he said softly. "May I come in a moment? I have something for Rolf."

Pleasant stepped aside to make room for Jeremiah to enter. Once fully inside, he took a moment to glance around, settling his gaze on the cypress boughs and eucalyptus that adorned the fireplace. "Smells like Christmas," he said. Then he noticed the open Bible that Rolf had been studying and the typed copy of Bettina's poem. "I'm sorry to disturb you, but a few days ago when he was practicing his part during a break at the shop I noticed that Rolf was having some trouble reading the small print in his Bible. I thought these might make it a bit easier for him."

From the pocket of his homespun trousers he produced a small leather case, snapped open the hinged lid and held up a pair of wire-rimmed eyeglasses. "They were my father's," he explained. "He used them to magnify the words when he read Scripture to us." He handed the glasses to Rolf. "Try them on."

As always, Rolf glanced first at Pleasant, seeking permission, and when she nodded, he accepted the glasses as if they were something fragile and precious. Carefully, he hooked them over his ears and peered up at her. "They make you look fuzzy," he reported.

Jeremiah laughed and reached for the Bible. "They are for close work like reading. Slide them down your nose a bit and look over the tops when you want to look at your mother."

Rolf followed his instructions.

"Now try reading this," Jeremiah said as he handed the boy the Bible.

Silently, his lips moving, Rolf read the text. Then he grinned and peered up at Pleasant. "They make the words bigger," he reported. "I can see them clearly now."

Pleasant had known that Rolf 's eyesight was not as good as it should be when she noticed his habit of squinting as he did his homework, but eyeglasses were expensive. She had planned that the income from the celery harvest would cover the need to buy shoes for all four children and eyeglasses for Rolf but there had been only enough income to pay the workers and buy the feed she needed for the chickens and other livestock.

"You shouldn't wear them except when you need them for reading," Jeremiah instructed. "You can keep them in this case between times." He handed Rolf the closed leather case.

"And you must take special care that they not get broken or lost," Pleasant added. "Herr Troyer has loaned you these glasses until we can have you fitted for a pair of your own." Pleasant spoke to Rolf but her purpose was to make it clear to Jeremiah that his gift was far too generous to be accepted as permanent. "Thank you," she said turning her attention to Jeremiah.

He glanced down at his shoes, suddenly shy. "I just thought—I mean he was squinting so and…"

She realized that the children had drifted back into the front room and now Rolf was eagerly reading the story from the Gospel according to Luke aloud while his siblings sat on the floor around him like a makeshift audience. She was alone in the hallway with Jeremiah. Outside the still-open front door, the last rays of the sunset had disappeared. Inside the hallway they were wrapped in the shadows cast by the single kerosene lamp and the fire that crackled in the front room.

"Gunther has invited John, Millie and me to join your family for Second Christmas," Jeremiah said.

"I'm glad," she replied and found that she meant it. The idea of sharing the day with him felt like a gift.

"Well, I should be going." He stepped onto the porch and started down the stairs.

"Will you come to see the children perform?" she asked, knowing that it was unusual for anyone who did not have a direct connection to the schoolchildren to attend the pageant.

He turned and although he was completely in shadow now, she thought she could almost hear his smile when he spoke. "I wouldn't miss it."

* * *

On the night of the pageant, the schoolhouse was filled to standing room only. Jeremiah had arrived late, having been delayed with a delivery of ice cream to the home of Potter Palmer for that family's annual Christmas Eve party. He could not help noticing the difference between the trappings that marked an *Englisch* Christmas and those of the Amish. The Palmer residence was festooned with greenery both inside and out. As he drove his wagon up the long driveway he could see a large decorated Christmas tree framed in the front window, and another smaller tree in a window that he passed on his way to the rear of the house.

In the kitchen, the cook and a housemaid were engaged in a lively discussion of what age was old enough for children to stop believing in the myth of Santa Claus. He had never understood the purpose of creating a tale of some magical creature whose job it was to determine whether or not a child had been good enough to deserve to find a stocking filled with gifts on Christmas morning. Christmas was a religious celebration and the idea of a gift was that it came unexpectedly to be sure. But a gift was the product of hard work, an expression of appreciation and love from one person to another.

He unloaded the wagon and followed the Palmer's butler to the large refrigerator where the ice cream would be stored until needed. Then on his way back to Celery Fields, he shook his head in wonder at the need for these outsiders to add their own secular interpretations to what had to be the greatest story ever told. Outside the small schoolhouse, he paused for a minute to consider the natural beauty of poinsettias and hibiscus in bloom, their colorful leaves and blossoms far more beautiful than the artificial lights that adorned the Palmer's Christmas tree.

The town was quiet, shops closed and what citizens weren't already inside the schoolhouse were no doubt gathered in their homes or at the homes of neighbors quietly—and simply—enjoying the blessings of the season. He could not deny the twinge of envy that ran through him in that moment. A family—mother, father, children—was possibly one of God's most precious gifts. It was also a blessing that he had long ago decided he would not seek, at least in the traditional way.

His reasons for opening the ice cream shop had been many. He had certainly understood how people would see that choice as unusual and perhaps even foolhardy given the times. But what he saw was the opportunity to surround himself in his daily life with families—parents, children, grandparents, cousins—without running the risk that he might one day turn out to be like his uncle. He certainly had seen some of the early signs that he was as capable of turning into the same hard and bitter—and sometimes cruel—man that his uncle had been. He had a quick temper that along with his small size had landed him in more than one fight with peers when he'd been a boy. And the older and bigger he had become, the more often he had had to restrain himself from striking back when his uncle unfairly punished him or one of his siblings.

No, he would not marry, he thought as he stepped inside the crowded schoolhouse.

And then he saw Pleasant.

She was seated on one of the benches where the children sat to receive their lessons. Will and Henry sat to either side of her, their short chubby legs swinging

back and forth, evidence of their excitement. Pleasant
smoothed each boy's cowlick and then turned their attention to the front of the room where Rolf had just stepped
up to the simple wooden lectern that Lydia Goodloe used
when teaching her students.

Self-consciously, he unfolded the stems of the eyeglasses and hooked them over his ears. There was a
titter of snickers that was instantly shushed by mothers around the room. Jeremiah saw Lydia signal Rolf
to speak louder as Levi and Hannah's son Caleb and a
girl that Jeremiah recognized as the oldest of Hilda and
Moses Yoder's children, slowly made their way to the
front of the room. The girl cradled a doll and sat on a
small stool while Caleb took up his place just behind her.
Jeremiah folded his arms and leaned against the back
wall of the classroom as the story unfolded. But his attention was not on the pageant. It was drawn again and
again to Pleasant Obermeier, whose profile he could observe without her knowing and who was surely the most
beautiful woman in the room.

He found himself mentally running down the list of
eligible men in the community, wondering if Pleasant
might not marry again someday. But he found that he
could not imagine her with any of those men. More than
that, he found that he did not wish to imagine her with
any other man and that thought stunned him.

Between his great-aunt Mildred and Roger Hadwell's
wife, it had not taken long to learn the story of Merle
Obermeier's similarities to Jeremiah's uncle when it
came to how he ran his household and raised his children. Once when Jeremiah had surprised Rolf practicing his part for the pageant instead of scrubbing out the
large tins that held the ice cream, the boy had instinc-

tively raised his hands in a protective gesture. Jeremiah had recognized that stance. He had used it often enough himself when his uncle had raised a hand to him.

"Those tins aren't going to scrub themselves," Jeremiah had commented and then gone back inside his shop. Through the window he had watched Rolf as he regained control of his rapid breathing, glanced around nervously and then closed his Bible and went back to work. Later, he had taken Rolf aside and quietly explained to him that if there was work to be done, he needed to attend to it as they had agreed. Once the tasks he'd been hired to complete were done, then he could use his time for homework or practicing his role for the pageant. And he had not missed the way the boy seemed almost weak with gratitude.

He turned his attention back to Pleasant, her features soft in the candlelight that illuminated the room as she watched Bettina take her brother's place at the lectern and deliver the poem she had memorized. And as Bettina spoke the poem aloud, he saw that Pleasant had sat forward a little and was mouthing the words along with her. Jeremiah suspected that she was probably unaware that she was doing this and that made the moment all the more poignant. She was a good mother and he had no doubt at all that she had been a good wife.

At first, Pleasant thought that Jeremiah had decided against attending the pageant and told herself that she was disappointed for the children. But then when the program ended she had turned to greet a neighbor and seen him. In fact, he was watching her and he had not looked away when she met his gaze. Instead, he had pushed himself away from his position leaning against the wall and started working his way through the throng of parents and children toward her.

Her first instinct was to flee, as if somehow his approach represented some danger to her. But she found that she couldn't move for the close quarters of benches and people and so she waited for him to reach her. Along the way, he paused to greet the Yoders and the Harnishers and others so that when he finally reached her and the twins, she had convinced herself that she had been mistaken to imagine that he had been watching her at all. He had simply made eye contact as any friend or neighbor might and she was a romantic fool.

"I'll get your glasses from Rolf," she told him and headed immediately for the front of the room where Lydia was surrounded by the excited participants of the program. She had to gain control of her emotions when it came to Jeremiah Troyer. In the weeks that had passed since the opening of his ice cream shop, she had fallen into the habit of being far too aware of his activities. At first she had told herself that she was only concerned about Rolf and that her son live up to his responsibilities. But Rolf had quickly settled into his new job and kept up with his schoolwork and chores at home as well.

Then she had tried convincing herself that they were in business together. She made the cones for his shop and it was only natural that she would be aware of when he might be coming to pick up the week's order or drop off a payment for her father. But the truth was that she looked forward to those occasions as she might well have looked forward to some beau coming to call when she was younger.

No, the plain fact was that she was drawn to Jeremiah in a way that no woman of her age or station in life should be. She had permitted herself to fall back into the romantic foolishness that had been her undoing before she married Merle. Yes, her life these days was difficult and lonely, and she would not deny that having someone to share her many responsibilities with would be a blessing. But a companion only—not someone like Jeremiah whose very smile could set her heart racing.

When she reached Lydia and the children, she took out the case for the glasses and handed it to Rolf. "Don't forget to say thank you," she murmured as her son reluctantly removed the glasses and carefully laid them in the case. Then he looked up at someone standing behind her.

"Thank you, Herr Troyer," he said. "They really helped a lot."

"Then keep them until you get fitted for a pair of your own," Jeremiah said. "I'm sure your teacher here would agree that if they help you with your schoolwork they are well worth wearing."

Lydia nodded. "You didn't stumble once in the reading tonight, Rolf. I have to agree that perhaps what I have thought might be a failure to learn your words has instead been a problem with seeing."

Rolf, Lydia and Jeremiah turned to Pleasant for her approval and agreement. "The glasses are a family heirloom, Lydia," she explained. "If they would be broken or damaged…"

"They can be replaced," Jeremiah said, his voice soft. "Although they are my father's glasses, it's the memory that is precious not the item." He smiled at Rolf and ruffled the boy's hair. "Besides, they make you look quite wise and grown-up," he added.

Rolf blushed and looked up at Pleasant. "They do help, Mama."

She could see that she was outnumbered and besides, what was the real problem? Was it that they were borrowed glasses? Or that they were evidence of her inability to afford glasses? Or that they somehow tied her family to Jeremiah? "Very well," she said. "But when you are not wearing them, they are safely stored in their case, all right?"

"Yes, Mama." Rolf's smile erased any doubt she might still be harboring. She would find a way to get him the glasses he needed and in the meantime she would not allow pride to keep her from accepting a neighbor's help.

She glanced around and saw that most people had started to file out of the classroom. "We should go," she told the children. "Tomorrow is going to be a full day."

"And the day after that," Bettina said with a twinkle in her large blue eyes. "Presents," she whispered to the twins who squealed with excitement and made a beeline for the door. "Come on, Rolf," Bettina urged as the two older children followed the twins up the aisle and out the door.

It seemed only natural for Pleasant to follow them, but when she realized that Jeremiah was walking out just behind her, she turned back to Lydia. "Coming?" she asked.

"Not just yet. You go on. I want to finish cleaning up here so everything is ready for the next school day."

"Perhaps Jeremiah could help," Pleasant suggested.

"No, thank you. You both worked all day already. I'll see you tomorrow, Pleasant, and you the day after, Jeremiah," she added with a smile.

Pleasant considered her half sister for a moment. She was such a lovely young woman—always thinking of others and that did not begin to take note of her outer beauty. She was the image of her late mother—the woman that Gunther had fallen madly in love with after Pleasant's mother died. The woman that Pleasant had so resented in those early years. But now she saw in Lydia what her father must have seen in Lydia and Greta's mother—a sweetness and beauty that was unmatched. And as she made her way out into the night, she could not help but wonder why Jeremiah Troyer had not seemed to take note of her half sister.

So when he fell into step with her as she and others made their way through the village and on to their homes, she found that God had given her a new purpose. Frankly, she did not understand why she hadn't seen it before. Clearly the woman that God had led Jeremiah Troyer to Florida to find was not Pleasant, but rather the beautiful and eligible Lydia. And if he had yet to recognize that then perhaps it was God's will that she help him see the light.

"Lydia is such a gifted teacher," she ventured as she and Jeremiah followed the stream of townspeople from the school.

"Hmm," Jeremiah agreed but it was clear that his thoughts were elsewhere, no doubt on business, Pleasant thought.

"She spends far too much time at the school and with the children, though," she added. "Just for this pageant alone she was working hours and hours."

No response. He walked beside her, his hands clasped behind his back.

"Guten abend," Hannah called out as Levi turned their buggy down the road that led to their farm.

"Merry Christmas," Jeremiah called back. "And to you, Pleasant," he added.

They had come to his shop and home and Pleasant felt compelled to make some last effort to bring her half sister's many virtues to his attention.

"Lydia would make a good wife," she blurted and then immediately clasped her hands over her mouth. It had been what she was thinking but not at all what she had intended to say.

He was looking at her but she could not see if he was smiling or shocked. "I expect she would," he said agreeably as if they were discussing the weather. "Did you have someone in mind, Pleasant?"

Now he was making fun of her—and rightly so. She had made an utter fool of herself. "It's an observation," she said. "Good night, Jeremiah," she added and hurried away, calling for her children to watch for buggies and wait for her.

"Merry Christmas, Pleasant," he replied and she was sure that she caught a hint of amusement in his tone.

Honestly, she chided herself as she hurried to catch up to the children—and put more distance between herself and Jeremiah, *you are becoming a busybody.* If he had any interest in Lydia then he was perfectly capable of pursuing that interest without her clumsy attempts at matchmaking. And certainly she had enough to worry about without concerning herself for one second with his personal business. Besides, it was Greta who had been mooning over the man, not Lydia. And the very idea that Greta would turn her affections from Josef Bontrager to Jeremiah was laughable. Those two were meant for each other.

No, Jeremiah Troyer was not for any one of the Goodloe women—not Greta, not Lydia and most definitely not her.

Chapter Eleven

It had been some time since Jeremiah had felt quite so lighthearted and at the same time confused. He had little doubt that it was the lovely widow Obermeier who was the cause of his jumbled emotions. He had made it all the way past thirty years and stuck to his decision formed early on that he would never marry, never allow himself to fall in love. From what he had observed over the course of his life there were far too many risks involved in taking such a step.

His parents, for example, had been deeply devoted to one another and the house he had known as a young boy had been filled with laughter and happiness. But then his father had died and his mother had changed, falling into a chasm of grief and sadness from which she had never recovered. His grandparents had been solemn people who frowned on any evidence of levity or the normal high spirits of children. It had not taken long after the family had moved in with his father's brother for his uncle to make clear his disapproval of such antics. If words did not make the point then he more often than not would resort to the switch. And it had not taken long at all to turn Jeremiah's siblings into the obedient, somber-faced offspring that his uncle seemed to prize.

Only Jeremiah had fought back—not physically, but emotionally, holding fast to the memory of that earlier time and that home filled with love and laughter. For a long time he dreamed of the day when he would marry and start a family of his own. But as the years went on and he learned more of his uncle's past, he came to understand that the man his uncle had become was not the man he had always been. The worries of life had changed him and his determination to assure that his children and those of his dead brother would have a secure future became the one thing that drove him.

For some time, Jeremiah had thought that he could be different, but the longer he lived in his uncle's house, the more the memory of life in his father's house faded. He had no idea how his father had managed to give his children a sense of security and responsibility and at the same time an understanding of the joy of life. Then one day he found himself chastising his younger brothers for some task not performed up to the high standards their uncle had set for them. He had heard in his voice the anger of his uncle and found his hand grasping a willow branch and brandishing it. He had felt rage and he had not known where it came from.

He had dropped the willow switch, apologized to his stunned siblings and walked away. And from that day forward he had done the work his uncle expected of him but refused to oversee the work of the others. He had also broken off his courtship of a neighboring farmer's daughter, a girl his uncle had thought far too flighty for him, winning him the older man's approval for once. And he had waited for the day when his younger brother was ready to take over as head of the family so that Jeremiah might leave the farm for good and make a life for himself.

And here he was. He had found his life's work, not as a farmer like his uncle and father, but as a businessman. Everything had fallen into place. His deal with the Palmer brothers had secured his future with his employers, for they were delighted to have him bring them back the business they had lost when the Amish farmers balked at dealing directly with an outsider. The ice cream shop was doing all right as well. He had found a home and a community that had taken him in, welcomed him without reservation. He had friends in the Harnishers and Hadwells and others in the community. He even had family here with John and Mildred. And yet...

Jeremiah lay back on his single bed and stared out the open window at a sky filled with stars. On that night so very long ago there had been a single brilliant star, guiding the wise men to the stable. He could use a guiding star. He closed his eyes and silently prayed for the wisdom to see the path that God wanted him to follow and the courage to follow it.

The year following Merle's death, Pleasant and the children had spent Christmas Day at her father's house. There they had followed the traditions of her childhood. Focusing on the celebration of the birth of Jesus, the day was spent in quiet reflection. At sunrise they took the buggy to the beach and walked together in silence as the gentle gulf waves swirled around their bare feet. Then back home Gunther read the Scriptures aloud, Pleasant told the older children stories while Lydia sat with the twins letting them draw pictures of their idea of the

Christmas story. Like many families, they fasted for most of the day, reminding themselves of those who were not nearly so blessed.

"I don't like being hungry," Henry told Pleasant as she and the children walked home at the end of the long day.

"Me, neither," Will chorused.

"And yet there are many people right here in this very country who do not have enough to eat," she reminded them.

"I know this girl in my class at school," Bettina said, "and I don't think she and her brother have enough to eat, Mama. They hardly have anything in their lunch buckets."

Pleasant knew the family. The man had married outside the faith and been shunned for it. He had a run-down house closer to the bay and he eked out a living finding work on commercial fishing boats when he could. He had continued to send his children to the Amish school and dress them in traditional clothing and the general feeling in the community had been to let them come.

"We have so much," Bettina continued. "Do you think we could take them something tomorrow, Mama?"

Pleasant considered the ramifications of such an act—for her children and even for her father's business if someone in the congregation found fault. Any act punishable by shunning was a serious offense and the power of the punishment lay in everyone in the community upholding the ban. "We'll see," she said and knew that the children saw her noncommittal as a way of saying "no."

But Bettina was not one to give up easily. "We could fill up a basket and then just leave it at their door," she suggested. "No one would have to know it was us."

Pleasant looked down at her children, their faces

raised to hers, their expressions hopeful. They wanted to do something good, something so in keeping with the way that Jesus had lived his life. Surely it would be the right thing to do. "We'd have to get up very early," Pleasant warned.

"But it's Second Christmas and we'll be so excited that we probably won't sleep at all," Bettina said as all four children pressed closer to Pleasant, waiting for her to agree to Bettina's plan.

"I do have a basket I'm not using," she mused. "But what to fill it with?"

"Oh, Mama, we have cans and jars of fruits and vegetables to spare," Bettina exclaimed.

"But we shouldn't just fill it with food," Pleasant continued. "If we are going to do this then I expect each of you to give something special." She could see each child starting to consider what might be the right thing.

"I'll be right back," Rolf muttered and took off at a run toward the bakery.

"Bring back the rest of the bread and rolls left from yesterday," Bettina called after him. "I have a doll and a book," she said then turned her attention to the twins, "And what about the puzzle Frau Yoder gave you—the one with too many pieces?"

Henry and Will nodded. "It's too hard for us," they agreed.

And as Rolf ran in one direction, the other three children hurried on to the house chattering away about what might be best to include in the basket. Pleasant had never been more proud of the children. She was well aware that Merle would have been horrified at the very idea that she might countenance any interaction with a family that had been shunned. Still, she couldn't help but think that he would have been proud as well. These were his children—loving, caring and good.

She had gotten the twins settled for the night and found a basket that she was filling with an assortment of jams and canned fruit and vegetables, when she heard footsteps and the low murmur of male voices through the open back door.

"Mama, Herr Troyer is going to help," Rolf announced breathlessly as he pulled Jeremiah into the kitchen. "I thought we could give them a special treat—ice cream—but I didn't think about how it would stay cold. But then I thought that we could put the basket on the porch and knock on the door and then hide until someone came out to get it and..." He gulped in air and glanced up at Jeremiah.

"I can pack the ice cream in ice and it should be fine," Jeremiah told her.

"But then they'll think the gift is from you," Bettina said as she laid her doll and a book and the twins' puzzle on the table next to the canned goods.

"It's not important who they think brought the gift," Pleasant reminded her. "Besides, they'll have the bread and rolls from the bakery and the ice cream from Herr Troyer...."

"And we can put in one of those dish towels from Yoder's store and a pencil from the hardware that has their name on it," Rolf added. "They won't be able to figure out who brought it."

Pleasant could see that Bettina was about to protest. "And that's the point, Bettina," she said softly. "The best gifts are those given without expectation of receiving anything in return—even acknowledgment of your good deed."

Bettina blushed. "I'm sorry. I just…"

"It's a wonderful thing you're doing," Jeremiah said. "Thank you for letting me be a part of it."

Satisfied, Bettina went back to planning the logistics of the delivery. "Rolf, you'll have to hitch up the wagon really early. I'll take care of getting the twins up and keeping them quiet so they won't spoil the surprise and…"

"Why don't I call for all of you just before dawn and we'll take a ride out there together," Jeremiah suggested. "I'll have the ice cream all packed in ice."

"That would be wonderful," Bettina exclaimed and for a moment, Pleasant could see the charmer that her daughter would one day become.

"Well, now that we've settled on a plan," she told the children, "I would suggest you get to bed. Dawn is going to come sooner than you may imagine."

She could hear the excited whispers of her two older children as they hurried down the hall and up to their rooms, leaving her alone with Jeremiah.

"Rolf forgot the bread and rolls," she said as she busied herself arranging things in the basket. "That's what he went to get…at the bakery."

"I can bring them in the morning. After all, the door is never locked, right?"

"Right," she murmured, still focusing on the basket. "You don't have to do this. I can explain to the children."

"Why wouldn't I want to be a part of something so perfectly tied to the season?"

"Well, not everyone would approve. The family has been shunned, after all. I don't even know if Bishop Troyer would approve and he's your family. Besides, you have a business to run and customers to please and if they knew you…"

He placed his hand on hers, stilling it from fussing further with the basket and forcing her to glance up at him.

"Pleasant," he said but stopped as their eyes met. He touched the tie of her prayer *kapp,* wrapping it loosely around his finger as he gazed down at her. He swallowed once and then again and she had to fight to keep from touching his cheek, burnished a golden brown after weeks of living in Florida.

Sun kissed, she thought, and felt the color rise to her cheeks as she realized that the kiss she was thinking of had nothing to do with the sun. She retreated a step so that she was free of his touch and forced a smile. "You should go," she said primly. "As I told the children, dawn will be here before we know it."

He nodded and turned to leave. And just before he went out the door he said, "By the way, just so we're clear on this, I have no interest in courting Lydia Goodloe."

"She's a good woman," Pleasant shot back, stopping him in his tracks.

He sighed heavily and turned to look at her through the screened door. "There are at least half a dozen good and eligible women in Celery Fields, Pleasant—including you. Should the time come when I'm so inclined, I prefer to do my own choosing."

And before she could even begin to come up with a response to that, he was gone.

Jeremiah was hardly surprised when the following morning Pleasant begged off going with the children and him to make their special delivery. "I still have pies to bake and bread rising," she protested as she stood in the yard while the children clamored aboard Jeremiah's wagon.

He knew he should be relieved. After all, he had just spent a mostly sleepless night imagining her shoulder brushing his as the wagon rumbled along the rutted road. And then after finally falling asleep he had been jolted awake with the thought that if they were seen together tongues would be wagging for weeks. Not so much about their errand to provide Christmas cheer to a shunned family. No, the very fact that Pleasant had been seen out riding with Jeremiah would be enough. Not even the buffer of the children could set the gossips to rest.

And as he hitched up the team of horses and drove through the darkness to Pleasant's house, he tried to come up with some reason why he couldn't go or she shouldn't go. But the truth was that he was so looking forward to having her next to him that his mind was a blank slate.

She, of course, had been the wiser of them, no doubt having considered the same hazards involved in the morning's adventure. She was risking enough allowing the children to go. Bettina and Rolf might be trusted to keep the secret but the twins had already revealed the name they had drawn and the gift they planned to give that person. The idea that those two would be able to keep quiet about something like this was simply ludicrous. And for that reason he decided that as soon as they had made the delivery and he had taken the children home, he would go immediately to his great-uncle's and tell him what they had done.

His great-uncle was just finishing his breakfast when

Jeremiah arrived. His great-aunt insisted on frying him some patties of cornmeal mush while he explained what he and the children had just done.

"And you say it was Bettina's idea," John said as he sipped his morning coffee and Mildred refilled Jeremiah's cup.

"Yes, but…"

"Stop worrying, Jeremiah. You must learn that things here in Florida tend to be a bit less…strict. You and the children did a good thing today. You shared your bounty with a family less fortunate. How can that be considered a wrong?"

"But he has been shunned."

John lifted a shoulder in a gesture of dismissal. "And yet there are the children to be considered. You have said that Pleasant's children each gave up a toy for the other family?"

"More than one from what I could see," Jeremiah said.

"Well, it's not something we can condone on a regular basis but the children are innocents in their parents' decision to marry. I see no reason why they should be punished."

And that was the end of the discussion. As if knowing that having made up his mind her husband was ready to move to other matters, Mildred handed Jeremiah a package wrapped in brown paper. "From your great-uncle and me," she said.

Jeremiah grinned and ripped open the paper. Inside the cardboard box was an ice cream scoop he'd admired when he and John had gone into Sarasota to see what the competition might be. "It's perfect," he announced, mimicking the scooping of ice cream with it. "Your turn," he added, setting the scoop on the table while he went out to his wagon and returned with gifts.

For John there was a new fishing rod and for Mildred a box of beeswax candles. And as the three of them sat around the table finishing their breakfast and discussing when John might try out his new fishing pole, Jeremiah was overcome with a sense of peace and contentment. The only label he could put to it was that he had finally come home. For this was how life had been when his father was alive—serene and amiable.

"Are you coming with us to Pleasant's for Christmas dinner?" Mildred asked and just like that Jeremiah was brought face-to-face with the turmoil he'd awakened with that morning, namely how best to limit contact with the widow Obermeier in the future. After all, he had come within a hair's breadth of kissing her the night before. For a man determined to remain a bachelor, that would not do.

"Of course he's coming," John boomed, pushing his chair back from the table. "There isn't a person in this community who would miss the opportunity to have one of Pleasant's meals. We are blessed to be invited."

Jeremiah wasn't at all sure that Pleasant would agree—not the way she had avoided meeting his eyes when he'd dropped the children off after their delivery. So when he pulled the bishop's buggy up to her house to let his great-uncle and aunt off later that afternoon, he spent more time than was really required stabling the horse in her barn. Rolf was there to help and Jeremiah used the opportunity to pass the time with the boy, recalling the joy they had both witnessed earlier that morning when the fisherman came out and found the basket and gifts.

"I thought they would see us for sure," Rolf said, his voice carrying more excitement than Jeremiah had ever heard him express.

Jeremiah was sure that the fisherman had seen them for he had stood in the open doorway of the wooden shack for several minutes after calling his wife and children to see the gifts. And when the rest of his family had gone back inside, he had stepped out into the dirt-packed yard, turned to face the direction where they were waiting and tipped his hat.

"Mama said Papa would have been real proud of us for what we did," Rolf said.

"You miss you father a lot, don't you?"

Rolf shrugged. "I think about him sometimes and wish there was some way he could know that I'm working hard and stuff."

"You honor his memory by doing well in your studies and being such a hard worker," Jeremiah told him.

Rolf went quiet and studied his bare feet. "Did your papa ever whip you?" he asked, his voice so soft that Jeremiah was unsure if he had heard him correctly.

"You mean a paddling?"

Rolf nodded.

"Not my father," he replied. "But my uncle sometimes…"

"Papa used to get so mad at me and I never could figure out how to make him proud," Rolf admitted.

Jeremiah wrapped his arm around the boy's thin shoulders. "He would be proud of you today, Rolf. Really proud to call you his son."

He let the boy swipe away tears and then added, "Now we'd best get up to the house before they send out a search party looking for us."

Rolf laughed and backhanded one last tear as he fell

into step with Jeremiah. "I think you might be right," he said as they crossed the yard together. "I think maybe if he'd lived long enough Papa would have liked me all right."

"I'm sure of it," Jeremiah said. But he wasn't—not really. From everything he'd heard about Merle Obermeier, he had been a hard and bitter man—a man who reminded Jeremiah a lot of his uncle. He wondered how many times Rolf had suffered the man's "whippings" and when he thought about the blows he had endured from his uncle being visited on Rolf, he felt his fists clench in rage. The kind of rage that he had fought to control all the time he had lived under his uncle's roof. The kind of rage that terrified him when it came over him and was at the very foundation of his determination never to marry and risk becoming what his uncle had been.

Chapter Twelve

Pleasant looked down the length of the long table laden with a feast that was the product of not only her hand, but those of her half sisters, Lydia and Greta, as well as Mildred Troyer. Later, she knew that they could anticipate visits from Hannah and her family as well as Hilda and Moses Yoder and their brood of seven. It would be a day filled with food, family and friends and, in her estimation, there could be no more precious gift than that.

She closed her eyes as everyone linked hands and bowed their heads in silent prayer. She had purposely seated Jeremiah at the far end of the table to the right of his great-uncle who held the place of honor at the head of the table where Merle would have sat. Of course, Merle would never have tolerated inviting so many extra people to share their holiday meal.

"We have six mouths of our own to feed without adding others," he had told her that first Christmas after they were married when she had suggested inviting her father and half sisters to share their dinner. "You've baked a pie to take when we go calling there later in the day. That will suffice."

Bishop Troyer's murmured "Amen" brought Pleasant back to the present with a jolt as all around her the room came suddenly alive with conversation, the clink of dishes being passed and food being served and the laughter of the children.

Pleasant was well aware that the year to come would be a challenging one but for now she was surrounded by loved ones and she felt a sense of peace and contentment such as she had not known for some time.

"No Brussels sprouts today, Frau Obermeier?" Jeremiah asked as Lydia passed him the bowl of green beans.

There were chuckles and smiles up and down the table, the tale of Jeremiah and the sprouts having been told in all three households at least once.

"Oh, you never know what might come with the next course, Herr Troyer," Pleasant replied, and encouraged by Jeremiah's look of surprise at her teasing, she continued, "I've been working on a special recipe for Brussels sprouts cones to serve your ice cream."

The twins made horrified faces and everyone laughed. "She's not serious," Bettina explained.

"On the other hand," Jeremiah said, "perhaps using that vegetable in ice cream might be something to try. I had a man call the other day who makes a soft drink with celery that he wanted me to serve in the shop."

"Celo," Gunther said, nodding.

The conversation turned then to the general state of business in Celery Fields as well as throughout the region as a whole. That led to a discussion of the prospects for rain and the possibility that the cooperative would be able to get the winter crops planted before the New Year.

"Enough talk of business," Mildred said after the men had dominated the conversation for most of the meal. "It's Christmas." She turned her attention to the children and added, "When I was a girl, long long ago, I lived in a place where it snowed and we would spend Second Christmas ice skating on the pond outside our back door."

"Was there a lot of snow?" Bettina asked, her eyes wide with the wonder of something she had never seen.

"There was," Mildred assured her. "Piles of it. Jeremiah, you must have had snow in Ohio at this time of year," she added.

"Piles and piles of it," he confirmed. "And yes, we went ice skating and sledding as well."

"What's 'sledding?'" Henry asked.

"You sit on a kind of wooden platform that's been fitted out with metal runners and slide down a hill on it," Jeremiah explained.

"And if you don't have a real sled," John said, "a piece of heavy cardboard will do—at least until it gets soaked through." He chuckled at the memory.

"Did you ever see snow, Mama?" Rolf asked.

"We had snow here once," she told them and then smiled. "Well, a few flakes. Remember, Papa, how Mama and I ran out to catch the flakes on our tongues?"

Gunther chuckled. "I remember that you were quite upset when they melted instantly—and your mother as well. I never saw anyone more frustrated than the two of you were." He shook his head at the memory. "Good times," he murmured, then he seemed to shake off the memory as he looked around the table and announced, "Well, are there any gifts to be opened or is this it?"

That set the children into immediate action as they scampered away from the table and claimed their spot on the braided rug in the front room and waited impatiently for the adults to follow their lead.

"Leave them," Pleasant told Mildred when the bishop's wife started clearing the table. "I don't think the children can contain their excitement much longer."

Mildred set down the plates she had gathered and followed Pleasant to the front room that had been decorated with potted poinsettias and cypress boughs. Several packages wrapped in brown paper that the children had illustrated with drawings added to the festive aura of the room. "Rolf, why don't you begin?" Pleasant suggested.

Rolf picked up a small package, crudely wrapped and tied with twine. He handed the package to Will. "I made it myself," he announced. "It's for your farm set."

Will tore off the paper, uncovering a wooden block that had been fashioned into a replica of a barn and painted a bright red. Pleasant saw the care with which Rolf had added details using black ink to mark the doors and window openings and pieces of sandpaper cut to simulate shingles for the roof.

"Thanks," Will murmured as he examined the piece.

"My turn," Bettina announced and handed Rolf a box covered in seashells. He opened the top to find nothing inside and looked at his sister with disappointment. "The box is the gift," she huffed with exasperation. "It's a place for you to keep your savings. Rolf is saving his earnings—the part he gets to keep—so that one day he can buy his own horse and buggy," she announced.

Rolf blushed. "Thank you, Bettina," he said softly and carefully replaced the lid on the box, running his fingers over the small white clam shells that everyone now could see had been glued in the shape of a buggy's wheel.

"I got Mama's name," Henry announced importantly and he pulled a small flat box from behind his back and presented it to Pleasant.

"What could it be?" she asked as she untied the ribbon.

"It's a new handkerchief," Henry said before she could fully open the box. "I did a whole bunch of chores for Frau Yoder and she let me pick it out."

"It's just what I needed," Pleasant assured him.

"Well, that's it," Gunther boomed, seeming to ignore the fact that Will was nearly in tears having not received a gift.

"What about Will?" Henry exclaimed and wrapped his arm around his twin.

"Oh, Will," Gunther exclaimed. "Did someone have Will's name?"

"Oh, Papa," Pleasant said, "stop teasing the boy." She handed Will his gift. "I had your name," she told him and her heart swelled when she saw the way he looked up at her, his eyes wide with surprise.

"What is it?" Henry asked, crowding close as Will unwrapped the box with great care. "Just rip it," Henry urged impatiently.

"It's a book," Will said, holding it up for everyone to see. "One I can read," he added as he thumbed through the pages. "I know this word," he pointed to a page. "See."

"I see it but what does it say?" Henry asked.

"See," Will repeated, tapping the word on the page. Henry rolled his eyes. "Okay, but…"

"The word is 'see,'" Bettina told her younger brother. Jeremiah leaned in closer to the twins from his position on a chair behind them. "Do you know that word?" he asked.

"Look?" Will guessed.

"That's right. And this one?"

Both twins studied the word for a long moment.

"What is the dog in the picture doing?" Jeremiah asked.

"Running," Henry said. "The word is running?"

"Shorter," Jeremiah coached.

"Run," the twins announced together and everyone applauded.

Watching Jeremiah teaching the boys, Pleasant felt her heart quicken. In the scene before her, she saw the only gift she had always truly longed for—a family—father, mother, children. Jeremiah would make such a good and patient father, she thought. Look how Rolf had blossomed under his tutelage. And Bettina had gotten in the habit of stopping by the ice cream shop after her chores at the bakery were done to tell Jeremiah her latest idea for some new ice cream flavor.

"Well," she said, her voice husky with emotion, "did anyone save room for dessert?"

"I did," the twins chorused, the book momentarily forgotten.

"Well then, I'm going to need some help clearing away the table," Pleasant said, leading the way back to the dining room.

It was later that evening, after the children had finally gone to sleep and the last of her company had gone home, that Pleasant was putting away the last of the dishes and savoring the memory of the day just past. Hannah and her family had arrived just in time for dessert and then stayed to visit. Then the Yoders had arrived and all the children had gone outside to play hide-and-seek while the men sat on the front porch discussing business and other news and the women gathered in the kitchen to put away the leftover food and wash and dry the dishes. And through it all, Pleasant could not seem to avoid thinking of Jeremiah. She heard the sound of his laughter as he joined in the game with the children and was touched by the way he leaned forward attentively listening to the talk of Gunther and John. It was almost as if he was as eager to learn from them as he had been to teach the twins earlier. But most of all she was all too aware of how often he had glanced her way, watching her as she moved through the rituals of the day and smiling as if they shared a secret when she worked up the nerve to meet his look directly.

She placed the last cup on its hook and then wrapped her hands around her sides, stretching her back. It had been a long day, but one filled with such joy that as tired as she was, she was reluctant to see it end. She needed sleep because she had been up before dawn and would be the following day as well. She unpinned her prayer *kapp* as she started down the hall toward the stairs. But then a light warm breeze fluttered through the open front door, drawing her outside for one more look, so she set her *kapp* on the small side table and stepped out onto the porch.

The street was deserted and most houses were completely dark but the sky was filled with stars and a sliver of a new moon. She closed her eyes and let the peace and silence surround her. When she heard the front gate open and close, she opened her eyes and moved from the shadows into the pool of light cast by the kerosene lamp inside her front door. "Who's there?" she asked, but felt no alarm, only concern that anyone out at this hour must be someone in need.

"It's me," Jeremiah said. "I didn't mean to disturb you," he added as he came up the path. "I thought that you and the children—I mean everyone seems to be sleeping and..."

She took a step closer, trying to see him in the dark. "Is something wrong, Jeremiah?"

"Not at all," he said. "I just..."

He was standing on the steps now, holding something in his hands. "I brought you this," he said and presented her with an orchid plant, its long tendril roots trailing over her hands even as she caught a whiff of the delicate flower's subtle perfume.

"It's beautiful but..." But what? Was she going to remind him that giving her a gift was inappropriate in their culture?

"It was growing out behind the shop in a thicket of pepper trees back there. I was going to give it to you to thank you for all the work you did to help make the ice cream shop's opening such a success, but that didn't seem like a good idea. I mean people might get the wrong idea and all."

As they would now, she thought, resisting the urge to take a quick look around to be sure no one was peering out a window or coming along the street. "Then why now?" she asked.

He glanced away and chuckled in that way that she had come to realize marked the evidence of his discomfort and shyness. "I'm not sure. It just seemed the right time. Today was very special for me, Pleasant. It's been a very long time since I felt so much a part of things—of a family. Thank you."

"You're welcome, but Jeremiah, surely you know by now that the entire community has come to respect you and see you as one of our own. Just in the short time you've been here you have somehow made yourself a part of us."

He stepped onto the porch and joined her in the pool of golden lamplight. "Could we sit a minute?" he asked, indicating the porch swing. "I have something I want to explain to you."

She should refuse. She should thank him again for the orchid and go back inside.

Instead she sat on the swing and waited for him to join her.

"After my father died," he began, then cleared his throat and started again. "Living with my uncle changed me."

"In what way?"

He was quiet for a long moment. "My uncle was a man who…" He shook his head and leaned forward, resting his elbows on his knees.

Although every instinct made her want to offer him some comfort, she resisted the urge to place her hand on his broad back. "Did you come to bring the orchid or perhaps there was something more, Jeremiah?"

He sighed. "That's just it. I did come to place that orchid in your tree so that you might discover it and not know that it came from me. I didn't want to cause you any concern about what others might think, Pleasant. But then you were here—it was almost like you were waiting for me, and all of a sudden I thought I must have come because I needed to tell you why I can never allow myself to have feelings for you."

Of all the things she might have imagined him saying,

this was surely the very last. Had he read her thoughts? Known that she had observed him, especially on the day just passed, and thought what a good father he might make? Had she revealed far too much of her own longing that it might still be possible for a man like him—handsome and gentle and kind—to love her?

She twisted her fingers together nervously. "You hardly owe me any explanation, Jeremiah," she said primly. "If this is about my comments regarding Lydia…"

To her shock he grasped her hands stilling them. "This is not about Lydia, Pleasant. It is you that I…" He shook his head miserably and released her hands.

"My uncle was a bitter man, Pleasant—a man who at a young age took on a great deal of responsibility. I can understand that now. He wasn't always so hard but in the time that we lived with him, the need to care for his own eight children and our family of seven—it was a lot to ask. Earlier today, Rolf asked me if my father had ever whipped me—his word—and admitted to me that your late husband had punished him on more than one occasion."

"You're not making any sense," Pleasant said, her heart racing with the unspoken fear that something was about to change for her, something that would spoil all of the peaceful contentment she had been feeling just minutes earlier.

"I don't want to become like my uncle—or like Merle, if I have understood Rolf correctly."

Pleasant was torn between the loyalty she felt she should have to her late husband and the realization that Rolf had turned to Jeremiah instead of her to admit how much his father had hurt him emotionally as well as physically. "Why would you think that might happen?"

"I have a temper—all the men in my family do. And sometimes that temper has been hard to manage and sometimes that temper has nearly brought me to strike out at others—my younger brothers, for example."

Pleasant was overcome with confusion. Why was he saying these things? Why tonight of all nights? Why was he determined to spoil this perfect day for her? She stood up. "I think you should go," she said stiffly. "Thank you for the orchid. I'll place it in the banyan tree early to-morrow. The children will be delighted." She took a step toward the door. "Good night, Jeremiah."

He caught her hand and spun her so that they were no more than inches apart. "I am trying to tell you that I care for you, Pleasant, but…"

"You have been kind to the children and to me, Jeremiah. Please don't concern yourself that I have taken that kindness for anything more than…"

He cupped her face in his hands and kissed her, and her instinct to protest was lost in the gentle pressure of his lips meeting hers. She closed her eyes and allowed herself this one moment of pure bliss, and she was still reeling from the tenderness of that kiss when he let her go and walked away.

Jeremiah's residence was dark when Pleasant went to the bakery the following morning. Clearly, he had left early for his shift at the ice plant. Business would be slower than usual as people recovered from the fes-tivities of the holiday and she wondered whether or not she should prepare the full weekly order of ice cream cones or if Jeremiah might decide to close the shop for a few days.

"Have you seen Jeremiah this morning?" she asked her father when he came to work on the accounts later that morning.

"He said something about having the early shift this week—said he needed to get his wagon loaded early for the delivery out to the co-op."

Vaguely, Pleasant recalled some conversation the day before about Jeremiah providing the ice necessary to properly preserve the winter celery crop that was almost ready to be harvested.

"He'll be back then," Pleasant murmured more to reassure herself than to respond to her father.

But Gunther laid down the paper he was studying and turned his attention to her. "I expect he will," he said. "Did you need something, Pleasant?"

She felt her cheeks growing red with embarrassment and moved closer to the hot ovens so her father might assign her rosy cheeks to the heat. "I just wondered about this week's order for cones."

"Good point. I can't imagine that he'll be wanting the full order. With the holiday and all we're already nearly half through the week." He scribbled a note on a piece of scrap paper and taped it to the top of his rolltop desk.

Pleasant smiled. This was her father's unique filing system—scraps of paper posted here and there plus stacks of files that littered the floor around him. But he knew where everything was and woe be it to anyone who tried to put his mess into some sort of logical order.

"I'll make half an order today and if he wants the rest I'll have time tomorrow," she announced as she began gathering the supplies she would need to make the cones.

"How are you doing, child?" Gunther asked after a moment, and Pleasant realized that he had not gone back to his work but had been watching her instead. "That was quite a spread you and the children put out for everyone yesterday. Are you sure that you didn't overdo?"

"The one thing the children and I do not lack for is food, Papa," she said as she cut lard into sugar. "At our weekly frolics, all the women have put up jars of fruit and canned vegetables to last everyone in the community for some time. And we still have the chickens for eggs and the cows to give us milk and…"

"The house needs work," Gunther reminded her.

"It's needed work for over a year now. We'll get to it."

"I imagine that the money that Jeremiah pays Rolf is a help."

"I put that money away for the children," Pleasant admitted. "For their future." She heard a horse snort and then the soft plodding of Jeremiah's team of Belgians entering the yard behind his shop. *He's back,* she thought and had to bear down on her mixing to restrain herself from going out to meet him.

"Looks like you can clear up the cone order for yourself," Gunther said as he reached up and ripped down the note he'd written himself and threw it in the wastebasket. "He's coming this way." And when Gunther pushed away from his desk and went to meet Jeremiah, it was all Pleasant could do not to collapse in the chair he had vacated, for suddenly her knees seemed to have turned to water.

Jeremiah had come to a decision. Living and working next door to Pleasant Obermeier was a bad idea. Going to her house for any reason was even worse. And worst—yet best—of all had been his impulsive act of kissing her. It had been all he could do to walk away from her after that. Every fiber of his being had screamed for him to stay, to touch the soft thick hair that swept back from her forehead and was always covered by her *kapp*. And after touching her face, his palms cradling the soft smoothness of her skin, he had had to drag his hands away and the clenched fists at his sides as he strode back down the street had not been clenched in anger, but rather in a need to maintain control, to keep himself from turning around and running back to her.

The kiss—her breath shallow and warm against his lips, the instant of resistance that turned quickly to surrender. He had acted out of frustration, hardly knowing what he was about to do before he had done it, and then it had been too late. He was lost. He had permitted the one thing he had promised himself he would never allow—he had opened his heart to the possibility of love.

"How did it go?" Gunther's booming voice jolted Jeremiah out of his reverie.

"Fine. Good. Is Pleasant here?"

"*Ja.* She has a question about the cones."

"The cones?" Of all the things Jeremiah had imagined that he and Pleasant might say to each other this morning, discussing ice cream cones was not even on the list.

"*Ja.* With Christmas and all, do you need the week's full order? She's started with half, but…"

So that was the way she had decided to handle things. Business as usual. It was probably best, but Jeremiah couldn't help but feel a little disappointed. "Half is good," he muttered. *Well, she's just being practical,* he told himself. After all he was the one who had told her he would never marry. Evidently, she had thought through his impulsive act and decided not to read anything into it. He turned back toward the wagon where the horses were pawing the ground, impatient to be free of their harness.

"I thought you wanted to see Pleasant about something," Gunther called after him.

"It'll keep until I get back," he said without breaking stride.

"You're going away?"

Jeremiah had reached his team of horses and began unhitching the wagon. "I want to go and see my family back in Ohio." *I need to remind myself why I resolved to remain single and why I left there in the first place.*

"What about the shop and your job?" Gunther had followed him and was helping him unhitch and stable the team.

"The shop can be closed until after the first of the year and I've asked for the time off. After all, harvesting won't get started in earnest until January."

Gunther nodded but he was looking at Jeremiah with concern. "Are you all right, Jeremiah?"

"Just need to see my family," Jeremiah replied. "Tell Pleasant not to worry. I'll leave a list of chores for Rolf to handle so he won't lose any of his weekly pay." He could see that Pleasant had come to the door of the bakery's kitchen and was watching them. "And that goes for paying you what we agreed as well, Gunther."

"You're leaving right away then?"

"There's a train I can take this afternoon."

"And the half order of cones Pleasant is making?"

Jeremiah had forgotten all about that. "Box them up and I'll take them with me. My former employer, Peter

Osgood, will enjoy tasting what we came up with and he can use the rest for serving his ice cream."

Gunther was shaking his head as if to say none of this made any sense but he would not insult Jeremiah by questioning him further. "I'll let Pleasant know," he said, patting the rump of one of the horses as he headed back to the bakery.

"And tell her…" *Tell her what? That you don't regret the kiss? That it doesn't change anything? That it changes everything and that's why you're running away?* "Thank her for yesterday," he finished lamely.

"Wouldn't hurt to do that yourself," he heard Gunther grumble as he walked away.

"Yeah, it would," he murmured as he watched Pleasant open the screen door to receive her father. "Just being in the same room with her right now would hurt more than you could possibly imagine."

Chapter Thirteen

Jeremiah had been gone a week when reports of the first cases of influenza were reported in South Carolina. Pleasant was immediately transported back to the virulent 1918 epidemic when her mother had been stricken down and eventually died of the virus. Now news of the deaths of a young mother and two schoolchildren in Georgia spread quickly and in spite of official assurances that this was nothing like the 1918 epidemic, Pleasant and other parents in Celery Fields considered how best to protect their loved ones—especially the children—from harm.

"We're taking the twins and Caleb and going to Wisconsin until this passes," Hannah told Pleasant one day. "We could take your children with us, Pleasant."

"I couldn't ask that of you," Pleasant exclaimed. "You have enough to worry about with your own three and then a new baby on the way."

"That's the main reason Levi insists on going," Hannah admitted as she eased herself onto Gunther's desk chair and let out a sigh of exhaustion. "I told him that he's being overly cautious, but you know Levi."

Pleasant saw the dreamy-eyed look her friend always got whenever she talked about her husband. "You should go," she said. "Levi's right and if his brother has room..."

When Caleb had run away with Levi's circus, Pleasant, Hannah and Gunther had spent several days staying with Levi's brother, Matthew, until arrangements could be made for them to return to Florida.

"Oh, Matthew and Mae have more than enough room and there's also Levi's old house on the circus grounds that's not being used. Plenty of room for your four—and you as well."

"I couldn't leave Papa, and who would mind the business? I mean these days it's all we have," she reminded her friend.

"Then let me take the children," Hannah pressed. "That will relieve you of some responsibility at a time when you need to mind your strength. If you get too run down then you're at risk as well and then what would the children do?"

It made perfect sense.

"Jake has given us the use of Levi's old private railway car for the trip. It will be an adventure for the children and once they reach Wisconsin they'll have the opportunity to see snow and go ice-skating." When Levi had decided to return to his Amish roots, he had sold his company to his business manager and longtime friend, Jake Jenkins. The two had remained close, spending time together during the months that the circus—and Jake—resided in nearby Sarasota.

"You make it sound so exciting," Pleasant said, wavering in spite of her doubts.

Hannah grinned. "Don't you remember what fun we had when we were there—and the journey itself?"

"You were a wreck worrying about Caleb for most of the time," Pleasant said with a grin.

"Well, that aside, we had some good times." She pushed herself to her feet. "Think about it. We're leaving on Friday." She pressed Pleasant's arm on her way to the door. "It's no bother, Pleasant, and I'd really like to do this for you. Levi and I both would. In fact, he was the one who suggested it."

Pleasant swallowed around the lump that had formed in her throat. *"Danke,"* she whispered, surprised to find herself near tears.

After Hannah left, Pleasant thought about the possibility. It was true that ever since she had learned of the disease and how it had already claimed three lives, she had laid awake nights worrying over the children and how best to keep them safe. The idea that she might be the one to fall ill had never occurred to her. What would the children do then? Who would care for them? Hilda Yoder had already taken her seven and gone to stay with her sister in Pennsylvania. Others had followed until the schoolhouse was practically empty and Bishop Troyer had told Lydia that the elders had decided to close the school for the time being.

Of course, no school meant no teacher's stipend and that meant that the financial situation for Pleasant and her extended family was even more dire. The picture was further complicated by the fact that with several families leaving to stay with out-of-town relatives, business at the bakery was practically nonexistent. Jeremiah had closed down the ice cream business when he left to visit his family and Pleasant really doubted that he would re-open once he returned—at least not until life got back to normal for the community.

*What if he didn't return? What if he decided to stay
in Ohio with his family? What if he decided that he'd
made a mistake leaving them and now with the threat
of another flu epidemic he'd be better off not coming
back at all?*

But surely his contract with the Palmer cooperative
would be hard to abandon. After all, by all reports it—
along with his job at the ice plant—would assure him of
a steady income. As he had promised he had left work for
Rolf and paid him in advance. But if he decided to per-
manently close the ice cream shop, Rolf would be dev-
astated. She thought about how hard the boy had worked
to live up to Jeremiah's expectations—or more likely the
expectations he demanded of himself in order to be able
to impress Jeremiah when his employer returned. That
reflected the years when Rolf had tried everything he
could think of to earn his father's approval—and failed.

Until the news of the spread of a new influenza,
Pleasant had been able to think of little else than the
night when she and Jeremiah had shared their first—and
only—kiss and he had told her the story of his uncle.
She understood that it was his fear that he might one day
follow in the man's path that had driven him to leave
town so suddenly and kept him away for over a week
now. He had admitted to having feelings for her—and
the children—feelings that he thought were not in their
best interests. And she had responded to his absence by
denying her own feelings for him, by assuring herself
that she did not think of him as more than a good friend
and neighbor. But every night when she said her prayers
she prayed for forgiveness for the lie she told herself
each day. For in spite of her determination to never again
permit herself to surrender to romantic foolishness, the

truth was that she had fallen deeply and irrevocably in love with Jeremiah Troyer.

It was impossible, of course. By his own report, he was determined never to marry and it was the height of arrogance to believe for one minute that he would choose her should he ever decide to change his mind. Under those circumstances she examined the kiss. What could he have possibly been thinking to act so impulsively? For she had no doubt that it had been impulsive—and that he had regretted his folly.

And yet the way he had cupped her cheeks with his palms had been so incredibly tender and surely a kiss delivered as an act of impulse would have been far more forceful. His lips pressed to hers had been soft and warm and ever so gentle. *Oh, stop being such a fool,* she chastised herself and headed for the bakery even though there was little for her to do there.

The bell over the door jangled as she opened and closed the bakery door. "Papa?" she called. "It's just me," she added as she headed for the kitchen.

She soaked a rag in hot water and started to wipe down the long worktable as she told her father about Hannah's offer. But when he didn't reply, she turned to see what had distracted him and found him hunched over his desk, his breathing shallow.

"Papa!" She knelt next to him and felt his forehead with the back of her hand. He didn't seem to be feverish, but he was very pale. "Papa, what is it?"

"Nothing," he replied weakly. "Just a little…" His eyes rolled back as he slid from the chair to the floor.

"Papa!" Pleasant ran to the front door and cried out for help, then returned to her father's side. He was grimacing in pain and moaning when Moses Yoder and Roger Hadwell came running.

"He needs a doctor," Moses announced.

"I'll go," Roger volunteered and Pleasant knew that he was on his way to the nearest house occupied by an *Englisch* family where they would have a telephone.

"Hurry," she called, then knelt beside her father pulling the cushion from his desk chair to place under his head. "The doctor's coming," she assured him. "It will be all right, Papa." She fought back tears and tried to smile so that he would not see how frightened she was. "I'll stay with you," she promised as she grasped her father's hand between both of hers.

"Do you want me to go get Lydia and Greta?" Moses asked, his voice somber.

At first the question irritated Pleasant. Gunther would be fine as soon as the doctor could tend to him and they could get him moved to the house. Then Lydia and Greta could be of some help but for now...

But then she glanced up at Moses and in his face she saw the truth. Her father might be dying. "Yes," she said and as she felt her father's hand go slack, she murmured, "Hurry, please."

"Oh, Papa," she whispered as soon as they were alone, "please don't leave us. We need you so." Like her father and every Amish person she had ever known, Pleasant did not believe in praying for personal favors, but seeing her strong, good and gentle father so helpless, she was sorely tempted to beg for his life.

"Pleasant?"

"Right here, Papa," she assured him.

"Send the children with Hannah."

So he had heard her. Through all his pain and discomfort as the force that might well end his life had struck, he had heard her say that Hannah and Levi were offering to take the children north until the danger of the influenza could pass. "Yes," she agreed clutching his hand.

"And the girls as well—they can look after the little ones." *The girls* had always been his way of referring to Lydia and Greta. He swallowed with great difficulty. "You go, too."

"No. There's too much to be done. We have the bakery and…"

He attempted a laugh that sounded more like a gurgle, then gathered his strength. "You'll need to start over, Pleasant—you and the girls and Merle's children. Go see the Palmers and see if you can sell them everything. Take Jeremiah with you so he can make a good deal for you. He knows them and…"

"Stop talking such foolishness," Pleasant chided as she wiped his brow and noticed how very white and thin his hair had grown. "We'll be all right. You'll be all right," she said, her voice choking on the words as she faced the reality that the doctor was not likely to make it in time.

"Do as I say," he countered and then opened his rheumy blue eyes and looked at her. "You're a good woman, Pleasant. Always caring for others. I wish…" He closed his eyes and drew in a long shuddering breath.

"Papa?" Pleasant leaned close to catch the words that came next.

"I wish," he whispered, "you to be happy."

"I am happy, Papa," she assured him, making no attempt now to hide her tears. "I have been so blessed and…"

The thunder of running feet came from two directions. At the same time that Moses, Lydia and Greta set the bell to jangling over the front door, Roger Hadwell came through the back door of the bakery with the doctor. Greta was nearly hysterical, clinging to her sister as the two of them stood aside to allow the doctor to examine their father. Knowing that she needed to give the doctor room, Pleasant reluctantly let go of Gunther's hand and went to stand with her half sisters. And as the three of them held on to each other, the doctor turned to them and shook his head. "I'm very sorry for your loss," he murmured before turning to speak quietly to Moses and Roger. The two men nodded and patted the doctor on his back and thanked him for coming as they walked him to the door. And as Pleasant looked at her grieving sisters, she realized that once again she was the one everyone would look to for answers to the question of what to do now. The problem was that she had no answers.

When Jeremiah stepped off the train after spending over two weeks with his mother and siblings in Ohio, he felt none of the optimism he had felt that first time he'd arrived at the station. This time no one was there to meet him since he hadn't let anyone know he was on his way back. The extreme change in temperature from the icy January winds that he'd left behind in Ohio to the balmy warmth of Florida took some getting used to as he carried his single valise up Main Street and headed east and north to Celery Fields.

He saw that there had been little or no rain to relieve the drought the area had suffered for months now. His throat felt choked and his eyes itched with the sandy dust that blew around him as he slowly made his way back home. For he had no doubt that Florida was his home now. There had been nothing left for him in Ohio. There among his own friends and family he had felt always like a visitor, an outsider observing people and places that should have seemed poignantly familiar, but that in truth only felt strange, even foreign.

Wiping sweat from his brow, he saw the cluster of buildings that formed the community of Celery Fields in the distance, took a firmer hold on his suitcase and quickened his step. But the closer he came, the more aware he became that the place seemed almost deserted. His pulse quickened. Had something happened in his absence? Had others closed up shop and gone back to their families in the Midwest?

Pleasant.

Now he found that he was running, stumbling a little as the suitcase knocked against his side. He dropped his suitcase next to the back door of the ice cream shop and hurried around to the front. The street was deserted, but at the far end he saw a line of people filing slowly out of Gunther's house, following a buggy used only for one reason—to carry the dead to their final resting place. When he saw Pleasant and her half sisters walking behind the buggy, he felt as if he'd been kicked by a horse. The body inside that coffin had to be Gunther's—a man he had known for too short a time and one who would be sorely missed by everyone in the community.

He fell into step with the last of the mourners thankful that he had worn his good suit for traveling and so was appropriately and respectfully attired to pay his last respects to Gunther. At the small cemetery, his great-uncle offered a few words of consolation and called for a final silent prayer. Jeremiah kept his eyes on Pleasant who was fully occupied tending to her youngest half sister. Greta seemed inconsolable and clung to Pleasant who stood next to her father's grave as the coffin was slowly lowered by ropes into the ground. As soon as the graveside part of the service was finished, the mourners slowly made their way back to Gunther's modest house. There would be a meal for everyone to share and then the people of Celery Fields would return to their regular routines. Death was just one more piece of God's overall plan for life on earth. The goal for the Amish was to live each day in such a way as to guarantee eternal happiness in Heaven. Certainly Gunther had achieved that.

"Good to have you back," Levi Harnisher said as he came alongside Jeremiah.

"I didn't know," Jeremiah said.

"It was sudden. Heart attack."

They walked on toward Gunther's house and Jeremiah became aware that several people he would have expected to see were not among the small gathering. "Where is Frau Yoder and…"

"There have been reports of a flu epidemic north of here—moving this way. Several of the women have taken their children and gone to stay with relatives up north until we know for sure that it's not like it was in 1918. Hannah is taking our children and Pleasant's to Wisconsin tomorrow."

"And Pleasant?"

"No. She'll stay here. Lydia and Greta have offered to go and care for the children. My former business partner is providing his private railroad car to take them to my brother's farm in Wisconsin."

"But she should go as well."

Levi shook his head as if this was an argument he and others had made and lost. "She's determined to stay.

Says there's no one else to take charge of the bakery or manage two houses or..."

Jeremiah picked up the pace, determined to have a word with Pleasant and convince her to go with the children and other women. "There's no reason for her to stay," he said. "I can easily...."

Levi grasped his arm. "Give her some time," he advised. "Gunther's death was a shock for everyone and I expect for Pleasant it was especially unexpected. She relied on him as much as he relied on her."

It was sound advice and counsel he knew he should heed. So it was hard to explain why after finally seeing her alone for the moment and expressing his sympathies for her loss, the first words that Jeremiah said to her were, "You should go to Wisconsin."

"There is work to be done here." She looked and sounded exhausted and all Jeremiah could think about was that in her present condition, she was as likely as anyone to contract the virus should it make its way to Celery Fields.

"I can do that," he said.

She looked directly at him for the first time and gave him a wan smile. "Indeed? You will collect the eggs, feed the livestock, milk the cows, bake the breads and other wares and..."

"Stop it," he said softly. "You know what I mean."

"No, I don't, Jeremiah. You've been gone. Things here are not the same. Not the same at all."

The look she gave him made him wonder if they were still discussing her father's death and the threat of a flu epidemic. "I am here for you, Pleasant. We all are."

Again, she managed the weak smile that seemed to take more of an effort than she needed at the moment.

"I know that and I appreciate it. Now please excuse me. I need to see about the children." She moved away from him. He watched as she paused to thank Hannah and the other women for all that they had done for her and realized that her response to him had been no different than her response to all the others who had gathered in Gunther's house to prepare the meals and care for the children.

He felt a wave of mild irritation at her unwillingness to accept help—no, to accept *his* help. But then he noticed that she was thinner than he remembered and her skin was so very pale, and the light that had glowed in her eyes was no longer there, and he wanted only to go to her, hold her and tell her everything was going to be all right.

"Herr Troyer?"

Jeremiah looked down at Rolf. The boy was wearing his Sunday clothes and clutching a piece of paper that Jeremiah recognized as the list of chores he'd left for the boy to take care of while he was gone. "Hello, Rolf."

"I have to go to Wisconsin tomorrow so I won't be able to work for you anymore."

"Until you come back," Jeremiah said.

Rolf shrugged and looked down at his shoes. Then he released a sigh worthy of a man three times his age. "What if we never come back?"

Jeremiah knelt so that he was eye to eye with the boy. "You'll be back. Your mother will see to that."

"She's not really our mother."

"Yes, she is—in every way that really counts," Jeremiah assured him.

Rolf eyed him suspiciously for a long moment.

"You can depend on her," Jeremiah stressed. "She

loves you and your sister and the twins as if you were her own children."

Rolf nodded. "Then why isn't she coming with us?"

Jeremiah had no answer for the boy. "She has her reasons. Remember what it was like when your father died?

"Well, her father just died and she's sad and she needs all of us to understand that and do whatever we can to make her feel better."

"I don't see how sending us away will make her feel better. Seems to me she's going to miss us a lot."

"You're right about one thing—she will miss you very much. But the other side of that is that she's doing this to make sure you and the others are safe from the virus that's been spreading this way."

"They closed the school down."

"Well, there you go. They would never close the school unless things were serious. Your mother just wants to do everything she can to protect you."

Jeremiah saw understanding dawn in the eyes of the boy. "She's taking care of us just like she promised," Rolf said. "Even though it makes her sad to see us go so far away."

"That's right, so you must promise to write to her and tell her all about Wisconsin. You're going to see snow and go ice skating and sledding...."

Rolf grinned. "I never thought about that. Real snow?"

Jeremiah stood up and ruffled the boy's hair. "The real stuff. There was a foot or more on the ground when I left Ohio a few days ago."

"I have to tell Bettina," Rolf said as he headed across the room to where Bettina was standing with Pleasant.

Jeremiah saw Pleasant look at Rolf, first with alarm

and then with relief as he breathlessly reported his news and then took off again, this time with Bettina and no doubt to find the twins. Pleasant smiled a genuine smile as she watched them go and then turned to look back at him. "Thank you," she mouthed.

Jeremiah nodded but he was thinking that there was no need to thank him. *It's the kind of thing you do when you care deeply about someone,* he thought. *The way I care about you.*

Chapter Fourteen

Pleasant had never imagined that a person could endure such unrelenting loneliness. Each day that passed seemed more like a month. She missed her father's hearty laughter, his mumbling to himself as she baked while he sat at his desk going over the accounts, and most of all she missed knowing that she could come to him with anything that might be troubling her. The absence of the children was by far the hardest to bear. The long silent days at the bakery followed by endless nights alone in the big empty house only accented her isolation. The whole community seemed deserted with so many of the women and children absent and the men trying to manage alone.

Jeremiah was barely around. She had thought that he might stop by or come to see the children and Hannah and her family off at the train station, but other than their brief encounter at her father's funeral, she had caught sight of him only now and then. He was gone all day and into the evening, the extra work he had taken on with the cooperative now demanding even more of his time. What time he wasn't working at the cooperative or at the ice plant, he spent making deliveries to his regular customers. He had posted a large sign in the window of the ice cream shop announcing that the creamery would reopen in spring and every Friday without fail, Pleasant found an envelope slipped through the bakery's mail slot with payment for the standing order of ice cream cones—cones she no longer made.

She had tried returning the money, taking it to his residence after closing the bakery for the day and after finding no one home, leaving the envelope with a note under his door. But the envelope and money had been back the following day. She was not in the mood to play his game so she started putting the money aside in a special tin box she kept in the bottom drawer of her father's desk. One day she would personally present him that box and its contents and if he refused it she would hand it over to the bishop as a donation for the congregation. Satisfied that she had solved the problem, she resolved not to give one more minute's thought to Jeremiah Troyer—and failed miserably.

For with her father's passing and Hannah leaving for Wisconsin, Pleasant realized that the two people she had relied on the most for conversation and counsel had been removed from her life. She even missed Hilda Yoder. That thought made her smile. After all the times she had wished Hilda would simply leave her alone and let her tend to her business and the children in her way, it was ironic that at this time she would have welcomed her sister-in-law's unannounced arrival and unsolicited guidance.

The truth was that without Gunther, Hannah or Hilda and the distraction of the children and their needs, she found she focused all of her thoughts on Jeremiah. She was far too aware of his comings and goings—even those that she did not witness. Shortly after she arrived at the bakery each morning she heard him hitch up his wagon. She strained to follow the laborious creaking of the wagon wheels as he drove away and counted it an especially good morning if she caught the sound of him clicking his tongue to urge the team of Belgians onward or a glimpse of him through the open door of the bakery.

By the time she closed the bakery for the day, he had not returned and she knew that after working his shift and making his deliveries, he would have spent long hours at the cooperative making sure the harvested crops were properly chilled and prepared for shipment. Sometimes when she sat alone on the front porch of Merle's house after dark, she saw a dim light in the ice cream shop at the opposite end of the street. She imagined him working on his accounts or perhaps he was relaxing from the day's backbreaking work by creating some new ice cream concoction to offer come spring.

They saw each other at the biweekly church services, but with so many of the women gone, Pleasant joined those women who were still in residence in the kitchen. In those homes where the woman of the house was absent and the male members of the family had not kept up with the housekeeping, Pleasant and the other women were well aware that in such a case, they would need to arrive early to make sure the womanless house was clean and ready for services. They would also need to stay late washing dishes and scrubbing pots and pans used for the meal served following services. She was relieved that on this particular Sunday services were to be held in Grace Hadwell's house and Grace along with Mildred Troyer worked side by side with Pleasant in the kitchen.

During services, Pleasant sat between Mildred and Grace and tried to find solace in the words of Bishop Troyer for her grief over the loss of her father and her abject loneliness without the chatter of her children around. But her mind wandered to other matters—the bakery and what to do with it. And what about her father's house? Would it be best to have Lydia and Greta move in with her or should they stay where they were?

Her eyes as well as her mind wandered until her gaze came to rest on Jeremiah. She was cognizant of his every twitch, the way his shoulders and back usually so ramrod straight seemed somehow to have folded in on him, and the way he stared at the floor rather than at the preacher who droned on about wandering in the wilderness. She supposed the lesson was about Moses and the chosen ones but the truth was that it seemed to be more immediate than that. She felt as if she were the wanderer, the lost one, for what was she going to do now?

Business at the bakery had fallen off even more with the absence of so many of the women and children, and with the school closed there was very little income for Lydia and Greta to live on once they returned. Then there was her house and the farm. She had to face the fact that for all intents and purposes she was now the head of Gunther's household as well as Merle's. She felt abandoned and bereft and she was so very tired of being the strong one.

Not that other members of the community hadn't rallied to her needs. Roger Hadwell had shown up one Saturday morning with a crew of neighbors to make much needed repairs to Merle's house and Josef Bontrager showed up every morning to feed and milk the cows, feed the chickens, clean out the chicken coop and barn and deliver the milk and eggs she would use for the day's baking. It was the way of her people—neighbor helping neighbor—and she did not think of these kind and generous acts as charity. Certainly she repaid them in kind through her work on Sunday mornings when there were services and with the bread and baked goods she handed Josef after he made his daily delivery.

Bishop Troyer called for the final prayer and Pleasant bowed her head, closing her eyes tight as she chided herself for not giving herself over to God's work instead of dwelling on her own unhappiness. There had been no reports of cases of influenza in the area for nearly a week now and that meant that perhaps the danger had passed and the children—and Hannah and Lydia and Greta— would soon be able to come home. The thought brought her a sense of peace and when she opened her eyes she smiled at Mildred Troyer who was sitting next to her.

But Mildred met her smile with a worried frown.

"Mildred, is anything the matter?" Pleasant asked.

"It's Jeremiah," Mildred admitted, casting a glance toward her great-nephew who was already making his way across the yard to his buggy. "I'm worried about his health. He's lost weight since coming back and he has this cough and he's working so very hard. John and I barely see him and frankly when he did show up this morning, I could not believe the difference in him."

Pleasant studied Jeremiah for a long moment and almost as if he felt her gaze he glanced her way, hesitated for a moment and then immediately continued on his way. "He does look tired," she admitted and did not add that she'd observed a brightness of his eyes that did not seem to come from any kind of pleasure at seeing her but rather appeared to be the glimmer of fever such as she had seen when the children had been ill with colds. "Perhaps Bishop Troyer could persuade him to see a doctor."

"You agree then?"

"I agree that he doesn't look well," Pleasant said.

"I'm so afraid that perhaps in his travels he contracted the virus," Mildred said and this time she covered her lips with her clenched fist and her voice was a whisper.

Alarm flooded through Pleasant like a sudden downpour. If Jeremiah were ill with the virus then there was no chance that the children would be able to return. More to the point if he were ill, he could be in serious danger. In addition to the early deaths reported in Georgia, there had been rumors of at least half a dozen additional deaths. The numbers were nowhere near as many as during the epidemic but even one death was enough to warrant concern. Her panic at the very idea that after everything else she might lose Jeremiah surprised her. Lose him? What did that mean? It wasn't as if they had any real connection. "He should be quarantined immediately until the doctor can examine him."

Mildred sighed. "Try and tell him that. He assures me that he's just tired from working such long hours— makes a joke about being soft." She hesitated a moment. "He has great respect for you, Pleasant. Perhaps you could speak with him?"

"I…"

"Please try to make him understand that he does himself no favors by working so hard that he becomes ill. His uncle is no longer alive to know of his successes and…"

"I don't understand."

Mildred sighed. "Oh, Pleasant, you, of all people understand. Jeremiah's uncle was a lot like Merle. There was no pleasing the man although certainly Jeremiah spent most of his youth trying—just as Rolf did with Merle."

Pleasant felt that she should defend her late husband's memory but this was the bishop's wife and certainly she had known Merle as well as anyone had. "All right," she agreed and Mildred's smile reflected her relief. "But I can't imagine that…"

"Just talk to him," Mildred urged.

Through the long afternoon after leaving services and returning to her house, Pleasant thought of little other than how best to approach Jeremiah with Mildred's concerns. He did not strike her as a man who would take kindly to meddling and certainly she would be meddling. Besides, it was the Sabbath, so there was no possibility that she could go to the bakery and hope to see him out in the yard or sitting on the stoop outside the ice cream shop. On the other hand, she needed to take care of some things at her father's house—a dwelling that sat not twenty yards to the other side of Jeremiah's shop and residence. Perhaps she would see him after all and it would be rude not to stop and exchange pleasantries.

Having settled on a plan, the outcome lay in God's hands, for unless Jeremiah made his presence known to her, there was little she could do to draw him out. It would certainly be totally inappropriate for her to knock at his door.

But knocking at his door was exactly what she found herself doing not twenty minutes later after she had entered Gunther's dim and shadowy house and found a large black snake coiled in a corner of the kitchen. There wasn't much that Pleasant feared in this world but she drew the line at snakes, even harmless ones as she suspected this one was.

"Pleasant?"

Jeremiah seemed confused when he opened the door, as if he had not quite awakened and yet before knocking she had heard him coughing and moving around his small kitchen. "I'm sorry to bother you, Jeremiah, but I was at my father's—I wanted to…. Well, it doesn't really matter why."

Jeremiah shook his head as if to clear it and in the afternoon light she saw that she had been right about his feverish eyes. "What's happened?" he asked, glancing toward Gunther's house as if expecting to see some catastrophe.

"There's a snake in the kitchen—a large one. Harmless probably but…"

Jeremiah smiled. "Well, well, well. I must say I never saw the day that you would be afraid of anything, Pleasant."

"I'm not afraid of the thing," she protested. "I simply don't like snakes." She tried to disguise an involuntary shudder and failed.

His grin broadened. "Give me a minute." He disappeared inside and returned a moment later with a large basket and a walking stick. "Are you coming or do you want to wait here?" he asked as he stepped past her and walked toward Gunther's open back door. "Chances are the thing has already vacated the premises since you left the door open."

Pleasant trudged along behind him, torn between hoping he was right and the fact that if the snake had simply disappeared how she would know for sure the thing wasn't lurking elsewhere in the house.

"Nope," Jeremiah called as soon as he stepped inside Gunther's kitchen. "Still here."

Pleasant edged closer, her hands and forearms wrapped in her apron as she tried to see what was happening. Then she heard a ruckus as if Jeremiah and the snake were engaged in combat and she shrieked. Just then Jeremiah emerged holding the basket in one hand and pushing the snake back inside it with the walking stick. "One snake removed," he announced but he made no further effort to dispose of the thing.

"Well, now what?" Pleasant asked.

Jeremiah picked up a flour sack from a stack on Gunther's back porch and after some effort he guided the snake into the bag and secured the top. "I could kill it," he offered.

Pleasant was horrified. "You wouldn't. That's one of God's own creatures and it's the Sabbath."

"I don't understand. Are you saying you want me to wait until it's no longer the Sabbath and then kill it?"

"I don't want you to kill it at all," she fumed. "Just…" She glanced around at the fields that stretched out beyond his shop and Gunther's house. "Just take it out there and let it go far away from the house and the school and anywhere else it might decide to nest."

"Yes, ma'am. But you'll have to come along."

"Why?"

"Because I want you to see that it's truly gone. I won't be the cause of you not getting your rest because you're imagining some snake crawling around."

"Very well," she huffed and started off through the nearest field. Behind her she heard him chuckle and then he started to cough.

She turned to see him doubled over as the coughing

racked his entire body. He dropped the flour sack and the tie loosened and she was aware that the snake was slithering off into the field but snake or no snake, she ran to Jeremiah. Supporting him with her arm around his waist she waited for the bout of coughing to end. She was aware that he was gasping for air and she looked around in a panic hoping to see some neighbor that she might call upon to help her get Jeremiah to a place where he could sit down and regain some of the strength that the deep racking cough had sapped.

But there was no one in sight. "All right," she said calmly. "You'll be all right." She might have been speaking to one of her own children. "Lean on me and let's get you back to the house."

He did as she instructed, leaning heavily against her as together they stumbled over the uneven ground to his rooms behind the ice cream shop. Every step of the way she scanned her surroundings for any sign of someone out and about who might help her get him safely home and then go for help. But the lanes leading off the main street of Celery Fields were even more deserted than usual. She tightened her grip on him and saw that her father's house was much closer than his place was. "Come on," she encouraged him. "Just a few more steps."

Thankfully, the back door to Gunther's house required only one small step up to reach. Once inside the kitchen she considered her next move and headed for her father's room just off the hall that led to the front of the house. There she moved as close as possible to the narrow bed and released her hold on Jeremiah, guiding his fall so that he landed on the bed. Somewhere along the way she realized that his hat had come off and she could see that his hair was soaked with perspiration as was his shirt.

"I'll get you some water," she said as she lifted his feet onto the bed, not caring that his shoes were caked with dirt from the fields. He rolled to his back and threw his forearm over his face to shut out the light which seemed to cause him actual pain. "Water," she murmured and hurried back to the kitchen.

She pumped water into a white enameled pan and threw a couple of dish towels over one shoulder. Next she filled a pitcher with water and set it and a glass in the pan of water so she could carry everything at once. Hurrying back down the hall she thought she heard Jeremiah call out. "Coming," she called back.

But when she reached the room he was lying flat on his back, his arm still covering his face and his breathing came in short bursts as if the air could not find its way through his lungs. She set the basin of water on the floor near the head of the bed and pulled a wooden armless rocker that Gunther had made for her mother, closer. Setting the pitcher and drinking glass aside for the moment, she soaked one towel and squeezed the excess water from it before gently swabbing his lips that she now realized were chapped and cracked. He sucked at the moisture as a man who had wandered for days in the desert might.

"Let me wipe your brow," she murmured as she gently pulled the towel free of his mouth and refolded it so that she could dab sweat from his cheeks and forehead. His arm fell heavily to his side but he kept his eyes closed and moaned when she laid the cool towel over them. "Jeremiah, you are very ill and I must go for help."

He rolled his head from side to side.

"I have some water here," she continued. "See if you can sip a little." She cradled the back of his neck with one arm while she maneuvered the glass to his lips with the other. A little water made it into his mouth while more of it trickled down his neck and as soon as he tried to swallow he started to cough. Pushing her hand away he curled onto his side and let the coughing spell have its way with him. When finally it passed he rolled to his back, gasping for breath once again.

Pleasant brushed his hair back from his forehead and in so doing realized that he was burning up. At the same time he was taken by such a chill that his entire body arched and his teeth chattered uncontrollably.

"Blankets," she instructed herself and spread the quilt that had been folded at the end of Gunther's bed over Jeremiah. Instinctively, he reached for it and pulled it closer. Pleasant raced to the bedroom her half sisters shared and grabbed the quilts from both beds. She spread them over Jeremiah, wiped his face and then laid a cool towel over his forehead and eyes.

"I have to go," she whispered, appreciating for perhaps the first time in her life the value of conveniences such as telephones that the *Englisch* world took for granted. "I'll be back," she promised and realized that Jeremiah's breathing had quieted and he was lying very still. "Don't you dare die on me, Jeremiah," she said in her normal voice, and as she ran from Gunther's house all the way to the bishop's home three streets away she was certain that she had only imagined the twitch of a smile that had seemed to relax Jeremiah's features.

Jeremiah was only dimly aware of the activity that surrounded him. He was having some trouble distin-

guishing reality from fantasy. Had he dreamed that
Pleasant had shown up at his door? Certainly he had
dreamed that many times before, wishing for it to be so.
And what about the snake? No, surely that had been real
for he had never been more aware of how the fever he'd
been fighting for a week now had sapped his strength as
he was when trying to wrestle that snake into the basket.

But everything after that was a blur. The light hurt
his eyes. Surely that was not a good sign. And he felt
as if he had been soaked in a hot shower, but then he
had thought himself cast out into the snow without his
coat. He was freezing. There was a woman's gentle voice
speaking to him as his mother once had. But then he had
heard Pleasant's unmistakable order that he was not to
die on her. The statement had made him smile, for only
Pleasant would take his dying so personally. And then
everything went quiet and he stopped trying to make
sense of things and gave in to sleep.

He was awakened by the low murmur of voices—
John speaking in English to another man who was
making little effort to monitor the volume of his voice.
"Pneumonia," he boomed. "No, not the influenza at all.
We haven't seen a case of that in at least a couple of
weeks now and none have been reported anywhere near
here. Your nephew is not contagious, sir, just a very
very sick man."

I can't be sick, Jeremiah mentally argued with the
man.

"Prolonged rest is the key," the man that Jeremiah
had to assume was the doctor announced. "I'll stop back
tomorrow."

Footsteps on the planked floors, a screen door opening and closing with a click, the start-up of a car en-

gine and the sound of the doctor's automobile driving away. Jeremiah waited to be sure the doctor was gone and then rolled to his side and pushed himself into a sitting position. Instantly, everything around him started to spin and shutting his eyes seemed the only recourse for making it stop.

"What do you think you're doing?" Pleasant asked, her tone that of a schoolteacher reprimanding an errant child. "Lie back down in that bed right now."

"I have work to do," Jeremiah said, opening his eyes and gripping the side of the bed just in case. He cleared his throat, trying to rid himself of the huskiness in his voice, and looked around for his shoes. He located them standing in a corner of the room underneath a hook that held his hat. "Where am I?"

"My father's house and if you don't even know where you are then it is beyond me how you think you might be able to concentrate on your work. Besides, it is the Sabbath. Now see if you can swallow a little of this chicken broth that your Aunt Mildred made for you."

He accepted the mug and sipped the hot broth while he watched her bustling around the room stacking towels and fresh linens on a small side table. "I thought I heard Uncle John speaking with the doctor."

"You did. The doctor will return tomorrow. Bishop Troyer has gone home to gather some things he will need while he stays the night with you. Tomorrow the doctor says you can be moved to the bishop's house for the duration."

"And what is the duration?"

She shrugged. "Whatever time it takes for you to heal. It could be a month or…"

"I don't have a month," Jeremiah protested and that

set off a coughing spell that racked his chest with indescribable pain and made breathing seem suddenly impossible. He gripped the mattress harder and waited for the coughing to pass, then gulped in air and fought for his next breath.

Pleasant removed the cup of broth from his hand and knelt next to him. "Slowly," she coached. "The doctor says that it's the panic that can make it worse." She drew in a deep breath of her own and slowly blew it out through pursed lips. And because that reminded him of the kiss they had shared and of his vow not to permit himself to think about that—or her—or the idea that there might be a future for them, he turned away from her.

"How did I get here—to Gunther's?" His voice was weak, barely more than a whisper now.

"There was a snake in the kitchen earlier when I came to check on the house and I came to your house—because it was the closest," she added defensively.

Jeremiah smiled. So the snake had been real as had her fear of it. "Thank you," he said.

Once again she was on her feet and moving around the room, adjusting a lamp shade, refolding a towel. "There's hardly any reason to thank me," she protested. "Had I not gotten you to take care of the snake, you probably would not have overexerted yourself and…"

"Or I might have laid there in my rooms and been unable to catch my breath and…"

"You are not going to die, Jeremiah Troyer. At least not in the near term unless, of course, you refuse to follow doctor's orders and insist on driving yourself too hard and making yourself even sicker in the bargain." Seemingly satisfied that she had properly stocked the sickroom, Pleasant sat down in the lone chair—a small rocking chair and picked up some mending.

"Are you staying as well?"

"I am waiting for the bishop to return. You are too weak to be left alone." She bent to her work, slowly removing the thread from the hem of a pair of boys' trousers.

With little strength and no other real choice, Jeremiah lay back on the bed and watched her. "You make a good nurse," he said.

"I know nothing about that profession," she replied around a half dozen straight pins that she had placed between her lips and was using to set the new hem. "Anyone would have done exactly as I did under the circumstances."

"I can't figure out how you managed to drag me back here. We were in the fields, weren't we?"

"Disposing of the snake—yes."

He had a sudden memory of her arm around his waist, her fingers gripping his side as she urged him to lean on her. "We must have looked like participants in a sack race coming across that field," he said with a chuckle.

"God was with us," she murmured, ducking her head to hide her smile.

He closed his eyes and pulled the quilt that he'd cast aside when he tried to sit up around his shoulders. Instantly, she was at his side. "Are you chilled?" She did not wait for an answer but spread the covers over him and then felt his forehead with the back of her hand.

Her skin was soft and smooth and so wonderfully cool against his brow that it calmed him. "Tired," he muttered. "So very tired."

"Then rest," she replied and readjusted the covers.

"Don't go," he said.

"I'm right here," she replied and he heard the creak of the cane seat of the rocking chair as she sat down next to him.

"Gut," he murmured. Pleasant was there. She would make sure he was all right. She would take care of everything—his job, his business...and him.

Chapter Fifteen

To Pleasant's surprise, Jeremiah turned out to be a very good patient. He took his medicine, followed the doctor's instructions to get plenty of rest and seemed content to allow his Aunt Mildred to mother him. He spent a week at Mildred and John's house and then moved back to his rooms behind the ice cream shop. Levi had organized the men of Celery Fields to cover Jeremiah's work from his shifts at the ice plant to the delivery of ice to homes in the area to the delivery of ice to the cooperative. All of this Pleasant learned from Mildred when the older woman stopped by the bakery after checking on Jeremiah.

For her part she kept her distance, taking comfort in the news of his recovery but stopping short of visiting him herself. She told herself that she was only doing what was proper, but in truth she knew that she had allowed herself to become too involved in his life—she had allowed herself to care for him in ways that were not appropriate and certainly not something that he would welcome given his determination never to marry.

So when the train carrying Hannah and the children

along with Lydia and Greta returned a week after Jeremiah had moved back to his place behind the ice cream shop, Pleasant was both ecstatic at having her children and dear friend home again and relieved that surely now her days would once again be so full that she would not have time to think about Jeremiah so much.

Hilda Yoder and her children had been back for three days now and Pleasant was anxious to have her own family home again. But she had not realized how very much she had missed the children until she saw them coming toward her at the station. Rolf looked as if he had grown another two inches in just the two weeks they had been away. And Bettina walked with a quiet grace that was new for her and reminded Pleasant of Levi's sister-in-law, Mae. The twins, however, did not seem to have changed at all. They ran pell-mell to her open arms, competing to be the first to report all of the new experiences they had shared.

Hannah and Lydia and Greta stood off to one side waiting their turn to be welcomed home while Caleb and Levi took charge of loading their luggage onto the buggy.

"Thank you so much," Pleasant said to Hannah after the twins had run off to tell Levi of their adventures.

"How are things here?" Hannah asked. "I understand that Jeremiah Troyer has fallen ill?"

Pleasant nodded. "Pneumonia. God has blessed him and the medicine—penicillin—that the doctor gave him seems to have brought him through the worst of it. He's doing much better but he's been left weak as a newborn kitten." She did not add that in spite of the efforts of Levi and the other men in the community to keep Jeremiah's agreement with the Palmer brothers, she had noticed the truck of a competing ice delivery service parked outside the offices of the cooperative as she followed Levi in her own buggy on their way to meet the train.

"He can't work then?"

"Not yet. But Levi and the others have helped out."

"And how is business at the bakery?"

Pleasant smiled. "Better since the threat of the flu passed. We're even getting orders again from merchants in Sarasota. Apparently, business there has started to improve with the arrival of the winter visitors. Not so many as in the past but some."

"So, once again God has blessed our community," Hannah said with a sigh of relief. "And I am more than a little anxious to get home and see how Levi has fared these last two weeks."

Pleasant smiled. "Your house is spotless."

"I doubt that but whatever its state it will be good to be home again." She smiled at her husband who helped her into the front seat of their buggy while Caleb took his place with his younger siblings in back. Once seated, Hannah's pregnancy became more obvious as she folded her hands over her stomach pressing the fullness of her skirt around it.

Pleasant waved to them as they drove away and then turned to her own family—grown now to include her two half sisters. It occurred to her that they had some decisions to make starting with whether or not Lydia and Greta would move in with her or stay in their father's house. Lydia was certainly of age to manage a household, but she also had the school to manage. Greta would no doubt marry Josef Bontrager as soon as that young man worked up his nerve to ask her and that would leave Lydia alone.

"Let's go home," Lydia said quietly as they watched the Harnisher family drive away. And as if she had been thinking the same thoughts as Pleasant, she added, "We can work out the details of where Greta and I will reside tomorrow. For today, I just want to be at home, all right?"

"Of course," Pleasant assured her and then orchestrated the loading of the four children and three adults into her small buggy. Greta rode in back with the twins cuddled in her lap and Rolf and Bettina crowded to either side of her while Lydia rode up front with Pleasant. The children continued to fill her in on everything they had seen and everyone they had met on their journey, but Pleasant saw that Jeremiah's competitor's truck was still at the cooperative as they passed and her thoughts wandered. "I need to make one stop," she said as she turned the buggy onto the sandy road that led to the low concrete building housing the offices of the cooperative.

Just as she pulled the buggy to a halt, a man exited the offices and got into the truck and drove away.

"I'll be right back," Pleasant said as she climbed down and walked stiffly toward the front door of the building. She had no idea what she was going to say or even who might be available to hear her out, but she would not stand by and let someone else take business away from Jeremiah.

"May I help you?" A young woman, her lips lined with lipstick and her hair artificially curled glanced up with surprise when Pleasant entered the small reception area.

"I wonder if the manager is available."

"Sorry. Everyone has gone for the day. I was just getting ready to close up myself and…"

"I saw a truck outside just now—a truck for the Venice Ice Company?"

To Pleasant's surprise, the woman blushed scarlet red and became more than a little agitated, wringing her hands and glancing around as if expecting someone to pop out of a closed doorway at any moment. "Please don't say anything," she said, her voice barely above a whisper. "Hank's my boyfriend and he just stopped by to…if my bosses knew that I was entertaining…please," she pleaded.

Relief flooded Pleasant. "Oh, I see. Then that young man was not here on business for…"

"No and there's the trouble, don't you see? He was supposed to be finishing up his delivery route but then he saw that the Palmers' car was gone and he…"

"Please don't feel you owe me any explanation, Miss." Pleasant turned back to the door.

"Shall I tell my bosses that you wanted to see them?"

"No. That won't be necessary," Pleasant replied. "Good day."

Outside, Pleasant ignored Lydia's curious glance as she climbed back into the buggy and took the reins.

"Is everything all right?"

"Yes. Perfectly all right now that my family is safely home again," Pleasant assured her; *and Jeremiah's business is apparently safe as well.*

The better Jeremiah felt the more restless he became and yet it was clear that he did not yet have the strength to manage the heavy work of his job at the ice plant or making deliveries. Levi stopped by daily to give him reports about who would be making the deliveries that day and who would be going to the cooperative to handle things there. Business throughout the region was improving and everyone was relieved about that. And Jeremiah was most appreciative of the ways his neighbors in Celery Fields had stepped in to help him while managing their own farms and businesses, but he felt the need to repay them in some way and sooner rather than later.

A few days earlier the doctor had given permission for him to move back to his rooms behind the ice cream shop. Mildred and John came by several times a day on the excuse of bringing him food or the need to do his laundry or some other housekeeping chore. He was well aware that his great-aunt and -uncle were more interested in checking up on him to make sure he didn't overdo than they were in delivering food or taking care of household matters. Still, he was relieved to be back in his own place waking each morning to the smell of fresh bread baking next door and thoughts of Pleasant.

He lay back on his narrow bed with his arms crossed behind his head and savored the aroma of Pleasant's rye bread. Later in the morning she would bake up some pies and other sweets to fill the display case in the front of the shop. He felt a sudden hunger for one of her molasses cookies and driven by that hunger he got himself dressed and walked slowly across the yard that separated her business from his. He refused to admit to himself that it wasn't molasses cookies drawing him to the bakery. It was the fact that it had been days since he'd seen Pleasant, much less talked to her, and he missed her.

"Guten morgen," he said and realized that his voice was still raspy from the effects of his illness and from lack of use. Pleasant spun around.

"I...*ja...guten morgen.*" She seemed unusually flustered by his presence, wiping her hands on a towel and looking anywhere but directly at him. "Should you be out like this?" she asked.

"The doctor suggested a few short walks as a way to regain my strength. From my shop to yours would seem to fit the bill. I had hoped there might be one of your molasses cookies available to give me the strength to make it home again." He opened the screen door and entered the kitchen but he was aware that he needed to be cautious in his movements. For reasons he didn't fully understand, Pleasant was as skittish around him as a newborn colt.

"I was just about to bake a batch," she said nodding to the trays lined up on the worktable. "I could bring you some once they cool."

"I'll wait if that's all right." He glanced toward Gunther's desk, the chair pushed in so that it did not invite anyone to sit there. "How's business?" he asked leaning against the doorway.

"Better," she said and seemed to relax. "For everyone, I think. For the bakery it means that some of the customers we had from Sarasota—shops and restaurants that carried our goods—have come back to us. And there are a surprising number of winter tourists in the area—some of them have found their way here. They come because they are curious to see how we live and then they stay to shop."

"I was thinking about reopening the ice cream shop," Jeremiah said.

Pleasant frowned. "That would be a great deal of work for you. Just churning the ice cream takes so much effort and…"

"I was thinking that maybe Rolf and Caleb Harnisher

could do that part of it." He waited to see how she would react to this idea.

"That might work but still there's everything else and you've been so ill and…"

"But I am better now, Pleasant, and I will get a little stronger every day. Besides, I would like to find some way to express my gratitude for everything that's been done for me."

"You know that no one expects repayment or thanks, Jeremiah. In fact…"

He nodded. "I understand that I have to take care in how I offer my gratitude, but that's the very reason reopening the ice cream shop might just be the answer. Uncle John mentioned the idea of a community picnic the other day and I was thinking that I could donate the ice cream for that as a way of letting folks know the ice cream shop is back in business. The question is whether with all you have to do, can you make the cones?"

"Of course, and speaking of that…" She went to Gunther's desk and opened a drawer. From far in the back of it she removed a tin box and handed it to him.

"What's this? A present?" He grinned.

"If that's how you choose to think of it but be assured that it is a gift you have given yourself."

Intrigued, he opened the box and his eyes widened when he saw the stack of money it contained. "What is this?"

"My father would never have accepted payment for goods never delivered," she explained, "and neither will I. Since you refused to stop leaving the weekly payment for cones never delivered I have kept the money here. And now that you are prepared to go back into business and apparently hire extra help, it is money I'm sure you can put to good use."

He closed the box and set it on the desk. "You are one stubborn woman, Pleasant Obermeier."

She apparently chose to ignore this, turning her attention to the ovens where she checked on the progress of the cookies. She slid one tray out and set it with a clatter on the worktable. He reached for a cookie and she swatted his hand away. "You'll burn yourself. Let them cool first."

He caught her hand in his and held on. It was an act of pure impulse but one that he did not regret. "Did you love him—your husband?" he asked and was as stunned as she obviously was at the question.

She pulled her fingers free of his and focused on removing the cookies from the pan to a large glass plate. At first he thought that she would ignore his question as she had his comment about her being stubborn, but after a moment she said, "Merle was not a man who believed in the kind of romantic love that I think you may mean."

"But you do believe in it?"

She pressed her lips into a thin line and then looked up at him. "I am a widow with four children and two half sisters who depend on me," she replied. "I have no time to think about such foolishness."

"Why not?" he pressed. "You're still relatively young and you have much to offer."

She placed the last cookie on the plate and then rested her hands on the edge of the worktable, her head bowed and her fingers clutching the table as if she drew strength from it. "Why are you doing this?" she whispered.

Why, indeed?

"Because I think perhaps it would be good to see

someone care for you the way you care for everyone around you, Pleasant. Because I would like to see you happy."

She swiped at her eyes with the back of her hand and he moved closer but she waved him away. "I have four beautiful children, Jeremiah. I have sisters that I have come to treasure and wonderful friends in a community that has sustained me through many difficult times. Why would you push me to want more?"

Because I have come to love you. The clarity of that admission was almost his undoing. Everything he had ever promised himself he would never allow was unraveled in those few words and yet the truth they held could not be denied. "Pleasant, we are two people walking through this life on parallel paths. Might we not see what would happen should we try walking the path together?"

Her eyes sparkled with unshed tears and disbelief as she looked up at him. "I do not need your pity, Jeremiah Troyer."

"I am not offering pity, Pleasant. I am offering my love."

She was speechless and did what he had observed was her natural reaction to such loss of control of the situation. She focused on something else. Placing two cookies in front of him she picked up the glass plate and headed to the front of the bakery. "You have been ill," she said as she deliberately put distance between them. "And such a serious illness—especially after the loss of a good friend—for certainly you and Gunther had become…"

He caught up with her and waited for her to place the plate of cookies in the display case before touching her lightly on her arm. "I am not delusional, Pleasant, and I know exactly what I just said. I will admit that it came as a surprise to me as it apparently did to you but that in no way changes the fact of it. I have feelings for you that go well beyond that of a neighbor for a neighbor. I believe that you return at least a portion of those same feelings and I am suggesting that we recognize that perhaps this is why God has brought us to this place at this time."

"Yet on Second Christmas you told me…"

"I also kissed you, Pleasant, and you kissed me back."

The bell over the bakery door announced the arrival of a customer and both Jeremiah and Pleasant jumped as if they had been caught doing something they shouldn't be doing.

"Well, Jeremiah," Hilda Yoder said as she eyed the two of them, "it would appear that you are indeed on the mend."

"Jeremiah was just…just…" Pleasant stuttered.

"I stopped by to see if Pleasant would have time to bake up an order of cones for my ice cream, Frau Yoder. I'm sure you've heard that the bishop has suggested a community picnic to celebrate the end to the threat of a flu epidemic and the return of the children and reopening of the school. It is my intention to provide the ice cream for that event."

"I see," Hilda said, still eyeing them both suspiciously.

"And I was just saying that I could definitely bake the cones once the bishop decides on the date for the picnic," Pleasant added as she edged around Jeremiah and moved closer to her former sister-in-law.

"That's what I came to tell you. The bishop was just in the store and said that the picnic is to be a week from Saturday." Hilda turned her full attention to Jeremiah. "Are you sure you're up to the challenge of this, Jeremiah? Churning ice cream to serve the entire community could…"

"I plan to hire help," Jeremiah told her. "Pleasant's son Rolf and Caleb Harnisher…and what about your eldest son? He's a good strong boy."

"I suppose that would be all right," Hilda replied and Jeremiah could see that she was pleased to be asked.

"Then it's all settled," he said. "And now if you'll excuse me, I expect my Aunt Mildred has gone to my house to prepare my lunch and she'll worry when she discovers that I'm not there. I'll just go out the back," he said as he turned away from Hilda so that she would not see the pleading look he gave Pleasant. "Think about it," he mouthed and when she nodded, his heart felt as if it might actually pound its way right out of his chest.

Think about it? As if she could think of anything else. Not even Hilda's chatter distracted her as she tried to find some order in the events of the past few minutes. Several people in the community had commented on the fact that Jeremiah seemed to be a man prone to sudden decisions and even rash actions. The evidence of that lay in his decision to pull up stakes and leave a perfectly good farming business to start over in Florida. Further evidence lay in his sudden decision to head north after the holidays. Speculation had run rampant that he had realized the folly of his decision and decided to return to his family and possibly reclaim his place there. Pleasant doubted if anyone would be surprised at the way in which he had orchestrated a complete about-face from his earlier lifelong bachelor status to ask her permission to court her. For that was what he was asking, wasn't it?

"Are you listening, Pleasant?" Hilda demanded.

"I apologize. I have a great deal on my mind and now with the addition of Jeremiah's…"

"Precisely," Hilda huffed. "As I was saying, you have become the focal point for some village gossip, Pleasant, and it does you no good to continue your contact with this man."

"It's business," Pleasant protested and felt she did not need to add that it was business she could use.

"And yet, I have learned that you were alone with the man when he fell ill, that you got him to your father's house and were in there for some time with him—alone—before additional help could arrive."

"Would you have had me leave the poor man lying in the fields?" Pleasant snapped. "I'm sorry, Hilda. That was uncalled for. I assure you that the relationship between Herr Troyer and myself is strictly…"

"I saw his hand on your arm when I entered the bakery, Pleasant."

Pleasant would not lie to cover the truth of Hilda's accusation so she remained silent.

"My dear, nothing would make Moses and me happier than to see you find a good man. You deserve that after everything Merle put you through."

Pleasant's eyes widened with shock, but Hilda waved away her surprise.

"Oh, I know what my brother was, Pleasant. I had hoped—we all had—that once he married you he might change, but…" She shook her head. "I know that he struck not only the children but you as well and I am sorry for that. His temper had always been uncontrollable. Even when we were children…"

"Oh, Hilda, are you saying that Merle struck you?"

Hilda nodded. "He always had to be in control and

whenever that control seemed threatened, he would lash out, usually at the ones nearest and dearest to him."

"And yet, he did love the children—and their mother," Pleasant reminded Hilda, feeling a duty to defend her late husband. When Hilda said nothing, Pleasant said, "I know you worry about me, Hilda, and I am grateful for that, but Jeremiah…"

Hilda held up her hand to stop her from saying anything further. "Mark my words, Pleasant, you need to watch yourself where that man is concerned. You have a reputation to maintain—a reputation that reflects on those children and now on your sisters as well."

Pleasant realized that Hilda was waiting for some kind of assurance that she had heard and would heed the warning so she chose her words with care. "I appreciate your advice as always, Hilda, but I assure you that you have nothing to be concerned about. It is business, nothing more."

"Suit yourself," Hilda said, "but a man puts his hand on you—well, it raises questions." And before Pleasant could say anything more, Hilda turned on her heel and left the bakery.

She was right, of course, Pleasant thought once she was alone again. Anyone could have walked in. Anyone could have glanced through the bakery windows and wondered why Jeremiah was standing behind the display case instead of in front of it and why he was standing there with her. And Hilda was right to remind Pleasant of her obligation to the children and to Lydia and Greta since she was now the head of both households.

Oh, but she was so very tired of the bonds that came with duty—the shoulds and could-nots. She loved her friends and family and certainly at her age she should know better than to indulge herself in some romantic fantasy. And yet the idea of being courted by a man as handsome and filled with joy as Jeremiah was—no! Not a man *like* Jeremiah, but Jeremiah himself. All her life she had lived by the traditions of her faith and she was not about to change now. And yet was there some possibility that Jeremiah had been right—that God had a plan for them? Surely there was no harm in getting to know each other a little better. If nothing else, he was good with the children and certainly Rolf needed the influence of a successful man in his life.

She put down the mixing bowl she'd been cradling in her arm while beating batter for a cake and smoothed her apron. Then she wrapped the cookies he'd left on the worktable in wax paper and stepped outside. To her relief, Jeremiah was outside as well for it would not do to call on him in his private residence without the buffer of either the children or another adult. He was standing outside the ice cream shop making notes on a folded piece of paper with a stub of a pencil.

"You forgot the cookies," she said and handed him the package.

"So I did. Thanks." He put down the paper and pencil and unwrapped the cookies. As he took a bite of one, he looked at her and a half smile skittered over his lips. "Best I ever had," he proclaimed, waving the half eaten cookie in her direction.

"I was wondering if you would be wanting the sample cones again? For the picnic?"

"What do you think?" He started on the second cookie.

"I wouldn't think so if the ice cream is for the picnic.

I just thought perhaps for the reopening of the shop you might want to repeat…"

"The regular cones will be fine," he said, dusting off the crumbs of cookies that had stuck to his fingers.

"All right," she said and paused. Back in the bakery she had been so clear about what she wanted to say to him but standing here not a foot from him was a different matter altogether.

"Was there something else, Pleasant?"

Was it her overactive imagination playing tricks on her once again or was there a hint of hope in that question?

"I—uh—about what we were discussing before Hilda came in."

He released a ragged sigh and frowned. "Look, I…"

"If you're feeling up to it, I thought perhaps you and the bishop and your Aunt Mildred might come over for supper this evening. We could discuss the plans for the picnic."

This time she did not need to imagine the interpretation of his expression. Disappointment lined the corners of his mouth and eyes as plainly as a smile might have. "So, it's business as always with you, is it, Pleasant?"

"No. That is… Oh, Jeremiah, why must you make things so difficult?"

He laughed incredulously. "Me? What about you?"

She straightened her spine, preparing to speak her piece and then get away from him as quickly as possible. "Courting in the true sense is out of the question. However…"

"Why?"

"However," she stressed, "I have decided that it would be good for us to know each other better. We are neighbors after all and business associates and the children are fond of you."

"You have decided?"

She truly wished he would stop challenging her with questions. *So leave.* But her feet remained rooted to the ground.

He took half a step closer. "And what if I have decided something entirely different, Pleasant?" He lowered his voice. "What if I have decided that one kiss simply will not do?"

She felt the blood rush to her cheeks at the very idea of repeating that kiss. "Stop it," she said but her voice failed her and the words came out on a whisper.

Jeremiah moved a step away from her. "I will come for supper."

"With the bishop," she amended.

"With the bishop," he agreed.

"Das ist gut," she said and forced herself to turn back toward the bakery.

"And afterward," he added when she was a good ten steps from him, "after the children are in bed and my uncle and aunt are safely home again, I will come back and you and I will start to tell one another our stories, Pleasant."

The idea of sitting with Jeremiah on her back porch after everyone else in the community was asleep and telling him all the things she had kept in her heart filled her with such a rush of joy that Pleasant found she could not speak. And so without looking back at him, she said only one word. *"Ja."*

Chapter Sixteen

Ever since Gunther's death, Pleasant had taken to closing the bakery on Mondays. She made use of that day to tend to household matters and she continued to participate in the weekly frolics the women of the community had established. On the Monday that followed a week of nightly visits from Jeremiah, she drove her buggy to the Harnisher farm, anxious to see Hannah even if she really couldn't talk to her friend about Jeremiah with the other women around.

She was so confused by him. As he had promised, he came to her back porch every night around nine and took a seat on the first step. He did not knock or otherwise make his presence known, just sat out there and waited for her to join him. "And what if I didn't come out here?" she'd asked him on the third night.

"Then I would assume you had something else to do and leave, but I would be back the next night and the one after that," he told her. "You don't have to worry, Pleasant. We're just going to talk—for now."

And the implied promise that somewhere down the road they might do more than talk—that there might be a repeat of that sweet kiss they had shared on Christmas, was the last thought Pleasant had as she drifted off to sleep each night and the first that she awoke to each morning.

After a week of his visits, she knew more about him than she had ever known about Merle and she had shared things with him that she had never told anyone else—not even her best friend, Hannah. But the fact was that she was falling deeply in love with Jeremiah and before she would risk disappointment in romance for a third time in her life, she needed the advice of someone who had known true love. How did a person know for certain?

As if Hannah had understood Pleasant's need to talk, she suggested that the other women take charge of the housecleaning while she and Pleasant worked in the garden. "That way we can make short work of both tasks and have time for some quilting and conversation before everyone needs to get home."

Only Hilda seemed about to object but seeing that she was alone in that, she bit her lip and took charge of organizing the other women while Hannah and Pleasant escaped to the large kitchen garden that Hannah had planted close to the house.

"All right," Hannah said as Pleasant knelt along the border of the garden and started pulling weeds. "Talk to me. Levi tells me that Jeremiah is courting you."

Pleasant sucked in her breath. "He said that?"

"The women aren't the only ones who talk, Pleasant. Besides, Levi and Jeremiah have become good friends." She set down a bucket of water for Pleasant to use in softening the hard ground. "So?"

"Courting is too strong a word. We are getting better acquainted. The children admire him—especially Rolf—and I need to make certain that…"

"Stop that," Hannah said with more irritation than Pleasant had ever heard from her. "You have waited your whole life for a man like Jeremiah—a good man—a man who will be good to you."

"How can you know that?"

"I know that he is not at all like Merle. I know from what you have told me and what he has told Levi that he has tried hard to be honest with you about his intentions."

"Oh, I don't know," Pleasant said. "At first he made it very clear that he was not going to marry—ever."

"And now?"

"Now he…he professes to love me," she said, her voice fading away with the wonder of saying those words aloud instead of savoring them in her heart when she was alone.

"And do you love him?"

There was no sense beating around the bush with Hannah. She seemed to be able to see through Pleasant's protests and excuses better than anyone Pleasant had ever known. "I love him," she admitted.

To her surprise, Hannah laughed. "Well, you don't have to make it sound like the worst thing that has ever happened to you. This is a good thing—he loves you and you love him." She dusted dirt off her hands and stood up. "So call it what you like—getting better acquainted or whatever suits you. He's courting you and you are permitting that courtship."

"Leading to what?" Pleasant asked the single question that had plagued her every night after Jeremiah returned to his house.

"Marriage, a father for those children, a companion for you to share the rest of your days with, a…"

"He has changed his mind once," Pleasant told her friend. "There is nothing to say that he won't realize his mistake and change it back to his decision never to marry."

"Oh, Pleasant, you are a woman of great faith. Surely you have prayed on this matter."

"Well, of course. I pray daily for the wisdom to make the decisions that will keep the children safe and secure and support Lydia and Greta until they are established in households of their own."

"And do you never pray for yourself?"

"That would be selfish and you know it."

Hannah leaned on a long-handled hoe. "You haven't a selfish bone in your body," she said. "You are praying for guidance in your dealings with the children and your sisters. How is that any different than praying for guidance in your personal dealings with Jeremiah?"

Pleasant bit her lip as she got to her feet and deposited a small pile of pulled weeds into the now-empty water bucket. "I don't want to be hurt yet again," she admitted.

Hannah relieved her of the bucket and started back toward the shed where she stored her gardening tools. "Think of it this way, Pleasant. You agreed to marry Merle even when you knew his interest in you was to gain a mother for his children rather than his undying love for you. Am I right?"

Pleasant nodded. "He made that plain enough."

"And now Jeremiah is making it plain that he has come to love you—as a woman he wishes to share his life with."

Pleasant felt her heart swell with hope. "Did he say those things to Levi?"

"He did, but more to the point, I would guess that he has said those things to you."

Pleasant could not deny the truth of that for every night when he was about to leave, he held her with such tenderness as if she were fragile and might disappear, and every night he murmured, "I love you, Pleasant." And although she had yet to say those words back to him, he had not stopped telling her that he loved her.

"Trust your heart, Pleasant," Hannah advised. "As I did with Levi."

Tears of happiness and gratitude filled Pleasant's eyes and in the shadow of the garden shed, she grinned at her friend. "You really think that...?"

"I really do," Hannah assured her as she squeezed Pleasant's hand.

And in that moment, Pleasant decided that the picnic would be the perfect venue for her to find a time to truly open her heart to Jeremiah Troyer. *And if he breaks it?* an inner voice nagged.

"He wouldn't," Pleasant whispered under her breath, and as she followed Hannah back to the house where the other women were waiting, she had never felt more certain that this time—with this man—things would be different.

John Troyer had picked the perfect day for a celebratory picnic. After a cold winter—even by Florida standards—the day was perfect with temperatures in the mid-seventies, blue skies and not a hint of humidity. Church elders had chosen a spot along a branch of the meandering Phillippi Creek for the event and by midmorning buggies filled with smiling adults and excited children had already started to arrive. By noon the area was packed with people of all ages, all similarly attired and all smiling broadly. Women, helped by their teen-aged daughters and granddaughters laid out a spread of food while the men and older boys wandered down to the creek to try their luck at fishing or pounded stakes into the hard ground for a game of horseshoes. The younger children needed no organized activity to fill their time. The place was rife with the possibility of adventure and the children made their own games.

"We're pioneers," Will announced when Pleasant asked what they were playing. She could not help thinking that in many ways the people of Celery Fields were indeed pioneers. Every adult present had migrated here from somewhere else. Only the children could claim to be native Floridians—and not all of them.

"And just what do pioneers do?" she called back to her son.

"Explore," Henry shouted with glee and took off running toward the banks of the creek.

"Be careful," Pleasant said and had taken a step to follow them when she felt Jeremiah's hand on her shoulder.

"I'll go," he said. "Just save me a place next to you for the picnic." He winked at her and instead of glancing around nervously to see who might be looking, Pleasant simply smiled. The fact was that after today—after she had finally told him she returned his feelings and was ready for the two of them to plan a future together—it wouldn't really matter what anyone else thought.

"Don't fall in the creek," she warned. "I believe somewhere along the way I heard you admit that you never learned to swim?"

He grinned and waved as he headed for the creek.

It was that kind of day, Pleasant decided. A day when everyone regardless of age felt a bit like a kid again. A day that invited friends to joke with one another. A perfect day for admitting to yourself and the world around you that you had fallen deeply in love and never in your entire life felt happier or more fulfilled. Pleasant just wished that her parents could be here to share in this moment of unadulterated joy.

She hummed to herself as she mixed up a salad from the bounty that several gardens had yielded. Nearby Hannah was squeezing fruit for the fresh lemonade, limeade and orangeade that they would all enjoy with their meal of cold fried chicken, beans simmering in pots over open fires and cold side dishes such as the salad she was making. For dessert there would be pies of all flavors and cakes that stood three layers high and cookies for the children to grab as they went back to their adventures.

She was just about to place the salad on the table when she looked toward the creek and her heart stopped. Jeremiah had just roughly snatched Henry into one arm and was raising a stick high over Will's head. Both boys were howling with fear. As he brought the stick down next to the boy, Pleasant dropped the salad and started to run.

Not again, she prayed as she ran, images of Merle's disciplining Rolf in the barnyard behind their house, a switch raised and lowered again and again striking the boy who refused to cry out.

"Stop that right now," she ordered when she was close enough to be heard.

Jeremiah looked at her and then slowly lowered Henry

back to the ground. "You're all right," she heard him murmur even as he cupped the back of Will's head. "It's over."

"Boys, come away from there this instant," Pleasant ordered and when they ran to her without question and clutched at her skirt, she felt that the one thing she had hoped to be wrong about had been confirmed. Jeremiah had lost his temper and her boys had been the object of his fury. Without a word to Jeremiah, she turned and shepherded them away from the creek. "Bettina, go find Rolf. We're leaving."

She saw disappointment reflected in the girl's eyes but her daughter did not question her. Instead, she ran to a cluster of older boys and pulled Rolf away. Pleasant saw the two of them whispering as they cast glances first at her and then at the creek bank where Jeremiah was still standing, no stick in sight.

"Why do we hafta go?" Henry wailed.

"We're all right," Will told her. "We promise to stay away from the creek, Mama."

Was that what had set Jeremiah off? Had he called for the twins to come away from the creek and they had refused? It would certainly have been enough to spark Merle's temper. She shuddered and snapped the reins to urge the horse away from the gawking crowd of friends and neighbors. Once again, Pleasant Goodloe Obermeier was no doubt going to be the main topic of gossip for the next several days.

Once again she had made a fool of herself and all because of some man.

Jeremiah stood watching her drive away thinking about the way she had looked at him. He understood what she thought she had seen. From that distance she would never have even noticed the alligator that had started to slowly snake its way along the bank to where the boys were playing. Jeremiah had had only seconds to act. He'd grabbed the boy closest to him and then with God's blessing had found the thick tree branch within easy reach.

Quietly he had told Will not to move and then with a force he had not thought himself capable of, he had struck the alligator across its long flat nose. Instantly, the thing had slithered back into the water, leaving Will a trembling mass on the shore and both boys in tears. But before he could comfort the boys, Pleasant had ordered them away from him—as if he would harm a hair on their golden heads.

But her doubt had been there in the glare with which she met his confused look. Her accusation had been silently hurled in the way she had turned away and herded the children back to the gathering, then without stopping to say a word to anyone, had loaded all four children into her buggy and driven away. She had not waited for explanations—she had not even considered that there might be one. She had simply assumed that he—like her late husband and like his uncle—was a man who could not control his temper.

He had lost her. Who was he kidding? He had never had her trust, her love—not really.

By the time he made his way back to the picnic, the speculation was rampant about why Pleasant had left so abruptly.

"One of the twins must have taken ill," Hilda Yoder announced. "The boy was in tears and who knows what those children might have been eating. Some wild berry out there in the brush. It happens when children are allowed to go unattended."

No one else seemed to have witnessed the scene that had made Pleasant drop the bowl she was carrying, scattering salad all over the ground and take off running toward the creek. By the time others had looked around it seemed that the twins were clinging to her as she brought them back to the family buggy and sent Bettina to find Rolf so they could leave. But Hannah Harnisher glanced at Jeremiah and raised her eyebrows in an unspoken question. Blessedly she did not ask that question aloud and he hoped that others had forgotten that he was with the boys and might offer an explanation for Pleasant's sudden departure.

"Jeremiah, you were down there with the twins," his great-aunt said and immediately others turned to him, seeking answers.

Not wanting to scare the other mothers, Jeremiah decided against talking about the alligator. "I'm not sure what happened," he said and that was not a lie. Until he could talk to Pleasant, his interpretation of her actions was pure conjecture. "But I'm certain that the boys will be fine."

Seemingly satisfied with this, Mildred turned to her husband. "Well, John, everyone is famished. Shall we eat?"

The bishop offered grace and Pleasant and her children were forgotten as everyone gathered to fill plates and find a spot in the shade to enjoy the picnic with friends and neighbors.

Jeremiah found that he didn't have much of an appetite and the fact that he had invited everyone to stop at the ice cream shop on their way home for a cone of his newest flavor—key lime vanilla—was no more appealing than the mounds of food that filled the plate Hannah handed to him.

"Will you join us, Jeremiah?" she invited, indicating a spot where Caleb and Levi and the Harnisher twins were settling to enjoy their food.

"Thank you." He was grateful for her kindness and knew that in spite of her curiosity, she would not pry. He could eat in peace and then make the excuse of needing to get back to town before everyone else came back for the promised ice cream.

He forced down half of the food and set his plate aside. He seemed incapable of thinking about anything other than the fact that in spite of everything they had shared these past evenings, Pleasant had assumed the worst. And the more he thought about the unfairness of her action, the more irritated he became. By the time he felt that he could reasonably make his escape, he was so upset with her that if she had been anywhere near him he might have taken her by the shoulders and forced her to hear him out. And then as likely as not, he would have kissed her.

Caleb Harnisher rode back to town with him and Jeremiah had his doubts that Rolf would be available to help out as they had planned.

"Want me to go get Rolf, sir?" Caleb asked as they passed Pleasant's house.

"No. I expect he's got other things he needs to do. Looks like it's just the two of us."

"Yes, sir."

But when he pulled his buggy into the yard behind his living quarters he saw Rolf waiting for them. As if nothing unusual had happened, the boy stepped forward to unhitch the horse and lead it into the barn.

"Your mother sent you?" Jeremiah asked as he watched Rolf wash up.

"I came on my own."

"Then go home."

"No, sir. I have a job to do. I'm not a quitter."

Jeremiah studied the small quiet boy for a long minute. "No, you're definitely not that," he said softly, recalling a time when he had stood up to his uncle in spite of the older man's threat to beat him within an inch of his life if Jeremiah dared disobey him. "Is everything all right at home? The twins are all right?"

"Yes, sir."

"And your mother?"

Rolf met his eyes directly. "She was crying in her room. Bettina tried to go to her, but she wouldn't let her in. I don't know what happened, sir, but she's very sad and I was thinking maybe I could take her some ice cream. She has a special fondness for key lime pie so I was thinking…"

"Good idea. Why don't you boys go fill two of those small buckets and set them in the icebox to take to your families once we're done here? Just to be sure we don't run out."

"Thank you, sir." Rolf and Caleb ran off to do as he had suggested. Jeremiah walked slowly to the front of his shop and then turned to look at the large white house that dominated the far end of the street. He focused on an upstairs window and thought about Pleasant there crying. And he couldn't help wondering if her tears were the product of the fear and disappointment he had seen in her eyes at the picnic or the product of her own regret at having judged him.

He opened the front door of his shop and called out to the boys. "I've got an errand to run. Get those cones lined up and ready and if I'm not back when the first customers arrive you know what to do."

"Yes, sir," came the chorus of young male voices from the back room.

He was halfway to Pleasant's house when he stopped walking. What was he doing? What was he going to say that would change anything? Even if he explained about the alligator, that wasn't the point. The point was that she had made an assumption—one based on things he had told her about his past and his fears that the temper of his uncle had been visited on him. Furthermore, she had good reason of her own to assume that he might have become irritated with the twins, so irritated that he had lost his temper and raised his hand to them. In their talks, she had confirmed what he had suspected— that her late husband had struck the children often— especially Rolf. She had even admitted that Merle had struck her when she tried to interfere. So what could he possibly say that would ever rid her of those memories and those fears?

And even if he did explain and she did accept his explanation, nothing could ever erase that look of doubt that he had seen in her eyes. She would always wonder, always be on her guard. He had no one to blame but himself. After all, instead of trying to show her that he was nothing like her late husband, he had done an excellent job of making sure that she understood that he, too, had a temper and he, too, came from a family where that temper could lash out at others—even loved ones.

No, he had done everything he could to convince her that he was not worthy of her love or trust.

He took one long look at her house and then turned around and walked back to the ice cream shop.

Pleasant had been unable to stem the rushing waves of tears that had consumed her almost as soon as she reached home. Bettina had taken the twins to the kitchen to wash their tear-stained faces and prepare them something to eat while Rolf had announced his intention to go to work. Pleasant had instinctively protested that decision but Rolf had stood firm, using her own words to make his argument. "You always told us that a promise is a promise and a job left undone is a broken promise," he reminded her. His eyes had challenged her to argue the point, and she had waved him away. Caleb would be there and soon everyone in town would be at the ice cream shop. Rolf would be fine.

Realizing that the children were out of harm's way, Pleasant felt exhaustion overwhelm her. Slowly she climbed the stairs, went into her room and closed the door. The tears had come then in a gush as if only her will to make sure the twins were rescued and all four children were safe had kept them at bay. Tears escalated into choking sobs and she was helpless to keep herself from making the guttural sounds of her misery.

"Mama?" Bettina knocked softly on the bedroom door.

"I'll be there in a bit," she managed.

"Mama?" She was surprised to hear Rolf's voice. "If you don't want me to go I'll stay. Herr Troyer...."

The mere utterance of his name was enough to make Pleasant double over. "No, you're right," she said, forcing her voice to remain steady. "A promise is…" But the rest was lost in a fresh deluge of sobbing.

She heard both children retreat downstairs, whispering to one another worriedly as they went. She stood at the window and watched Rolf trudge up the street to the ice cream shop. She remained there, unable to move or to make any decision beyond the ones she had already made. Once again she had misread the signs. Once again she had given her heart to the wrong man.

She saw Jeremiah pull his buggy past the bakery and on into the backyard of the ice cream parlor. She waited—for what she could not have said—her sobs coming now in intermittent shudders that racked her entire body. After what seemed a very long time she saw Jeremiah start to walk up the street, his hat tipped back as he looked straight at her house, as he seemed to be looking straight through the upstairs window where she stood.

He walked with purpose and she felt a glimmer of hope. Perhaps there was some plausible explanation although she could not think what it might be. Perhaps he had realized the error of his ways and come to apologize. Perhaps…

Suddenly, he stopped in the middle of the deserted street. He stood there for a long moment, his fists clenched at his sides and then he turned around and walked back to his shop.

"No," she whispered, her fist jammed against her lips. "We can work this out." But she had thought the same of Merle and had finally had to admit defeat when her husband had turned on her.

She remained standing at the window until the street was lined on both sides with parked buggies and at the far end of the street a crowd had gathered around the ice cream shop. She was still standing there when the last of the buggies pulled away and still there when she saw Rolf walking home carrying a tin bucket that she knew would be filled with ice cream. She dabbed at the remnants of her crying jag with the hem of her apron and went downstairs to make supper for her family, more certain than she had ever been that God's plan for her life was to make safe and secure the lives of those blessed children.

Chapter Seventeen

"Where did you run off to yesterday?" Hannah asked the following day as the community gathered for the bi-weekly service.

"I…it was the twins."

"Yes, they had quite a scare. I couldn't believe it when Caleb told us last night what had happened."

Pleasant was confused. How could Caleb…?

"Rolf told him that according to the twins, the alligator was huge and headed right for Will. The boys were so blessed that Jeremiah was there and of course, it was only his quick thinking that spared them both." Hannah shuddered. "You have much to be thankful for today, Pleasant."

Alligator?

"Will you excuse me a moment, Hannah?" she asked and did not wait for permission as she hurried outside in search of any one of her children. She saw Rolf returning from the Yoders' barn where he had led their horse to the trough. "Rolf, walk with me a minute," she invited and put her hand around the boy's thin shoulder as she guided him a little ways from the house.

"Services will be starting," he reminded her.

"I know and we'll be there in time. But I need you to tell me what happened yesterday at the picnic with the twins and Herr Troyer."

His eyes widened. "You saw. Will and Henry had gone down to the creek bank and they were playing a game there and you sent Herr Troyer to fetch them and when he got there he saw this alligator coming up the bank. He grabbed Henry and a big stick and he hit that 'gator smack across the snout and that thing made a bee-line right back into the creek." He spoke with increasing enthusiasm as the details unfolded. "Then you got there and well, you know the rest."

Jeremiah had not been disciplining the boys. He had saved them.

Pleasant closed her eyes tight against the memory of her horror and the way she had looked at him, how she had assumed the worst of him without even considering that there might be some other explanation for his actions.

"Mama? Everybody's inside," Rolf said, nodding toward the Yoder house where Pleasant could hear voices raised in the opening hymn.

"Yes. We should go," she said but her mind was definitely not on church. All she could think about was how she could ever possibly get Jeremiah to forgive her.

He was sitting in his usual place at the end of the second row of benches close to the door. Rolf squeezed in next to Caleb in the row ahead of the women while Pleasant took her place between Bettina and Lydia.

"Is everything all right?" Lydia whispered and Pleasant nodded.

But nothing would ever be all right again, she thought.

For now she understood why Jeremiah had walked half-way to her house and then changed his mind and turned back. What was there to say? Even once he explained what really happened, there was no taking back the look of mistrust and doubt that he must have read in her eyes. How could she possibly convince him that she did trust him when in her heart of hearts she had to admit that for that instant she had not? She had believed the worst of him, believed him capable of striking her child.

Oh, Jeremiah, she thought as she stared at his proud straight back, *how can I ever make this up to you?* A day earlier she had been filled with excitement, planning to admit her love for him at last. On this day she still loved him—perhaps more than she had even imagined she could—but she understood beyond all doubt that in an instant she had ruined everything they might have shared.

The service that she wished would go on and on so that she could at least have some cause to be in the same room with him seemed to be over in the blink of an eye. Before she knew it everyone had scattered to attend to the after-services rituals of resetting the benches and preparing the meal they would all share. But instead of joining the other women in the kitchen, Pleasant followed Jeremiah out to the yard.

She was relieved to see him walk a little away from the other men and then realized that he was going home. Heedless of the looks her actions garnered from the other men or of the gossip that was sure to ensue once the men talked to their wives, she caught up to Jeremiah.

"I owe you an apology," she began and even to her ears her voice sounded tight and insincere. She understood that it was a case of nerves at not having taken time to plan what she might say to him, but when he glanced back at her and then kept walking without commenting on her presence, she knew that she was only making matters worse.

Yet she could not seem to stop herself. She was practically running to keep pace with his long and determined strides. "Please, Jeremiah, let me explain."

He stopped so abruptly that she almost ran into him and when she looked up at him, she was forced to take half a step back so that she could withstand the fury and accusation in his expression. He was looking at her now, boring into her with eyes that glinted with anger and hurt.

"Let you explain?" he repeated with a mirthless laugh. "Oh, that's a good one, Frau Obermeier. Would that be as in the way you gave me the opportunity to explain yesterday?"

"I…oh, Jeremiah, I…"

"Let's be clear about where we stand with one another, Frau Obermeier.…"

"Stop calling me that," she hissed, her own temper rising to the bait he offered.

He kept on talking as if she hadn't spoken. "We have a business arrangement. I need you to supply the cones for my shop because I have foolishly built my reputation of the combination of those cones and my ice cream. Besides, I shook hands with your father on the matter and I will not go back on that."

"My father is no longer here. I run the bakery now," she reminded him.

"And yet because I trust that you are a woman of honor, I assume that you will hold to whatever agreements your father may have made while he was living."

"This is not about business and we both know it."

"That's where you're wrong, Pleasant."

She noted the use of her given name and took hope from the fact that his voice had softened. He was looking at her as he had those evenings when they had sat talking for hours, as he had when he had gently caressed her cheek before saying good-night.

"The only thing we have between us is business. Now, forgive me, but yesterday was a difficult day and I would like to take the rest of this Sabbath to consider whether or not I made a mistake in coming here altogether or whether my mistake was simply one of falling in love against my better judgment."

Pleasant was incapable of either calling out to him or going after him as he resumed his march back to town, leaving her standing in the middle of the lane that led back to the Yoders' house. On the previous day she had thought that she couldn't possibly have more tears to shed. As she watched Jeremiah walk away, she had to wonder if her tears would ever stop.

For the week following the church service, Jeremiah made sure that his days were filled with business that kept him away from Celery Fields. He not only needed to put as much distance as his current situation would allow between Pleasant and him, he also wanted to avoid the unasked questions in the eyes of his friends and especially his uncle and aunt.

But in spite of his best efforts, thoughts of Pleasant stalked him hour after hour. The nights were the worst. He had quickly gotten used to going to her house in the evenings after the town was quiet and her children were in bed. There, the two of them would sit together on her back porch, looking up at the starlit sky or listening to the rain. There, they had slowly told their stories—her childhood a happy one until her mother died suddenly and unexpectedly in the influenza epidemic of 1918, when she had just turned eighteen. His childhood similarly happy while his father was alive but cut even shorter when his father died. The loss of a parent had changed everything for each of them. Gunther had remarried within a year and his new wife had presented him with two beautiful daughters—Lydia and Greta. Pleasant's brother had married Hannah and moved to his own farm on the edge of the community. In Ohio, Jeremiah's mother had taken him and his siblings to live with his father's brother, where he had quickly and painfully learned that his tendency toward inquisitiveness and natural thirst for knowledge did not sit well at all with his uncle's old-style ways.

It had been these similar experiences that had drawn them closer and led to long conversations about the future she hoped for her children and his dreams of making his mark in Florida. From there it was a natural leap to talk of a future together—at least he had hinted at that. He realized now that she had remained reserved although the night before the picnic she had for once not dismissed such talk as the idealistic ramblings of a dreamer.

More than once she had chided him in a gentle teasing way about his tendency to act first and consider the full consequences afterward. She had illustrated her observation by reminding him of his decision to leave a perfectly stable situation in Ohio to pursue a profession about which he knew very little in a state he'd never even visited. And the night before the picnic he had kissed her before leaving her, noting with a smile that he had a reputation for being spontaneous to maintain. And he had foolishly believed in his own dreams—that they could share a life together. One that would include her adopted children and perhaps, with God's blessing, children of their own.

That's what he had been thinking the day of the picnic as he'd wandered down to the creek bank where the twins were playing. He had imagined teaching them things and watching them grow into fine young men— the kind of young man that Rolf was already becoming. And then he had seen the alligator. He had acted purely on instinct, his fear for the safety of one or both of those children blocking out everything else. There had been no time to consider his actions. No time to think that they could be misinterpreted. No time for anything but to strike out at the present danger. He had brought the tree branch down with such force that the 'gator had been momentarily stunned—long enough for him to grab the second boy and haul both clear of the threat. His breathing had come in heaves as if he had just run a long distance in the blazing sun.

And then he had looked up and seen her and in her expression he had read their fate. She believed the worst— without reason or cause, she had simply assumed. With the benefit of time he had told himself that given her experience with Merle, perhaps it was understandable. But he could not get past the fact that he was not Merle—not like Merle in any way from everything he knew about the man. How could she not see that?

Day after day he was aware of her early morning arrival at the bakery, the smell of bread baking, the spicy scent of molasses cookies that followed him as he left to work his shift and then make his deliveries. Night after night he replaced those scents with memories of the softness of her cheeks cupped in his hands and the feathery touch of a wisp of her hair against his face.

He loved her—in spite of everything, he loved her. And because he loved her he never again wanted to be the cause of that expression of abject fear and disillusionment that he had seen in her face the day of the picnic. Rolf had told him of her tears and that news had very nearly been his undoing. But what did he have to offer her that could possibly assure her that he was not like her late husband? What assurance could he give himself that over time he might not become the hardened and embittered man his uncle had become? No, it was best to leave her alone. In time, he hoped that they might settle back into the comfortable if slightly contentious friendship they had known when they first met. Neighbors and business associates—nothing more.

Having made his decision, he snapped the reins and urged the team of Belgians homeward—back to Celery Fields. Back to the loneliness of his rooms. Back to another night where sleep would not come without dreams of Pleasant.

The days passed in a vacuum of work and loneliness. Pleasant could not fathom how it could be possible that a man she had known for only a few months could have filled her life to such a level that without him she felt as dried up and useless as the fields behind her house. She tried to keep up a front for the sake of the children, but their sudden silences and tentative reactions whenever she entered a room spoke volumes.

She tried to cheer herself with the fact that business at the bakery was improving every week, Lydia was back to teaching and earning her stipend and even Greta had gotten a job in the Yoders' general store. On Mondays, she and the other women still took turns staging a frolic at one of the houses and for a few brief hours, she was able to focus on others and even enjoy a laugh now and again.

But running the bakery was solitary work and with Jeremiah's place right next door—even if he was absent most of the time—she had more than enough time to think about what might have been. She had developed the habit of arriving at the bakery even earlier hoping to catch sight of Jeremiah—perhaps exchange a greeting. Anything that might start to rebuild what she had destroyed with one look. She longed to see him sitting on the steps leading to the bakery, waiting for her, and chided herself for her foolishness in believing that would ever happen.

She trudged down the street in the dark of predawn and felt the weight of her unhappiness with every step. She might have been carrying the five gallon buckets of lard that she used in her baking so slumped were her shoulders and ponderous her steps. With a sigh, she navigated the three shallow steps leading to the bakery's back door and as she did every morning, glanced over to Jeremiah's kitchen window before going inside and propping the door open for the day.

There was a light in his window but no sign of him and she wondered as she always did if he ever stood drinking his coffee and looking over to see if she was there. *Probably not.*

She thought she caught a movement in the shadows by the barn and hesitated. Perhaps he, too, was getting an early start. "Jeremiah?" she called, taking a step toward the edge of the porch. But there was no answer and at the same time she saw a shadow pass by the light in Jeremiah's kitchen. With a heavy sigh, she went into the bakery kitchen and sat down at her father's desk.

She had arrived so early that it was too soon to start the baking. She had some accounts that needed her attention and decided to take care of those first. The first streaks of daylight were visible through the window but she lit the kerosene lamp and set it on the desk. She had just bent to pull the heavy ledger from the bottom drawer of the desk when she heard footsteps crossing the back porch.

"Hello?" she called and peered around the high back of the rolltop desk. The screen door squeaked open and then shut. "Jeremiah?" The word was no more than a prayer that he would be the one standing hesitantly in the doorway, but she already could see that the man who had entered her kitchen was shorter and heavier than Jeremiah was.

She stood up and reached for the lantern, lifting it to the top of the desk so that it would throw more light. "May I help you?" she asked when what she wanted to say was, "Get out of here now!"

The man was dressed in mismatched old clothes, a battered fedora pulled low over his forehead. The stench of him reached her from across the room. "You alone?" he growled.

"I think you should leave," she said, forcing herself to her full height and clutching the edge of the desk as she tried to think of how best to protect herself. "There's some bread by the front door—take it if you're hungry and…"

The man gurgled a laugh that sounded as if he might

become hysterical. "Hungry? You have no idea, lady. And I'll take the bread—when I'm ready."

He had begun to walk around the kitchen as if perfectly within his rights to do so. He picked up a large knife that Pleasant used for chopping dried fruit and nuts. Brandishing it, he started toward her. "Money, lady. Whatever you've got."

"I..."

He raised the knife and moved within inches of her. "Now!"

She considered her options and saw a chance to put some distance between them, perhaps make it to the door and cry out for help. "The cash box is there in that bottom drawer," she said, inching away.

He grabbed her wrist and twisted it painfully. "So, get it out," he sneered, his unshaven face inches from hers.

She took the box from the drawer and set it on the writing surface of the desk. She opened it and waited for him to lower the knife so he could fill his pockets.

But to her horror, he merely glanced at the money and then closed the lid and looked at her with a smile that made her nauseous. "You're a pretty one, aren't you? And so clean and proper like all your kind." He ran the point of the knife under the edge of her prayer covering and Pleasant closed her eyes.

"Yeah, pray, little lady. For all the good it will do you." He moved against her so that she was blocked between him and the desk. She felt his rough hand cup her jaw, pinching it painfully to force a pucker to her lips.

She braced herself against the desk and felt the handle of the knife within reach. She closed her fingers around it and waited for his next move.

The sound of the bell jangling over the door in the

front of the shop signaled someone's arrival. *Please don't let it be Rolf and the other children,* she prayed as she grasped the knife even more firmly.

"Keep quiet," the man demanded and then changed his mind. "Send them away."

"We're not open yet," she called, her voice shaking almost uncontrollably.

"Sorry," Jeremiah called. "I'll come back later then."

"No," she whispered but the bell jangled and the door closed and the man holding her captive grinned.

"Now where were we?" he muttered as he clutched her face once again and wrapped his other arm around her crushing her to him.

"I believe you were leaving," Jeremiah said, his voice not two inches away from the man's back.

Pleasant's entire body melted against the desk with relief as the vagrant spun around to face Jeremiah. But then she heard the man's sickening laugh.

"You're one of her kind—you won't fight. Bunch of cowards hiding behind religion." He spat out each word as he taunted Jeremiah by getting right in his face. "Come on, put 'em up. Best man wins the little lady."

A look crossed Jeremiah's face that was so terrible in its fury that Pleasant almost cried out to him. She saw that his fists were clenched tight at his sides. He moved half an inch closer to the man so that he was towering over him. "Leave now," he said and it was the quiet menace in his tone that made the words a threat.

"Or what?" The vagrant was standing his ground but he seemed less certain.

Realizing that she was free to move away from him, Pleasant grabbed the knife and ran to Jeremiah's side. He wrapped his arm around her and pulled her tight against him, holding on to her as if he would never let her go.

The vagrant grinned. "Oh, my apologies. This is your woman then?"

"That is none of your business," Jeremiah replied. "Right now you have a choice—leave and never come to this area again or stay and I will restrain you while she goes for the authorities."

"You and what army?"

Jeremiah released Pleasant so quickly that she staggered and by the time she had recovered her balance he had bodily lifted the vagrant, plopped him into her father's desk chair and wheeled the chair as close to the desk as he could. Now he was leaning against the back of the chair pressing it and the man into the edge of the desk.

"I can't breathe," the man protested.

"Then you have one last chance to make this right. Leave now and we'll consider the matter resolved, but if ever I see you around here again…"

"I'm just so hungry and there's no work and…" He was whining now.

"Get yourself cleaned up then and come back here tomorrow and I'll find you work," Jeremiah said. "The rest will be up to you."

The vagrant twisted his head around to see if Jeremiah could possibly be serious. "You don't mean that," he sneered.

"I do." He eased up slightly on the pressure he'd put on the chair. "Those of my faith stand by their word. How about you? Are you a man who can be trusted?" He signaled Pleasant to pass him the knife—a decision she questioned but when he raised his eyebrows as if to ask would she doubt him again, she handed him the knife.

When he set the vagrant free and offered him the knife, Pleasant could not restrain a gasp. The man held up both palms, refusing the gesture. Jeremiah then tossed the knife onto the worktable. The clatter of it was the only sound in the room.

The vagrant looked first at Jeremiah and then at Pleasant. "I apologize, ma'am. Don't know what got into me—just so hungry and tired." Wearily he walked toward the door, his back bent into the posture of a man twice his age.

"Wait," Pleasant called and hurried into the shop then returned with three loaves of day-old bread. She put them into a flour sack bag and handed it to him. Then she took three dollars from the cash box and gave him that as well. "You can pay for a room and a bath and a proper meal," she suggested.

Tears ran down the man's weathered face and he became so emotional that all he could do was nod as he made his escape, leaving Pleasant and Jeremiah alone for the first time since that fateful day at the picnic.

"Thank you for coming," she said, focusing on the floor rather than him. "I don't know…" Suddenly the enormity of what had just happened—what might have happened had he not come to her rescue—struck Pleasant with a force that left her trembling.

"Pleasant, I'm right here," he said and when she looked up, he was holding his arms open to her and before he could change his mind, she ran to him and said the words she had been holding inside for all this time.

"I love you so, Jeremiah. Whatever becomes of us, I

do love you—I think I have loved you from the day you first walked into this bakery."

"Good," he whispered, his lips tickling her ear, "because I love you and we will find a way, Pleasant. Whatever our pasts, together we can find our way to a future if you'll have me." He placed his forefinger under her chin and lifted her face to meet his. "You have my word on it," he told her.

"Will we marry?" she asked unable to believe what was happening.

He grinned. "Why, Pleasant Goodloe Obermeier, are you proposing to me?"

She blushed but stood her ground. "Will you have me?" she replied with a sassy tilt of her head.

All trace of teasing disappeared instantly from his expression. "All I want in this life is to spend the rest of my days loving you, Pleasant. We've been proud fools, the two of us and wasted precious time. I'll talk to my Uncle John right away—that is, if you'll say yes."

She smiled and stroked his cheek. "You'll look quite distinguished with a beard, Jeremiah," she said dreamily, reminding them both that married men of their faiths wore beards.

"Is that a yes?"

"What was the question again?"

"Will you marry me?" He enunciated each word, savoring each syllable.

"Yes," she whispered and wrapped her arms around his neck as she stood on tiptoe to kiss him. "Yes, a thousand times, yes."

He lifted her and twirled around the bakery kitchen with her until they heard the unmistakable clatter of the wagon that would be Rolf bringing the milk and eggs and Bettina taking the twins to Hilda's for the day.

"Shall we tell the children now?" she asked.

And like children themselves, they ran hand in hand out to the backyard so that when Rolf drove the wagon around the bakery, they were standing together to greet him and the other children.

Bettina's shrieks of sheer delight brought Moses Yoder and the Hadwells at a run to see what had happened and after that, news of the pending nuptials of Jeremiah Troyer and Pleasant Goodloe Obermeier spread like wildfire through the town.

"Well, high time," Hilda announced to Pleasant when she heard the news. "The two of you have been walking on thin ice—spending so much time together, and alone at that. People were beginning to talk."

Pleasant knew that the person leading that talk was Hilda herself but she was far too happy to allow anyone—especially Hilda—to dampen her spirits. "He'll be a good father to Merle's children," she told Hilda.

"You won't allow the children to forget their father," she stated firmly and it was not a question but more of a command.

"Of course not. They will keep his name—your family name."

"Because although I know my brother could be—difficult," Hilda continued as if Pleasant had not spoken, "he was their father and they need to remember that."

Pleasant could not help but notice that Hilda felt no need to make the same demands regarding the children's mother—a woman she had never cared for and one she was certain had tricked her brother into marriage. Pleasant had long ago learned that it did no good at all to remind Hilda how much Merle had loved his first wife, how he had grieved for her and how he had chosen Pleasant not out of love but out of the practical need for someone to raise his children.

"I will see that all four children continue to honor their parents' memory," she assured Hilda.

"And when you and Jeremiah have your own?" Hilda demanded.

Pleasant pressed her hand on her sister-in-law's forearm. "We will still be a family, Hilda. Just one that has grown as your family has grown over the years."

Hilda snorted. "My children are all of one parentage."

"And equally loved as will Merle's children be and any offspring that Jeremiah and I may be blessed to birth." She sighed, weary of Hilda's constant tendency to always see the negative. "Can you not be happy for me, Hilda? I love this man as you love Moses, and he loves me."

To her astonishment, Hilda's eyes softened to a girlish dreamy look. "He does at that," she said softly. "Everyone has been saying as much for weeks now. Hannah talks about the two of you as if you invented true love."

Pleasant laughed. "Oh, Hilda, I am so very happy."

"Well, then I am happy for you. You've had many hard times, Pleasant, and everyone admires the way you have moved forward in spite of everything you've had to face. It seems to me that it's about time you were given the opportunity to enjoy your life a bit." And having made this pronouncement Hilda spent the next several days presenting Pleasant with her ideas for exactly how, where and when the wedding should take place.

Chapter Eighteen

~❦~

Jeremiah was not particularly happy about the idea of moving into the house that Pleasant had shared with her first husband. On the other hand, he could hardly expect her to bring the children and come live with him. One solution he had considered was suggesting that they move into Gunther's house, but that brought up the question of sharing the initial weeks of the marriage not only with four children but also with Pleasant's two half sisters.

He stopped at the Harnisher farm on his way back to town. Levi was a good listener and if asked would likely offer some suggestions for Jeremiah's dilemma.

"What would you think about starting fresh?" Levi asked.

"Leave Celery Fields?"

"No, but with a house that neither you nor Pleasant has occupied and one that would comfortably house the children."

"I'm listening," Jeremiah said.

"A man who used to work for me when I had the circus—Hans Winters—has decided to go back north per-manently. He and my former secretary plan to marry and settle there in Wisconsin."

Jeremiah had met Hans once at Levi's farm. "So he wants to sell his place?" He nodded toward the house that sat a hundred yards down the road from Levi's house.

"He does. He'd make you a fair price. He's just that kind of a man."

Jeremiah looked out over the land that surrounded them and then down the long road that led into town. "I don't know. Pleasant has the bakery and I have my businesses and those are all in town. Living out here..."

"Peace and quiet," Levi said, "and Pleasant would be close to Hannah and her kids would have our kids as neighbors."

"You make a good case," Jeremiah admitted. "But then there's the house that Merle left her and the land..."

"Things are changing, Jeremiah. You might want to talk to the Palmer brothers. Word has it that they've been quietly buying up the land of those who have given up and gone back north. Merle's place might not be good farmland but it is prime real estate for an area that's growing."

Jeremiah thanked Levi for his suggestions and started back to town, but as he passed the house that Hans Winters owned, he slowed his team of horses to a walk. The house was smaller than the one that Pleasant occupied with the children now, but it was a charming house nonetheless. There was a screened front porch where two rocking chairs sat at an angle to one another. Jeremiah imagined sitting there with Pleasant in the evenings and on Sunday afternoons as together they watched the children playing or just enjoyed the sunset.

Almost without realizing what he was doing he

turned the horses onto the road that led to the house and five minutes later he was knocking on the door. An hour after that he walked out of the house—a house he now owned or would own as soon as he delivered the down payment to Hans Winters. Levi's former butler followed him out to the porch and watched as Jeremiah climbed aboard his wagon.

"Remember, you can always change your mind," Hans told him.

"I won't change my mind," Jeremiah assured him, but he wasn't so sure about Pleasant. If there was one thing he understood it was that where he was spontaneous and some would even say impulsive, she was far more cautious. She thought about the smallest details of any decision she made—how it would affect the children, how it would impact Lydia and Greta now that Gunther had died, what it would mean for managing the business that her father had built. He thought about all of that as he allowed the horses to find their way back to town.

Pleasant was in the bakery when he got there. He could see through the open door that she was hardly alone. The children were there as were Hilda Yoder and Greta. It was not at all the right time to tell his future wife that he had bought her a house. A house that was two miles from town—and the bakery. A house that she had never seen except from the outside. A house that she might not think was at all suitable for their needs. But he and Hans Winter had shaken hands and that had sealed the bargain between them.

Jeremiah sighed and climbed down from his wagon. Sooner or later he was going to have to tell her what he had done and perhaps the buffer of the children and the others was a blessing in disguise. He crossed the yard and mounted the steps to the bakery.

"Well, I don't trust them," Hilda announced as he entered the room.

"Don't trust who?" he asked.

"The Palmers," Hilda replied with a derisive snort. "They go around offering to buy people's houses as if there were no sentimental value at all."

"They made a very generous offer," Greta argued.

"And how would you know what is generous and what is insulting?" Hilda asked.

"Josef says that..."

Hilda dismissed the mention of the young carpenter with a wave of her hand. "The question before you, Pleasant, is what will you do?"

"About?" Jeremiah asked, trying hard to make sense of the conversation that had continued as if he were not there.

Pleasant glanced at him and then down at her hands. "Mr. Potter Palmer has offered to buy my—Merle's—house and land," she said softly.

"And what did you say?"

"I told him I would need to discuss it with you—and the children, of course. After all, that is their inheritance."

"Not to mention the only home those children have ever known," Hilda grumbled.

"Well, the children are here," Jeremiah said, nodding to Rolf who was sitting at Gunther's desk working on a column of figures, and Bettina who was grinding nuts at the far end of the worktable. He had passed the twins out in the yard playing a game of marbles. "Why don't you ask them what they think?"

Rolf and Bettina exchanged a look and stopped pretending to be otherwise occupied. Rolf chewed the stub of his pencil. "Where would we live then?" he asked, and Bettina nodded, abandoning her work to move closer to Pleasant.

"Well, we could live in the house where I grew up," Pleasant said slowly, trying to put the best possible face on the idea. "You know that house almost as well as you know our own and…"

"You mean live with our teacher in her house?" Rolf looked decidedly alarmed at this idea.

"I would be there and so would Jeremiah once we marry and…"

"Or," Jeremiah hastened to add, "we might just buy a new house—one where we could start fresh as a family."

"I like that idea," Bettina said. "What kind of a house? Could it be in the country?"

"You mean, close to where Caleb Harnisher lives?" Rolf asked and he grinned at his sister whose cheeks had taken on a most becoming rosy glow.

"No," she protested. "I just happen to like the country."

Jeremiah drew in his breath and took the plunge. Facing Pleasant instead of the children he started to describe the house. "What if there were a perfect house not a hundred yards from Hannah and Levi." He glanced at Bettina and added softly, "And Caleb."

"You're talking about the house where Hans lives?" Pleasant asked.

Jeremiah nodded. "I stopped by there today and well, I sort of bought the place."

Greta clapped her hands excitedly while Hilda

scowled at him. "How does one 'sort of' buy something as momentous as a house, Jeremiah Troyer?"

But the only reaction he needed or wanted was Pleasant's and to his astonishment, she burst out laughing. "Oh, Jeremiah, you never cease to surprise me. You bought us a house?"

Jeremiah nodded and held his breath, hoping her laughter was not of the hysterical variety.

"That is so romantic," Greta whispered to Bettina as Rolf rolled his eyes.

"Hans Winters's house?" Pleasant asked.

Again, Jeremiah could manage only a nod.

"I love that house," she said softly. "I always have."

Hilda cleared her throat loudly. "Am I to understand, Pleasant, that you are going to sell Merle's legacy for his children to the highest bidder?"

Pleasant faced her sister-in-law. "That is precisely what I intend to do, Hilda, for what greater legacy could Merle have left his children than one that secures their future? With the money that Mr. Palmer has offered there will be more than enough for Rolf and each of the twins to one day own a business or property of their own—and Bettina…"

"I'm going to run the bakery," the girl announced.

Hilda's lips thinned for a long moment as she worked through her feelings that somehow this might be disloyal to her late brother.

"Pleasant is right, Hilda," Jeremiah assured her. "Merle's house needs work and the land hasn't produced a viable crop in…"

"Oh, don't speak to me as if I can't possibly see God's hand in all of this, Jeremiah," Hilda huffed.

Pleasant placed a gentle hand on Hilda's shoulder. "I'm going to need your help, Hilda. Hans has lived there alone all this time and the place will surely need a woman's touch."

"No doubt." She turned to go then paused and looked up at Jeremiah. "You bought her a house?"

"I did."

"But how did you know—I mean, what if she…"

Jeremiah looked at Pleasant. "Sometimes, Hilda, you just have to put your doubts aside and know that whatever happens, the person you love will understand that you acted out of love—always out of love."

He was so blinded by the smile that Pleasant gave him that he was only vaguely aware that Hilda had scurried off or that Bettina and Rolf had run outside to tell the twins that they would be moving or that Greta had made some excuse about needing to attend to something in the front of the bakery. There was only Pleasant and him. He held out his arms and she came to him and in that moment he saw them standing here years from now, their arms around each other as they looked back over a life shared and forward toward the days still to come.

"I thought it was impossible for you to make me any happier than you already have," she said. "But…"

He chuckled and kissed her temple. "If I had known buying you a house would have this effect I would have bought you half a dozen houses."

"Not just any house," she protested. "This house— our house."

"Our family," he reminded her as he nodded toward the back door of the bakery where the four children stood watching them. He kept one arm around Pleasant and spread the other to welcome the children, and in moments the six of them were dancing in a circle of delight, their laughter and excitement the only music any of them needed.

* * *

It rained all week before the wedding and even that seemed to Pleasant to be a sign that God had blessed this union. The community desperately needed the rain and the steadiness of the downpour seemed to promise no letup until the earth had once again drunk its fill. She had decided to hold the ceremony at her father's house. After all, that was the place she had always thought of as "home" and it was tradition for weddings to take place in the home of the bride. She had always felt a little like a visitor in Merle's house, furnished as it was with all of the things his first wife had chosen—furnishings that Merle had forbade Pleasant from moving from their assigned position.

At her father's house surrounded by happy memories, she felt such a sense of peace and calm and Jeremiah had agreed that it was the perfect setting in which to be married. Lydia and Greta were delighted to have the house used for such a joyous occasion and even the children got caught up in the preparations. Pleasant had to keep reminding Bettina that this was a second wedding.

"Not for Jeremiah," Bettina reminded her. They had agreed that the children should start to call him by his given name within the family and continue to refer to him as Herr Troyer when others were around. "This is his first wedding and just because he's a man that doesn't mean we shouldn't take that into consideration."

Pleasant was so busy with the bakery and the sale of Merle's property to the Palmers and making herself a new dress for the wedding that she had little time to pay attention to the whispered conversations Bettina was constantly holding with either Rolf, Greta or Lydia—

conversations that stopped abruptly the moment she entered the room.

But two days before the wedding was to take place she was surprised to see Hannah enter the bakery, her lovely face wreathed in a smile. "Come with me," she instructed.

"I can't...the bakery."

"Yes, you can," Mildred Troyer announced as she took up Pleasant's usual position behind the worktable and began cutting out cookies from the pastry that Pleasant had just finished rolling out. She used the open mouth of a glass jar, efficiently plopping it into the dough, giving it a twist and then repeating the process. "I can mind the bakery for a few hours. You go with Hannah. Go on, now."

"I don't understand," Pleasant said when they exited the bakery. Caleb was waiting out in front with Hannah's buggy.

"You will," Hannah said as she climbed into the buggy and waited for Pleasant to join her. "Well, come on."

They headed for the Harnisher farm and then bypassed it and pulled into the lane leading to the house that Jeremiah had bought from Hans Winters. "What's going on?" Pleasant asked, her suspicions on high alert when she saw several buggies lined up outside the house and a welcoming party of friends, neighbors and customers lining the walkway to the front porch.

"Just wait," Caleb said, giving her what for him amounted to a radiant grin. He hopped down and then offered her his hand to assist her down from the buggy. Hannah hooked arms with her and practically pulled her up the walkway as everyone shouted, "Surprise!"

Bettina ran to her and took hold of her free hand. "Wait 'til you see, Mama. It's all so perfect."

"We'll start the tour here," Lydia announced, pointing to two bentwood rockers on the small front porch. "Hans said to tell you that he wished he could be here to give these to you and Jeremiah himself. He wanted them to be his wedding gift to you."

"Oh, how lovely," Pleasant crooned, running the flat of her hand over the smooth wood.

"There's more," Bettina said, tugging her through the front door.

Inside, Pleasant blinked several times with disbelief as she took in the polished wood floors, a fully furnished sitting room. "Everyone helped furnish this room," Hannah told her, "and look how perfectly the bits and pieces came together—as if they belonged here."

"I don't know what to say," Pleasant murmured, glancing shyly at all the faces pressed in at the front door to watch as she discovered her surprise. "You are all just too kind."

"The dining room table and chairs are our gift," Greta told her. "Mine and Lydia's and the children's."

"It's so beautiful," Pleasant said, "but..."

"Josef Bontrager found the set discarded behind an abandoned house in Sarasota. He repaired it and we all sanded and refinished the pieces," Lydia explained.

Pleasant moved closer to the table with six chairs surrounding it and already set as if just waiting for a family to sit down. "These are Mama's dishes," she whispered as she picked up a plate and studied it.

"Papa had them boxed up and stored in the attic," Lydia told her, "along with several other things you've yet to discover." She nodded toward the hall that led to three small bedrooms.

The first two were already set up to welcome the children. The third at the end of the hall would be hers to share with Jeremiah. A double bed there had been made up with a quilt that she recognized as one made by her mother.

"And there's the kitchen," Bettina said when she saw the first tear trickle down Pleasant's cheek. "You'll love the kitchen, Mama," she promised.

And indeed she did for sitting at the kitchen table was her husband-to-be, sipping from a mug of steaming coffee and grinning up at her. "Welcome home," he said softly and when she started to cry in earnest, he stood up. "Now, now, anything you don't like can be changed or moved or gotten rid of."

"Don't you dare touch one dish or chair," she warned, sniffing back her tears. "It's perfect."

Around her everyone smiled with relief.

"Thank you," she said, finding her voice in spite of her tears. "Thank you so very much. Jeremiah and the children and I feel so truly blessed that we have all of you with us as we start our life together in this beautiful house."

"And as soon as we are married, you're all invited for ice cream and shoo-fly pie," Jeremiah added.

Everyone laughed at that and there was some good-natured ribbing about how Jeremiah was always thinking about business before the others got back into their buggies and went on about their day. Hannah was the last to leave, taking Lydia, Greta and Pleasant's children with her.

"I'll assume you can get Pleasant back to the bakery, Jeremiah," she said with a teasing laugh.

"I do know the way," he replied. "On the other hand, it might be fun to get lost at least for a little while."

Pleasant felt the heat of pleased embarrassment rise to her throat. "Stop that," she chided, but inside she was smiling at the realization that with God's blessing she and Jeremiah would have days and months and years to spend together in this place, surrounded by their children and the dear friends they had made.

"I thought maybe I could hang a swing there in that tree for the twins," Jeremiah said as they walked back to the house. He offered her the choice of rocking chairs on the porch and then sat in the other one next to her. He took her hand. "And speaking of children, do you think there's enough room?"

"Plenty. Rolf and the twins can be in that front room—it's a little larger and then Bettina can have the smaller room next to ours." She blushed as she realized they were talking about such intimate things as sharing a bedroom—a bed—and not yet married. "I mean..."

"I was thinking beyond right now," Jeremiah admitted as he leaned forward and took both her hands in his. "What about when we have children? Where will they be?"

"I...that is..." She was already overwhelmed with the blessing of spending the rest of her days with this wonderful man.

"You don't want more children?" he asked, frowning.

"More? I've never had..." The way he looked away and his mouth tightened and she realized that he must be thinking that once again she doubted him, remembering what he had told her about his uncle and his fears.

She tightened her grip on his hands and leaned closer. "Of course, we're going to have children together, Jeremiah," she said as she brushed an errant strand of his hair away from his cheek. "And the matter of where they will sleep will resolve itself. You'll see."

He bowed his head and before raising it, he lifted her fingers to his lips and kissed them. "I love you, Pleasant," he murmured.

She leaned in and kissed his cheek. "And I love you, Jeremiah and that, with God's help, is all either of us will ever need to find our way through life's challenges."

They sat together for a long time then, rocking their chairs in unison and staring out at the tree where he would hang a swing for the twins—and the little ones to come. Words were not necessary—their fingers intertwined spoke volumes about their love for each other and their gratitude for the blessings they had been given.

* * * * *

WE HOPE YOU ENJOYED THESE
LOVE INSPIRED®
AND
LOVE INSPIRED® HISTORICAL BOOKS.

Whether you love heart-pounding suspense, historically rich stories or contemporary heartfelt romances, Love Inspired® Books has it all!

Look for new titles available every month from Love Inspired®, Love Inspired® Suspense and Love Inspired® Historical.

Love Inspired®

www.LoveInspired.com

Love Inspired®

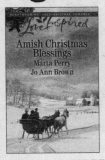

Save $1.00

on the purchase of any
Love Inspired®,
Love Inspired® Suspense or
Love Inspired® Historical book.

Available wherever books are sold, including
most bookstores, supermarkets, drugstores
and discount stores.

Save $1.00

**on the purchase of any Love Inspired®, Love Inspired® Suspense
or Love Inspired® Historical book.**

Coupon valid until February 28, 2017. Redeemable at participating retail outlets
in the U.S. and Canada only. Limit one coupon per customer.

52614460

Canadian Retailers: Harlequin Enterprises Limited will pay the face value
of this coupon plus 10.25¢ if submitted by customer for this product only. Any
other use constitutes fraud. Coupon is nonassignable. Void if taxed, prohibited
or restricted by law. Consumer must pay any government taxes. Void if copied.
Inmar Promotional Services ("IPS") customers submit coupons and proof of
sales to Harlequin Enterprises Limited, P.O. Box 3000, Saint John, NB E2L 4L3,
Canada. Non-IPS retailer—for reimbursement submit coupons and proof of
sales directly to Harlequin Enterprises Limited, Retail Marketing Department,
225 Duncan Mill Rd., Don Mills, ON M3B 3K9, Canada.

U.S. Retailers: Harlequin Enterprises
Limited will pay the face value of
this coupon plus 8¢ if submitted by
customer for this product only. Any
other use constitutes fraud. Coupon is
nonassignable. Void if taxed, prohibited
or restricted by law. Consumer must pay
any government taxes. Void if copied.
For reimbursement submit coupons
and proof of sales directly to Harlequin
Enterprises, Ltd 482, NCH Marketing
Services, P.O. Box 880001, El Paso,
TX 88588-0001, U.S.A. Cash value
1/100 cents.

5 65373 00076 2   (8100)0 12237

® and ™ are trademarks owned and used by the trademark owner and/or its licensee.

© 2016 Harlequin Enterprises Limited

LIINC1COUP1116

SPECIAL EXCERPT FROM

Love Inspired

Could a Christmastime nanny position for the ranch foreman's son turn into a full-time new family for one Texas teacher?

Read on for a sneak preview of the third book in the **LONE STAR COWBOY LEAGUE: BOYS RANCH** *miniseries,* **THE NANNY'S TEXAS CHRISTMAS** *by Lee Tobin McClain.*

"Am I in trouble?" Logan asked, sniffling.

How did you discipline a kid when his whole life had just flashed before your eyes? Flint schooled his features into firmness. "One thing's for sure, tractors are going to be off-limits for a long time."

Logan just buried his head in Flint's shoulder.

As they all started walking again, Flint felt that delicate hand on his arm once more.

"You doing okay?" Lana Alvarez asked.

He shook his head. "I just got a few more gray hairs. I should've been watching him better."

"Maybe so," Marnie said. "But you can't, not with all the work you have at the ranch. So I think we can all agree—you need a babysitter for Logan." She stepped in front of Lana and Flint, causing them both to stop. "And the right person to do it is here. Miss Lana Alvarez."

"Oh, Flint doesn't want—"

"You've got time after school. And a Christmas vacation coming up." Marnie crossed her arms, looking

LIEXP1116